MW00778409

AGAINST NATURE

(À REBOURS)

By J. K. HUYSMANS

Against Nature (À Rebours)
By J. K. Huysmans

Print ISBN 13: 978-1-4209-6567-4
eBook ISBN 13: 978-1-4209-6568-1

This edition copyright © 2019. Digireads.com Publishing.

All rights reserved. No part of this publication may be reproduced,
distributed, or transmitted in any form or by any means, including
photocopying, recording, or other electronic or mechanical methods,
without the prior written permission of the publisher, except in the case
of brief quotations embodied in critical reviews and certain other
noncommercial uses permitted by copyright law.

Cover Image: a detail of "Landscape of Seine-et-Oise; Paysage de
Sein-et-Oise", by Gustave Loiseau (1865-1935), c. 1906 (oil on canvas)
/ Photo © Christie's Images / Bridgeman Images.

Please visit *www.digireads.com*

Introduction

I

In trying to represent the man who wrote the extraordinary books grouped around "A Rebours" and "En Route," I find myself carried back to the decline of the Latin world. I recall those restless Africans who were drawn into the vortex of decadent Rome, who absorbed its corruptions with all the barbaric fervour of their race, and then with a more natural impetus of that youthful fervour threw themselves into the young current of Christianity, yet retaining in their flesh the brand of an exotic culture. Tertullian, Augustine, and the rest gained much of their power, as well as their charm, because they incarnated a fantastic mingling of youth and age, of decayed Latinity, of tumultuously youthful Christianity. Huysmans, too, incarnates the old and the new, but with a curious, a very vital difference. Today the *rôles* are reversed; it is another culture that is now young, with its aspirations after human perfection and social solidarity, while Christianity has exchanged the robust beauty of youth for the subtler beauty of age. "The most perfect analogy to our time which I can find," wrote Renan to his sister amid the tumults of Paris in 1848, a few weeks after Huysmans had been born in the same city, "is the moment when Christianity and paganism stood face to face." Huysmans had wandered from ancestral haunts of mediæval peace into the forefront of the struggles of our day, bringing the clear, refined perceptions of old culture to the intensest vision of the modern world yet attained, but never at rest, never once grasping except on the purely aesthetic side of the significance of the new age, always haunted by the memory of the past and perpetually feeling his way back to what seems to him the home of his soul.—The fervent seeker of those early days, indeed, but *à rebours!*

This is scarcely a mere impression; one might be tempted to say that it is strictly the formula of this complex and interesting personality. Coming on the maternal side from an ordinary Parisian bourgeois stock, though there chanced to be a sculptor even along this line, on the paternal side he belongs to an alien aristocracy of art. From father to son his ancestors were painters, of whom at least one, Cornelius Huysmans, still figures honourably in our public galleries, while the last of them left Breda to take up his domicile in Paris. Here his son, Joris Karl, has been the first of the race to use the pen instead of the brush, yet retaining precisely those characters of "veracity of imitation, jewel-like richness of colour, perfection of finish, emphasis of character," which their historian finds in the painters of his land from the fourteenth century onwards. Where the Meuse approaches the Rhine valley we find the home of the men who, almost alone in the north, created painting and the arts that are grouped around painting, and evolved religious music. On the side of art the Church had found its chief builders in the men of these valleys, and even on the spiritual side also, for here is the northern home of mysticism. Their latest child has fixed his attention on the feverish activities of Paris with the concentrated gaze of a stranger in a strange land, held by a fascination which is more than half repulsion, always missing something, he scarcely knows what. He has ever been seeking the satisfaction he had missed, sometimes in the aesthetic vision of common things, sometimes in the refined Thebaïd of his own visions, at length more joyfully in the survivals of mediæval mysticism. Yet as those early Africans still retained their acquired Roman instincts, and that fantastic style which could not be shaken off, so Huysmans will surely retain to the last the tincture of Parisian modernity.

Yet we can by no means altogether account for Huysmans by race and environment. Every man of genius is a stranger and a pilgrim on the earth, mirroring the world in his mind as in those concave or convex mirrors which elongate or abbreviate absurdly all who approach them. No one ever had a keener sense of the distressing absurdity of human affairs than M. Huysmans. The Trocadero is not a beautiful building, but to no one else probably has it appeared as an old hag lying on her back and elevating her spindle shanks towards the sky. Such images of men's works and ways abound in Huysmans' books, and they express his unaffected vision of life, his disgust for men and things, a shuddering disgust, yet patient, half-amused. I can well recall an evening spent some years ago in M. Huysmans' company. His face, with the sensitive, luminous eyes, reminded one of Baudelaire's portraits, the face of a resigned and benevolent Mephistopheles who has discovered the absurdity of the Divine order but has no wish to make any improper use of his discovery. He talked in low and even tones, never eagerly, without any emphasis or gesture, not addressing any special person; human imbecility was the burden of nearly all that he said, while a faint twinkle of amused wonderment lit up his eyes. And throughout all his books until almost the last "l'éternelle bêtise de l'humanité" is the ever-recurring refrain.

Always leading a retired life, and specially abhorring the society and conversation of the average literary man, M. Huysmans has for many years been a government servant—a model official, it is said—at the Ministry of Foreign Affairs. [deputy espionage chief] Here, like our own officials at Whitehall, he serves his country in dignified leisure— on the only occasion on which I have seen him in his large and pleasant *bureau*, he was gazing affectionately at Chéret's latest *affiche*, which a lady of his acquaintance had just brought to show him—and such duties of routine, with the close contact with practical affairs they involve, must always be beneficial in preserving the sane equipoise of an imaginative temperament. In this matter Huysmans has been more fortunate than his intimate friend Villiers de l'Isle-Adam, who had wandered so far into the world of dreams that he lost touch with the external world and ceased to distinguish them clearly. One is at first a little surprised to hear of the patient tact and diplomacy which the author of "A Rebours" spent round the death-bed of the author of "Contes Cruels" to obtain the dying dreamer's consent to a ceremony of marriage which would legitimate his child. But Huysmans' sensitive nervous system and extravagant imagination have ever been under the control of a sane and forceful intellect; his very idealism has been nourished by the contemplation of a world which he has seen too vividly ever to ignore. We may read that in the reflective deliberation of his grave and courteous bearing, somewhat recalling, as more than one observer has noted, his own favourite animal, the cat, whose outward repose of Buddhistic contemplation envelops a highly-strung nervous system, while its capacity to enjoy the refinements of human civilization comports a large measure of spiritual freedom and ferocity. Like many another man of letters, Huysmans suffers from neuralgia and dyspepsia; but no novelist has described so persistently and so poignantly the pangs of toothache or the miseries of *maux d'estomac*, a curious proof of the peculiarly personal character of Huysmans' work throughout. His sole preoccupation has been with his own impressions. He possessed no native genius for the novel. But with a very sound instinct he set himself, almost at the outset of his career, to describe intimately and faithfully the crudest things of life, the things most remote from his own esoteric tastes but at that time counted peculiarly "real." There could be no better discipline for an idealist. Step by step he has left the region of vulgar actualities to attain his proper sphere, but the marvellous and slowly won power of expressing the spiritually impalpable in concrete imagery is the fruit of that laborious apprenticeship. He was influenced in his novels at first by Goncourt, afterwards a little by Zola, as he sought to reproduce his own vivid and personal vision of the world. This vision is like that of a man with an intense exaltation of the senses, especially the senses of sight and smell. Essentially Huysmans is less a novelist than a poet, with an instinct to use not verse but prose as his medium. Thus he early fell under the influence of Baudelaire's prose-poems. His small and slight first volume, "Le Drageoir à Epices," bears witness to this influence, while yet revealing a personality clearly distinct from Baudelaire's. This personality is already wholly revealed in the quaint audacity of the little prose-poem entitled "L'Extase." Here, at the very outset of Huysmans' career, we catch an unconscious echo of mediæval asceticism, the voice, it might be, of Odo of Cluny, who nearly a thousand years before had shrunk with horror from embracing a "sack of dung"; "quomodo ipsum stercoris saccum amplecti desideramus!" "L'Extase" describes how the lover lies in the wood clasping the hand of the beloved and bathed in a rapture of blissful emotion; "suddenly she rose, disengaged her hand, disappeared in the bushes, and I heard as it were the rustling of rain on the leaves"; at once the delicious dream fled and the lover awakes to the reality of commonplace human things. That is a parable of the high-strung idealism, having only contempt for whatever breaks in on its ideal, which has ever been the mark of Huysmans. Baudelaire was also such a hyperæsthetic idealist, but the human tenderness which vibrates beneath the surface of Baudelaire's work has been the last quality to make itself more than casually felt in Huysmans. It is the defect which vitiated his early work in the novel, when he was still oscillating between the prose-poem and the novel, clearly conscious that while the first suited him best, only in the second could mastery be won. His early novels are sometimes portentously dull, with a lack of interest, or even attempt to interest, which itself almost makes them interesting, as frank ugliness is. They are realistic with a veracious and courageously abject realism, never like Zola's, carefully calculated for its pictorial effectiveness, but dealing simply with the trivialest and sordidest human miseries. His first novel "Marthe"—which inaugurated the long series of novels devoted to state-regulated prostitution in those slaughterhouses of love, as Huysmans later described them, where Desire is slain at a single stroke,—sufficiently repulsive on the whole, is not without flashes of insight which reveal the future artist, and to some readers indeed make it more interesting than "La Fille Elisa," which the Goncourts published shortly afterwards. Unlike the crude and awkward "Marthe"—though that book reveals the influence of the Goncourts—"La Fille Elisa" shows the hand of an accomplished artist, but it is also the work of a philanthropist writing with an avowed object, and of a fine gentleman ostentatiously anxious not to touch pitch with more than a finger-tip. The Preface to "Marthe" contains a declaration which remains true for the whole of Huysmans' work: "I set down what I see, what I feel, what I have lived, writing it as well as I am able, *et voilà tout!*" But it has ever been a dangerous task to set down what one sees and feels and has lived; for no obvious reason except the subject, "Marthe" was immediately suppressed by the police. This first novel remains the least personal of Huysmans' books; in his next novel, "Les Sœurs Vatard"— a study of Parisian work-girls and their lovers—a more characteristic vision of the world begins to be revealed, and from that time forward there is a continuous though irregular development both in intellectual grip and artistic mastery. "Sac au Dos," which appeared in the *Soirées de Médan*, represents a notable stage in this development, for here, as he has since acknowledged, Huysmans' hero is himself. It is the story of a young student who serves during the great war in the Garde Mobile of the Seine, and is invalided with dysentery before reaching the front.

There is no story, no striking impression to record—nothing to compare with Guy de Maupassant's incomparably more brilliant "Boule-de-Suif," also dealing with the fringe of war, which appears in the same volume—no opportunity for literary display, nothing but a record of individual feelings with which the writer seems satisfied because they are interesting to himself. It is, in fact, the germ of that method which Huysmans has since carried to so brilliant a climax in "En Route." All the glamour of war and the enthusiasm of patriotism are here—long before Zola wrote his "Débâcle"—reduced to their simplest terms in the miseries of the individual soldier whose chief aspiration it becomes at last to return to a home where the necessities of nature may be satisfied in comfort and peace.

The best of Huysmans' early novels is undoubtedly "En Ménage." It is the intimate history of a young literary man who, having married a wife whom he shortly afterwards finds unfaithful, leaves her, returns to his bachelor life, and in the end becomes reconciled to her. This picture of a studious man who goes away with his books to fight over again the petty battles of bachelorhood with the *bonne* and the *concierge* and his own cravings for womanly love and companionship, reveals clearly for the first time Huysmans' power of analyzing states of mind that are at once simple and subtle. Perhaps no writer surprises us more by his revealing insight into the commonplace experiences which all a novelist's traditions lead him to idealize or ignore. As a whole, however, "En Ménage" is scarcely yet a master's work, a little laboured, with labour which cannot yet achieve splendour of effect. Nor can a much slighter story, "A Vau l'Eau," which appeared a little later, be said to mark a further stage in development, though it is a characteristic study, this sordid history of Folantin, the poor, lame, discontented, middle-aged clerk. Cheated and bullied on every side, falling a prey to the vulgar woman of the street who boisterously takes possession of him in the climax of the story, all the time feeling poignantly the whole absurdity of the situation, there is yet one spot where hope seems possible. He has no religious faith; "and yet," he reflects, "yet mysticism alone could heal the wound that tortures me." Thus Folantin, though like André in "En Ménage" he resigns himself to the inevitable stupidity of life, yet stretches out his hands towards the Durtal of Huysmans' latest work.

In all these novels we feel that Huysmans has not attained to full self-expression. Intellectual mastery, indeed, he is attaining, but scarcely yet the expression of his own personal ideals. The poet in Huysmans, the painter enamoured of beauty and seeking it in unfamiliar places, has little scope in these detailed pictures of sordid or commonplace life. At this early period it is still in prose-poems, especially in "Croquis Parisiens," that this craving finds satisfaction. Huysmans took up this form where Baudelaire and Mallarmé had left it, and sought to carry it yet further. In that he was scarcely successful. The excess of tension in the tortured language with which he elaborates his effects too often holds him back from the goal of perfection. We must yet value in "Croquis Parisiens" its highly wrought and individual effects of rhythm and colour and form. In France, at all events, Huysmans is held to inaugurate the poetic treatment of modern things—a characteristic already traceable in "Les Sœurs Vatard"—and this book deals with the aesthetic aspects of latter-day Paris, with the things that are "ugly and superb, outrageous and yet exquisite," as a type of which he selects the Folies-Bergère, at that time the most characteristic of Parisian music-halls, and he was thus the first to discuss the aesthetic value of the variety stage which has been made cheaper since. For the most part, however, these *Croquis* are of the simplest and most commonplace things—the forlorn Bièvre district, the poor man's *café*, the roast-chestnut seller—extracting the beauty or pathos or strangeness of all these things. "Thy garment is the palette of settings suns, the rust of old copper, the brown gilt of Cordovan leather, the sandal and saffron tints of the autumn foliage. . . . When I contemplate thy coat of mail I think of Rembrandt's pictures, I see again his superb heads, his sunny flesh, his gleaming jewels on black velvet. I see again his rays of light in the night, his trailing gold in the shade, the dawning of suns through dark arches." The humble bloater has surely never before been sung in language which recalls the Beloved of the "Song of Songs."

In 1884 "A Rebours" appeared. Not perhaps his greatest achievement, it must ever remain the central work in which he has most powerfully concentrated his whole vision of life. It sums up the progress he had already made, foretells the progress he was afterwards to make, in a style that is always individual, always masterly in its individuality. Technically, it may be said that the power of "A Rebours" lies in the fact that here for the first time Huysmans has succeeded in uniting the two lines of his literary development: the austere analysis in the novels of commonplace things mostly alien to the writer, and the freer elaboration in the prose-poems of his own more intimate personal impressions. In their union the two streams attain a new power and a more intimately personal note. Des Esseintes, the hero of this book, may possibly have been at a few points suggested by a much less interesting real personage in contemporary Paris, the Comte de Montesquiou-Fezensac, but in the main he was certainly created by Huysmans' own brain, as the representative of his author's hyperæsthetic experience of the world and the mouthpiece of his most personal judgments. The victim of over-wrought nerves, of neuralgia and dyspepsia, Des Esseintes retires for a season from Paris to the solitude of his country house at Fontenay, which he has fitted up, on almost cloistral methods, to soothe his fantasy and to gratify his complex aesthetic sensations, his love of reading and contemplation. The finest pictures of Gustave Moreau hang on the walls, with the fantastic engravings of Luyken, and the strange visions of Odilon Redon. He has a tortoise curiously inlaid with precious stones; he delights in all those exotic plants which reveal Nature's most unnatural freaks; he is a sensitive amateur of perfumes, and considers that the pleasures of smell are equal to those of sight or sound; he possesses a row of little barrels of liqueurs so arranged that he can blend in infinite variety the contents of this instrument, his "mouth-organ" he calls it, and produce harmonies which seem to him comparable to those yielded by a musical orchestra. But the solitary pleasures of this palace of art only increase the nervous strain he is suffering from; and at the urgent bidding of his doctor Des Esseintes returns to the society of his abhorred fellow-beings in Paris, himself opening the dyke that admitted the "waves of human mediocrity" to engulf his refuge. And this wonderful confession of aesthetic faith—with its long series of deliberately searching and decisive affirmations on life, religion, literature, art—ends with a sudden solemn invocation that is surprisingly tremulous: "Take pity, O Lord, on the Christian who doubts, on the skeptic who desires to believe, on the convict of life who embarks alone, in the night, beneath a sky no longer lit by the consoling beacons of ancient faith."

"He who carries his own most intimate emotions to their highest point becomes the first in file of a long series of men"; that saying is peculiarly true of Huysmans. But to be a leader of men one must turn one's back on men. Huysmans' attitude towards his readers was somewhat like that of Thoreau, who spoke with lofty disdain of such writers as "would fain have one reader before they die." As he has since remarked, Huysmans wrote "A Rebours" for a dozen persons, and was himself more surprised than any one at the wide interest it evoked. Yet that interest was no accident. Certain aesthetic ideals of the latter half of the nineteenth century are more quintessentially expressed in "A Rebours" than in any other book. Intensely personal, audaciously independent, it yet sums up a movement which has scarcely now worked itself out. We may read it and re-read, not only for the light which it casts on that movement, but upon every similar period of acute aesthetic perception in the past.

II

The aesthetic attitude towards art which "A Rebours" illuminates is that commonly called decadent. Decadence in art, though a fairly simple phenomenon, and world-wide as art itself, is still so ill understood that it may be worth while to discuss briefly its precise nature, more especially as manifested in literature.

Technically, a decadent style is only such in relation to a classic style. It is simply a further development of a classic style, a further specialization, the homogeneous, in Spencerian phraseology, having become heterogeneous. The first is beautiful because the parts are subordinated to the whole; the second is beautiful because the whole is subordinated to the parts. Among our own early prose-writers Sir Thomas Browne represents the type of decadence in style. Swift's prose is classic, Pater's decadent. Hume and Gibbon are classic, Emerson and Carlyle decadent. Roman architecture is classic, to become in its Byzantine developments completely decadent, and St. Mark's is the perfected type of decadence in art; pure early Gothic is classic in the highest degree, while later Gothic, grown weary of the commonplaces of structure, is again decadent. In each case the earlier and classic manner—for the classic manner, being more closely related to the ends of utility, must always be earlier—subordinates the parts to the whole, and strives after those virtues which the whole may best express; the later manner depreciates the importance of the whole for the benefit of its parts, and strives after the virtues of individualism. All art is the rising and falling of the slopes of a rhythmic curve between these two classic and decadent extremes.

Decadence suggests to us going down, falling, decay. If we walk down a real hill we do not feel that we commit a more wicked act than when we walked up it. But if it is a figurative hill then we view Hell at the bottom. The word "corruption"—used in a precise and technical sense to indicate the breaking up of the whole for the benefit of its parts—serves also to indicate a period or manner of decadence in art. This makes confusion worse, for here the moralist feels that surely he is on safe ground. But as Nietzsche, with his usual acuteness in cutting at the root of vulgar prejudice, has well remarked (in "Die Fröhliche Wissenschaft"), even as regards what is called the period of "corruption" in the evolution of societies, we are apt to overlook the fact that the energy which in more primitive times marked the operations of the community as a whole has now simply been transferred to the individuals themselves, and this aggrandizement of the individual really produces an even greater amount of energy. The individual has gained more than the community has lost. An age of social decadence is not only the age of sinners and degenerates, but of saints and martyrs, and decadent Rome produced an Antoninus as well as a Heliogabalus. No doubt social "corruption" and literary "corruption" tend to go together; an age of individualism is usually an age of artistic decadence, and we may note that the chief literary artists of America—Poe, Hawthorne, Whitman—are for the most part in the technical sense decadents.

Rome supplies the first clear types of classic and decadent literature, and the small group of recent French writers to whom the term has been more specifically applied were for the most part peculiarly attracted by later Latin literature. So far as I can make out, it is to the profound and penetrating genius of Baudelaire that we owe the first clear apprehension of the legitimate part which decadence plays in literature. We may trace it, indeed, in his own style, clear, pure, and correct as that style always remains, as well as in his literary preferences. He was a good Latinist, and his favourite Latin authors were Apuleius, Juvenal, Petronius, St. Augustine, Tertullian, and other writers in prose and verse of the early Christian Church. He himself wrote a love-poem in rhymed Latin verse, adding to it a note concerning the late Latin decadence regarded as "the supreme sign of a vigorous person already transformed and prepared for the spiritual life....In this marvellous tongue," he added, "solecism and barbarism seem to me to render the forced negligence of a passion which forgets itself and mocks at rules. Words taken in a new meaning reveal the charming awkwardness of the northern barbarian kneeling before the Roman beauty." But the best early statement of the meaning of decadence in style—though doubtless inspired by Baudelaire—was furnished by Gautier in 1868 in the course of the essay on Baudelaire which is probably the most interesting piece of criticism he ever achieved:

"The poet of the 'Fleurs du Mal' loved what is improperly called the style of decadence, and which is nothing else but art arrived at that point of extreme maturity yielded by the slanting suns of aged civilizations: an ingenious complicated style, full of shades and of research, constantly pushing back the boundaries of speech, borrowing from all the technical vocabularies, taking colour from all palettes and notes from all keyboards, struggling to render what is most inexpressible in thought, what is vague and most elusive in the outlines of form, listening to translate the subtle confidences of neurosis, the dying confessions of passion grown depraved, and the strange hallucinations of the obsession which is turning to madness. The style of decadence is the ultimate utterance of the Word, summoned to final expression and driven to its last hiding-place. Unlike the classic style it admits shadow. . . One may well imagine that the fourteen hundred words of the Racinian vocabulary scarcely suffice the author who has undertaken the laborious task of rendering modern ideas and things in their infinite complexity and multiple colouration."

Some fifteen years later, Bourget, again in an essay on Baudelaire ("Essais de Psychologie Contemporaine"), continued the exposition of the theory of decadence, elaborating the analogy to the social organism which enters the state of decadence as soon as the individual life of the parts is no longer subordinated to the whole. "A similar law governs the development and decadence of that other organism which we call language. A style of decadence is one in which the unity of the book is

decomposed to give place to the independence of the page, in which the
page is decomposed to give place to the independence of the phrase,
and the phrase to give place to the independence of the word." It was at
this time (about 1884) that the term "decadent" seems first to have been
applied by Barrès and others to the group of which Verlaine,
Huysmans, Mallarmé were the most distinguished members, and in so
far as it signified an ardent and elaborate search for perfection of detail
beyond that attained by Parnassian classicality it was tolerated or
accepted. Verlaine, indeed, was for the most part indifferent to labels,
neither accepting nor rejecting them, and his work was not bound up
with any theory. But Huysmans, with the intellectual passion of the
pioneer in art, deliberate and relentless, has carried both the theory and
the practice of decadence in style to the farthest point. In practice he
goes beyond Baudelaire, who, however enamoured he may have been
of what he called the phosphorescence of putrescence, always retained
in his own style much of what is best in the classic manner. Huysmans'
vocabulary is vast, his images, whether remote or familiar, always
daring—"dragged," in the words of one critic, "by the hair or by the
feet, down the worm-eaten staircase of terrified Syntax,"—but a heart-
felt pulse of emotion is restrained beneath the sombre and extravagant
magnificence of this style, and imparts at the best that modulated surge
of life which only the great masters can control.

Des Esseintes's predilections in literature are elaborated through
several chapters, and without question he faithfully reflects his
creator's impressions. He was indifferent or contemptuous towards the
writers of the Latin Augustan age; Virgil seemed to him thin and
mechanical, Horace a detestable clown; the fat redundancy of Cicero,
we are told, and the dry constipation of Caesar alike disgusted him;
Sallust, Livy, Juvenal, even Tacitus and Plautus, though for these he
had words of praise, seemed to him for the most part merely the
delights of pseudo-literary readers. Latin only began to be interesting to
Des Esseintes in Lucan, for here at least, in spite of the underlying
hollowness, it became expressive and studded with brilliant jewels. The
author whom above all he delighted in was Petronius—who reminded
Des Esseintes of the modern French novelists he most admired—and
several eloquent pages are devoted to that profound observer, delicate
analyst, and marvellous painter who modelled his own vivid and
precise style out of all the idioms and slang of his day. After Petronius
there was a gap in his collection of Latin authors until the second
century of our own era is reached with Apuleius and the sterner
Christian contemporaries of that jovial pagan, Tertullian and the rest, in
whose hands the tongue that in Petronius had reached supreme maturity
now began to dissolve. For Tertullian he had little admiration, and none
for Augustine, though sympathizing with his "City of God" and his
general disgust for the world. But the special odour which the

Christians had by the fourth century imparted to decomposing pagan Latin was delightful to him in such authors as Commodian of Gaza, whose tawny, sombre, and tortuous style he even preferred to Claudian's sonorous blasts, in which the trumpet of paganism was last heard in the world. He was also able to maintain interest in Prudentius, Sedulius, and a host of unknown Christians who combined Catholic fervour with a Latinity which had become, as it were, completely putrid, leaving but a few shreds of torn flesh for the Christians to "marinate in the brine of their new tongue."

Des Esseintes is no admirer of Rabelais or Molière, of Voltaire or Rousseau. Among the older French writers he read only Villon, D'Aubigné, Bossuet, Bourdaloue, Nicole, and especially Pascal. Putting these aside, his French library began with Baudelaire, whose works he had printed in an edition of one copy, in episcopal letters, in large missal *format*, bound in flesh-coloured pig-skin; he found an unspeakable delight in reading this poet who, "in an age when verse only served to express the external aspects of things, had succeeded in expressing the inexpressible, by virtue of a muscular and sinewy speech which more than any other possessed the marvellous power of fixing with strange sanity of expression the most morbid, fleeting, tremulous states of weary brains and sorrowful souls." After Baudelaire the few French books on Des Esseintes's shelves fall into two groups, one religious, one secular. Most of the French clerical writers he disregarded, for they yield a pale flux of words which seemed to him to come from a schoolgirl in a convent. Lacordaire he regarded as an exception, for his language had been fused and moulded by ardent eloquence, but for the most part the Catholic writers he preferred were outside the Church. For Hello's "Homme," especially, he cherished profound admiration, and an inevitable sympathy for its author, who seemed to him "a cunning engineer of the soul, a skilful watchmaker of the brain, delighting to examine the mechanism of a passion and to explain the play of the wheel-work," and yet united to this power of analysis all the fanaticism of a Biblical prophet, and the tortured ingenuity of a master of style—an ill-balanced, incoherent, yet subtle personality. But above all he delighted in Barbey d'Aurévilly, shut out from the Church as an unclean and pestiferous heretic, yet glorying to sing her praises, insinuating into that praise a note of almost sadistic sacrilege, a writer at once devout and impious, altogether after Des Esseintes's own heart, so that a special copy of the "Diaboliques," in episcopal violet and cardinal purple, printed on sanctified vellum with initials adorned by satanic tails, formed one of his most cherished possessions. In D'Aurévilly's style alone he truly recognized the same gaminess, the speckled morbidity, the flavour as of a sleepy pear which he loved in decadent Latin and the monastic writers of old time. Of contemporary secular books he possessed not many; certain selected works of the three great French novelists of his time—Flaubert, Goncourt, and Zola—for in all three he found in various forms, that "nostalgie des au-delà" by which he was himself haunted. With Baudelaire, these three were, in modern profane literature, the authors by whom he had chiefly been moulded. The scanty collection also included Verlaine, Mallarmé, Poe, and Villiers de l'Isle-Adam, whose firm fantastic style and poignantly ironic attitude towards the utilitarian modern world he found entirely to his taste. Finally, there only remained the little anthology of prose-poems. Des Esseintes thought it improbable that he would ever make any additions to his library; it seemed impossible to him that a decadent language—"struggling on its death-bed to repair all the omissions of joy and bequeath the subtlest memories of pain"—would ever go beyond Mallarmé.

We have to recognize that decadence is an aesthetic and not a moral conception. The power of words is great, but they need not befool us. The classic herring should suggest no moral superiority over the decadent bloater. We are not called upon to air our moral indignation over the bass end of the musical clef. We may well reserve our finest admiration for the classic in art, for therein are included the largest and most imposing works of human skill; but our admiration is of little worth if it is founded on incapacity to appreciate the decadent. Each has its virtues, each is equally right and necessary. One ignorant of plants might well say, on gazing at a seed-capsule with its seeds disposed in harmonious rows, that there was the eternally natural and wholesome order of things, and on seeing the same capsule wither and cast abroad its seeds to germinate at random in the earth, that here was an unwholesome and deplorable period of decay. But he would know little of the transmutations of life. And we have to recognize that those persons who bring the same crude notions into the field of art know as little of the life of the spirit.

III

For some years after the appearance of "A Rebours" Huysmans produced nothing of any magnitude. "En Rade," his next novel, the experience of a Parisian married couple who, under the stress of temporary pecuniary difficulties, go into the country to stay at an uncle's farm, dwells in the memory chiefly by virtue of two vividly naturalistic episodes, the birth of a calf and the death of a cat. More interesting, more intimately personal, are the two volumes of art criticism, "L'Art Moderne" and "Certains," which Huysmans published at about this period. Degas, Rops, Raffaelli, Odilon Redon are among the artists of very various temperament whom Huysmans either discovered, or at all events first appreciated in their full significance, and when he writes of them it is not alone critical insight which he reveals, but his own personal vision of the world.

To Huysmans the world has ever been above all a vision; it was no accident that the art that appeals most purely to the eyes is that of which he has been the finest critic. One is tempted, indeed, to suggest that this aptitude is the outcome of heredity. He has been intensely preoccupied with the effort to express those visible aspects of things which the arts of design were made to express, which the art of speech can perhaps never express. The tortured elaboration of his style is chiefly due to this perpetual effort to squeeze tones and colours out of this foreign medium. The painter's brain holds only a pen and cannot rest until it has wrung from it a brush's work. But not only is the sense of vision marked in Huysmans. We are conscious of a general hyperæsthesia, an intense alertness to the inrush of sensations, which we might well term morbid if it were not so completely intellectualized and controlled. Hearing, indeed, appears to be less acutely sensitive than sight, the poet is subordinated to the painter, though that sense still makes itself felt, and the heavy multicoloured paragraphs often fall at the close into a melancholy and poignant rhythm laden with sighs. It is the sense of smell which Huysmans' work would lead us to regard as most highly developed after that of sight. The serious way in which Des Esseintes treats perfumes is charactertistic, and one of the most curious and elaborate of the "Croquis Parisiens" is "Le Gousset," in which the capacities of language are strained to define and differentiate the odours of feminine arm-pits. Again, earlier, in a preface written for Hannon's "Rimes de Joie," Huysmans points out that that writer—who failed to fulfil his early promise—alone of contemporary poets possessed "la curiosité des parfums," and that his chief poem was written in honour of what Huysmans called "the libertine virtues of that glorious perfume," opoponax. This sensitiveness to odour is less marked in Huysmans' later work, but the dominance of vision remains.

The two volumes of essays on art incidentally serve to throw considerable light on Huysmans' conception of life. For special illustration we may take his attitude towards women, whom in his novels he usually treats, from a rather conventionally sexual point of view, as a fact in man's life rather than as a subject for independent analysis. In these essays we may trace the development of his own personal point of view, and in comparing the earlier with the later volume we find a change which is significant of the general evolution of Huysmans' attitude towards life. He is at once the ultra-modern child of a refined civilization and the victim of nostalgia for an ascetic mediævalism; his originality lies in the fact that in him these two tendencies are not opposed but harmonious, although the second has only of late reached full development. In a notable passage in "En Rade," Jacques, the hero, confesses that he can see nothing really great or beautiful in a harvest field, with its anodyne toil, as compared with a workshop or a steamboat, "the horrible magnificence of machines, that one beauty which the modern world has been able to create." It is so that Huysmans views women also; he is as indifferent to the feminine ideals of classic art as to its literary ideals. In *L'Art Moderne*, speaking with admiration of a study of the nude by Gauguin, he proceeds to lament that no one has painted the unclothed modern woman without falsification or premeditated arrangement, real, alive in her own intimate personality, with her own joys and pains incarnated in the curves of her flesh, and the lash of childbirth traceable on her flanks. We go to the Louvre to learn how to paint, he remarks, forgetting that "beauty is not uniform and invariable, but changes with the age and the climate, that the Venus of Milo, for instance, is now not more beautiful and interesting than those ancient statues of the New World, streaked and tattooed and adorned with feathers; that both are but diverse manifestations of the same ideal of beauty pursued by different races; that at the present date there can be no question of reaching the beautiful by Venetian, Greek, Dutch, or Flemish rites; but only by striving to disengage it from contemporary life, from the world that surrounds us." "Un nu fatigué, délicat, affiné, vibrant" can alone conform to our own time; and he adds that no one has truly painted the nude since Rembrandt. It is instructive to turn from this essay to that on Degas, written some six years later. It may fairly be said that to Degas belongs the honour of taking up the study of the nude at the point where Rembrandt left it; and like Rembrandt, he has realized that the nude can only be rightly represented in those movements, postures, and avocations by which it is naturally and habitually exposed. It is scarcely surprising, therefore, that Huysmans at once grasped the full significance of the painter's achievement. But he has nothing now to say of the beauty that lies beneath the confinement of modern garments, "the delicious charm of youth, grown languid, rendered as it were divine by the debilitating air of cities." On the contrary, he emphasizes the vision which Degas presents of women at the bathtub revealing in every "frog-like and simian attitude" their pitiful homeliness, "the humid horror of a body which no washing can purify." Such a glorified contempt of the flesh, he adds, has never been achieved since the Middle Ages. There we catch what had now become the dominant tone in Huysmans' vision; the most modern things in art now suggest to him, they seem to merge into, the most mediæval and ascetic. And if we turn to the essay of Félicien Rops in the same volume—the most masterly of his essays—we find the same point developed to the utmost. Rops in his own way is as modern and as daring an artist of the nude as Degas. But, as Huysmans perceives, in delineating the essentially modern he is scarcely a supreme artist, is even inferior to Forain, who in his own circumscribed region is insurpassable. Rops, as Huysmans points out, is the great artist of the symbolical rather than the naturalistic modern, a great artist who furnishes the counterpart to Memlinc and Fra Angelico. All art, Huysmans proceeds, "must gravitate, like humanity which has given birth to it and the earth which carries it, between the two poles of Purity and Wantonness, the Heaven and the Hell of art." Rops has taken the latter pole, in no vulgar nymphomaniacal shapes, but "to divulge its causes, to summarize it Catholically, if one may say so, in ardent and sorrowful images"; he has drawn women who are "diabolical Theresas, satanized saints." Following in the path initiated by Baudelaire and Barbey d'Aurévilly, Huysmans concludes, Rops has restored Wantonness to her ancient and Catholic dignity. Thus is Huysmans almost imperceptibly led back to the old standpoint from which woman and the Devil are one.

"Certains" was immediately followed by "Là-Bas." This novel is mainly a study of Satanism, in which Huysmans interested himself long before it attracted the general attention it has since received in France. There are, however, three lines of interest in the book, the story of Gilles de Rais and his Sadism, the discussion of Satanism culminating in an extraordinary description of a modern celebration of the Black Mass, and the narration of Durtal's *liaison* with Madame Chantelouve, wherein Huysmans reaches, by firm precision and triumphant audacity, the highest point he has attained in the analysis of the secrets of passion. But though full of excellent matter, the book loses in impressiveness from the multiplicity of these insufficiently compacted elements of interest.

While not among his finest achievements, however, it serves to mark the definite attainment of a new stage in both the spirit and the method of his work. Hitherto he had been a realist, in method if not in spirit, and had conquered the finest secrets of naturalistic art; by the help of "En Ménage" alone, as Hennequin, one of his earliest and best critics has said, "it will always be possible to restore the exact physiognomy of Paris today." At the outset of "Là-Bas" there is a discussion concerning the naturalistic novel and its functions which makes plain the standpoint to which Huysmans had now attained. Pondering the matter, Durtal, the hero of the book, considers that we need, on the one hand, the veracity of document, the precision of detail, the nervous strength of language, which realism has supplied; but also, on the other hand, we must draw water from the wells of the soul. We cannot explain everything by sexuality and insanity; we need the soul and the body in their natural reactions, their conflict and their union. "We must, in short, follow the great highway so deeply dug out by Zola, but it is also necessary to trace a parallel path in the air, another road by which we may reach the Beyond and the Afterward, to achieve thus, in one word, a spiritualistic naturalism." Dostoievsky comes nearest to this achievement, he remarks, and the real psychologist of the century is not Stendhal but Hello. In another form of art the early painters—Italian, German, especially Flemish—realized this ideal. Durtal sees a consummate revelation of such spiritual naturalism in Matthæus Grünewald's crucifixion at Cassel—the Christ who was at once a putrid and unaureoled corpse and yet a manifest god bathed in invisible light, the union of outrageous realism and outrageous idealism. "Thus from triumphal ordure Grünewald extracted the finest mints of dilection, the sharpest essences of tears." One may say that the tendency Huysmans here so clearly asserts had ever been present in his work. But in his previous novels his own native impulse was always a little unduly oppressed by the naturalistic formulas of Goncourt and Zola. The methods of these great masters had laid a burden on his work, and although the work developed beneath, and because of, that burden, a sense of laborious pain and obscurity too often resulted. Henceforth this disappears. Huysmans retains his own complexity of style, but he has won a certain measure of simplicity and lucidity. It was a natural development, no doubt furthered also by the position which Huysmans had now won in the world of letters. "A Rebours," which he had written for his own pleasure, had found an echo in thousands of readers, and the consciousness of an audience inspired a certain clarity of speech. From this time we miss the insults directed at the *bêtise* of humanity. These characteristics clearly mark Huysmans' next and perhaps greatest book, in which the writer who had conquered all the secrets of decadent art now sets his face towards the ideals of classic art.

In "En Route," indeed, these new qualities of simplicity, lucidity, humanity, and intensity of interest attain so high a degree that the book has reached a vast number of readers who could not realize the marvellous liberation from slavery to its material which the slow elaboration of art has here reached. In "A Rebours" Huysmans succeeded in taking up the prose-poem into his novel form, while at the same time certainly sacrificing something of the fine analysis of familiar things which he had developed in "En Ménage." In "En Route" he takes the novel from the point he had reached in "A Rebours," incorporates into it that power of analysis which has now reached incomparable simplicity and acuity, and thus wields the whole of the artistic means which he has acquired during a quarter of a century to one end, the presentation of a spiritual state which has become of absorbing personal interest to himself.

I well remember hearing M. Huysmans, many years ago, tell how a muddle-headed person had wished to commission him to paint a head of Christ. It seemed then a deliciously absurd request to make of the author of "A Rebours," and his face wore the patient smile which the spectacle of human stupidity was wont to evoke, but I have since thought that that muddle-headed person was wiser than he knew. As we look back on Huysmans' earlier work it is now easy to see how he has steadily progressed towards his present standpoint. "En Route" does not represent, as some might imagine, the reaction of an exhausted debauchee or even the self-deception of a disappointed man of the world. The temperament of Durtal is that of André and Folantin and Des Esseintes; from the first, in the "Drageoir à Epices," Huysmans has been an idealist and a seeker, by no means an ascetic, rather a man whose inquisitive senses and restless imagination had led him to taste of every forbidden fruit, but never one to whom the vulgar pleasures of life could offer any abiding satisfaction. The more precise record of Des Esseintes's early sexual life may help us here; while for the penultimate stage Durtal's relations with Madame Chantelouve in "Là-Bas," and the mingled attraction and repulsion which he felt for her, are certainly significant. In "En Route" Durtal magnifies his own wickedness, as Bunyan did in his "Grace Abounding"; the saints have always striven to magnify their wickedness, leaving to the sinners the congenial function of playing at righteousness. To trace the real permanence of Huysmans' attitude towards religion it is enough to turn back to "A Rebours." Des Esseintes had been educated by the Jesuits, and it sometimes seemed to him that that education had put into him some extra-terrestrial ferment which never after ceased to work, driving him in search of a new world and impossible ideals. He could find no earthly place of rest; he sought to build for himself a "refined Thebaïd" as a warm and comfortable ark wherein to find shelter from the flood of human imbecility. He was already drawn towards the Church by many bonds, by his predilection for early Christian Latinity, by the exquisite beauty of the ecclesiastical art of the Middle Ages, by his love for monastic mediæval music, "that emaciated music which acted instinctively on his nerves and seemed to him precious beyond all other. Just as Nietzsche was always haunted by the desire for a monastery for free-thinkers, so Des Esseintes dreamed of a hermitage, of the advantages of the cloistered life of convents, wherein men are persecuted by the world for meting out to it the just contempt of silence.

Des Esseintes, and even the Durtal of "Là-Bas," always put aside these thoughts with the reflection that, after all, the Church is only an out-worn legend, a magnificent imposture. In "En Route" Durtal has taken a decisive step. He has undergone that psychological experience commonly called "conversion." It is only of recent years that the phenomena of conversion have been seriously studied, but we know at all events that it is not intellectual, not even necessarily moral transformation, though it may react in either direction, but primarily an emotional phenomenon; and that it occurs especially in those who have undergone long and torturing disquietude, coming at last as the spontaneous resolution of all their doubts, the eruption of a soothing flood of peace, the silent explosion of inner light. The insight with which this state is described in "En Route" seems to testify to a real knowledge of it. No obvious moral or intellectual change is effected in Durtal, but he receives a new experience of reposeful faith, a conviction deeper than all argument. It is really the sudden emergence into consciousness of a very gradual process, and the concrete artistic temperament which had been subjected to the process reacts in its own way. A more abstract intelligence would have asked: "But, after all, is my faith true?" Durtal, in the presence of the growing structure of sensory and imaginative forms within him, which has become as it were a home, feels that the question of its truth has fallen into the background. Its perfect fitness has become the affirmation of its truth. Henceforth it is the task of his life to learn how best to adapt himself to what he recognizes as his eternal home. "En Route" represents a stage in this adaptation.

By a rare chance—a happier chance than befell Tolstoi under somewhat similar circumstances—a new development in artistic achievement has here run parallel, and in exquisite harmony, with the new spiritual development. The growing simplicity of Huysmans' work has reached a point beyond which it could not perhaps be carried without injury to his vivid and concrete style. And the new simplicity of spirit, of which it is the reflection, marks the final retreat into the background of that unreasonable contempt for humanity which ran through nearly all the previous books, and now at last passes even into an ecstasy of adoration in the passages concerning old Simon, the monastery swine-herd. Huysmans has chiefly shown his art, however, by relying almost solely for the interest of his book on his now consummate power of analysis. This power, which we may perhaps first clearly trace in "Sac au Dos," has developed in "En Ménage" into a wonderful skill to light up the unexplored corners of the soul and to lay bare those terrible thoughts which are, as he has somewhere said, the lamentable incarnation of "the unconscious ignominy of pure souls." In his earlier masterpiece, "A Rebours," however, it is little seen, having mostly passed into aesthetic criticism. The finest episode of emotional analysis here is the admirable chapter in which Des Esseintes's attempt to visit London is narrated. All his life he had wished to see two countries, Holland and England. He had been to Holland, and with visions from Rembrandt and Teniers he had returned disillusioned. Now he went to Galignani's, bought an English Baedeker, entered the bodega in the Rue de Rivoli to drink of that port which the English love, and then proceeded to a tavern opposite the Gare St. Lazare to eat what he imagined to be a characteristic English meal, surrounded by English people, and haunted by memories of Dickens. And as time went by he continued to sit still, while all the sensations of England seemed to pass along his nerves, still sat until at last the London mail had started. "Why stir," he asked himself, "when one can travel so magnificently in a chair? . . . Besides, what can one expect save fresh disillusionment, as in Holland? . . . And then I have experienced and seen what I wanted to experience and see. I have saturated myself with English life; it would be madness to lose by an awkward change of place these imperishable sensations. . . . He called a cab and returned with his portmanteaux, parcels, valises, rugs, umbrellas, and sticks to Fontenay, feeling the physical and mental fatigue of a man who returns home after a long and perilous journey." There could be no happier picture of the imaginative life of the artistic temperament. But in "En Route" analysis is the prime element of interest; from first to last there is nothing to hold us but this searching and poignant analysis of the fluctuations of Durtal's soul through the small section which he here travels in the road towards spiritual peace. There could, for instance, be no better statement than this of one of the mystic's secrets: "There are two ways of ridding ourselves of a thing which burdens us, casting it away or letting it fall. To cast away requires an effort of which we may not be capable, to let fall imposes no labour, is simpler, without peril, within reach of all. To cast away, again, implies a certain interest, a certain animation, even a certain fear; to let fall is absolute indifference, absolute contempt; believe me, use this method, and Satan will flee."

"En Route" is the first of a trilogy, and the names of the succeeding volumes, "La Cathédrale" and "L'Oblat," sufficiently indicate the end of the path on which Durtal, if not indeed his creator, has started. But however that may prove, whatever Huysmans' own final stage may be, there can be little doubt that he is the greatest master of style, and within his own limits the subtlest thinker and the acutest psychologist who in France today uses the medium of the novel. Only Zola can be compared with him, and between them there can be no kind of rivalry. Zola, with his immense and exuberant temperament, his sanity and width of view, his robust and plebeian art, has his own place on the high-road of modern literature. Huysmans, an intellectual and aesthetic aristocrat, has followed with unflinching sincerity the by-path along which his own more high-strung and exceptional temperament has led him, and his place, if seemingly a smaller one, is at least as sure; wherever men occupy themselves with the literature of the late nineteenth century they will certainly sometimes talk about Zola, sometimes read Huysmans. Zola's cyclopean architecture can only be seen as a whole when we have completed the weary task of investigating it in detail; in Huysmans we seek the expressiveness of the page, the sentence, the word. Strange as it may seem to some, it is the so-called realist who has given us the more idealized rendering of life; the concentrated vision of the idealist in his own smaller sphere has revealed not alone mysteries of the soul but even the exterior secrets of life. True it is that Huysmans has passed by with serene indifference, or else with contempt, the things which through the ages we have slowly learnt to count beautiful. But on the other hand, he has helped to enlarge the sphere of our delight by a new vision of beauty where before to our eyes there was no beauty, exercising the proper function of the artist who ever chooses the base and despised things of the world, even the things that are not, to put to nought the things that are. Therein the decadent has his justification. And while we may accept the pioneer's new vision of beauty, we are not called upon to reject those old familiar visions for which he has no eyes, only because his gaze must be fixed upon that unfamiliar height towards which he is leading the men who come after.

IV

Huysmans very exquisitely represents one aspect of the complex modern soul, that aspect which shrinks from the grosser forces of Nature, from the bare simplicity of the naked sky or the naked body, the "incessant deluge of human foolishness," the eternal oppression of the commonplace, to find a sedative for its exasperated nerves in the contemplation of esoteric beauty and the difficult search for the mystic peace which passes all understanding. "Needs must I rejoice beyond the age," runs the motto from the old Flemish mystic Ruysbroeck set on the front of "A Rebours," "though the world has horror of my joy and its grossness cannot understand what I would say." Such is decadence; such, indeed, is religion, in the wide and true sense of the word. Christianity itself, as we know it in the western church, sprang from the baptism of young barbarism into Latin decadence. Pagan art and its clear serenity, science, rationalism, the bright, rough vigour of the sun and the sea, the adorable mystery of common life and commonplace human love, are left to make up the spirit that in any age we call "classic."

Thus what we call classic corresponds on the spiritual side to the love of natural things, and what we call decadent to the research for the things which seem to lie beyond Nature. "Corporea pulchritudo in pelle solummodo constat. Nam si viderent homines hoc quod subtus pellem est, sicut lynces in Beotia cernere interiore dicuntur, mulieres videre nausearent. Iste decor in flegmate et sanguine et humore ac felle constitit." That is St. Odo of Cluny's acute analysis of woman, who for man is ever the symbol of Nature: beauty is skin-deep, drowned in excretions which we should scarcely care to touch with the finger's tip. And for the classic vision of Nature, listen to that fantastic and gigantic Englishman, Sir Kenelm Digby. He has been admitted by her maids to the bed-chamber of Venetia Stanley, the famous beauty who afterwards became his wife; she is still sleeping, and he cannot resist the temptation to undress and lie gently and reverently beside her, as half disturbed in her slumber she rolled on to her side from beneath the clothes; "and her smock was so twisted about her fair body that all her legs and best part of her thighs were naked, which lay so one over the other that they made a deep shadow where the never-satisfied eyes wished for the greatest light. A natural ruddiness did shine through the skin, as the sunbeams do through crystal or water, and ascertained him that it was flesh that he gazed upon, which yet he durst not touch for fear of melting it, so like snow it looked. Her belly was covered with her smock, which it raised up with a gentle swelling, and expressed the perfect figure of it through the folds of that discourteous veil. Her paps were like two globes—wherein the glories of the heaven and the earth were designed, and the azure veins seemed to divide constellations and kingdoms ... out of that darkness did glisten a few drops of sweat like diamond sparks...."

They play with the same counters, you observe, these two, Odo and Digby, with skin, sweat, and so forth, each placing upon them his own values. Idealists both of them, the one idealizes along the line of death, the other along the line of life which the whole race has followed, and both on their own grounds are irrefutable, the logic of life and the logic of death, alike solidly founded in the very structure of the world, of which man is the measuring-rod.

The classic party of Nature seems, indeed, the stronger—in seeming only, and one recalls that, of the two witnesses just cited, the abbot of Cluny was the most venerated man of his age, while no one troubled even to publish Digby's "Memoirs" until our own century— but it carries weakness in its very strength, the weakness of a great political party formed by coalition. It has not alone idealists on its side, but for the most part also the blind forces of robust vulgarity. So that the more fine-strung spirits are sometimes driven to a reaction against Nature and rationalism, like that of which Huysmans, from "L'Extase" onwards, has been the consistent representative. At the present moment such a reaction has attained a certain ascendancy.

Christianity once fitted nearly every person born into the European world; there must needs be some to whom, in no modern devitalized form but in its purest essence, it is still the one refuge possible. No doubt conditions have changed; the very world itself is not what it was to the mediæval man. For the mediæval man,—as still today for the child in the darkness,—his dreams and his fancies, every organic thrill in eye or ear, seemed to be flashed on him from a world of angels and demons without. The average man of those days—not the finer or the coarser natures, it may well be—might be said to be the victim of a species of madness, a paranoia, a sytematized persecutional delusion. He could not look serenely in the face of the stars or lie at rest among the fir-cones in the wood, for who knew what ambush of the Enemy might not lurk behind these things? Even in flowers, as St. Cyprian said, the Enemy lay hidden. There was only one spot where men might huddle together in safety—the church.

Huysmans, notwithstanding a very high degree of intellectual subtlety, is by virtue of his special aesthetic and imaginative temperament carried back to the more childlike attitude of this earlier age. The whole universe appears to him as a process of living images; he cannot reason in abstractions, cannot *rationalize*; that indeed is why he is inevitably an artist. Thus he is a born leader in a certain modern emotional movement.

That movement, as we know, is one of a group of movements now peculiarly active. We see them on every hand, occultism, theosophy, spiritualism, all those vague forms on the borderland of the unknown which call to tired men weary of too much living, or never strong enough to live at all, to hide their faces from the sun of nature and grope into cool, delicious darkness, soothing the fever of life. It is foolish to resent this tendency; it has its rightness; it suits some, who may well cling to their private dream if life itself is but a dream. At the worst we may remember that, however repugnant such movements may be, to let fall remains a better way of putting Satan to flight than to cast away. And at the best one should know that this is part of the vital process by which the spiritual world moves on its axis, alternating between darkness and light.

Therefore soak yourself in mysticism, follow every intoxicating path to every impossible Beyond, be drunken with mediævalism, occultism. Yet be sure that Nature is your home, and that from the farthest excursions you will return the more certainly to those fundamental instincts which are rooted in the zoological series at the summit of which we stand. For the whole spiritual cosmogony finally rests, not indeed on a tortoise, but on the emotional impulses of the mammal vertebrata which constitute us men.

HAVELOCK ELLIS

Preface

Written Twenty Years After The Novel

I suppose all men of letters are like myself in this, that they never re-read their works once they have appeared.

Nothing in fact is more disenchanting, more painful than to examine one's phrases again after an interval of years. They have been in bottle, so to speak, and form a deposit at the bottom of the book; and, most times, volumes are not like wines which improve with age; once clarified in the fulness of time, the chapters grow flat and their bouquet evaporates.

Such is the impression certain bottles stacked in the "Against the Grain" bin made upon me when I had to uncork them.

Now, sadly enough, I endeavour to recall, as I turn over the pages, what precise state of mind I could have been in at the time I wrote them.

Naturalism was then at full tide; but that school, which was destined to perform the never-to-be-forgotten good service of showing real personages in accurate surroundings, was condemned to go on repeating itself, marking time for ever on the same spot.

It would allow, in theory at any rate, almost no exception; it was therefore bound to limit its range to the delineation of everyday existence, forced, under pretext of making its characters alive, to create beings as like as they could possibly be made to the general average of people. This ideal was, in its class, realized in a masterpiece which has been, far more than *L'Assommoir*, the type and paragon of Naturalism, viz, the *Education Sentimentale* of Gustave Flaubert. This book was for all of us, men of the *Soirées de Médan*, a veritable Bible; but it brought little grist to our mill. It was done and ended, a thing not to be begun again even by Flaubert himself. Consequently we found ourselves reduced in those days to tack about, to prowl round all the countryside by roads more or less thoroughly explored before.

Virtue being, we are compelled to admit, an exception here below, was for that very reason barred from the Naturalistic author's scheme. Not possessing the orthodox Christian conception of the Temptation and Fall, we had no knowledge from what struggles and what tribulations it had arisen; the soul's heroism, triumphant over snares and pitfalls, was inappreciable by us. It would never have occurred to us to describe this combat, with its ups and down, its feints and flank attacks, not to speak of its skilled auxiliaries arming themselves very often far from the individual against whom the Evil One's assault is directed, in the quiet of some remote Cloister; to us Virtue seemed the attribute of creatures devoid of intelligent curiosity or wanting in common sense,—hardly a stimulating subject, in any case, to treat from the point of view of art.

Remained the Vices; but here the area capable of cultivation was restricted. It was confined to the territories of the Seven Deadly Sins, and even of these seven, one only, that against the Sixth Commandment, was fairly accessible.

The rest had been cropped cruelly bare, and hardly a grape was left to pluck in those vineyards. Avarice, for instance, had been squeezed to the last drop of liquor by Balzac and Hello. Pride, Anger, Envy had played their parts in every publication of the Romantics, and as dramatic *motifs* had been so violently distorted by the abuse of stage exigencies that it would have called for a veritable genius to rejuvenate them in a book. As for Gluttony and Idleness, these seemed to lend themselves to realization rather in subsidiary characters, to be more suitable to supers than to leading actors or prima donnas in the novel of manners.

The truth is that Pride would have been the most magnificent of all sins to study, in its infernal ramifications of cruelty towards others and false humility, that Gluttony, towing in its wake Lust and Idleness, and Theft would have supplied subjects for surprising investigations, if only writers had examined these offences with the lamp and blow-pipe of the Church and possessing Faith. But as a fact not one of us was qualified for the task. We were therefore driven to handle and re-handle the sin of all others most easily laid bare, Lust, in all its various manifestations; God knows we did our best, but this amusement was in the nature of things short-lived. Invent what one chose, the story could be summed up in half-a-dozen words,—to wit, why did Monsieur So-and-So commit or not commit adultery with Madame This or That? If you wished to be distinguished and stand out as a writer of the most polite taste, you made the work of the flesh take place between a Marquise and a Count; if on the other hand, you wanted to pose as a popular author, a writer knowing what's what, you chose a lover from the slums and the first street girl to hand. Only the frame was different. High life, it appears to me, has carried the day at present in the reader's good graces, for I notice that for the moment he hardly cares to regale himself on plebeian or middle-class amours, but still continues to savour the scruples and hesitations of the Marquise on her way to meet her seducer at a dainty little flat, whose aspect changes according to the varying fashion in furniture. Will she fall? Will she not fall? This is called a study in Psychology. Well, I have no objection.

Nevertheless I must own that, if I happen to open a book and come upon this everlasting seduction and not less everlasting adultery, I make haste to shut it again, being in no sort of way anxious to know how the promised idyll will finish. Any volume that does not contain authenticated documents, any book that does not teach me something, loses all interest in my eyes.

At the date when "Against the Grain" was published, in 1884 that is to say, the state of things therefore was this: Naturalism was getting more and more out of breath by dint of turning the mill for ever in the same round. The stock of observations that each writer had stored up by self-scrutiny or study of his neighbours was getting exhausted. Zola, who was a first-rate scene-painter, got out of the difficulty by designing big, bold canvases more or less true to life; he suggested fairly well the illusion of movement and action; his heroes were devoid of soul, governed simply and solely by impulses and instincts, which greatly simplified the work of analysis. They moved about, carried out sundry summary activities, peopled the scene with tolerably convincing sketches of lay-figures that became the principal characters of his dramas. In this fashion he celebrated the Central Markets, and the big stores of Paris, the railways and mines of the country at large; and the human beings wandering lost amid these surroundings played no more than the part of utility men and supers therein. But Zola was Zola—an artist a trifle ponderous, but endowed with powerful lungs and massive fists.

The rest of us, less robust and concerned about a more subtle method and a truer art, were constrained to ask ourselves the question whether Naturalism was not marching up a blind alley and if we were not bound soon to knock up against an impassable wall.

To tell the truth, these reflections did not actually occur to me till much later. I was striving in vain to escape from a *cul-de-sac* in which I was suffocating, but I had no settled plan, and "Against the Grain," which, by letting in fresh air, let me get away from a literature that had no door of escape, is a purely unpremeditated work, imagined without any preconceived ideas, without definite intentions for the future, without any predetermined plan whatever.

It had appeared to me at first in the light of a brief fantasy, under the form of an extravagant tale; I saw in it something like a pendant to *A vau-l'eau* transferred into another milieu; I pictured to myself a Monsieur Folantin, more cultured, more refined, more wealthy and who has discovered in artificiality a relief from the disgust inspired by the worries of life and the American habits of his time; I outlined him winging a swift flight to the land of dreams, seeking refuge in the illusion of extravagant fancies, living alone and aloof, remote from his own country, amid the association called up by memory of more cordial epochs, and less villainous surroundings. The more I pondered over it, the more the subject grew and the more it seemed to demand long and patient researches. Each chapter became the extract of a speciality, the sublimate of a different art; I found it condensing into a "meat essence" of precious stones, of perfumes, of flowers, of literature religious and lay, of profane music and plain-song.

The strange thing was that, without having had an inkling of this at the beginning, I was led by the very nature of my task to study the Church under many aspects. It was in fact impossible to go back to the only really characteristic eras humanity has ever known, the Middle Ages that is, without realizing that She embraced everything, that art existed only in Her and by Her. Being outside the Faith, I looked upon Her with some suspicion, surprised at Her greatness and glory, asking myself how a Religion which seemed to me only made for children had been able to suggest such marvellous works.

I prowled a little round Her in a groping way, guessing more than I saw, reconstructing a whole for myself with the fragments I recovered in Museums and old books. And to-day as I skim, after more lengthy and more trustworthy investigations, the pages of "Against the Grain," that deal with Catholicism and religious art, I note that that miniature panorama I then sketched on leaves of block-books, is accurate. What I depicted then was succinct, wanting elaboration, but it was veracious. I have confined myself subsequently to enlarging and developing my outline drawings.

I might quite well sign my name at the present moment to the pages of "Against the Grain" relating to the Church, for they appear in very deed to have been written by a Catholic.

Yet I supposed myself far from Religion all the time! I did not dream that from Schopenhauer, whom I admired beyond all reason, to Ecclesiastes and the Book of Job was only a step. The premises as to Pessimism are identical, only when it comes to action, the Philosopher shirks away. I like his ideas on the horror of existence, on the stupidity of the world, on the harshness of fate; I like them just as well in the Holy Books. But Schopenhauer's observations end in nothing; he leaves you, so to say, in the lurch; his aphorisms, in fact, are but a *hortus siccus* of lifeless specimens. The Church for her part explains origins and causes, certifies results, offers remedies; she is not satisfied with giving you a spiritual consultation, she treats you and cures you, while the German quack, after clearly showing you that the complaint you suffer from is incurable, turns his back on you with a sardonic grin.

His Pessimism is no different from that of the Scriptures from which he borrowed it. He has said no more than Solomon or than Job, no more even than the Imitation, which long before his day summed up his whole philosophy in a sentence:—"Verily it is a wretched thing to be alive on the earth!"

Looked at from a distance, these similarities and dissimilarities stand out clearly, but at that period, if I saw them at all, I paid no heed; the necessity of coming to a conclusion did not appeal to me; the road laid down by Schopenhauer was practicable and offered diversified views. I travelled contentedly along it, without a thought of where it led. In those days I had no real illumination as to debts to be paid, no apprehension of penalties to be exacted; the mysteries of the Catechism struck me as childish; like the mass of Catholics, indeed, I was entirely ignorant of my religion; I failed to realize that everything is mysterious, that we live only in mystery, that if chance existed, chance would be yet more mysterious than Providence. I could not admit the fact of pain inflicted by a God, I persuaded myself that Pessimism could act as the consoler of lofty souls. What foolishness! Of all notions *this* had the smallest basis of experience, was the lease of a "human document," to use a phrase dear to Naturalism. Never yet has Pessimism consoled either the sick of body or the afflicted of soul!

I smile when after so many years I re-read the pages where these theories, determinedly false, are affirmed.

But what strikes me most forcibly in this perusal is another fact: all the romances I have written since "Against the Grain" are contained in embryo in that book. The successive chapters are nothing more nor less than the priming of the volumes that followed. The chapter on the Latin Literature of the Decadence I have, if not developed, at any rate probed deeper into, when treating of the Liturgy in *En Route* and *L'Oblat*.

I shall now reprint it without any alteration save in connexion with St. Ambrose, whose watery prose and turgid rhetoric I continue to dislike. I still think him what I called him then, a "tiresome Christian Cicero," but, in compensation, as a poet he is charming; his hymns and those of his school are among the finest the Church has preserved. I will add that the literature, of a rather special sort it is true, of the Hymnary might well have found a place in the reserved compartment of that chapter.

No more than in 1884 am I at the present moment enamoured of the Classical Latin of Maro and the "Chick-pea," (Cicero); as in the days of "Against the Grain," I prefer the language of the Vulgate to that of the Augustan Age, nay, even to that of the Decadent Period more curious though it be with its gamey flavour and its discolourations as of over-high venison. The Church, which after disinfecting and rejuvenating it, created, to deal with an order of ideas hitherto unexpressed, a vocabulary of grandiloquent words and diminutives of exquisite tenderness, appears to me to have fashioned Herself a diction far superior to the dialect of Paganism, and Durtal still holds the same views on this point as did Des Esseintes.

The chapter on precious stones I have recapitulated in *La Cathédrale*, in the second case treating the matter from the point of view of the symbolism of gems. I have there given life to the dead stones of "Against the Grain." Of course I do not deny that a fine emerald may be admired for the flashes that sparkle in the fire of its green depths, but, if we are ignorant of the idiom of symbols, is it not an unknown being, a stranger, a foreigner with whom no talk can be had and who has no word to say himself, because we do not understand his language? But he is surely something more and better than that.

Without admitting with an old writer of the sixteenth century, Estienne de Clave, that precious stones propagate their species, like human beings, with a seed disseminated in the womb of mother earth, we may truly say that they are minerals with a meaning, substances that talk,—that in one word they are symbols. They have been regarded under this aspect from the remotest times and the tropology of gems is one branch of that Christian symbolism so absolutely forgotten by priests and laymen alike in our own day, and which I have endeavoured to reconstruct in its main features in my volume on the basilica of Chartres.

The chapter in "Against the Grain" is therefore only superficial, a flush-bezel setting, so to speak. It is not what it should be, a display ranging beyond the mere material stones, it is made up of caskets of jewels more or less well described, more or less artistically arranged in a show-case,—but that is all, and that is not enough.

The painting of Gustave Moreau, the engravings of Luyken, the lithographs of Bresdin and Redon make the same impression on me now as then. I have no modification to make in the arrangement of the little collection.

As for the terrible Chapter VI, the number of which corresponds, without any preconceived purpose on my part, to the Commandment it offends against, as also for some portions of Chapter IX that may be classed with it, I should obviously not write them in the same vein again. They should at least have been accounted for, in a more studious spirit, by that diabolic perversity of the will which affects, especially in matters of sensual aberration, the exhausted brains of sick folk. It would seem, in fact, that nervous invalids expose fissures in the soul's envelope whereby the Spirit of Evil effects an entrance. But this is a riddle that remains unsolved; the word hysteria explains nothing; it may suffice to define a material condition, to mark invincible disturbances of the senses, it does not account for the spiritual consequences attached to the phenomena and, more particularly, the sins of dissimulation and falsehood that are almost always engrafted on them. What are the details and attendant circumstances of this malady of sinfulness, in what degree is the responsibility diminished of the individual whose soul is attacked by a sort of demoniac possession that takes root in the disorganization of his unhappy body? None can tell: on this point Medicine talks mere folly, Theology holds her peace.

In default of a solution which manifestly he could not supply, Des Esseintes should have viewed the question from the point of view of sinfulness and expressed at any rate some regret. He refrained from abusing himself, and he did wrong; but then, though educated by the Jesuits, whose panegyrist he is,—and a more ardent one than Durtal,— he had grown subsequently so recalcitrant to the Divine constraints, so obstinately resolved to wallow in the mire of his carnal appetites!

In any case, these chapters seem to be mark-stakes unconsciously planted to indicate the road Là-Bas was to follow. It is noteworthy moreover that Des Esseintes' library contained a certain number of old books of magic and that the ideas expressed in Chapter VII of "Against the Grain" on sacrilege are the hooks on which to hang a subsequent volume treating the subject more thoroughly.

As for this book *Là-Bas*, which frightened so many people, neither should I write it, if I had to do the thing again, in the same manner, now I am become a Catholic once more. There is no doubt indeed that the wicked and sensual side therein developed is reprehensible; but at the same time I declare I have glazed over things, I have said nothing of the worst; the documents it embodies are in comparison with those I have omitted, but which I have among my papers, very insipid sweetmeats, very tasteless tit-bits.

I believe, nevertheless, that in spite of its cerebral aberrations and its abdominal follies, the work, by mere virtue of the subject it laid bare, has done good service. It has recalled attention to the wiles of the Evil One, who had succeeded in getting men to deny his existence; it has been the starting-point of all the studies, revived of late years, on the never-changing procedure of Satanism; it has helped, by exposing them, to put an end to the odious practices of sorcery; it has taken sides, in fact, and fought a very strenuous fight for the Church against the Devil.

To come back to "Against the Grain," of which this book is only a succedaneum, I may repeat in connexion with the flower chapter what I have already stated with regard to precious stones.

"Against the Grain" considers them only from the point of view of shapes or colours, in no wise from that of the significations they disclose; Des Esseintes chose only rare orchids, strange blossoms, but without a tongue. It is fair to add that he would have found it hard to give speech in the book to a flora attacked by aphasia, a dumb flora, for the symbolic language of plants died with the Middle Ages, and the vegetable creoles cherished by Des Esseintes were unknown to the allegorists of those days.

The counterpart of this flower study I have written since in *La Cathédrale*, when dealing with that liturgical horticulture which has suggested such quaint pages in the works of St. Hildegard, St. Meliton and St. Eucher.

It is different with the question of odours, the mystic emblems of which I have expounded in the same book.

Des Esseintes had concerned himself only with lay perfumes, simple scents or extracts, and profane perfumes, compound essences or bouquets.

He might have extended his experiments to the aromas of the

Church, incense, myrrh and that strange Thymiama mentioned in the Bible and which is still noted in the ritual books as proper to be burned, together with incense, under the mouths of Church bells when they are baptised, after the Bishop has washed them with holy water and made the sign of the cross on them with the Holy Chrism and the oil of the sick. But this fragrant essence seems forgotten even by the Church, and I imagine a *curé* would be not a little startled if asked for Thymiama.

Yet the recipe is given in Exodus. The Thymiama was compounded of styrax, galbanum, incense and onycha, and this last ingredient would seem to be nothing else but the operculum of a certain shell of the tribe of the "purples" which is dredged up in the Indian seas.

Now it is difficult, not to say impossible, given the insufficient description of this shell and the locality it comes from, to prepare an authentic Thymiama. This is a pity, for had it been otherwise, this lost perfume would have surely called up before Des Esseintes' imagination sumptuous pictures of the religious festivals and liturgical rites of Eastern lands.

As for the chapters on contemporary literature, lay and clerical, they still, in my opinion, remain, as does that on Latin literature, well founded. That dealing with profane writing has helped to set in due relief several poets very little known to the public of that day,— Corbière, Mallarmé, Verlaine. I have nothing to retract in what I wrote nineteen years ago; I still keep my admiration for these authors; the admiration I professed for Verlaine has even increased. Arthur Rimbaud and Jules Laforgue would have well deserved to figure in Des Esseintes' florilegium, but at that date they had not yet printed anything and it was only long after that their works saw the light.

I do not anticipate, on the other hand, that I shall ever come to appreciate the modern religious authors scourged in "Against the Grain." Nothing will ever change my view that the criticism of the late lamented Nettement is idiotic and that Mine. Augustin Craven and Mlle. Eugénie de Guérin are blue-stockings of a very lymphatic sort and pious pedants of a very barren kind. Their juleps strike me as insipid; Des Esseintes has passed his taste for spices on to Durtal, and I think they would come to a good understanding together, both of them, at the present moment, to prepare, in lieu of these emulsions, an essence savoury with the stimulating condiment of art.

Nor have I changed my mind about the literature of the confraternity of the Poujoulats and Genoudes, but I should be less severe nowadays on the Père Chocarne, named among a miscellaneous lot of pious scribblers, for he has at any rate composed some pithy pages on Mysticism in his introduction to the works of Saint Jean de la Croix; in the same way I should deal more gently with De Montalembert who, despite his lack of talent, has bestowed on the world a work, incoherent indeed and ill-arranged, but still moving, on the monastic orders. Above all I should not now describe the visions of Angèle de Foligno as silly, insipid stuff; the exact contrary is the truth, but I must plead in my excuse that I had then read them only in Hello's translation. Now the latter was possessed with a mania for pruning, sugaring, softening down the mystics for fear of offending the mock modesty of Catholic readers. He has set under the press a work, strong and full of sap, to extract therefrom only a vapid and colourless juice, feebly warmed up again in a pipkin over the poor night-light of his style.

So much being allowed, that as a translator Hello showed himself a molly-coddle and a pious fraud, it is only fair to add that when he was working on original matter he was an originator of fresh ideas, a sagacious commentator, an analyst of true power. He was indeed, among the writers of his type, the only thinker; I came to the support of Aurévilly in commending the work of this writer, so incomplete, but so interesting, and "Against the Grain" has, I think, had some share in securing what little success his best book, *L'Homme*, won after his death.

The conclusion arrived at in this chapter on modern ecclesiastical literature was that among the geldings of religious art, there was only one stallion, to wit Barbey d'Aurévilly; and this opinion remains absolutely and entirely accurate. He was the one and only artist, in the proper sense of the word, that Catholicism produced at that period; he was a great prose stylist, an admirable novelist whose boldness set all beadledom screaming, enraged by the explosive vehemence of his phraseology.

To conclude the list, if ever chapter can be considered the starting-point of other books, it is surely the one on plain. chant which I afterwards amplified in all my publications, in *En Route* and above in *L'Oblat*.

As result of this brief review of each of the special articles exhibited in the show-cases of "Against the Grain" the conclusion is forced upon us,—the book was priming for my Catholic propaganda, which is implicit in it in its entirety, though in embryo.

Indeed the misunderstanding and stupidity of sundry pedants and agitated members of the priesthood strike me, yet once again, as unfathomable. Year after year they clamoured for the destruction of the book, the copyright of which, by-the-bye, I do not own, without ever realizing that the mystic volumes that came after it are incomprehensible without being as it is, I reiterate the statement, the root from which they all sprang. Besides this, how it is possible to appreciate the work of an author in its entirety, if it is not taken from its first beginnings and followed up step by step; above all, how is it possible to realize the progress of God's Grace in a soul, if the traces of its passage are neglected, if the first tokens left by its presence are effaced?

One thing at any rate is certain, that "Against the Grain" marked a definite rupture with its predecessors, with *Les Sœurs Vatard, En Ménage, A vau-l'eau*, that with it I entered on a path the goal of which I did not so much as suspect.

More sagacious than the Catholics, Zola saw this clearly. I remember how, after the first appearance of "A Rebours," I went to spend a few days at Médan. One afternoon when we were out walking, the two of us, in the country, he stopped suddenly, and his face grown dark, reproached me for having written the book, declaring I was dealing a terrible blow at Naturalism, that I was leading the school astray, that, into the bargain, I was burning my ships with such a book, inasmuch as no class of literature was possible of this sort, where a single volume exhausted the subject; finally, as a friend—he was the best of good fellows—he urged me to return to the beaten track, to put myself in harness and write a study of manners.

I listened to what he said, thinking that he was at one and the same time right and wrong—right, when he accused me of undermining Naturalism and entirely blocking my own road; wrong, in this sense that the novel as he conceived it seemed to me moribund, worn to a shadow by the wearisome repetitions that, whether he liked it or no, possessed no interest for me.

There were many things Zola could not understand; in the first place, the craving I felt to open the windows, to escape from surroundings that were stifling me; secondly, the desire that filled me to shake off preconceived ideas, to break the limitations of the novel, to introduce into it art, science, history; in a word not to use this form of literature except as a frame in which to put more serious kinds of work. For my part, the thing that seemed to me most indispensable at that period was to do away with the traditional plot of intrigue, even to eliminate love and woman altogether, to concentrate the ray of light on a single character, to strike out a new line at any price.

Zola vouchsafed no answer to the arguments by which I endeavoured to convince him, but went on repeating over and over again the one phrase:—"I cannot allow that a man may change his ways of working and his view of art; I cannot allow that he may burn what he once adored."

Well, well! has *he* not too played the part of the good Sicambrian? He has, as a matter of fact, if not modified his methods of composition and writing, at least varied his manner of conceiving humanity and explaining life. After the black pessimism of his first books, have we not had, under colour of socialism, the self-satisfied optimism of his latest productions?

It must be freely confessed that nobody ever showed less

comprehension of the soul than the "Naturalists" who undertook the task of investigating it. They saw existence all of a piece; they would have nothing to do with it except as manifested under probable conditions. But I have learned since by experience to know that the improbable is not always, in this world, exceptional, that the adventures of Rocambole are sometimes as true to nature as those of Gervaise and Coupeau. But the mere thought that Des Esseintes might be as truly drawn as the dramatis personae of his own novels disconcerted and came near to angering Zola.

So far, in these few pages of introduction, I have spoken of "Against the Grain" mainly from the point of view of literature and art. Now I must discuss it from that of God's Grace, show how large a share the unconscious, the workings of a soul ignorant of its own tendencies, may often have in the production of a book.

The definite set of "Against the Grain" towards Catholicism, manifest and clearly-marked as it is, remains, I confess, an insoluble problem to me.

I was not brought up in the schools of any religious order, but just in a Lycée. I was never a pious boy, and the influences of childish associations, of first Communion, of religious teaching, which often loom so large in conversion, never had any effect on me. What still further complicates the difficulty and defies analysis is this: in the days when I wrote "Against the Grain," I never set foot in a church, I did not know a single Catholic who regularly performed his religious duties, I had not a single priest among my acquaintance; I felt no Divine impulse drawing me towards the Church, I lived calmly and comfortably in my own style; it seemed to me perfectly natural to satisfy the calls of my sensual appetites, and the thought never so much as entered my head that that sort of amusement was forbidden.

"Against the Grain" appeared in 1884, and I set off to be converted at a Trappist House in 1892; nearly eight years had elapsed before the seeds of the book had germinated. Give two years, or even three, of the working of Grace,—a working slow and secret, only occasionally visible; there would still remain five years at least during which I can remember having felt no Christian stirrings at all, no remorse for the life I was leading, no wish to alter it. Why, by what impulse, have I been incited to take a road at that time shrouded in darkness from my view? I am utterly unable to say; nothing, save perhaps an ancestry not unconnected with Béguinages and Religious Houses and the prayers of a very devout Dutch family, which however I knew hardly anything of, will account for the purely unconscious unction of the concluding cry, the pious appeal of the last page of "Against the Grain."

Yes, I am quite aware, there are people of very sturdy fibre who trace out plans, organize beforehand itineraries of existence and follow them; it is even to be understood, if I am not mistaken, that by force of will any end may be reached. I can quite believe it, but for me, I confess, I have never been either tenacious of purpose as a man or worldly wise as an author. My life and my writings have something of passive receptivity about them, some unknown element, some trace of direction from outside myself which cannot be questioned.

Providence was merciful to me and the Virgin kind. I confined myself simply to not resisting them when they gave token of their purposes; I merely obeyed; I was led by what they call "extraordinary ways." If any man can have the certainty of the worthless thing he would be without God's help, it is I.

Persons who do not belong to the Faith will object that, with such ideas, one is like to end in fatalism and the negation of all scientific psychology.

Not so, for Faith in Our Lord is not fatalism. Free will remains free. I could if I chose, continue to yield to the temptations of the senses and stay on at Paris, instead of going to suffer tribulations at a Trappist Monastery. God doubtless would not have insisted; but, while certifying that the will is intact, we must nevertheless allow that the Saviour has much to do in the matter, that he harasses the sinner, tracks him down, *shadows* him, to use a forcible phrase of the police; but I say again, one can, at one's own risk and peril, reject his offices.

As to Psychology, the thing is otherwise. If we regard it, as I am doing, from the point of view of a conversion, it is, in its preliminaries, impossible to unravel; certain points tangible, but the rest, no; the subterranean workings of the soul are beyond our ken. There was no doubt at the date when I was writing "Against the Grain," a shifting of the soil, a delving of the earth, to lay the foundations, of which I was all unconscious. God was digging to lay His wire, and he was at work only in the darkness of the soul, in the night. Nothing was visible on the surface; it was only years after that the spark began to run along the wires. Then I could feel my soul stirred by the shock; as yet it was neither very painful nor very distinct. The Church offices, mysticism, art were the vehicles and the means; it occurred mostly in churches, at Saint Séverin in particular, where I used to go out of curiosity, for lack of other things to do. I experienced as I watched the services only an inward tremor, the little shiver one feels on seeing, hearing or reading a fine work of art; but there was no definite movement, no positive impulse to come to a decision.

Only, little by little, I was shaking myself loose from my shell of impurity; I was beginning to have a disgust of myself, but at the same time I kicked against the articles of the Faith. The objections I raised in my own mind seemed irresistible; and lo! one fine morning when I woke they were solved,—I never knew how. I prayed for the first time, and the catastrophe was over.

For such as do not believe in the Grace of God, all this seems folly. For those who have experienced its effects, no surprise is possible; or, if surprise there were, it could continue only over the period of incubation, the period when one sees nothing and notices nothing, the period of the clearing of the ground and laying of the foundations of which one never had even a suspicion.

I can understand, in fact, up to a certain point what befell between the year 1891 and the year 1895, between *Là-Bas* and *En Route*, nothing at all between the year 1884 and the year 1891, between "Against the Grain" and *Là-Bas*.

If I failed to understand them myself, a fortiori others could not understand the impulses that moved Des Esseintes. "Against the Grain" fell like an aerolite into the literary fairground, to be received with mingled amazement and indignation; the Press completely lost their heads; such an outburst of incoherent ravings had never been known before. After first calling me a misanthropic impressionist and describing Des Esseintes as a maniac and lunatic of a complex sort, the Schoolmasters, with M. Lemaître at their head, were furious that I had not eulogized Virgil, and declared in authoritative tones that the decadent exponents of the Latin tongue in the Middle Ages were simply "drivellers and idiots." Other would-be critics were kind enough to advise me that it would do me a world of good to be confined in a hydropathic establishment and suffer the discipline of cold douches. Then, the public lecturers took their turn to join in the abuse. At the Salle des Capucines, the high archon Sarcey was crying in bewilderment: "I am quite ready to be hanged if I understand one blessed word of the book." Finally, to make all complete, the serious reviews, such as the *Revue des Deux Mondes*, deputed their fugleman, M. Brunetiere, to liken the novel to the vaudevilles of Waflard and Fulgence.

In all this hurly-burly, a single writer alone saw clear, Barbey d'Aurévilly, who, be it said, had no personal acquaintance with me. In an article in the *Constitutionnel*, bearing date July 28th, 1884, and which has been reprinted in his Le *Roman Contemporain* published in 1902, he wrote:—

"After such a book, it only remains for the author to choose between the muzzle of a pistol or the foot of the cross."

The choice has been made.

J. K. HUYSMANS

1903.

Notice

To judge by such family portraits as were preserved in the Château de Lourps, the race of the Floressas des Esseintes had been composed in olden days of stalwart veterans of the wars, grim knights with scowling visages. Imprisoned in the old-fashioned picture frames that seemed all too narrow to contain their broad shoulders, they glared out alarmingly at the spectator, who was equally impressed by the fixed stare in the eyes, the martial curl of the moustaches and the noble development of the chests encased in enormous steel cuirasses.

These were ancestral portraits; those representing subsequent generations were conspicuous by their absence. There was a gap in the series, a gap which one face alone served to fill and so connect the past and present,—a mysterious, world-weary countenance. The features were heavy and drawn, the prominent cheekbones touched with a spot of rouge, the hair plastered to the head and entwined with a string of pearls, the slender neck rising from amid the pleatings of a stiff ruff.

Already in this picture of one of the most intimate friends of the Duc d'Epernon and the Marquis d'O, the vitiation of an exhausted race, the excess of lymph in the blood, were plainly to be traced.

No doubt the gradual degeneration of this ancient house had followed a regular and unbroken course; the progressive effemination of the men had gone on continuously from bad to worse. Moreover, to complete the deteriorating effect of time, the Des Esseintes had for centuries been in the habit of intermarrying among themselves, thus wasting the small remains of their original vigour and energy.

Sole surviving descendant of this family, once so numerous that it covered nearly all the domains of the Ile-de-France and of La Brie, was the Duc Jean des Esseintes, a frail young man of thirty, anæmic and nervous, with hollow cheeks, eyes of a cold, steely blue, a small but still straight nose, and long, slender hands.

By a curious accident of heredity, this last scion of a race bore a strong resemblance to the far-off ancestor, the mignon of Princes, from whom he had got the pointed beard of the very palest possible blonde and the ambiguous look of the eyes, at once languid and energetic in expression, which marked the portrait.

His childhood had been beset with perils. Threatened with scrofulous affections, worn out with persistent attacks of fever, he had nevertheless successfully weathered the breakers of puberty, after which critical period his nerves had recovered the mastery, vanquished the languors and depressions of chlorosis and permitted the constitution to reach its full and complete development.

The mother, a tall, silent, white-faced woman, died of general debility; then the father succumbed to a vague and mysterious malady.

At the time Des Esseintes was approaching his seventeenth birthday.

The only recollection he retained of his parents was one of fear rather than of anything resembling gratitude or affection. His father, who generally resided in Paris, was almost a total stranger; his mother he only remembered as a chronic invalid, who never left the precincts of a shuttered bedroom in the Château de Lourps. It was only on rare occasions that husband and wife met, and of these meetings all he recalled was the drab, colourless dulness,—his father and mother seated on either side of a table lighted only by a deeply shaded lamp, for the Duchess could not endure light and noise without suffering from nervous attacks. In the semi-darkness, they would exchange two or three sentences at most; then the Duke would slip away with a yawn and take his departure by the first available train.

At the Jesuits' College to which Jean was sent to be educated, his life proved pleasanter and less trying. The Fathers made much of the lad, whose intelligence amazed them; yet. in spite of all their efforts, they entirely failed to induce him to pursue any definite and disciplined course of study. He, devoted himself eagerly to certain tasks, acquired a precocious mastery of the Latin tongue; but on the other hand, he was absolutely incapable of construing three words of Greek, displayed no aptitude whatever for living languages and showed himself a perfect fool directly any attempt was made to teach him the merest rudiments of the physical sciences.

His family pretty much washed their hands of him; occasionally his father would pay him a visit at the College, but, "Good day, good evening, be a good boy and work hard," was about all he ever said to him. His summer holidays he used to spend at the Château de Lourps, where his presence quite failed to rouse his mother from her reveries; she hardly seemed to see him or, if she did, would gaze at him for a few moments with a painful smile, then sink back again into the artificial night in which the heavy curtains drawn across the windows wrapped the apartment.

The domestics were old and tiresome. The boy, left to himself, would turn over the books in the library on wet days, or on fine afternoons take long walks in the country.

It was his great delight to make his way down into the valley to Jutigny, a village standing at the foot of the hills,—a little cluster of cottages with thatched roofs tufted with moss. He would lie out in the meadows under the lee of the tall hayricks, listening to the dull rumble of the water-mills, filling his lungs with the fresh air of the Voulzie. Sometimes he would wander as far as the peat-workings, to the hamlet of Longueville with its hovels painted green and black; at another time climb the wind-swept hills and gaze out over the vast prospect. There he had below him on one side the valley of the Seine, losing itself in immensity and melting into the blue haze of the far distance; on the other, high on the horizon line, the churches and Castle keep of Provins that seemed to shake and shiver in a sunlit dust-cloud.

He spent the hours in reading or dreaming, drinking his fill of solitude till nightfall. By dint of constantly brooding over the same thoughts, his mind gained concentration and his still undeveloped ideas ripened towards maturity. After each vacation, he went back more thoughtful and more stubborn to his masters. These changes did not escape their notice, clear-sighted and shrewd, taught by their profession to sound the deepest depths of the human soul, they were well aware of the qualities and limitations of this alert but indocile intelligence; they realized that this pupil of theirs would never enhance the fame of the House, and as his family was wealthy and appeared to take little interest in his future, they soon abandoned all idea of directing his energies towards any of the lucrative careers open to the successful student. Though he was ready enough to enter with them into those theological disputations that attracted him by their subtleties and casuistical distinctions, they never even thought of preparing him for Holy Orders, for despite their efforts, his faith remained feeble. In the last resort, out of prudence and a fear of the unknown, they left him to himself to work at such studies as he chose and neglect the rest, unwilling to alienate this independent spirit by petty restrictions such as lay ushers are so fond of imposing.

So he lived a perfectly contented life, scarcely conscious of the priests' fatherly yoke. He pursued his Latin and French studies after his own fashion, and, albeit Theology found no place in the curriculum of his classes, he completed the apprenticeship to that science which he had begun at the Château de Lourps in the library of books left by his great great-uncle Dom Prosper, erstwhile Prior of the Canons Regular of Saint-Ruf.

The time, however, arrived when he must quit the Jesuit College; he was coming of age and would be master of his fortune; his cousin and guardian, the Comte de Montchevrel, gave him an account of his stewardship. The intimacy thus established was of short duration, for what point of contact could there be between the two, one of whom was an old man, the other a young one? Out of curiosity, lack of occupation, courtesy, Des Esseintes kept up relations with this family, and on several occasions, at his hotel in the Rue da la Chaise, endured evenings of a deadly dulness at which good ladies of his kin, as ancient as the hills, conversed about quarterings of nobility, heraldic scutcheons and ceremonial observances of years gone-by.

Even more than these worthy dowagers, the men, gathered round a whist-table, betrayed their hopeless nullity; these descendants of the old *preux chevaliers*, last scions of the feudal houses, appeared to Des Esseintes under the guise of a parcel of snuffling, grotesque greybeards, repeating *ad nauseam* a wearisome string of insipid outworn platitudes.

Just as when you cut the stalk of a fern, you can see the mark of a lily, really a fleur-de-lis seemed to be the one and only impress left on the softened pulp that took the place of brains in these poor old heads.

The young man was filled with an ineffable pity for these mummies buried in their rococo catafalques; for these crusty dandies who lived with eyes for ever fixed on a vaguely defined Land of Promise, an imaginary Canaan of good hope.

After a few experiences of the kind, he firmly resolved, in spite of all invitations and reproaches, never again to set foot in this society.

Thereupon he began to spend his days among young men of his own age and rank. Some of these, who had been brought up like himself at religious seminaries, had retained from this training a special character of their own. They attended church, communicated at Easter, frequented Catholic clubs and dropping their eyes in mock modesty, hid from each other, as if they had been crimes, their enterprises with women. For the most part they were witless fellows, with a sufficiency of good looks, but without a spark of mind or spirit; prime dunces who had exhausted their masters' patience, but had nevertheless fulfilled the latters' ambition to send out into the world obedient and pious sons of the Church.

Others, reared in the Colleges of the State or at *Lycées*, were more outspoken and less of hypocrites, but they were neither more interesting nor less narrow-minded. These were men of pleasure, devotees of operettas and races, playing lansquenet and baccarat, stalking fortunes on horses and cards,—all the diversions in fact that empty-headed folks love. After a year's trial of this life an enormous weariness resulted; he was sick and tired of these people whose indulgences struck him as paltry and commonplace, carried out without discrimination, without excitement, without any real stirring of blood or stimulation of nerves.

Little by little, he left off frequenting their society, and approached the men of letters, with whom his mind must surely find more points of sympathy and feel itself more at ease in their company. It was a fresh disappointment; he was revolted by their spiteful and petty judgments, their conversation that was as hackneyed as a church-door, their nauseous discussions invariably appraising the merit of a work solely according to the number of editions and the amount of profit on the sales. At the same time, he discovered the apostles of freedom, the wiseacres of the bourgeoisie, the thinkers who clamoured for entire liberty,—liberty to strangle the opinions of other people,—to be a set of greedy, shameless hypocrites, whom as men of education he rated below the level of the village cobbler.

His scorn of humanity grew by what it fed on; he realized in fact that the world is mostly made up of solemn humbugs and silly idiots. There was no room for doubt; he could entertain no hope of discovering in another the same aspirations and the same antipathies, no hope of joining forces with a mind that, like his own, should find its satisfaction in a life of studious idleness; no hope of uniting a keen and doctrinaire spirit such as his, with that of a writer and a man of learning.

His nerves were on edge, he was ill at ease; disgusted at the triviality of the ideas exchanged and received, he was growing to be like the men Nicole speaks of, who are unhappy everywhere; he was continually being chafed almost beyond endurance by the patriotic and social exaggerations he read every morning in the papers, overrating the importance of the triumphs which an all-powerful public reserves always and under all circumstances for works equally devoid of ideas and of style.

Already he was dreaming of a refined Thebaïd, a desert hermitage combined with modern comfort, an ark on dry land and nicely warmed, whither he could fly for refuge from the incessant deluge of human folly.

One passion and one only, woman, might have arrested him in this universal disdain that was rising within him; but this too was exhausted. He had tasted the sweets of the flesh with the appetite of a sick man, an invalid debilitated and full of whimsies, whose palate quickly loses savour. In the days when he had consorted with the coarse and carnal-minded men of pleasure, he had participated like the rest in some of those unconventional supper parties where tipsy women bare their bosoms at dessert and beat the table with dishevelled heads; he had been a visitor likewise behind the scenes, had had relations with actresses and popular singers, had endured, added to the natural and innate folly of the sex, the frantic vanity of women of the stage; then he had kept mistresses already famous for their gallantry and contributed to swell the exchequer of those agencies that supply, for a price, highly dubious gratifications; last of all, sick and satiated with this pretence of pleasure, of these stale caresses that are all alike, he had plunged into the nether depths, hoping to revive his flagging passions by sheer force of contrast, thinking to stimulate his exhausted senses by the very foulness of the filth and beastliness of low-bred vice.

Try what he would, an overpowering sense of ennui weighed him down. But still he persisted, and presently had recourse to the perilous caresses of the experts in amorousness. But his health was unable to bear the strain and his nerves gave way; the back of the neck began to prick and the hands were tremulous,—steady enough still when a heavy object had to be lifted, but uncertain if they held anything quite light such as a wineglass.

The physicians he consulted terrified him. It was indeed high time to change his way of life, to abandon these practices that were draining away his vitality. For a while, he led a quiet existence; but before long his passions awoke again and once more piped to arms. Like young girls who, under the stress of poverty, crave after highly spiced or even repulsive foods, he began to ponder and presently to practise abnormal indulgences, unnatural pleasures. This was the end; as if all possible delights of the flesh were exhausted, he felt sated, worn out with weariness; his senses fell into a lethargy, impotence was not far off.

So he found himself stranded, a lonely, disillusioned, sobered man, utterly and abominably tired, beseeching an end of it—an end the cowardice of his flesh forbade his winning.

His projects of finding some retreat far from his fellows, of burying himself in a hermit's cell, deadening, as they do the noise of the traffic for sick people by laying down straw in the streets, the inexorable turmoil of life, these projects more and more attracted him.

Besides, it was quite time to come to some definite decision for other reasons; he reckoned up the state of his finances and was appalled at the result. In reckless follies and riotous living generally, he had squandered the major part of his patrimony, while the balance, invested in land, brought him in only an insignificant revenue.

He determined to sell the Château de Lourps, which he never visited and where he would leave behind him no tender memories, no fond regrets; by this means he paid off all claims on the rest of his property, bought Government annuities and so secured himself an annual income of fifty thousand francs, while reserving, over and above, a round sum to buy and furnish the little house where he proposed to steep himself in a peace and quiet that should last his lifetime.

He searched the outer suburbs of the capital and presently discovered a cottage for sale, above Fontenay-aux-Roses, in a remote spot, far from all neighbours, near the Fort. His dream was fulfilled; in this district, still unspoilt by intruders from Paris, he was secure against all harassment; the very difficulties of communication—the place was wretchedly served by a grotesquely inefficient railway at the far end of the little town and a rustic tramway that went and came according to a self-appointed time table—were a comfort to him.

As he thought over the new existence he meant to make for himself, he experienced a lively sense of relief, seeing himself just far enough withdrawn for the flood of Paris activity not to touch his retreat, yet near enough for the proximity of the metropolis to add a spice to his solitariness. Indeed, in view of the well-known fact that for a man to find himself in a situation where it is impossible for him to visit a particular spot is of itself quite enough to fill him with an instant wish to go there, he was really guarding himself, by thus not entirely barring the road, from any craving to renew intercourse with the world or any regret for having abandoned it.

He set the masons to work on the house he had bought; then suddenly one day, without telling a soul of his plans, he got rid of his

furniture, dismissed his servants and disappeared without leaving any
address with the concierge.

Chapter One

More than two months slipped by before the time came when Des Esseintes found it feasible to immerse himself definitely in the peace and silence of his house at Fontenay; purchases of all kinds still kept him perambulating the Paris streets, tramping the town from end to end.

And yet, what endless inquiries had he not instituted, what lengthy lucubrations had he not indulged in, before finally entrusting his new home to the hands of the upholsterers!

He had long been an expert in the right and wrong combinations and contrasts of tints. In other days, when he was still in the habit of inviting women to his house, he had fitted up a boudoir where, amid dainty carved furniture of the light-yellow camphor-wood of Japan, under a sort of tent of pink Indian satin, the flesh tints borrowed a soft, warm glow from the artfully disposed lights sifting down through the rich material.

This room, where mirrors hung on every wall, reflecting backwards and forwards from one to another an infinite succession of pink boudoirs, had enjoyed a great renown among his various mistresses, who loved to bathe their nakedness in this flood of warm crimson amid the aromatic odours given off by the Oriental wood of the furniture.

But, quite apart from the miracles wrought by this artificial atmosphere in the way of transfusing, or so it seemed, a new blood into tired veins and freshening up complexions tarnished and worn by the habitual use of cosmetics and too frequent nights of love, he also tasted in his own person, in this luxurious retreat, special and peculiar satisfactions, pleasures exaggerated and rendered in a way more entrancing by the recollections of evil days overpast and vexations now outlived.

So, in a spirit of hate and scorn of his unhappy boyhood, he had suspended from the ceiling of the room we speak of, a little cage of silver wire in which a cricket was kept prisoner to chirp as they had been used to do in old days among the cinders in the great fireplaces at the Château de Lourps. Whenever he heard this sound, which he had so often listened to on many an evening of constraint and silence in his mother's chamber, all the miseries of a wretched and neglected childhood would come crowding before the eye of memory. At such times, roused from his reveries by the movements of the woman he was fondling mechanically at the moment and whose words and laughter interrupted his thoughts of the past and recalled him to reality, there as he lay in the pink boudoir, a sudden commotion would shake his soul, a longing for revenge on dreary hours endured in former times, a mad craving to befoul with base and carnal acts his recollections of bygone family life, an overmastering temptation to assuage his lustful propensities on the soft cushion of a woman's body, to drain the cup of sensuality to its last and bitterest dregs.

Other times again, when despondency weighed heavy on his spirit, when on rainy Autumn days he felt a sick aversion for everything,—for the streets, for his own house, for the dingy mud-coloured sky, for the stony-looking clouds, he would fly to this refuge, set the cricket's cage swinging gently to and fro and watch its movement repeated *ad infinitum* in the surrounding mirrors, till at last his eyes would grow dazed and he seemed to see the cage itself at rest, but all the room tossing and turning, filling the whole apartment with a dizzy whirl of pink walls.

Then, in the days when Des Esseintes still deemed it incumbent on him to play the eccentric, he had also installed strange and elaborate dispositions of furniture and fittings, partitioning off his salon into a series of niches, each differently hung and carpeted, and each harmonizing in a subtle likeness by a more or less vague similarity of tints, gay or sombre, refined or barbaric, with the special character of the Latin and French books he loved. He would then settle himself down to read in whichever of these recesses displayed in its scheme of decoration the closest correspondence with the intimate essence of the particular book his caprice of the moment led him to peruse.

Last fancy of all, he had prepared a lofty hall in which to receive his tradesmen. These would march in, take seats side by side in a row of church stalls; then he would mount an imposing pulpit and preach them a sermon on dandyism, adjuring his bookmakers and tailors to conform with the most scrupulous fidelity to his commandments in the matter of cut and fashion, threatening them with the penalty of pecuniary excommunication if they failed to follow out to the letter the instructions embodied in his monitories and bulls.

He won a great reputation as an eccentric,—a reputation he crowned by adopting a costume of black velvet worn with a gold-fringed waistcoat and sticking by way of cravat a bunch of Parma violets in the opening of a very low-necked shirt. Then he would invite parties of literary friends to dinners that set all the world talking. In one instance in particular, modelling the entertainment on a banquet of the eighteenth century, he had organized a funeral feast in celebration of the most unmentionable of minor personal calamities. The dining-room was hung with black and looked out on a strangely metamorphosed garden, the walks being strewn with charcoal, the little basin in the middle of the lawn bordered with a rim of black basalt and filled with ink; and the ordinary shrubs superseded by cypresses and pines. The dinner itself was served on a black cloth, decorated with baskets of violets and scabiosæ and illuminated by candelabra in which tall tapers flared.

While a concealed orchestra played funeral marches, the guests were waited on by naked negresses wearing shoes and stockings of cloth of silver besprinkled with tears.

The viands were served on black-bordered plates,—turtle soup, Russian black bread, ripe olives from Turkey, caviar, mule steaks, Frankfurt smoked sausages, game dished up in sauces coloured to resemble liquorice water and boot-blacking, truffles in jelly, chocolate-tinted creams, puddings, nectarines, fruit preserves, mulberries and cherries. The wines were drunk from dark-tinted glasses,—wines of the Limagne and Roussillon vintages, wines of Tenedos, the Val de Penas and Oporto. After the coffee and walnuts came other unusual beverages, kwas, porter and stout.

The invitations, which purported to be for a dinner in pious memory of the host's (temporarily) lost virility, were couched in the regulation phraseology of letters summoning relatives to attend the obsequies of a defunct kinsman.

But these extravagances, that had once been his boast, had died a natural death; nowadays his only feeling was one of self-contempt to remember these puerile and out-of-date displays of eccentricity,—the extraordinary clothes he had donned and the grotesque decorations he had lavished on his house. His only thought henceforth was to arrange, for his personal gratification only and no longer in order to startle other people, a home that should be comfortable, yet at the same time rich and rare in its appointments, to contrive himself a peaceful and exquisitely organized abode, specially adapted to meet the exigencies of the solitary life he proposed to lead.

When at length the new house at Fontenay was ready and fitted up in accordance with his wishes and intentions by the architect he had engaged; when nothing else was left save to settle the scheme of furniture and decoration, once again he passed in review, carefully and methodically, the whole series of available tints.

What he wanted was colours the effect of which was confirmed and strengthened under artificial light; little he cared even if by daylight they should appear insipid or crude, for he lived practically his whole life at night, holding that then a man was more truly at home, more himself and his own master, and that the mind found its only real excitant and effective stimulation in contact with the shades of evening; moreover, he reaped a special and peculiar satisfaction from finding himself in a room brilliantly lighted up, the only place alive and awake among surrounding houses all buried in sleep and darkness,—a sort of enjoyment that is not free from a touch of vanity, a selfish mode of gratification familiar enough to belated workers when, drawing aside the window curtains, they note how all about them the world lies inert, dumb and dead.

Slowly, one by one, he sifted out the different tones.

Blue, by candle light, assumes an artificial green tinge; if deep blue, like cobalt or indigo, it becomes black; if light, it changes to grey; it may be as true and soft of hue as a turquoise, yet it looks dull and cold.

Yes, it could only be employed as a supplement to help out some other colour; there could be no question of making blue the dominating note of a whole room.

On the other hand, the iron greys are even more sullen and heavy; the pearl greys lose their azure tinge and are metamorphosed into a dirty white; as for the deep greens, such as emperor green and myrtle green, these suffer the same fate as the blues and become indistinguishable from black. Only the pale greens therefore remained, peacock green for instance, or the cinnabars and lacquer greens, but then in their case lamplight extracts the blue in them, leaving only the yellow, which for its part shows only a poor false tone and dull, broken sheen.

Nor was it any use thinking of such tints as salmon-pink, maize, rose; their effeminate note would go dead against all his ideas of self-isolation; nor again were the violets worth considering, for they shed all their brightness by candle light; only red survives undimmed at night,—but then what a red! a sticky red, like wine-lees, a base, ignoble tint! Moreover, it struck him as quite superfluous to resort to this colour, inasmuch as after imbibing a certain small dose of santonin, a man sees violet, and it becomes the easiest thing in the world to change about at will and without ever altering the actual tint of his wall hangings.

All these colours being rejected, three only were left, viz. red, orange, yellow.

Of these three, he preferred orange, so confirming by his own example the truth of a theory he used to declare was almost mathematically exact in its correspondence with the reality, to wit: that a harmony is always to be found existing between the sensual constitution of any individual of a genuinely artistic temperament and whatever colour his eyes see in the most pronounced and vivid way.

In fact, if we leave out of account the common run of men whose coarse retinas perceive neither the proper cadence peculiar to each of the colours nor the subtle charm of their various modifications and shades; similarly leaving on one side those bourgeois eyes that are insensible to the pomp and splendour of the strong, vibrating colours; regarding therefore only persons of delicate, refined visual organs, well trained in appreciation by the lessons of literature and art, it appeared to him to be an undoubted fact that the eye of that man amongst them who has visions of the ideal, who demands illusions to satisfy his aspirations, who craves veils to hide the nakedness of reality, is generally soothed and satisfied by blue and its cognate tints, such as mauve, lilac, pearl-grey, provided always they remain tender and do not overpass the border where they lose their individuality and change into pure violets and unmixed greys.

The blustering, swaggering type of men, on the contrary, the plethoric, the sanguine, the stalwart go-ahead fellows who scorn compromises and by-roads to their goal, and rush straight at their object whatever it is, losing their heads at the first go-off, these for the most part delight in the startling tones of the reds and yellows, in the clash and clang of vermilions and chromes that blind their eyes and surfeit their senses.

Last comes the class of persons, of nervous organization and enfeebled vigour, whose sensual appetite craves highly seasoned dishes, men of a hectic, over-stimulated constitution. *Their* eyes almost invariably hanker after that most irritating and morbid of colours, with its artificial splendours and feverish acrid gleams,—orange.

What Des Esseintes' final choice then would be hardly admitted of a doubt; but indubitable difficulties still remained unsolved. If red and yellow are accentuated under artificial light, this is not always the case with their composite, orange, which is a hot-headed fellow and often blazes out into a crimson or a fire red.

He studied carefully by candle light all its different shades, and finally discovered one he thought should not lose equilibrium or refuse to fulfil the offices he claimed of it.

These preliminaries disposed of, he made a point of eschewing, so far as possible, at any rate in his study, the use of Oriental stuffs and rugs, which in these days, when rich tradesmen can buy them in the fancy shops at a discount, have become so common and so much a mark of vulgar ostentation.

Eventually he made up his mind to have his walls bound like his books in large-grained crushed morocco, of the best Cape skins, surfaced by means of heavy steel plates under a powerful press.

The panelling once completed, he had the mouldings and tall plinths painted a deep indigo, a blue lacquer like what the coach-builders use for carriage bodies, while the ceiling, which was slightly coved, was also covered in morocco, displaying, like a magnified *œil-de-bœuf*, framed in the orange leather, a circle of sky, as it were, of a rich blue, wherein soared silver angels, figures of seraphim embroidered long ago by the Weavers' Guild of Cologne for an ancient cope.

After the whole was arranged and finished, all these several tints fell into accord at night and did not clash at all; the blue of the woodwork struck a stable note that was pleasing and satisfying to the eye, supported and warmed, so to say, by the surrounding shades of orange, which for their part shone out with a pure, unsullied gorgeousness, itself backed up and in a way heightened by the near presence of the blue.

As to furniture, Des Esseintes had no long or laborious searches to undertake, inasmuch as the one and only luxury of the apartment was to be books and rare flowers; while reserving himself the right later on to adorn the naked walls with drawings and pictures, he confined himself for the present to fitting up almost all round the room a series of bookshelves and bookcases of ebony, scattering tiger skins and blue-foxes' pelts about the floor: and installing beside a massive money-changer's table of the fifteenth century, several deep-seated, high-backed armchairs, together with an old church lectern of wrought iron, one of those antique service-desks whereon the deacon of the day used once to lay the Antiphonary, and which now supported one of the ponderous volumes of du Cange's *Glossarium mediæ et infimæ Latinitatis.*

The windows, the glass of which was coarse and semi-opaque, bluish in tinge and with many of the panes filled with the bottoms of bottles, the protuberances picked out with gilt, allowed no view of the outside world and admitted only a faint dim "religious" light. They were further darkened by curtains made out of old priestly stoles, the dull dead gold of whose embroideries faded off into a background of a subdued, almost toneless red.

To complete the general effect, above the fireplace, the screen of which was likewise cut from the sumptuous silk of a Florentine dalmatic, midway between two monstrances of gilded copper in the Byzantine style which had come originally from the Abbaye-aux-Bois at Bièvre, stood a marvellously wrought triptych, each of the three separate panels carved with a lacelike delicacy of workmanship; this now contained, guarded under glass let into the triple frame, copied on real vellum in beautiful missal lettering and adorned with exquisite illuminations, three pieces of Baudelaire's: right and left, the sonnets called "The Lovers' Death" and "The Enemy," in the middle, the prose poem that goes by the English title of "Anywhere out of the World."

Chapter Two

After the sale of his household goods, Des Esseintes kept on the two old servants who had looked after his invalid mother and between them had filled the double office of general *factotum* and hall-porter at the Château de Lourps. The latter had, up to the date of its being put up for sale, remained empty and untenanted.

He took with him to Fontenay this pair of domestics broken in to play the part of sick-nurses, trained to the methodical habits of wardsmen at a hospital, accustomed to administer at stated hours spoonfuls of physic and doses of medicinal draughts, subdued to the rigid quietude of cloistered monks, shut off from all communication with the outer world, content to spend their lives in close rooms with doors and windows always shut.

The husband's duty was to keep the rooms clean and fetch the provisions, the wife's to attend to the cooking. Their master gave up the first floor of the house for their accommodation, made them wear thick felt shoes, had double doors installed with well-oiled hinges and covered the floors with heavy carpeting so as to prevent his hearing the faintest sound of their footsteps overhead.

Then he arranged with them a code of signals, fixing the precise significance of different rings on his bell, few or many, long or short, and appointed a particular spot on his writing-desk where each month the account books were to be left; in fact, made every possible disposition so as to avoid the obligation of seeing them or speaking to them more often than was absolutely indispensable.

More than this, as the woman must needs pass along the front of the house occasionally on her way to an outhouse where the wood was stored and he was resolved not to suffer the annoyance of seeing her commonplace exterior, he had a costume made for her of Flemish grogram, with a white mutch and a great black hood to muffle face and head, such as the *Béguines* still wear to this day at Ghent. The shadow of this mediæval coif gliding by in the dusk gave him a conventual feeling, reminding him of those peaceful, pious settlements, those abodes of silence and solitude buried out of sight in a corner of the bustling, busy city.

He fixed the hours of meals, too, in accordance with a never varying schedule; indeed his table was of the plainest and simplest, the feebleness of his digestion no longer permitting him to indulge in heavy or elaborate repasts.

At five o'clock in winter, after dusk had closed in, he ate an abstemious breakfast of two boiled eggs, toast and tea; then came dinner at eleven; he used to drink coffee, sometimes tea or wine, during the night, and finally played with a bit of supper about five in the morning, before turning in.

These meals, the details and menu of which were settled once for all at the beginning of each season of the year, he took on a table placed in the middle of a small room communicating with his study by a padded corridor, hermetically closed and allowing neither smell nor sound to penetrate from one to the other of the two apartments it served to connect.

The dining-room in question resembled a ship's cabin with its wooden ceiling of arched beams, its bulkheads and flooring of pitch-pine, its tiny window-opening cut through the woodwork as a porthole is in a vessel's side.

Like those Japanese boxes that fit one inside the other, this room was inserted within a larger one,—the real dining-room as designed by the architect.

This latter apartment was provided with two windows; one of these was now invisible, being hidden by the bulkhead or partition wall, which could however be dropped by touching a spring, so that fresh air might be admitted to circulate freely around and within the pitch-pine enclosure; the other was visible, being situated right opposite the porthole contrived in the woodwork, but was masked in a peculiar way, a large aquarium filling in the whole space intervening between the porthole and the real window in the real house-wall. Thus the daylight that penetrated into the cabin had first to pass through the outer window, the panes of which had been replaced by a single sheet of plain mirror glass, then through the water and last of all through the glazing of the porthole, which was permanently fixed in its place.

At the hour when the steaming samovar stood on the table, the moment when in Autumn the sun would be setting in the west, the water in the aquarium, dull and opaque by daylight, would redden and throw out fiery flashes as if from a glowing furnace over the light-coloured walls.

Sometimes, of an afternoon, if Des Esseintes happened to be up and about at that time of day, he would turn the taps connected with a system of pipes and conduits that enabled the tank to be emptied and refilled with fresh water, and then by pouring in a few drops of coloured essences, he could enjoy at his pleasure all the tints, green or grey, opaline or silvery, that real rivers assume according to the hue of the heavens, the greater or less ardour of the sun's rays, the more or less threatening aspect of the rain-clouds, in a word according to the varying conditions of season and weather.

This done, he could picture himself in the 'tween-decks of a brig as he gazed curiously at a shoal of ingenious mechanical fishes that were wound up and swam by clockwork past the port-hole window and got entangled in artificial water-weeds; at other times, as he inhaled the strong smell of tar with which the room had been impregnated before he entered it, he would examine a series of coloured lithographs on the walls, of the sort one sees in packet-boat offices and shipping agencies, representing steamers at sea bound for Valparaiso or the River Plate, alongside framed placards giving the itineraries of the Royal Mail Steam Packet services and of the various Ocean liners, freighting charges and ports of call of the Transatlantic mail boats, etc.

Then presently, when he was tired of consulting these time tables, he would rest his eyes by looking over the collection of chronometers and mariner's compasses, sextants and dividers, binoculars and charts scattered about the table, whereon figured only a single book, bound in sea-green morocco, the "Adventures of Arthur Gordon Pym," specially printed for his behoof on pure linen-laid paper, hand picked, bearing a sea-gull for water mark.

In the last resort, he could turn his gaze upon a litter of fishing-rods, brown tanned nets, rolls of russet-coloured sails, a miniature anchor made of cork painted black, all heaped together near the door that communicated with the kitchen by a passage padded, like the corridor joining the dining-room and study, in such a way as to absorb every unpleasant smell and disturbing noise.

By these means he could procure himself, without ever stirring from home, in a moment, almost instantaneously, all the sensations of a long voyage; the pleasure of moving from place to place, a pleasure which indeed hardly exists save as a matter of after recollection, almost never as a present enjoyment at the moment of the actual journey, this he could savour to the full at his ease, without fatigue or worry, in this improvised cabin, whose ordered disorder, whose transitional look and temporary arrangement, corresponded closely enough with the nature of the flying visits he paid it and the limited time he devoted to his meals, while it offered an absolute contrast to his working-room,—a fixed and final spot, a place of system and settled habit, a room manifestly contrived for the definite enjoyment of a life of cloistered and learned leisure. In fact it appeared to him a futile waste of energy to travel when, so he believed, imagination was perfectly competent to fill the place of the vulgar reality of actual prosaic facts. To his mind it was quite possible to satisfy all the cravings commonly supposed to be the hardest to content under the normal conditions of life, and this merely by a trifling subterfuge, by a more or less close simulation of the object aimed at by these desires. Thus it is a sufficiently well-known fact that in these days the epicure who frequents those restaurants that have a reputation for the excellence of their cellars is really and truly gratifying his palate by drinking rare vintages artificially manufactured out of common, cheap wines treated after M. Pasteur's methods. Now, whether genuine or faked, these wines have the same aroma, the same colour, the same bouquet, whence it follows that the pleasure experienced in imbibing these fictitious, doctored beverages is absolutely identical with the satisfaction that would be enjoyed from tasting the pure, unsophisticated liquor now unprocurable even at its weight in gold.

Transferring this artful sophistication, this clever system of adulteration, into the world of the intellect, there is no doubt we can, and just as easily as in the material world, enjoy false, fictitious pleasures every whit as good as the true; no doubt, for instance, a man can undertake long voyages of exploration sitting in his armchair by the fireside, helping out, if needful, his recalcitrant or sluggish imagination by the perusal of some work descriptive of travels in distant lands; no doubt again that it is quite possible,—without ever stirring from Paris,—to obtain the health-giving impression of sea-bathing. In two words, all that is required in this last case is simply to take a walk to the

"Bain Vigier," on a pontoon moored right out in the middle of the
Seine.

There, by just salting your bath and mixing with the water,
according to the formula given in the Pharmacopœia, a compound of
sulphate of soda, hydrochlorate of magnesia and lime; by drawing from
a box carefully secured by a screw-top a ball of twine or a scrap of
rope's end bought for the purpose at one of those great marine store
dealers' emporiums whose huge warehouses and cellars reek with the
salty smell of the sea and sea-ports; by inhaling these odours which the
twine or ropes end are bound to retain; by examining a lifelike
photograph of the casino and industriously reading the "Guide Joanne"
describing the beauties of the seaside resort where you would like to
be; by letting yourself be lulled by the waves raised in the bath by the
passing river steamers as they steer close past the bathing pontoon, by
listening to the sobbing of the wind as it blusters through the arches of
the bridges and the dull rumble of the omnibuses rolling six feet above
your head across the Pont Royal; just by doing and suffering these
simple things, the illusion is undeniable, overmastering, perfect; you
are as good as at the seaside.

The whole secret is to know how to set about it, to be able to
concentrate the mind on a single point, to attain to a sufficient degree of
self-abstraction to produce the necessary hallucination and so substitute
the vision of the reality for the reality itself.

To tell the truth, artifice was in Des Esseintes' philosophy the
distinctive mark of human genius.

As he used to say, Nature has had her day; she has definitely and
finally tired out by the sickening monotony of her landscapes and
skyscapes the patience of refined temperaments. When all is said and
done, what a narrow, vulgar affair it all is, like a petty shopkeeper
selling one article of goods to the exclusion of all others; what a
tiresome store of green fields and leafy trees, what a wearisome
commonplace collection of mountains and seas!

In fact, not one of her inventions, deemed so subtle and so
wonderful, which the ingenuity of mankind cannot create; no Forest of
Fontainebleau, no fairest moonlight landscape but can be reproduced
by stage scenery illuminated by the electric light; no waterfall but can
be imitated by the proper application of hydraulics, till there is no
distinguishing the copy from the original; no mountain crag but painted
pasteboard can adequately represent; no flower but well chosen silks
and dainty shreds of paper can manufacture the like of!

Yes, there is no denying it, she is in her dotage and has long ago
exhausted the simple-minded admiration of the true artist; the time is
undoubtedly come when her productions must be superseded by art.

Why, to take the one of all her works which is held to be the most
exquisite, the one of all her creations whose beauty is by general

consent deemed the most original and most perfect,—woman to wit, have not men, by their own unaided effort, manufactured a living, yet artificial organism that is every whit her match from the point of view of plastic beauty? Does there exist in this world of ours a being, conceived in the joys of fornication and brought to birth amid the pangs of motherhood, the model, the type of which is more dazzlingly, more superbly beautiful than that of the two locomotives lately adopted for service on the Northern Railroad of France?

One, the Crampton, an adorable blonde, shrill-voiced, slender-waisted, with her glittering corset of polished brass, her supple, catlike grace, a fair and fascinating blonde, the perfection of whose charms is almost terrifying when, stiffening her muscles of steel, pouring the sweat of steam down her hot flanks, she sets revolving the puissant circle of her elegant wheels and darts forth a living thing at the head of the fast express or racing seaside special!

The other, the Engerth, a massively built, dark-browed brunette, of harsh, hoarse-toned utterance, with thick-set loins, panoplied in armour-plating of sheet iron, a giantess with dishevelled mane of black eddying smoke, with her six pairs of low, coupled wheels, what overwhelming power when, shaking the very earth, she takes in tow, slowly, deliberately, the ponderous train of goods waggons.

Of a certainty, among women, frail, fair-skinned beauties or majestic, brown-locked charmers, no such consummate types of dainty slimness and of terrifying force are to be found. Without fear of contradiction may we say: man has done, in his province, as well as the God in whom he believes.

Thoughts like these would come to Des Esseintes at times when the breeze carried to his ears the far-off whistle of the baby railroad that plies shuttlewise backwards and forwards between Paris and Sceaux. His house was within a twenty minutes' walk or so of the station of Fontenay, but the height at which it stood and its isolated situation left it entirely unaffected by the noise and turmoil of the vile hordes that are inevitably attracted on Sundays by the neighbourhood of a railway station.

As for the village itself, he had hardly seen it. Only at night, from his window, he had looked out over the silent landscape that stretches down to the foot of a hill on the summit of which rise the batteries of the Bois de Verrières.

In the shadow, to right and left, loomed other dimly seen masses, terracing the hillside and dominated by other far-off batteries and fortifications, the high revetments of which seemed in the moonlight as if washed in with silver pigment upon a dark background of sky.

The plain lay partly in the shadows cast by the hills, while the centre, where the moonlight fell, looked as if it were powdered with starch and smeared with cold-cream; in the warm air that fanned the pale grass and brought with it a spicy perfume, the trees stood out clearly silhouetted with their shaggy leaves and thin stems, which threw black bars of shadow across the chalky earth strewed with pebbles that sparkled like shards of broken crockery.

The artificial, rather theatrical air of this landscape was to Des Esseintes' taste; but after that one afternoon devoted to the search for a house at the hamlet of Fontenay, he had never again trodden its streets by daylight. In fact, the green-cry of this district inspired him with no sort of interest, not offering even the dainty, melancholy charm to be found in the pitiful, sickly vegetation that has so sore a struggle to live on the rubbish-heaps of suburban spots near the ramparts.

Besides, on that memorable day, he had caught sight of paunchy citizens with flowing whiskers and smartly dressed individuals with moustaches, carrying their heads high, as if they were something sacrosanct, evidently magistrates or military officers; and after such a sight, his usual horror of the human face had been still further accentuated.

During the last months of his residence in Paris, at the period when, utterly disillusioned, depressed by hypochondria, eaten up by spleen, he had reached such a pitch of nervous irritability that the mere sight of an unpleasant object or disagreeable person was deeply graven on his brain and several days were needed to efface the impress, even to a slight degree, of the human form that had formed one of his most agonizing torments when passed casually in the street.

In positive fact, he suffered pain at the sight of certain types of face, resented almost as insults the condescending or crabbed expressions of particular visages, and felt himself sorely tempted to box the ears of such and such a worthy citizen who strolled by with half closed lids and a magisterial air, another who stood swinging his cane and admiring himself in the shop windows, or yet another who seemed to be pondering the fate of the universe, as he absorbed with frowning brows the titbits and gossipy paragraphs of his morning paper.

He scented such a depth of stupidity, such a lively hatred of all his own ideals, such a contempt for literature and art and everything he himself adored, implanted and profoundly fixed in the meagre brains of these tradesmen preoccupied to the exclusion of all else by schemes of swindling and money-grubbing and only accessible to the ignoble distraction that alone appeals to mean minds, politics, that he would rush back home in a fury and lock himself up with his books.

Worst of all, he loathed with all his powers of hate the new types of self-made men, the hideous boors who feel themselves bound to talk loud and laugh uproariously in restaurants and cafés, who elbow you, without apology, on the pavements, who, without a word of polite excuse or so much as a bow, drive the wheels of a child's go-cart between your legs.

Chapter Three

One division of the shelves fixed against the walls of his blue and orange working-room was occupied exclusively by Latin works,—those works which minds broken in to conventionality by listening year after year to the miserable teaching of School and College lecturers designate under the generic name of "The Decadence."

The truth is, the Latin language, as it was written at the period which learned professors still persist in calling the "Golden Age," roused his interest scarcely at all. That idiom, confined within such narrow limits, with its carefully counted, almost invariable turns of phrase, without suppleness of syntax, without colour or light and shade; that idiom, ironed smooth on every seam, pruned of the rugged but often picturesque expressions of earlier epochs, could at a pinch enunciate the pompous nullities, the vague commonplaces repeated *ad nauseam* by the rhetoricians and poets of that day, but so lacking was it in originality, so instinct with tediousness, that we must, in our studies of language and literature, come down to the French style of the age of Louis XIV, to find one so wilfully emasculated, so solemnly tiresome and sapless.

Among other authors, the gentle Virgil, he whom school ushers name the Swan of Mantua, presumably because he was *not* born in that city, appeared to him as one of the most terrible of pedants, one of the most dismal twaddlers Antiquity ever produced; his shepherd swains, all washed and beribboned, taking turn and turn about to empty over the unfortunate reader's head their slops of sententious, chilly verses, his Orpheus whom he compares with a weeping nightingale, his Aristæus blubbering over bees, his Æneas, that weak-kneed, fluent personage who stalks, like a shadow figure at a show, with wooden gestures behind the ill-fitted and badly oiled screen of the poem, set him beside himself with exasperation. He might indeed have put up with the tedious fiddle-faddle these marionettes exchange by way of dialogue as a stage device; he might even have excused the impudent plagiarisms perpetrated on Homer, Theocritus, Ennius, Lucretius, the flagrant theft Macrobius has revealed to us of the whole Second Book of the Æneid, copied almost word for word from a poem of Pisander's, he might have forgiven, in fact, all the indescribable dulness of this farrago of borrowed verses; but what revolted him more than all was the false ring of those hexameters, with their tinny tinkle like the rattle of a cracked pot, with their longs and shorts weighed out by the pound according to the unalterable laws of a pedantic, barren prosody; it was the framework of these stiff and formal lines that was beyond all bearing, with their official stamp and cringing subservience to grammatical propriety, these verses each mechanically bisected by an

unmodifiable caesura, then stopped off at the tail, always in precisely
the same way, by a dactyle knocking up against a final spondee.

Borrowed from the cast-iron system perfected by Catullus, that
unvarying metrical scheme, unimaginative, inexorable, stuffed full of
useless verbiage and endless amplifications, an array of ingeniously
contrived pegs each fitting into its corresponding and expected hole,
that poor trick of the Homeric "standing epithet," dragged in again and
again without rhyme or reason, all that scanty vocabulary with its dull,
flat tones, were a torment to his sensibility.

It is only fair to add that, if his admiration for Virgil was decidedly
lukewarm and his appreciation of the light lucubrations of Ovid
anything but marked, the disgust he felt for the elephantine graces of
Horace, the twaddle of this unmitigated lout who smirks at his audience
with the painted face and villainous jests of a superannuated clown,
was limitless.

In prose, his enthusiasm was not a whit greater for the redundant
figures and nonsensical digressions of "Chick-Pea" (Cicero); the
braggadocio of his apostrophes, the claptrap of his never-ending
appeals to patriotism, the exaggerated emphasis of his harangues, the
ponderousness of his style, well-fed and full-fleshed, but run to fat and
devoid of bones and marrow, the intolerable litter of his sonorous
adverbs opening every sentence, the monotonous structure of his portly
periods tied awkwardly to each other by a thread of conjunctions, worst
of all his wearisome habits of tautology, were anything but attractive to
him. Cæsar again was little more to his taste, for all his reputation for
conciseness; his was the opposite excess,—a dry-as-dust aridity, a
deadly dulness, an unseasonable constipation of phrase that passes
belief.

The end of it all was that he could find mental pabulum neither
among these writers nor among that other class which still forms the
delight of dilettante scholars,—Sallust, who indeed is less insipid than
most of the rest; Livy, sentimental and pompous; Seneca, turgid and
jejune; Suetonius, lymphatic and horrifying; Tacitus, the most nervous
in his studied concision, the most biting, the most sinewy of them all.
In poetry, Juvenal, despite some vigorously conceived lines, Persius,
despite his mysterious insinuations, both left him cold. Neglecting
Tibullus and Propertius, Quintilian and the two Plinies. Statius, Martial
of Bilbilis, Terence even and Plautus, whose jargon, full as it is of
neologisms, made-up words and diminutives, might have pleased him,
had not his low wit and coarse jocosity repelled him, Des Esseintes
only began to be interested in the language of Rome on the appearance
of Lucan, with whom it took on a wider range, becoming henceforth
more expressive and less harsh; that author's laboured workmanship,
his verse, veneered with enamels, studded with jewels, caught his
fancy, albeit his exclusive preoccupation with form, his tinkling

sonorities, his metallic brilliancies, did not entirely hide from his eyes this author's, vacuity of thought and the emptiness of the wind-bag phrases that plump out the carcase of the "Pharsalia."

The writer he really loved and who made him reject for good and all from among the books he read, Lucan and his sounding periods, was Petronius.

Petronius was an acute observer, a delicate analyst, a marvellous delineator; calmly, without prejudice, without animosity, he described the daily life of Rome, setting down in the lively little chapters of the *Satyricon* the manners, customs and morals of his day.

Noting facts as they occurred, putting them down in positive black and white, he disclosed the trivial, every-day existence of the commonalty, its incidents, its bestialities, its sensualities.

Here, we have the Inspector of Lodgings coming to inquire the names of the travellers lately arrived; there, it is a brothel where men are prowling round naked women standing beside placards giving name and price, while through the half-open doors of the rooms the couples can be seen at work; elsewhere again, now in country houses full of insolent luxury, amid a mad display of wealth and ostentation, now in poverty-stricken taverns with their brokendown pallet-beds swarming with fleas, the society of the period runs its race,—debauched cut-purses like Ascyltos and Eumolpus on the look-out for a piece of luck; old wantons of the male sex with their tucked-up gowns and cheeks plastered with ceruse and acacia red; minions of sixteen, plump and curly-headed; women frantic with hysteria; legacy hunters offering their boys and girls to gratify the lustful caprices of rich men; all these and more gallop across the pages, quarrel in the streets, finger each other at the baths, belabour each other with fisticuffs like the characters in a pantomime.

All this told with an extraordinary vigour and precision of colouring, in a style that borrows from every dialect, that cribs words from every language imported into Rome, that rejects all the limitations, breaks all the fetters of the so-called "Golden Age," that makes each man speak in his own peculiar idiom—freemen, without education, the vernacular Latin, the argot of the streets; foreigners, their barbarian lingo, saturated with African, Syrian, Greek expressions; idiotic pedants, like the Agamemnon of the *Satyricon*, a rhetoric of invented words. All these people are drawn with a free pencil, squatted round a dining-table, exchanging the imbecile conversation of tipsy revellers, mouthing dotards' wise saws and pointless proverbs, all eyes turned upon Trimalchio, the giver of the feast, who sits picking his teeth, offers the company chamber-pots, discourses of his insides, begging his guests to make themselves at home.

This realistic romance, this slice cut from the raw of Roman life, without one thought, whatever people may say, whether of reforming or satirizing society, without any moral purpose whatever or idea of moralizing, this tale,—there is neither intrigue nor action in it,—bringing before the reader the love adventures of male prostitutes, analyzing with calm address the joys and griefs of these amours and these amorous couples, depicting in language wrought to the perfection of a piece of goldsmith's work, without the writer once showing himself, without a word of comment, without one phrase of approbation or disapproval of his characters' deeds and thoughts, the vices of a decrepit civilization, an Empire falling to ruin, rivetted Des Esseintes' attention; he saw in the refinements of its style, the keenness of its observation, its closely knit, methodical construction, a strange likeness, a curious analogy with the three or four modern French novels that he could stomach.

We may be sure he bitterly regretted the loss of the *Eustion* and the *Albutia*, two works by Petronius mentioned by Planciades Fulgentius, but now vanished beyond possibility of recovery; however, the bibliophile side of him came in to console the scholarly, as he fondled in reverent hands the example he owned of the superb edition of the *Satyricon*, the octavo edition bearing date 1585 printed by J. Dousa at Leyden.

After Petronius, his collection of Latin authors came to the Second Century of the Christian era, skipping over the declaimer Fronto, with his old-fashioned turns of speech and his ill-adjusted, ill-polished style, leaving on one side the *Noctes Atticæ* of Aulus Gellius, his disciple and friend, a sagacious and inquisitive mind, but as a writer embarrassed by a sticky, glutinous style,—only stopping when he reached Apuleius, the editio princeps of which author he possessed the folio printed at Rome in 1469.

This African rhetorician was his delight; the Latin language was surely at its best and richest in him, rolling along in a full, copious flood, fed by many tributary streams from all the Provinces of the Empire, and combining all these different elements to form one strange, exotic dialect, hardly dreamed of before; in it new mannerisms, new details of Latin society found expression in new turns of phrase, invented in the stress of conversation in a little Roman town in a corner of Africa. Moreover, the man's bonhomie,—he was a fat, jovial boon companion, there could be no doubt of that,—and the warm-blooded exuberance of his southern nature tickled our hero's fancy. He had the air of a gay and genial comrade, not mealy-mouthed by any means, alongside of the Christian apologists, his contemporaries,—the soporific Minutius Felix, a pseudo-classic, ladling out in his Octavius Cicero's heavy periods, grown heavier than ever, or even Tertullian himself, whom he kept on his shelves more perhaps for the sake of the Aldine edition of his works than for any love of the matter.

Well equipped as he was for Theological disquisitions, the

argumentations of the Montanists against the Catholic Church, the polemics of the latter against gnosticism, left him cold; so, despite the preciosity of Tertullian's style, a style rigorously compressed, full of quibbles and amphibologies, based on a liberal use of participles, emphasized by continual antitheses, crammed with puns and plays upon words, variegated with words borrowed from the language of jurisprudence and the diction of the Greek Fathers, he hardly ever now opened the *Apologetica* or the *Tractate on Patience*; the most he ever did was to skim through a page or two of the *De Cultu Feminarum*, in which Tertullian charges the sex not to bedeck their persons with jewels and precious stuffs and forbids them to make use of cosmetics because they are thereby trying to correct and improve on Nature.

These ideas, the precise opposite of his own, made him smile; though the part played by Tertullian as Bishop of Carthage seemed to him suggestive in the way of pleasant day-dreams. In a word, it was really the man more than his works that attracted him.

He had, in truth, lived in stormy times, at a period of fearful stress and strain, under Caracalla, under Macrinus, under that amazing personage, the High-Priest of Emessa, Elagabalus; and he had gone on calmly and quietly writing his sermons, composing his dogmatic treatises, preparing his apologies and homilies, while the Roman Empire was tottering to its foundations, while the frantic follies of Asia and the foul vices of Paganism were at their worst; he was preaching with an air of perfect self-possession carnal abstinence, frugality of diet, sobriety of dress at the very moment when, treading on powder of silver and sand of gold, his head crowned with a tiara, his robes studded with precious stones, Elagabalus was at work, among his eunuchs, at women s tasks, calling himself by the title of Empress and every night lying with a new Emperor, selecting him for choice from the ranks of the Court barbers and scullions, or the charioteers from the Circus.

This contrast delighted him; then the Latin language, after attaining to supreme maturity in Petronius, was beginning to break up; the literature of Christianity was claiming its place, bringing in along with new ideas new words, unfamiliar constructions, strange verbs, adjectives of far-fetched meanings, abstract nouns, hitherto scarce in the Roman tongue, and of which Tertullian had been one of the first to introduce the usage.

Only this degeneration, which was carried further after Tertullian's death by his pupil St. Cyprian, by Arnobius, by the muddy Lactantius, was eminently unattractive. It was a gradual decay, slow and incomplete, marked by awkward attempts to return to the emphasis of the Ciceronian periods, not yet possessing that special raciness which in the Fourth and still more in the succeeding Centuries the odour of Christianity will give to the Pagan tongue, as it decomposes little by little, acquires a stronger and stronger aroma of decay, dropping bit by bit to pieces *pari passu* with the crumbling of the civilization of the Ancient World, with the collapse, before the advance of the Barbarian hordes, of the Empires rotted by the putrescence of the ages.

Only one Christian poet, Commodian of Gaza, was to be found in his library as representative of the art of the Third Century. The *Carmen Apologeticum*, written about 259 A.D., is a compendium of rules of conduct, tortured into acrostics, composed in rude hexameters, divided by a caesura after the fashion of heroic verse, but without any attention to quantity or the rules of hiatus and often eked out with rhymes of the kind ecclesiastical Latin later on afforded numerous examples of.

These strained, sombre verses, with their touch of savagery, full of common, vernacular expressions, of words deflected from their original meanings, appealed to him, interested him even more than the style, over-ripe and already decadent, the historians Ammianus Marcellinus and Aurelius Victor, of the letter-writer Symmachus and the compiler and grammarian Macrobius; he even preferred them to the lines, correctly scanned, and the variegated and superbly picturesque diction of Claudian, Rutilius and Ausonius.

These were in their day the masters of the art; they filled the dying Empire with their swan songs,—the Christian Ausonius with his *Cento Nuptialis* and his copious and elaborate poem on the Moselle; Rutilius, with his hymns to the glory of Rome, his anathemas against the Jews and against the Monks, his itinerary of Cisalpine Gaul, where he manages sometimes to render certain aspects of the beauties of Nature, the vague charm of landscapes reflected in water, the mirage of mists, the flying vapours about the mountain tops.

Then there is Claudian, a kind of *avatar* of Lucan, who dominates all the Fourth Century with the terrific clarion of his verse—a poet who wrought a striking and sonorous hexameter, beating out, amid showers of sparks, the right epithet at a blow, attaining a certain grandeur, filling his work with a puissant breath of life. In the Western Empire falling more and more into ruin, amid the confusion of the repeated disasters that fall upon it, unchecked by the constant threat of invasion by the Barbarians now pressing in hordes at the very gates of the Empire whose bolts and bars are cracking under the strain, he revivifies Antiquity, sings of the Rape of Proserpine, lays on his brilliant colours, goes by with all his fires ablaze in the gathering gloom that is overspreading the world.

Paganism lives again in him, sounding its last fanfare, raising its last great poet high above the Christianity that is from his day onwards utterly to submerge the language and for ever after remain absolute arbiter and master of poetry,—with Paulinus, pupil of Ausonius, with the Spanish priest Juvenous, who paraphrases the Gospels in verse, with Victorinus, author of the *Macchabæi*, with Sanctus Burdigalensis,

who in an Eclogue copied from Virgil makes the herdsmen Egon and
Buculus deplore the maladies of their flocks. Then these are succeeded
by all the series of the Saints,—Hilary of Poitiers, the champion of the
faith of Nicæa, the Athanasius of the West, as he was called;
Ambrosius, the author of indigestible homilies, the wearisome
Christian Cicero; Damasus, the fabricator of epigrams cut and polished
like precious stones; Jerome, the translator of the Vulgate, and his
adversary Vigilantius of Comminges who attacks the worship of the
saints, the abuse of miracles and the practice of fasts, and already
preaches, using arguments the ages will go on repeating one to the
other, against monastic vows and the celibacy of the clergy.

At last, in the Fifth Century, comes Augustine, Bishop of Hippo.
Him Des Esseintes knew only too well, for he was the writer of all
others most highly reputed by the Church, the founder of Christian
orthodoxy, the theologian whom good Catholics regard as an oracle, a
sovereign authority. Result: he never opened his books any more, albeit
he had celebrated, in his *Confessions*, his disillusionment with this
world and with groans of pious contrition; in his *Civitas Dei*, had
endeavoured to assuage the woeful distress of the age by seductive
promises of better things to come in a future life. In the years when he
was an active theologian, he was already a tired man, sated with his
own preachings and jeremiads, weary of his theories on predestination
and grace, exhausted by his fights against the schisms.

Des Esseintes liked better to dip into the *Psychomachia* of
Prudentius, the inventor of the allegorical poem, destined later on to
flourish uninterruptedly in the Middle Ages, or the Works of Sidonius
Apollinaris, whose correspondence, stuffed with sallies, points of wit,
archaisms, enigmas, attracted him. He was always ready to read the
panegyrics, wherein, in support of his pompous praises, he invokes the
deities of Paganism, and in spite of his better judgment, could not but
acknowledge a weakness for the affectations and hidden meanings of
these poems put together by an ingenious mechanic who loves his
machine, scrupulously oils its working parts, and is prepared at a pinch
to invent new ones just as complicated and as useless as the old.

After Sidonius, again, he kept on familiar terms with the panegyrist
Merobaudes; Sedulius, author of rhymed poems and alphabetical
hymns of which the Church has appropriated portions to incorporate in
her offices; Marius Victor, whose dark and dismal tractate on the
Perversity of Morals is lit up here and there by lines that glitter like
phosphorus; Paulinus of Pella, the poet of that icy production the
Eucharisticon; Orientius, Bishop of Auch, who in the distichs of his
Monitoria rails at the licence of women, whose faces, he declares,
destroy the nations.

The interest that Des Esseintes felt in the Latin language remained
as strong as ever even now when, rotten through and through, it hung a

decaying carcase, losing its limbs, distilling its pus, barely keeping, in the utter corruption of its body, a few sound parts which the Christians abstracted to preserve them in the salt pickle of their new dialect.

The second half of the Fifth Century was come, the appalling period when unspeakable troubles afflicted the world. The Barbarians were ravaging Gaul; Rome, paralyzed, sacked by the Visigoths, felt her life frozen within her veins as she saw her outlying limbs, the East and the West, struggling in a sea of blood, growing more and more exhausted from day to day.

Amid the general dissolution, amid the assassinations of Caesars that follow close on each other's heels, amid the uproar of slaughter that rolls from end to end of Europe, a wild hurrah broke forth, terrifying men's hearts, and drowning all other sounds. On the banks of the Danube, thousands of men, perched on little horses, wrapt in rat-skin coats, hideous Tartars with immense heads, flat noses, chins furrowed with wounds and scars, jaundiced, hairless faces, are rushing down helter-skelter on the provinces of the Lower Empire, overwhelming everything in the whirlwind of their advance.

Civilization disappeared in the dust of their gallop, in the smoke of their fires. Darkness fell upon the world and the peoples trembled in consternation as they heard the dread host rush by with a sound of thunder. The horde of Huns swept over Europe, precipitated itself on Gaul, to be overwhelmed on the plains of Châlons where Aëtius heaped up its dead in a fearful carnage. The land was gorged with blood,—a very sea of rolling purple; two hundred thousand corpses barred the road and broke the onrush of this avalanche that, turned aside, fell like a thunderclap on Italy, whose ruined cities flamed up to heaven like so many fired hay-ricks.

The Eastern Empire crumbled under the shock; the expiring life it still dragged out in decrepitude and corruption was extinguished. The last end of the universe indeed seemed near at hand; the cities Attila had passed over were decimated by plague and famine. The Latin tongue, too, seemed to be perishing amid the ruins of a world.

Years rolled by; presently the Barbarian idioms grew more regular, began to emerge from their uncouth envelopes, to develop into true languages; Latin, rescued in the general cataclysm by the Monasteries, was limited to the Religious Houses and the secular cures. Only here and there a few poets appeared, cold, difficult versifiers,—the African Dracontius with his *Hexameron*; Claudius Mamert, with his liturgical poems; Avitus of Vienna; then presently biographers, such as Ennodius, who relates the miracles of St. Epiphanes, the acute and venerated diplomatist, the upright and vigilant pastor, such as Eugippus, who has recorded for us the incomparable life of St. Severin, the mysterious anchorite, the humble ascetic, who appeared like an angel of mercy to the mourning nations, mad with pain and fear; then again writers like Veranius of the Gévaudan, who composed a little treatise on Continence, like Aurelian and Ferreolus who compiled Church canons; historians like Rotherius of Agde, famed for a History of the Huns, now lost.

Works of the next succeeding centuries were few and far between on Des Esseintes' shelves. Still the Sixth Century was represented by Fortunatus, Bishop of Poitiers, whose hymns and the *Vexilla Regis*, hacked out of the ancient carcase of the Latin language, and flavoured with the aromatic spices of the Church, haunted his thoughts on certain days; by Boëtius Gregory of Tours, and Jornandes. Then, in the Seventh and Eighth Centuries, inasmuch as, (over and above the Low Latin of the Chroniclers, such as Fredegarius and Paul the Deacon, and verses comprised in the Bangor Antiphonary, one hymn in which, the one that forms an acrostic and has one and the same rhyme ending every line, composed in honour of St. Comgill, he sometimes looked at), contemporary literature was almost exclusively confined to Lives of the Saints,—the legend of St. Columba by the cenobite Jonas and that of the Blessed Cuthbert compiled by the Venerable Bede from the notes of an anonymous monk of Lindisfarne, he confined himself to turning over at odd moments the pages of these Hagiographers and re-reading extracts from the Lives of St. Rusticula and St. Radegonde, related, the former by Defensorius, Synodite of Ligugé, the latter by the modest and simple-hearted Baudonivia, a Nun of Poitiers.

However, certain singular productions of Latin literature in Anglo-Saxon lands were more to his liking; there was for instance the whole series of the enigmas of Aldhelm, of Tatwine, of Eusebius, those inheritors of Symphosius' mantle, and in especial the riddles composed by St. Boniface in the form of acrostics, where the answer is given by the initial letters of the lines of each stanza.

His predilection grew less and less towards the end of these two Centuries; finding small pleasure indeed in the ponderous prose of the Carlovingian Latinists, the Alcuins and Eginhards, he contented himself, by way of specimens of the language of the Ninth Century, with the anonymous chronicler of St. Gall, with Freculf and Reginon, with the poem on the Siege of Paris indited by Abbo Le Courbé, with the *Hortulus*, the didactic poem of the Benedictine Walafrid Strabo, whose canto devoted to the glorification of the pumpkin, symbol of fecundity, charmed his sense of humour. Another favourite was the poem of Ermold the Black, celebrating the exploits of Louis le Débonnaire, a poem written in regular hexameters, in a severe, black style, in a diction of iron tempered in monastic waters, with here and there threads of sentiment imbedded in the hard metal; yet another, the *De Viribus Herbarum*, a poem of Macer Floridus on simples, which particularly delighted him by its poetical recipes and the extraordinary virtues he attributes to certain herbs and flowers,—to the aristolochia or birthwort, for example, which mixed with beef and laid as a plaster on a woman's abdomen is an infallible specific to make her bear a male child, or the borage, which sprinkled in an infusion about a dining hall, ensures the guests being all merry, or the peony, the pounded root of which cures head-ache for good and all, or the fennel, which, applied to a woman's bosom, clarifies her discharges and stimulates the sluggishness of her periods.

Except for a few special volumes, unclassed, certain works, modern or undated, cabalistic, medical and botanical, sundry odd tomes of Migne's Patrology, preserving Christian poems not to be found elsewhere, and Wernsdorff's Anthology of the Minor Latin Poets, except for Meursius, Forberg's Manual of Classical Erotology, the Moechialogy and the Diaconals for the use of Father Confessors, which he would take down from the shelves to dust at long intervals, with these exceptions, his Latin collections stopped with the beginning of the Tenth Century.

For truly the quaint originality, the complex simplicity of Christian Latinity had likewise come to an end. Henceforth the fiddle-faddle of philosophers and scholiasts, the vain logomachies of the Schoolmen, were to reign in undisputed mastery. The sooty masses of chronicles and books of history, the leaden lumps of the Cartularies, were to rise in more and more mountainous heaps, while the stammering grace, the clumsy but often exquisite simplicity of the Monks setting in a pious hotchpotch the poetical relics of Antiquity were no more, the fabrication of verses of refined sweetness, of substantives smelling of incense, of quaint adjectives, roughly shaped out of gold, in the barbarous, fascinating taste of Gothic jewelry, ceased. The old editions, fondly cherished by Des Esseintes, came to an end,—and making a prodigious jump over the centuries, he loaded the rest of his shelves with modern, vernacular works that, heedless of the slow progression of the ages, came down at once to the French of the present day.

Chapter Four

A carriage stopped late one afternoon before the house at Fontenay. As Des Esseintes never received a visitor; as even the postman did not venture within these deserted precincts, never having either newspaper, review or letter to leave there, the servants hesitated, asking themselves if they ought to open. But presently, at the repeated summons of the bell outside the wall pulled with a vigorous hand, they went so far as to draw aside the judas let into the door; this done, they beheld a Gentleman whose whole breast was covered, from neck to waist, with a vast buckler of gold.

They informed their master, who was at breakfast.

"By all means," said he, "bring the gentleman in,"—for he

remembered having on one occasion given his address to a lapidary to enable the man to deliver an article he had ordered.

The Gentleman came in, made his bow and deposited in the dining-room, on the pitch-pine flooring, his gold shield, which swayed backwards and forwards, rising a little bit from the ground and extending at the extremity of a snake-like neck a turtle's head which next instant it drew back in a scare under its shell.

This turtle was the result of a whim that had suddenly occurred to Des Esseintes a short while before his leaving Paris. Looking one day at an Oriental carpet with iridescent gleams of colour and following with his eyes the silvery glints that ran across the web of the wool, the colours of which were an opaque yellow and a plum violet, he had told himself: it would be a fine experiment to set on this carpet something that would move about and the deep tint of which would bring out and accentuate these tones.

Possessed by this idea, he had strolled at random through the streets; had arrived at the Palais-Royal, and in front of Chevet's window had suddenly struck his forehead,—a huge turtle met his eyes there, in a tank. He had bought the creature; then, once it was left to itself on the carpet, he had sat down before it and gazed long at it, screwing up his eyes.

Alas! there was no doubt, the negro-head hue, the raw sienna tone of the shell dimmed the sheen of the carpet instead of bringing out the tints; the dominant gleams of silver now barely showed, clashing with the cold tones of scraped zinc alongside this hard, dull carapace.

He gnawed his nails, searching in vain for a way to reconcile these discordances, to prevent this absolute incompatibility of tones. At last he discovered that his original notion of lighting up the fires of the stuff by the to-and-fro movements of a dark object set on it was mistaken; the fact of the matter was, the carpet was still too bright, too crude, too new-looking. Its colours were not sufficiently softened and toned down; the thing was to reverse the proposed expedient, to deaden the tints, to stifle them by the contrast of a brilliant object that should kill everything round it, casting the flash of gold over the pale sheen of silver. Thus looked at, the problem was easier to solve. Accordingly he resolved to have his turtle's back glazed over with gold.

Once back from the jeweller's who had taken it in to board at his workshop, the beast blazed like a sun in splendour, throwing its flashing rays over the carpet, whose tones were weak and cold in comparison, looking for all the world like a Visigothic targe inlaid with shining scales, the handiwork of some Barbaric craftsman.

At first, Des Esseintes was enchanted with the effect; but he soon came to the conclusion that this gigantic jewel was only half finished, that it would not be really complete and perfect till it was incrusted with precious stones.

He selected from a collection of Japanese curios a design representing a great bunch of flowers springing from a thin stalk, took it to a jeweller's, sketched out a border to enclose this bouquet in an oval frame, and informed the dumb-founded lapidary that every leaf and every petal or the flowers was to be executed in precious stones and mounted in the actual scales of the turtle.

The choice of the stones gave him pause; the diamond had grown singularly hackneyed now that every business man wears one on his little finger; Oriental emeralds and rubies are less degraded and dart fine, flashing lights, but they are too reminiscent of those green and red eyes that shine as head-lights on certain lines of Paris omnibuses; as for topazes, burnt or raw, they are cheap stones, dear to the humble housewife who loves to lock up a jewel-case or two in a glass cupboard; of another sort, the amethyst, albeit the Church has given it something of a sacerdotal character, is yet a stone spoilt by its frequent use to ornament the red ears and bulbous hands of butchers' wives who are fain at a modest cost to bedeck their persons with genuine and heavy jewels. Alone among all these, the sapphire keeps its fires inviolate, unharmed by the folly of tradesmen and money-grubbers. The brilliance of its fire that sparkles from a cold, limpid background has to some degree guaranteed against defilement its discreet and haughty nobility. But unfortunately by artificial light its bright flames flash no longer; the colour sinks back into itself and seems to go to sleep, only to wake and sparkle again at daybreak.

No, not one of these stones satisfied Des Esseintes; besides, they were all too civilized, too familiar. He preferred other, more startling and uncommon, sorts. After fingering a number of these and letting them trickle through his hands, he finally picked out a series of stones, some real, some artificial, the combination of which should produce a harmony, at once fascinating and disconcerting.

He combined together the several parts of his bouquet in this way: the leaves were set with stones of a strong and definite green colour,— chrysoberyls, asparagus green; peridots, leek green; olives, olive green; springing from twigs of almandine and ouvarovite of a purple red, gems throwing out sparkles of a clear, dry brilliance like the incrustations of tartar that glitter on the insides of wine-casks.

For the blossoms that stood isolated, far removed from the stalk, he used an ashen blue, rejecting, however, definitely the Oriental turquoise that is used for brooches and rings, and which, along with the commonplace pearl and the odious coral form the delight of vulgar souls; he selected exclusively those European turquoises that, strictly speaking, are only a fossil ivory impregnated with coppery infiltrations and whose sea-green blue is heavy, opaque, sulphurous, as if jaundiced with bile.

This done, he could now proceed to incrust the petals of such blossoms as grew in the middle of the bunch, those in closest neighbourhood of the stem, with certain translucent stones, possessing a glassy, sickly sheen with feverish, vivid bursts of fire.

Three gems, and only three, he employed for this purpose,— Ceylon cat's-eyes, cymophanes and sapphirines.

All three were stones that flashed with mysterious, incalculable sparkles, painfully drawn from the chill interior of their turbid substance,—the cat's eye of a greenish grey, striped with concentric veins that seem to be endowed with motion, to stir and shift every instant according to the way the light falls; the cymophane with bluish waterings running across the milky hue that appears afloat within; the sapphirine that lights up blue, phosphorescent fires on a dull, chocolate-brown background.

The lapidary took careful notes and measures as to the exact places where the stones were to be let in. "And the edges of the shell?" he presently asked Des Esseintes.

The latter had thought at first of a border of opals and hydrophanes. But these stones, interesting as they are by their curious variations of colour and changes of sparkle, are too difficult and untrustworthy to deal with; the opal has a quite rheumatic sensitiveness, the play of its rays is entirely modified according to the degree of moisture, and of heat and cold, while the hydrophane has no fire, refuses to light up the grey glow of its furnace except in water, after it has been wetted.

Finally he settled on stones whose hues would supplement each other,—the hyacinth of Compostella, mahogany red; the aquamarine, sea green; the balass ruby, vinegar rose; the Sudermania ruby, pale slate-colour. Their comparatively feeble play of colours would suffice to light up the deadness of the dull, grey shell, while leaving its full value to the brilliant bouquet of jewelled blossoms which they framed in a slender garland of uncertain splendours.

Des Esseintes stood gazing at the turtle where it lay huddled together in one corner of the dining-room, flashing fire in the dim half light.

He felt perfectly happy; his eyes were intoxicated with the splendours of these flowers flashing in jewelled flames against a golden background. Then, contrary to his use, he had an appetite and was dipping his slices of toast spread with super-excellent butter in a cup of tea, an impeccable blend of Si-a-Fayoun, Mo-you-tann and Khansky,— yellow teas, imported from China into Russia by special caravans.

This liquid perfume he drank from those cups of Oriental porcelain known as egg-shell china, so delicate and transparent are they; in the same way, just as he would have nothing to say to any other save this adorably dainty ware, he refused to use as dishes and plates anything else but articles of genuine antique silver-gilt, a trifle worn so that the underlying silver shows a little here and there under the film of gold, giving a tender, old-world look as of something fading away in a quiet death of exhaustion.

After swallowing his last mouthful, he went back to his study, whither he directed a servant to bring the turtle, which obstinately declined to make the smallest effort towards locomotion.

Outside the snow was falling. In the lamplight, ice arabesques glittered on the dark windows and the hoar-frost sparkled like crystals of sugar on the bottle-glass panes speckled with gold.

A deep silence wrapped the little house that lay asleep in the darkness.

Des Esseintes stood lost in dreams; the logs burning on the hearth filled the room with hot, stifling vapours, and presently he threw the window partly open.

Like an overhanging canopy of reversed ermine, the sky rose before him, a black curtain dappled with white.

An icy wind was blowing, that sent the snow spinning before it and soon reversed this first arrangement of black and white. The sky returned to the correct heraldic blazon, became a true ermine, white dappled with sable, where the black of night showed here and there through the general whiteness of the snowy mantle of descending snowflakes.

He closed the window again. But this quick change, without any intermediate transition, from the torrid heat of the room to the cold of mid-winter had given him a shock; he crouched back beside the fire and thought he would swallow a dose of spirits to restore his bodily temperature.

He made his way to the dining-room, where in a recess in one of the walls, a cupboard was contrived, containing a row of little barrels, ranged side by side, resting on miniature stocks of sandal wood and each pierced with a silver spigot in the lower part.

This collection of liquor casks he called his *mouth organ*. A small rod was so arranged as to connect all the spigots together and enable them all to be turned by one and the same movement, the result being that, once the apparatus was installed, it was only needful to touch a knob concealed in the panelling to open all the little conduits simultaneously and so fill with liquor the tiny cups hanging below each tap.

The organ was then open. The stops, labelled "flute," "horn," "vox humana," were pulled out, ready for use. Des Esseintes would imbibe a drop here, another there, another elsewhere, thus playing symphonies on his internal economy, producing on his palate a series of sensations analogous to those wherewith music gratifies the ear.

Indeed, each several liquor corresponded, so he held, in taste with the sound of a particular instrument. Dry curaçao, for instance, was like the clarinet with its shrill, velvety note; kummel like the oboe, whose timbre is sonorous and nasal; crême de menthe and anisette like the flute, at one and the same time sweet and poignant, whining and soft. Then, to complete the orchestra, comes kirsch, blowing a wild trumpet blast; gin and whisky, deafening the palate with their harsh outbursts of comets and trombones; liqueur brandy, blaring with the overwhelming crash of the tubas, while the thunder peals of the cymbals and the big drum, beaten might and main, are reproduced in the mouth by the rakis of Chios and the mastics.

He was convinced too that the same analogy might be pushed yet further, that quartettes of stringed instruments might be contrived to play upon the palatal arch, with the violin represented by old brandy, delicate and heady, biting and clean-toned; with the alto, simulated by rum, more robust, more rumbling, more heavy in tone; with vespetro, long-drawn, pathetic, as sad and tender as a violoncello; with the double-bass, full-bodied, solid and black as a fine, old bitter beer. One might even, if anxious to make a quintette, add yet another instrument,—the harp, mimicked with a sufficiently close approximation by the keen savour, the silvery note, clear and self-sufficing, of dry cumin.

Nay, the similarity went to still greater length, analogies not only of qualities of instruments, but of keys were to be found in the music of liquors; thus, to quote only one example, Bénédictine figures, so to speak, the minor key corresponding to the major key of the alcohols which the scores of wine-merchants' price-lists indicate under the name of green Chartreuse.

These assumptions once granted, he had reached a stage, thanks to a long course of erudite experiments, when he could execute on his tongue a succession of voiceless melodies; noiseless funeral marches, solemn and stately; could hear in his mouth solos of crême de menthe, duets of vespetro and rum.

He even succeeded in transferring to his palate selections of real music, following the composer's *motif* step by step, rendering his thought, his effects, his shades of expression, by combinations and contrasts of allied liquors, by approximations and cunning mixtures of beverages.

Sometimes again, he would compose pieces of his own, would perform pastoral symphonies with the gentle black-current ratafia that set his throat resounding with the mellow notes of warbling nightingales; with the dainty cacao-chouva, that sung sugarsweet madrigals, sentimental ditties like the "Romances d'Estelle"; or the "*Ah! vous di-rai-je maman*," of former days.

But tonight, Des Esseintes had no wish to "taste" the delights of music; he confined himself to sounding one single note on the keyboard of his instrument, filling a tiny cup with genuine Irish whisky and taking it away with him to enjoy at his leisure.

He sank down in his armchair and slowly savoured this fermented spirit of oats and barley—a strongly marked, almost poisonous flavour of creosote diffused itself through his mouth.

Little by little, as he drank, his thoughts followed the impression thus re-awakened on his palate, and stimulated by the suggestive savour of the liquor, were roused by a fatal similarity of taste and smell to recollections half obliterated years ago.

The acrid, carbolic flavour forcibly recalled the very same sensation that had filled his mouth and burned his tongue while the dentists were at work on his gums.

Once started on this track, his recollections, at first wandering vaguely over all the different practitioners he had had to do with, drew to a point, converging on one of the whole number, the eccentric memory of whose proceedings was graven with particular emphasis on his memory.

The thing had happened three years before: seized in the middle of the night with an abominable toothache, he had done everything a man does in such a case,—plugging his jaws with cotton-wool, stumbling against the furniture, pacing up and down his room like a madman.

It was a molar that had been stopped again and again, and was past cure; only the dentist's forceps could end his misery. In a fever of agony, he waited for daylight, firmly resolved to bear the most atrocious operation if only it would put an end to his sufferings.

Still holding his jaws between his hands, he asked himself what to do. The dentists he usually consulted were well-to-do practitioners who could not be seen at a moment's notice; a visit must be arranged beforehand, a regular appointment made. "That is out of the question, I cannot wait," he told himself; so he made up his mind to go to the first dentist he could find, to resort to any common, low-class tooth-drawer, one of those fellows with fists of iron, who, ignorant as they may be of the art (a mighty useless art, be it said by the way) of attending to decayed teeth and stopping hollow ones, know how to extirpate with unparalleled rapidity the most obstinate of aching stumps. Places of the sort open at daybreak, and there is no waiting. Seven o'clock struck at last. He dashed out of doors, and remembering a name he knew of such a mechanic calling himself a dentist and living at the corner of a neighbouring street, he hurried thither, biting his handkerchief and keeping back his tears as best he might.

Arrived in front of the house, which was advertised by a huge wooden placard, whereon the name "Gatonax" sprawled in enormous yellow letters on a black background and two little glazed cases in which artificial teeth were ranged in symmetrical lines in gums of pink composition joined together by mechanical springs of brass wire, he stood panting for breath, the sweat rolling from his temples; a horrid spasm shook him, a shudder ran over his skin,—and lo! relief came, the pain stopped, the tooth ceased to ache.

He halted irresolute on the pavement. But eventually he mastered his terror, climbed a dark staircase, mounting four steps at a time to the third floor. There he found on a door an enamelled plaque repeating in sky-blue lettering the same legend as on the board below. He pulled the bell; then, appalled at the great red blotches of expectoration he caught sight of on the steps, he suddenly turned tail, resolved to endure toothache all his life long, when a fearful screech reached his ears through the partition and re-echoed in the well of the staircase, nailing him to the spot in a trance of horror, while at the same instant a door opened and an old woman begged him to come in.

Shame had won the day over fear; he was shown into a dining-room; then another door opened noisily, admitting a formidable grenadier of a man, dressed in a frock coat and black trousers that seemed carved in wood. Des Esseintes followed him into an inner sanctum.

From that moment his sensations had been vague. Confusedly he remembered dropping into an armchair before a window, and stammering out, as he put a finger to his tooth: "It has been stopped already; I am afraid there's nothing can be done."

The man had cut short this explanation peremptorily, inserting an enormous fore-finger into his mouth; then, muttering something from under his lacquered, pointed moustaches, he had picked up an instrument from a table.

Thereupon the drama had begun. Clinging to the arms of the operating chair, Des Esseintes had felt a sensation of cold in his cheek, then his eyes had seen three dozen candles all at once, and so unspeakable were the tortures he was enduring, he had started beating the floor with his feet and bellowing like an animal under the slaughterer's knife.

There was a loud crack, the molar had broken in coming away; he thought they were pulling off his head, smashing in his skull; he lost all control of himself, howled at the top of his voice; fought furiously against the man who now came at him again as if he would plunge his arm to the bottom of his belly; had then suddenly stepped back a pace and lifting the patient bodily by the tooth still sticking in his jaw, had let him fall back again violently in a sitting posture into the chair; next moment he was standing up blocking the window, and puffing and panting as he brandished at the end of his pincers a blue tooth with a red thread hanging from it.

Half fainting, Des Esseintes had spit out a basin full of blood, waved away the old woman who now came in offering him the stump of his tooth, which she was preparing to wrap up in a piece of newspaper, and had fled, after paying two francs, taking his turn to leave his signature in bloody spittle on the steps; then he was once more in the street, a happy man, feeling ten years younger, ready to be interested in the veriest trifles.

"B'rrr. . . ." he shivered, horrified at these dismal reminiscences. He sprang up to break the horrid nightmare of his thoughts, and coming back to everyday matters, began to feel anxious about the turtle.

It still lay quite still; he touched it, it was dead. Accustomed no doubt to a sedentary life, an uneventful existence spent under its humble carapace, it had not been able to support the dazzling splendour imposed on it, the glittering garment in which it had been clad, the pavement of precious stones wherewith they had inlaid its poor back like a jewelled pyx.

Chapter Five

Simultaneously with his craving to escape a hateful world of degrading restrictions and pruderies, the longing never again to see pictures representing the human form toiling in Paris between four walls or roaming the streets in search of money, had obtained a more and more complete mastery over his mind.

Having once divorced himself from contemporary existence, he was resolved to suffer in his hermit's cell no spectres of old repugnances and bygone dislikes; accordingly he had chosen only to possess pictures of a subtle, exquisite refinement, instinct with dreams of Antiquity, reminiscent it may be of antique corruption, but at any rate remote from our modern times and modern manners.

He had selected for the diversion of his mind and the delight of his eyes works of a suggestive charm, introducing him to an unfamiliar world, revealing to him traces of new possibilities, stirring the nervous system by erudite phantasies, complicated dreams of horror, visions of careless wickedness and cruelty.

Of all others there was one artist who most ravished him with unceasing transports of pleasure,—Gustave Moreau.

He had purchased his two masterpieces, and night after night he would stand dreaming in front of one of these, a picture of Salomé.

The conception of the work was as follows: A throne, like the high altar of a Cathedral, stood beneath an endless vista of vaulted arches springing from thick-set columns resembling the pillars of a Romanesque building, encased in many coloured brickwork, incrusted with mosaics, set with lapis lazuli and sardonyx, in a Palace that recalled a basilica of an architecture at once Saracenic and Byzantine.

In the centre of the tabernacle surmounting the altar, which was approached by steps in the shape of a recessed half circle, the Tetrarch Herod was seated, crowned with a tiara, his legs drawn together, with hands on knees.

The face was yellow, like parchment, furrowed with wrinkles, worn with years; his long beard floated like a white cloud over the starry gems that studded the gold-fringed robe that moulded his breast.

Round about this figure, that sat motionless as a statue, fixed in a hieratic pose like some Hindu god, burned cressets from which rose clouds of scented vapour. Through this gleamed, like the phosphoric glint of wild beasts' eyes, the flash of the jewels set in the walls of the throne; then the smoke rolled higher, under the arcades of the roof, mingling its misty blue with the gold dust of the great beams of sunlight pouring in from the domes.

Amid the heady odour of the perfumes, in the hot, stifling atmosphere of the great basilica, Salomé, the left arm extended in a gesture of command, the right bent, holding up beside the face a great lotus-blossom, glides slowly forward on the points of her toes, to the accompaniment of a guitar whose strings a woman strikes, sitting crouched on the floor.

Her face wore a thoughtful, solemn, almost reverent expression as she began the wanton dance that was to rouse the dormant passions of the old Herod; her bosoms quiver and, touched lightly by her swaying necklets, their rosy points stand pouting; on the moist skin of her body glitter clustered diamonds; from bracelets, belts, rings, dart sparks of fire; over her robe of triumph, bestrewn with pearls, broidered with silver, studded with gold, a corselet of chased goldsmith's work, each mesh of which is a precious stone, seems ablaze with coiling fiery serpents, crawling and creeping over the pink flesh like gleaming insects with dazzling wings of brilliant colours, scarlet with bands of yellow like the dawn, with patterned diapering like the blue of steel, with stripes of peacock green.

With concentrated gaze and the fixed eyes of a sleep walker, she sees neither the Tetrarch, who sits there quivering, nor her mother, the ruthless Herodias, who watches her, nor the hermaphrodite or eunuch who stands sabre in hand on the lowest step of the throne, a terrible figure, veiled to below the eyes, the sexless dugs of the creature hanging like twin gourds under his tunic barred with orange stripes.

The thought of this Salomé, so full of haunting suggestion to the artist and the poet, had fascinated Des Esseintes for years. How often had he read in the old Bible of Pierre Variquet, translated by the Doctors in Theology of the University of Louvain, the Gospel of St. Matthew where it recounts in brief, naive phrases the beheading of the Precursor; how often had he dreamed dreams between the simple lines:

"But when Herod's birthday was kept, the daughter of Herodias danced before them, and pleased Herod.

"Whereupon, he promised with an oath to give her whatsoever she would ask.

"And she, being before instructed of her mother, said 'Give me here John Baptist's head in a charger.'

"And the king was sorry: nevertheless, for the oath's sake, and them which sat with him at meat, he commanded it to be given her.

"And he sent, and beheaded John in the prison.

"And his head was brought in a charger, and given to the damsel: and she brought it to her mother."

But neither St. Matthew, nor St. Mark, nor St. Luke, nor any other of the Sacred Writers had enlarged on the maddening charms and the active allurements of the dancer. She had always remained a dim, obliterated figure, lost with her mysterious fascination in the far-off mist of the centuries, not to be realized by exact and pedestrian minds, only appealing to brains shaken and sharpened, made visionary as it were by hysteria; she had always eluded the grasp of fleshy painters, such as Rubens who travestied her as a Flemish butcher's wife; always baffled the comprehension of writers who have never yet succeeded in rendering the delirious frenzy of the wanton, the subtle grandeur of the murderess.

In the work of Gustave Moreau, going for its conception altogether beyond the meagre facts supplied by the New Testament, Des Esseintes saw realized at last the Salomé, weird and superhuman, he had dreamed of. No longer was she merely the dancing-girl who extorts a cry of lust and concupiscence from an old man by the lascivious contortions of her body; who breaks the will, masters the mind of a King by the spectacle of her quivering bosoms, heaving belly and tossing thighs; she was now revealed in a sense as the symbolic incarnation of world-old Vice, the goddess of immortal Hysteria, the Curse of Beauty supreme above all other beauties by the cataleptic spasm that stirs her flesh and steels her muscles,—a monstrous Beast of the Apocalypse, indifferent, irresponsible, insensible, poisoning, like Helen of Troy of the old Classic fables, all who come near her, all who see her, all who touch her.

So understood, she belonged to the ancient Theogonies of the Far East; no longer she drew her origin from Biblical tradition; could not even be likened to the living image of Babylonish Whoredom, or the Scarlet Woman, the Royal Harlot of Revelations, bedecked like her with precious stones and purple, tired and painted like her; for *she* was not driven by a fateful power, by a supreme, irresistible force, into the alluring perversities of debauch.

Moreover, the painter seemed to have wished to mark his deliberate purpose to keep outside centuries of history; to give no definite indication of race or country or period, setting as he does his Salomé in the midst of this strange Palace, with its confused architecture of a grandiose complexity; clothing her in sumptuous, fantastic robes, crowning her with a diadem of no land or time shaped like a Phoenician tower such as Salammbô wears, putting in her hand the sceptre of Isis, the sacred flower of Egypt and of India, the great lotus-blossom.

Des Esseintes strove to fathom the meaning of this emblem. Did it bear the phallic signification the primordial religions of India give it; did it proclaim to the old Tetrarch a sacrifice of a woman's virginity, an exchange of blood, an incestuous embrace asked for and offered on the express condition of a murder? Or was it intended to suggest the allegory of Fertility, the Hindu myth of Life, an existence held betwixt the fingers of woman, snatched away and defiled by the lustful hands of man, who is seized by a sudden madness, bewildered by the cry of the flesh?

Perhaps, too, in arming his enigmatic goddess with the revered lotus-flower, the painter had thought of the dancing harlot of all times, the mortal woman the temple of whose body is defiled,—cause of all the sins and all the crimes; perhaps he had remembered the sepulchral rites of ancient Egypt, the ritual ceremonies of the embalmment, when surgeons and priests stretch the dead woman's body on a slab of jasper, then with curved needles extract her brains through the nostrils, her entrails through an incision opened in the left side; finally, before gilding the nails and teeth, before coating the corpse with bitumen and precious essences, insert into her sexual parts, to purify them, the chaste petals of the divine flower.

Be this as it may, an irresistible fascination breathed from the canvas; but the water-colour entitled "The Apparition" was perhaps even yet more troubling to the senses.

In it, Herod's Palace towered aloft like an Alhambra on light columns iridescent with Moorish chequer-work, joined as with silver mortar, consolidated with cement of gold; arabesques surrounded lozenges of lapis lazuli and wound all along the cupolas, where on marquetries of mother-of-pearl, wandered glittering rainbows, flashes of prismatic colour.

The murder had been done; now the headsman stood there impassive, his hands resting on the pommel of his long sword, stained with blood.

The decapitated head of the Saint had risen up from the charger where it lay on the flags, and the eyes were gazing out from the livid face with its discoloured lips and open mouth; the neck all crimson, dripping tears of gore.

A mosaic encircled the face whence shone an aureola darting gleams of fire under the porticoes, illuminating the ghastly lifting of the head, revealing the glassy eyeballs, that seemed fixed, glued to the figure of the dancing wanton.

With a gesture of horror, Salomé repulses the appalling vision that holds her nailed to the floor, balanced on her toe tips; her eyes are dilated, her hand grips her throat convulsively.

She is almost naked; in the ardour of the dance the veils have unwound themselves, the brocaded draperies of her robes have slipped away; she is clad now only in goldsmith's artistries and translucent gems; a gorget clips her waist like a corselet; and for clasp a superb, a wondrous jewel flashes lightnings in the furrow between her bosoms; lower, on the hips, a girdle swathes her, hiding the upper thighs, against which swings a gigantic pendant, a falling river of carbuncles and emeralds; to complete the picture: where the body shows bare betwixt gorget and girdle, the belly bulges, dimpled by the hollow of the navel that recalls a graven seal of onyx with its milky sheen and tint as of a rosy finger-nail.

Beneath the ardent rays flashing from the Precursor's head, every facet of her jewelled bravery catches fire; the stones burn, outlining the woman's shape in flaming figures; neck, legs, arms, glitter with points of light, now red as burning brands, now violet as jets of gas, now blue as flames of alcohol, now white as moonbeams.

The dreadful head flashes and flames, bleeding always, dripping gouts of dark purple that point the beard and hair. Visible to Salomé, alone, it embraces in the stare of its dead eyes neither Herodias, who sits dreaming of her hate satiated at last, nor the Tetrarch, who, leaning rather forward with hands on knees, still pants, maddened by the sight of the woman's nakedness, reeking with heady fumes, dripping with balms and essences, alluring with scents of incense and myrrh.

Like the old King, Des Esseintes was overwhelmed, over-mastered, dizzied before this figure of the dancing-girl, less majestic, less imposing, but more ensnaring to the senses than the Salomé of the oil painting.

In the callous and pitiless statue, in the innocent and deadly idol, the emotion, the terror of the human being had dawned; the great lotus-flower had disappeared, the goddess vanished; an atrocious nightmare now gripped the throat of the mime, intoxicated by the whirl of the dance, of the courtesan, petrified, hypnotized by terror.

In this, she was altogether feminine, obedient to her temperament of a passionate, cruel woman; she was active and alive, more refined and yet more savage, more hateful and yet more exquisite; she was shown awakening more powerfully the sleeping passions of man; bewitching, subjugating more surely his will, with her unholy charm as of a great flower of concupiscence, born of a sacrilegious birth, reared in a hothouse of impiety.

As Des Esseintes used to maintain: never before at any epoch had the art of water-colour succeeded in reaching such a brilliancy of tint; never had the poverty of chemical pigments been able thus to set down on paper such coruscating splendours of precious stones, such glowing hues as of painted windows illumined by the noonday sun, glories so amazing, so dazzling of rich garments and glowing flesh tints.

And, falling into a reverie, he would ask himself what were the origin and antecedents of the great painter, the mystic, the Pagan, the man of genius who could live so remote from the outside world as to behold, here and now in Paris, the splendid, cruel visions, the magic apotheoses of other ages.

Who had been his predecessors? This Des Esseintes found it hard to say; here and there, he seemed influenced by vague recollections of Mantegna and Jacopo de Barbari; here and there, by confused memories of Da Vinci and the feverish colouring of Delacroix. But in the main, the effect produced by these masters' work on his own was imperceptible; the real truth was that Gustave Moreau was a pupil of no man. Without provable ancestors, without possible descendants, he remained, in contemporary art, a unique figure. Going back to the ethnographic sources of the nations, to the first origins of the mythologies whose blood-stained enigmas he compared and unriddled, reuniting, combining in one the legends derived from the Far East and metamorphosed by the beliefs of other peoples, he thus justified his architectonic combinations, his sumptuous and unexpected amalgamations of costumes, his hieratic and sinister allegories, made yet more poignant by the restless apperceptions of a nervous system altogether modern in its morbid sensitiveness; but his work was always painful, haunted by the symbols of superhuman loves and superhuman vices, divine abominations committed without enthusiasm and without hope.

There breathed from his pictures, so despairing and so erudite, a strange magic, a sorcery that moved you to the bottom of the soul, like that of certain of Baudelaire's poems, and you were left amazed, pensive, disconcerted by this art that crossed the last frontier-lines of painting, borrowing from literature its most subtle suggestions, from the art of the enameller its most marvellous effects of brilliancy, from the art of the lapidary and the engraver its most exquisite delicacies of touch. These two images of Salomé, for which Des Esseintes' admiration was boundless, were living things before his eyes where they hung on the walls of his working study on special panels reserved for them among the shelves of books.

But this was by no means the end of the purchases of pictures he had made with a view to beautifying his solitude.

True he had sacrificed all the first storey of his house, the only one above the ground floor, and occupied none of its rooms for his personal use, but the latter even by itself demanded a large number of pictures to cover the nakedness of its walls.

This ground floor was distributed as follows: A dressing-room, communicating with the bedroom, occupied one angle of the building; from the bedroom you passed into the library, from the library into the dining-room, which formed the other angle.

These rooms, making up one front of the house, extended in a straight line, pierced with windows giving on the valley of Aunay.

The opposite side of the edifice consisted of four rooms exactly corresponding, so far as size and disposition went, with the former. Thus a kitchen stood at the corner, answering to the dining-room; a large vestibule, serving as entrance hall to the dwelling, matched the library; a kind of boudoir, the bedroom; the closets and bathrooms, the dressing-room.

All these latter rooms looked out on the side opposite to the valley of Aunay, towards the Tour du Croy and Châtillon.

As to the staircase, it was built against one side of the house, on the outside, so that the servants' footsteps, trampling up the steps, reached Des Esseintes deadened and less noisy.

He had had the boudoir hung with tapestry of a vivid red, and on each of the four walls were displayed in ebony frames prints by Jan Luyken, an old Dutch engraver, almost unknown in France.

The works he possessed of this artist, at once fantastic and depressing, vigorous and brutal, included the series of his *Religious Persecutions*, a collection of appalling plates representing all the tortures which the savagery of religious intolerance has invented, plates exhibiting all the horrors of human agony,—men roasted over braziers, skulls laid open by sword cuts, pierced with nails, riven asunder with saws, bowels drawn out of the belly, and twisted round rollers, finger-nails torn out one by one with pincers, eyes put out, eyelids turned back and transfixed with pins, limbs dislocated or carefully broken bones laid bare and scraped for hours with knives.

These productions, replete with abominable imaginations, stinking of the stake, reeking with blood, echoing with curses and screams of agony, made Des Esseintes' flesh creep as he stood stifled with horror in the red boudoir.

But, over and above the qualms of disgust they provoked, over and above the dreadful genius of the man and the extraordinary vividness he gave his figures, there were likewise to be found among the thronging multitudes that people his marvellous drawings, among the hosts of spectators sketched with a dexterity of hand reminding us of Callot, but with a power that amusing but trivial draughtsman never possessed, curious reconstructions of the life of other places and periods; architecture, costumes, manners and customs in the days of the Maccabees, at Rome during the persecutions of the Christians, in Spain under the Inquisition, in France in the Middle Ages and at the date of the St. Bartholomew and the Dragonnades, were all noted with a scrupulous exactitude, and put on paper with a supreme skill.

These prints were mines of curious information; a man could look at them for hours and never weary; profoundly suggestive of ideas, they often helped Des Esseintes to kill the time on days when books refused to interest him.

Moreover, Luyken's own life was yet another attraction to him, explaining indeed the wildness of his work. A fervent Calvinist, a hidebound sectary, a fanatic of hymns and prayers, he composed religious poems, which he illustrated with his burin, paraphrased the Psalms in verse, lost himself in deep studies of the Bible, from which he would emerge, haggard and enraptured, his brain haunted by bloody pictures, his mouth full of the maledictions of the Reformation, and roused to an ecstasy by its songs of terror and fury.

Added to this, he was one who scorned this world, gave up his goods to the poor, lived on a crust of bread himself; in the end, he had taken boat along with an old servant-maid, carried away by a fanatic admiration of the man, put to sea at a venture, landing wherever his vessel came ashore and preaching the Gospel to all peoples, trying to live without eating, a madman and a savage almost at the last.

In the adjoining room, the vestibule, a larger apartment panelled with cedar wood the colour of a cigar-box, were ranged in rows other engravings and drawings equally extraordinary.

Bresdin's *Comedy of Death* was one, where in an impossible landscape, bristling with trees, coppices and thickets taking the shape of demons and phantoms, swarming with birds having rats' heads and tails of vegetables, from a soil littered with human bones, vertebrae, ribs and skulls, spring willows, knotted and gnarled, surmounted by skeletons tossing their arms in unison and chanting a hymn of victory, while a Christ flies away to a sky dappled with little clouds; a hermit sits pondering, his head between his hands, in the recesses of a grotto; a beggar dies worn out with privations, exhausted with hunger, stretched on his back, his feet extended towards a stagnant pool.

Another was the *Good Samaritan* by the same artist, an immense pen-and-ink drawing, lithographed,—a wild entanglement of palms, service-trees, oaks, growing all together in defiance of seasons and climates, an outburst of virgin forest, crammed with apes, owls and screech-owls, cumbered with old stumps shapeless as roots of coral,—a magic wood, pierced by a clearing dimly revealing far away, beyond a camel and the group of the Samaritan and the man who fell by the wayside, a river and behind it again a fairylike city climbing to the horizon line, rising to meet a strange-looking sky, dotted with birds, woolly with rolling clouds, swelling, as it were, with bales of vapour.

You would have thought it the work of an Early Italian master or a half-developed Albert Durer, composed under the influence of opium.

But, much as he admired the delicacy of detail and the imposing conception of this plate, Des Esseintes was more particularly attracted by the other pictures that decorated the room. These were signed Odilon Redon.

In their light frames of unpainted pear-wood, with a gold beading, they contained productions of an inconceivable eccentricity,—a head in a Merovingian style, placed upon a cup; a bearded man, having something about him recalling at one and the same time a Buddhist priest and an orator at a public meeting, touching with the tip of his finger a colossal cannonball; a horrible spider, with a human face lodged in the middle of its body. Then there were crayons that went further yet in the horrors of a nightmare dream. Here it was an enormous die that winked a mournful eye; there, a series of landscapes,—barren, parched, burnt-up plains, riven by earthquakes, rising in volcanic heights wreathed with wild clouds under a livid, stagnant sky. Sometimes even the subjects seemed to be borrowed from the dreams of science, to go back to prehistoric times; a monstrous flora spread over the rocks; everywhere were erratic blocks, glacial mud streams, and amongst them human beings whose ape-like type,—the heavy jaws, the projecting arches of the brows, the receding forehead, the flattened top of the skull, recalled the ancestral head, the head of the earliest quaternary period, when man was still a fruit-eater and speechless, a contemporary of the mammoth, the woolly-haired rhinoceros and the giant bear. These drawings passed all bounds, transgressing in a thousand ways the established laws of pictorial art, utterly fantastic and revolutionary, the work of a mad and morbid genius.

In fact, there were some of these faces, staring out with great, wild, insane eyes, some of these shapes exaggerated out of all measure or distorted as if seen refracted through water, that evoked in Des Esseintes' memory recollections of typhoid fever, remembrances that had stuck persistently in his head of hot nights of misery and horrid childish nightmares.

Overcome by an indefinable sense of distress before these designs,—the same distress he had formerly experienced at the sight of certain *Proverbs* of Goya's which they resembled, as also after reading some of Edgar Allan Poe's stories, whose mirages of hallucination and effects of terror Odilon Redon seemed to have transferred into a sister art, he would rub his eyes and gaze at a radiant figure that, amid these frenzied designs, rose calm and serene, a figure of *Melancholia*, seated before a round sun's disk, on rocks, in an attitude of depression and despondency.

Then the gloom would be dissipated as if by magic; a pleasing sadness, a languor of gentle mournfulness, would fill his thoughts, and he would meditate for hours before this work, which, with its splashes of colour-wash gleaming amid the heavy chalks, struck a brilliant note of liquid green and pale gold to relieve the unbroken black of all these crayons and engravings.

Besides this series of Redon's works, covering nearly all the panels of the vestibule, he had hung in his bedroom an extravagant design, a sketch by Théocopuli, a Christ with livid flesh tints, the drawing of which was exaggerated, the colouring crude, the vigour excessive and undisciplined, an example of that painter's second manner, when he was tormented with the one haunting idea of avoiding any resemblance to Titian at all costs.

This gloomy work of art, with its tints of dead black and unhealthy green, corresponded in Des Esseintes' ideas with certain conclusions he came to with regard to the furnishing of the same apartment.

There existed, according to him, two ways and only two of arranging a bedroom; either to make it a place for pleasure, contrived to excite the passions for nightly adventure; or else to regard it as a retreat dedicated to sleep and solitude, a home of quiet thoughts, a kind of oratory.

In the first case, the Louis XV. style, was pre-eminently the one for refined minds, for people exhausted above all by stress and strain of mental sensibility; indeed, only the Eighteenth Century has known how to envelope woman in a vicious atmosphere, shaping its furniture on the model of her charms, copying the contortions of her ardour, imitating the spasms of her amorousness in the waving lines and intricate convolutions of wood and copper, adding a spice to the sugar-sweet languor of the blonde by the vivid, bright tone of its ornamentation, mitigating the salty savour of the brunette by tapestries of subdued, liquid, almost insipid hues.

A chamber of the sort he had already included in his Paris abode, with the broad, white bed that gives an added titillation, an enhanced satisfaction to the depraved senses of an old voluptuary, that is like a cynic's grin in face of pretended chastity, before Greuze's innocent sprigs of girlhood, before the artificial purity of naughty sheets that seem spread for children and young virgins.

In the other case,—and now that he was determined to break with the agitating memories of his past life, this was the only one possible,—he must contrive a bed-chamber to resemble a monk's cell in a Religious House; but here came difficulty upon difficulty, for he refused absolutely to endure for his personal occupation the austere ugliness that marks such refuges for penitence and prayer.

By dint of turning the question over this way and that and looking at it from every side, he arrived at the conclusion that the result to be aimed at amounted to this—to arrange by means of objects cheerful in themselves a melancholy whole, or rather, while preserving its character of plain ugliness, to impress on the general effect of the room thus treated a kind of elegance and distinction; to reverse, in fact, the optical delusion of the stage, where cheap tinsel plays the part of expensive and sumptuous robes, to gain indeed precisely the opposite effect, using costly and magnificent materials so as to give the impression of common rags; in a word, to fit up a Trappist's cell that should have the look of the genuine article, and yet of course be nothing of the sort.

He set about the task as follows: to imitate the ochre wash that is the invariable mark of administrative and clerical direction, he had the walls hung with saffron silk; to represent the chocolate brown of the wainscot, the regulation colour for suchlike places, he panelled the lower part of these same walls with wood painted a rich, deep purple. The effect was charming, recalling—though how different really!—the bald stiffness of the pattern he was copying,—with modifications. The ceiling, in the same way, was covered with unbleached white cloth, giving the appearance of plaster, but without its crude shiny look; then for the cold tiles of the floor; he mimicked these very successfully, thanks to a carpet with a pattern of red squares, interspersed with spots of a whitish hue where the occupants' sandals might have been supposed to leave their mark.

This room he furnished with a little iron bedstead, a sham hermit's couch, constructed out of old pieces of wrought and polished iron, its plainness relieved at head and foot by a leaf and flower ornamentation,—tulips and vine-tendrils intertwined, once part of the balustrade of the great staircase of an old chateau.

By way of night-table, he installed an antique prie-Dieu, the inside of which would hold a utensil, while the top supported a book of offices of the Church; he erected against the opposite wall a state pew, surmounted by an open-work canopy decorated with ornaments carved in the solid wood; he used candelabra that had come from a desecrated church, in which he burned real wax tapers purchased at a special house patronized by the clergy, for he felt a genuine repugnance for all the modern methods of illumination, whether petroleum, rock-oil, gas or composite candles, all alike in their crude, dazzling effects.

In bed in the morning, as he lay with his head on the pillow before falling asleep, he would gaze at his Théocopuli, the painful colouring of which modified to some degree the soft cheerfulness of the yellow silk on the walls and gave it a graver tone; at these times, he could easily picture himself living a hundred leagues from Paris, far from the world of men, in the depths of a Monastery.

And, after all, the illusion was not difficult to sustain for truly he was living a life largely analogous to that of a Monk. In this way, he enjoyed the advantages of confinement in a cloister, while he escaped its inconveniences,—the quasi-military discipline, the lack of comfort, the dirt and herding together and the monotonous idleness. Just as he had made his cell into a warm, luxurious bedchamber, so he had procured himself an existence carried on under normal conditions, without hardship or incommodity, sufficiently occupied, yet free from irksome restraints.

Like an eremite, he was ripe for solitude, harassed by life's stress, expecting nothing more of existence; like a monk again, he was overwhelmed with an immense fatigue, a craving for peace and quiet, a longing to have nothing more to do henceforth with the vulgar, who were in his eyes all utilitarians and fools.

In short, though he was conscious of no vocation for the state of grace, he felt in himself a genuine sympathy for the folks shut up in Monasteries, persecuted by a society that hates them and can never forgive the well-grounded contempt they entertain for it nor the wish they manifest to redeem, to expiate by long years of silence the ever-increasing licentiousness of its grotesque or silly conversations.

Chapter Six

Buried in a vast hooded armchair, his feet resting on the silver-gilt balls of the fire-dogs, his slippers roasting before the burning logs that shot out bright, crackling flames as if lashed by the furious blast of a blow-pipe, Des Esseintes laid down on a table the old quarto he was reading, stretched himself, lit a cigarette and presently lapsed into a delicious reverie, his mind hurrying full chase in pursuit of old-time reminiscences. For months he had not given these a thought, but now they were suddenly revived by the associations of a name that recurred without apparent reason to his memory.

Once more he could see with surprising clearness his friend D'Aigurande's embarrassment when once, at a gathering of confirmed old bachelors, he had been forced to confess to the final completion of the arrangements for his marriage. Everybody protested and drew a harrowing picture for his benefit of the abominations of sleeping two in a bed. Nothing availed; he had lost his head, he believed implicitly in the good sense of his future wife and would have it he had discovered in her quite exceptional gifts of tenderness and devotion.

Among them all, Des Esseintes had been the only one to encourage him in his design,—this after learning the fact that his comrade's fiancée wished to live at the corner of a newly constructed boulevard, in one of those modern flats that are built on a circular ground-plan.

Convinced of the merciless influence exerted by petty vexations, more disastrous as these are for highly strung temperaments than the great sorrows of life, and basing his calculations on the fact that D'Aigurande possessed no fortune of his own, while his wife's dowry was all but non-existent, he foresaw in this harmless wish an indefinite vista of ludicrous miseries to come.

D'Aigurande proceeded in due course to buy furniture all made on the round,—console-tables hollowed out at the back so as to form a semicircle, curtain-poles curved like a bow, carpets cut crescent-shaped,—a whole suite of furniture made specially to order. He spent twice as much as other people; then presently, when his wife, finding herself short of money for her dress, got tired of living in this round-house and removed to an ordinary square habitation at a lower rent, no single piece of furniture would fit in or look right. Little by little, these unconscionable chairs and tables and chests of drawers gave rise to endless squabbles; conjugal happiness, already worn thin by the friction of a life in common, grew week by week more and more ambiguous; mutual recriminations followed, as they found it impossible to live in their drawing-room where sofas and console-tables refused to touch the wall and, in spite of wedges and props, shook and shivered whenever you came near them. Funds were lacking for repairs and improvements, which, to tell the truth, were quite impracticable. Everything became a subject of bitterness and quarrelling, from the drawers that had warped in the wobbling furniture to the petty thefts of the maidservant who took advantage of her master and mistress's squabbles to rob the cash-box. In one word, their life grew unbearable; he sought amusement out of doors, she tried to find in the arms of lovers an anodyne for the wretchedness of her overcast and monotonous life. By common consent, they cancelled the settlements and petitioned for a separation.

"Yes, my plan of campaign was quite correct," Des Esseintes had told himself on hearing the news; he enjoyed the same satisfaction a strategist feels when his manoeuvres, planned long beforehand, end in victory.

Now, sitting there before his fire and thinking over the break-up of this household which he had helped by his advice to bring together, he threw a fresh armful of wood onto the hearth, and so off again full cry in his dreams.

Belonging to the same order of ideas, other memories now began to crowd upon him.

It was some years ago now since one evening in the Rue de Rivoli, he had come across a young scamp of sixteen or so, a pale-faced, quick-eyed child, as seductive as a girl. He was sucking laboriously at a cigarette, the paper of which was bursting where the sharp ends of the coarse *caporal* had come through. Cursing the stuff, the lad was rubbing kitchen matches down his thigh; they would *not* light, and soon he came to the end of the box. Catching sight of Des Esseintes who was watching him, he came up, touching his peaked cap, and asked politely for a light. Des Esseintes offered some of his own scented Dubeques, after which he entered into conversation with the lad and urged him to tell the story of his life.

Nothing could well be more ordinary; his name was Auguste Langlois, and he worked at making pasteboard boxes; he had lost his mother and had a father who beat him unmercifully.

Des Esseintes' thoughts were busy as he listened. "Come and have a drink," he said,—and took him to a café where he regaled him with goes of heady punch. The child drank his liquor without a word. "Look here," broke in Des Esseintes suddenly, "would you like some fun this evening? I'll pay the piper." And he had thereupon carried off the youngster to Madame Laure's, a lady who kept an assortment of pretty girls on the third floor of a house in the Rue Mosnier; there was a series of rooms with red walls diversified by circular mirrors, the rest of the furniture consisting mainly of couches and wash-basins.

There, petrified with surprise, Auguste as he fingered his cloth cap, had stared with round eyes at a battalion of women whose painted lips exclaimed all together:

"Oh! the little lad! Why, he is sweet!"

"But, tell us, my angel, you're not old enough yet, surely?" a brunette had interjected, a girl with prominent eyes and a hook nose who filled at Mine. Laure's establishment the indispensable rôle of *the handsome Jewess*.

Quite at his ease, and very much at home, Des Esseintes was talking familiarly in a low voice with the mistress of the house.

"Don't be afraid, stupid," he turned to the child to say; "come now, make your choice, it's *my* treat,"—and he pushed the lad gently towards a divan, onto which he fell between two women. They drew a little closer together, on a sign from Madame Laure, enveloping Auguste's knees in their peignoirs and bringing under his nose their powdered shoulders that emitted a warm, heady perfume. The child never stirred, but sat there with burning cheeks, a dry mouth and downcast eyes, darting from under their lids downward glances of curiosity, that refused obstinately to leave the upper part of the girls' thighs.

Vanda, the handsome Jewess, kissed him, giving him good advice, telling him to do what father and mother told him, while her hands were straying all the time over the lad's person; a change came over his face and he threw himself back in a kind of transport on her bosom.

"So it's not on your own account you've come tonight," observed Madame Laure to Des Esseintes. "But where the devil did you get hold of that baby?" she added, when Auguste had disappeared with the handsome Jewess.

"In the street, my dear lady."

"Yet you're not drunk," muttered the old woman. Then, after thinking a bit, she proceeded, with a motherly smile: "Ah, I understand; you rascal, you like 'em young, do you?"

Des Esseintes shrugged his shoulders.—"You're wide of the mark! oh! miles away from it," he laughed; "the plain truth is I am simply trying to train a murderer. Now just follow my argument. This boy is virgin and has reached the age when the blood begins to boil; he might, of course, run after the little girls of his neighbourhood, and still remain an honest lad while enjoying his bit of amusement; in fact, have his little share of the monotonous happiness open to the poor. On the contrary, by bringing him here and plunging him in a luxury he had never even suspected the existence of and which will make a lasting impression on his memory; by offering him every fortnight a treat like this, I shall make him acquire the habit of these pleasures which his means forbid his enjoying; let us grant it will take three months for them to become absolutely indispensable to him—and by spacing them out as I do, I avoid all risk of satiating him—well, at the end of the three months, I stop the little allowance I am going to pay you in advance for the benevolence you show him. Then he will take to thieving to pay for his visits here; he will stop at nothing that he may take his usual diversions on this divan in this fine gas-lit apartment.

"If the worst comes to the worst, he will, I hope, one fine day kill the gentleman who turns up just at the wrong moment as he is breaking open his desk; then my object will be attained, I shall have contributed, so far as in me lay, to create a scoundrel, an enemy the more for the odious society that wrings so heavy a ransom from us all."

The woman gazed at the speaker with eyes of amazement. "Ah! so there you are!' he exclaimed, as he saw Auguste creeping back into the room, red and shy, skulking behind the fair Vanda. "Come, youngster, it is getting late, make your bow to the ladies." Then he explained to him on their way downstairs that, once every fortnight, he might pay a visit to Madame Laure's without putting hand in pocket. Finally, on reaching the street, as they stood together on the pavement, he looked the abashed child in the face and said:

"We shall not meet again after this; do you go back hot foot to your father, whose hand is itching for work to do, and never forget this half divine command: 'Do unto others as you would *not* have them do unto you.' With that to guide you you will go far."

"Good night, sir."

"But whatever you do, do not be ungrateful, let me hear tidings of you soon as may be,—in the columns of the Police News."

"The little Judas!" Des Esseintes muttered to himself on this occasion, as he stirred the glowing embers; "to think that I have never once seen his name in the newspapers! True, it has been out of my power to play a sure game; that I have foreseen, yet been unable to prevent certain contingencies,—old mother Laure's little tricks, for instance, pocketing the money and not delivering the goods; the chance of one of the women getting infatuated with Auguste, and, when the three months was up, letting him have his whack on tick; or even the possibility of the handsome Jewess's highly-spiced vices having scared the lad, too young and impatient to brook the slow and elaborate preliminaries, or stand the exhausting consummations of her caprices. Unless, therefore, he has been in trouble with the criminal courts since I have been at Fontenay where I never read the papers, I am dished."

He got up from his chair and took two or three turns up and down the room.

"It would be a thousand pities all the same," he mused, "for, by acting in this way, I had really been putting in practice the parable of lay instruction, the allegory of popular education, which, while tending to nothing else than to turn everybody into Langlois, instead of definitely and mercifully putting out the wretched creatures' eyes, tries its hardest to force them wide open that they may see all about them other lots unearned by any merit yet more benignant, pleasures keener and more brightly gilded, and therefore more desirable and harder to come at."

"And the fact is," went on Des Esseintes, pursuing his argument, "the fact is that, pain being the effect of education, seeing that it grows greater and more poignant the more ideas germinate, the more we endeavour to polish the intelligence and refine the nervous system of the poor and unfortunate, the more we shall be developing the germs, always so fiercely ready to sprout, of moral suffering and social hatred."

The lamps were smoking. He turned them up and looked at his watch. Three o'clock in the morning. He kindled a cigarette and plunged himself again in the perusal, interrupted by his dreaming, of the old Latin poem *De Laude Castitatis*, written, in the reign of Gondebald, by Avitus, Bishop Metropolitan of Vienne.

Chapter Seven

After this evening when, without any apparent cause, he had dwelt upon the melancholy memory of Auguste Langlois, Des Esseintes lived his whole life over again.

He was now incapable of understanding one word of the volumes he perused; his eyes themselves refused to read; it seemed to him that his mind, satiated with literature and art, declined absolutely to absorb any more.

He lived on himself, fed on his own substance, like those hibernating animals that lie torpid in a hole all the winter; solitude had acted on his brain as a narcotic. At first, it had nerved and stimulated him, but its later effect was a somnolence haunted by vague reveries; it checked all his plans, broke down his will, led him through a long procession of dreams which he accepted with passive endurance without even an attempt to escape them.

The confused mass of reading and meditation on artistic themes which he had accumulated since he had lived alone as a barrier to arrest the current of old recollections, had been suddenly carried away, and the flood was let loose, sweeping away present and future, submerging them under the waves of the past, drowning his spirit in a vast lake of melancholy, on the surface of which floated, like grotesque derelicts, trivial episodes of his existence, ridiculously unimportant incidents.

The book he was holding tumbled on to his knees; he did not try to resume it, but sat reviewing, full of fear and disgust, the years of his dead past; his thoughts pivoted, like swirling waters round a stake that stands firm and immovable in their midst, about the memories connected with Madame Laure and Auguste. What a time that was!— the period of evening parties, of race-meetings, of card-playing, of love scenes, ordered in advance and served to the minute, at the stroke of midnight, in his pink boudoir! His mind was obsessed by glimpses of faces, looks, unmeaning words that stuck in his memory in the way popular tunes have of doing, which for a while you cannot help humming over and over, but are as suddenly forgotten without your being aware of it.

This epoch was of short duration; then followed a siesta of memory, during which he buried himself once more in his Latin studies, anxious to efface every last trace of these recollections of by-gone years.

But the game was fairly started; a second phase followed almost immediately on the first, when his thoughts clung persistently about his boyhood, and especially the part of it spent with the Jesuit fathers.

These memories were more distant, yet clearer than the others, engraved on his heart more deeply and more ineffaceably; the leafy park, the long garden walks, the flower beds, the benches, all the material details rose before him.

Then the gardens filled with a throng of boys and masters; he could hear the former's shouts at play, the latter's laughter as they mingled in the lads' sports, playing tennis with tucked-up cassocks, the skirts passed between their legs, or else talking under the trees to their pupils without the least affectation of superiority, as if conversing with comrades of their own age.

He recalled that paternal yoke which discountenanced any form of punishment, declined to inflict impositions of five hundred or one thousand lines, was content to have the unsatisfactory task done over again while the rest of the class were at recreation, more often than not preferred a mere reprimand, watched over the growing child with an active but loving care, striving to please his tastes, agreeing to walks in whatever direction he liked on Wednesday half-holidays, seizing the opportunity offered by all the little semi-official feast-days of the Church to add to the ordinary fare at meals a treat of cakes and wine or organize a country expedition,—a yoke under which the pupil was never brutalized, but was admitted to open discussion, was treated in fact like a grown man, while still being pampered like a spoilt child.

In this way the Fathers succeeded in gaining a real ascendancy over the young, moulded to some extent the minds they cultivated, guided them in the desired direction, engrafted particular modes of thought on their intelligence, secured the development of their character after the required pattern by an insinuating, wheedling method of treatment which they continued to pursue afterwards, making a point of following their subsequent course of life, backing them in their career, keeping up an affectionate correspondence with them,—letters of the sort the Dominican Lacordaire knew well how to write to his former pupils at Sorrèze.

One by one, Des Esseintes went over the points of the training he had undergone, as he himself supposed without result; he quite appreciated its merits, albeit his temperament, recalcitrant and stubborn, carping and critical, eager to argue out every proposition, had prevented his being modelled by their discipline or ruled by what they taught him. Once outside the College walls, his scepticism had grown more acute; his intercourse with legitimist society, intolerant and narrow to the last degree, his talks with puzzle-headed church officials and half educated priests whose blunders tore away the veil so cleverly contrived by the Jesuits, had still further fortified his spirit of independence and increased his distrust in any and every form of belief.

He deemed himself, in a word, released from every tie, free from every obligation; all he had hitherto preserved, differing herein from all his friends who had been educated at Lycées or lay boarding-schools, was a highly favourable memory of his school and school-masters; yet now, he was actually examining his conscience, beginning to ask himself if the seed heretofore fallen on barren ground was not showing signs of fructifying.

The fact is for some days he had been in an indescribably strange state of mind. For a brief moment he was a believer, an instinctive convert to religion; then, after the shortest interval of reflexion, all his attraction towards the Faith would evaporate. But all the time and in spite of everything, he was anxious and disturbed in spirit.

Yet he was perfectly well aware, if he looked into his own heart, that he could never have the humility and contrition of a truly Christian soul; he knew beyond all possibility of doubt that the moment of which Lacordaire speaks, the moment of grace, "when the final ray of right penetrates the soul and draws together to a common centre the truths that lie dispersed therein," would never come for him; he experienced none of that craving for prayer and mortification without which, if we are to listen to the majority of priests, no conversion is possible; he felt no wish to supplicate a God, whose loving-kindness seemed to him highly problematical. At the same time the sympathy he still had for his former instructors was sufficient to interest him in their works and teachings; the inimitable accents of conviction he remembered, the ardent voices of men of superior intelligence he recalled, haunted his mind and made him doubt his own ability and strength of intellect. Living the lonely life he now did, with no fresh food for thought, no novel impressions to stimulate imagination, no exchange of sensations coming from outside, from meeting friends or society, from living the same life as other men, confined within an unnatural prison-house which he refused to escape from, all sorts of problems, never thought of during his residence in Paris, demanded a solution with irritating persistency.

His study of the Latin works he delighted in, works almost without exception written by bishops and monks, had no doubt played their part in determining this crisis. Surrounded by a cloistered atmosphere, wrapt in a fragrance of incense that intoxicated his brain, he had got into an overwrought condition of nerves, and then, by a natural association of ideas, these books had ended by dimming his recollections of his life as a young man, while throwing into high relief those connected with his boyhood among the Fathers.

"There is no difficulty," Des Esseintes told himself with an effort after self-examination, "in accounting for this irruption of the Jesuit element at Fontenay; ever since I was a child, and without my knowing it myself, I have had this leaven, which had not previously fermented; is not this inclination I have always felt towards religious thoughts and things perhaps a proof of this?"

But his efforts were all directed to persuading himself of the contrary, annoyed as he was to find himself no longer absolute master of his own soul. He sought for motives to account for the change in himself; yes, he must have been forcibly drawn in the direction of the priesthood because the Church, and the Church only, has preserved the art, the lost beauty of the centuries; she has stereotyped, even in the cheap modern reproductions, the patterns of metal work, preserved the charm of chalices slim and tall as petunias, of sacred vessels of exquisite curves and contours, safeguarded, even in aluminium, in sham enamel, in coloured glass, the grace of the models of olden days. As a matter of fact, the main part of the precious objects exhibited in the Musée de Cluny, having escaped by a miracle the foul savagery of the sans-culottes, come from the old Abbeys of France. Just as in the Middle Ages the Church saved from barbarism, philosophy, history and letters, so she has saved plastic art, brought down to our own days those wondrous patterns in ecclesiastical robes and jewelry which the manufacturers of Church furniture and ornaments do their best to spoil, though they can never quite ruin the original beauty of form and colour. There was therefore no cause for surprise in the fact that he had sought eagerly for these antique curios, that like many another collector, he had acquired suchlike relics from the shops of the Parisian antiquaries and the stores of country dealers.

But, despite all the good reasons he could call up to his aid, he could not quite manage to convince himself. No doubt, after due consideration, he still continued to look upon religion merely as a superb myth, as a magnificent imposture; and yet, heedless of all his excuses and explanations, his scepticism was beginning to wear thin.

There was the fact, odd as it might seem: he was less confident at the present moment than he had been in his boyhood, in the days when the Jesuits exercised direct supervision over his training, when their teaching had to be received, when he was entirely in their hands, was theirs, body and soul, without family ties, without any outside influences of any kind to react against their ascendancy. Moreover, they had instilled in him a certain taste for the marvellous that had slowly and stealthily taken root in his soul, and was now coming to a head in this solitary life that could not but exert its influence on his silent, self-centred nature, for ever moving within the narrow limits of certain fixed ideas.

By dint of examining the processes of his thought, of striving to connect its threads together and discover its causes and conditioning circumstances, he eventually persuaded himself that its activities during his life in the world of men had their origin in the education he had received. Thus, his tendencies to artificiality, his longings for eccentricity, were these not, after all, results of plausible studies, supra-terrestrial refinements, semi-theological speculations; in ultimate analysis they amounted to the same thing as religious enthusiasms, aspirations towards an unknown universe, towards a far-off beatitude, just as ardently to be desired as that promised to believers by the Scriptures.

He pulled himself up short, broke off the thread of his reflexions. "Come, come," he chid himself angrily, "I am more seriously hit than I thought: here I am argufying with myself, like a casuist."

He remained pensive, troubled by a secret fear. No doubt, if Lacordaire's theory was correct, he had nothing to dread, seeing that the magic touch of conversion does not come about in an instant; to produce the explosion, the ground must have been long and systematically mined. But if the novelists talk about the thunderclap of love at first sight, there is also a certain number of theologians who speak of the thunderclap of religion. Admitting the truth of this doctrine, no man then was safe against succumbing. There was no room left for self-analysis, no use in weighing presentiments, no object gained by taking preventive measures; the psychology of mysticism was futile. It was so *because* it was so, and there was no more to be said.

"Why, I am growing crazy," Des Esseintes told himself; "the dread of the disease will end by bringing on the disease itself, if this goes on."

He managed to shake off the influence of these preoccupations to some extent, but other morbid symptoms supervened. Now it was the subject matter of various discussions that haunted him to the exclusion of everything else. The College garden, the school lessons, the Jesuit

Fathers sank into the remote background, his whole mind was dominated by abstractions, his thoughts were busy, in spite of himself, with contradictory interpretations of dogmas, with long forgotten apostasies, denounced in his work on the Councils of the Church by Père Labbe. Fragments of these schisms, scraps of these heresies, which for centuries divided the Western and the Eastern Churches, haunted his memory. Here it was Nestorius, protesting against the Virgin's bearing the title of Mother of God, because in the mystery of the Incarnation, it was not God, but rather the human creature, she had carried in her womb; there it was Eutyches, maintaining that the image of Christ could not be like that of the rest of mankind, inasmuch as the Divinity had been domiciled in his body and had thereby changed its nature utterly and entirely; elsewhere again other quibblers would have it that the Redeemer had had no human body at all, that the language of the Holy Books on this point must be understood figuratively, while yet again Tertullian was found positing his famous quasi-materialistic axiom: "Nothing is incorporal save what is not; whatever is, has a body that is proper to itself," till finally we come to the old, old question debated for years: was the Christ bound alone to the cross, or did the Trinity, one in three persons, suffer, in its threefold hypostasis, on the gibbet of Calvary? All these difficulties tormented him, pressing for an answer,—and mechanically, like a lesson already learnt by rote, he kept asking himself the questions and repeating the replies.

For several succeeding days, his brain was seething with paradoxies and subtleties, puzzling over a host of hairsplitting distinctions, wrestling with a tangle of rule as complicated as so many points of law, open to any and every interpretation, admitting of every sort of quirk and quibble, leading up to a system of celestial jurisprudence of the most tenuous and burlesque subtlety. Then the abstract side fell in its turn into abeyance, and a whole world of plastic impressions took its place, under the influence of the Gustave Moreaus hanging on the walls.

He beheld a long procession pass before his eyes of prelates, archimandrites, patriarchs, blessing the kneeling multitudes with uplifted arms of gold, wagging their white beards in reading of the Scriptures and in prayer; he saw dim crypts receive the silent ranks of innumerable penitents; he looked on while men raised vast cathedrals where white-robed monks thundered from the pulpit. In the same fashion as de Quincey, after a dose of opium, would at the mere sound of the words "Consul Romanus" recall whole pages of Livy, would see the consuls coming on in solemn procession and the pompous array of the Roman legionaries marching stately by, so Des Esseintes, struck by some theological phrase, would halt in breathless awe as he pondered the flux and reflux of Nations, and beheld the forms of bishops of other days standing forth in the lamplit gloom of basilicas; visions like these kept him entranced, travelling in fancy from age to age, coming down at last to the religious ceremonies of the present day, enfolded in an endless flood of music, mournful and tender.

Now he was beyond all self-justification, the thing was decided beyond appeal; it was just an indefinable impression of veneration and fear; the artistic sense was dominated by the well-calculated scenes of Catholic ceremonial. At these memories his nerves quivered; then, in a sudden mood of revolt, of swift revolution, ideas of monstrous depravity would attack him,—thoughts of the profanities foreseen in the Confessors' Manual, degraded and filthy abuses of the holy water and the consecrated oil. Face to face with an omnipotent God now stood up a rival full of energy, the Demon; and he thought a hideous glory must needs result from a crime committed in open church by a believer fiercely resolved, in a mood of horrid merriment, of a sadic satisfaction, to blaspheme, to overwhelm with insult and recrimination the things most deserving veneration; mad doings of magic, the black mass, the witches' sabbath, horrors of demoniac possession and exorcism rose before his imagination; he began to ask himself if he were not guilty of sacrilege in possessing articles once consecrated to holy uses,—church service-books, chasubles, pyx-covers. And, strange to say, this notion of living in a state of sin afforded him a sense of proud satisfaction and pleasure; he found a delight in these acts of sacrilege,—after all a possibly innocent sacrilege; in any case not a very serious offence, seeing he really loved these articles and put them to no base usage. Thus he comforted himself with prudent, coward considerations, his half-hearted condition of soul forbidding open crimes, robbing him of the needful courage to accomplish real sins, deliberate, damning iniquities.

Eventually, little by little, these casuistries disappeared. He looked out, as it were, from the summit of his mind, over the panorama of the Church and her hereditary influence over humanity, as old as the centuries; he pictured her to himself, solitary and impressive, proclaiming to mankind the horror of life, the inclemency of fate; preaching patience, contrition, the spirit of sacrifice; essaying to heal men's sores by exhibiting the bleeding wounds of the Christ; guaranteeing divine privileges, promising the best part of paradise to the afflicted; exhorting the human creature to suffer, to offer to God as a holocaust his tribulations and his offences, his vicissitudes and his sorrows. He saw her truly eloquent, a mother to the unfortunate, a pitiful father to the oppressed, a stern judge to oppressors and tyrants.

At this point, Des Esseintes recovered footing. Doubtless he was content to accept this admission of social rottenness, but his mind revolted against the vague remedy offered, the hope of another life. Schopenhauer was more exact; his doctrine and the Church's started from a common point of view; he, too, took his stand on the

wickedness and baseness of the world; he, too, cried out, with the
Imitation of Our Lord, in bitterness of spirit: "Verily it is a pitiful thing
to be alive on the earth!" He, too, preached the nullity of existence, the
advantages of solitude; warned humanity that, whatever it did,
whichever way it turned, it must still be unhappy,—the poor man,
because of the sufferings that spring from privations; the rich, by
reason of the invincible ennui engendered by abundance. But he
proclaimed no panacea, consoled you, as a cure for inevitable evils,
with no alluring bait.

Nor did he maintain the revolting dogma of original sin; did not try
to convince you of the existence of a God supremely good and kind
who protects the scoundrel, succours the fool, crushes infancy,
brutalizes old age, chastises the innocent; he did not extol the benefits
of a Providence which has invented that abomination, useless,
incomprehensible, unjust and inept, physical pain; far from
endeavouring, like the Church, to justify the necessity of torments and
trials, he exclaimed in his indignant pity: "If a God had made this
world, I should not like to be that God; the misery of the world would
break my heart."

Schopenhauer had seen the truth! What were all the evangelical
pharmacopoeias beside his treatises of spiritual hygiene? He made no
professions of healing, offered the sick no compensation, no hope; but
his theory of Pessimism was, after all, the great consoler of chosen
intellects, of lofty souls; it revealed society as it was, insisted on the
innate foolishness of women, pointed you out the beaten tracks, saved
you from disillusions by teaching you to restrict, so far as possible,
your expectations; never, if you felt yourself strong enough to check
the impulse, to let yourself come to the state of mind of believing
yourself happy at last if only, when you least expected it, heaven did
not send crashing on your head some murderous tile from the
housetops.

Setting out from the same starting-point as the *Imitation*, this
theory found the very same goal, but without losing itself on the road
among mysterious mazes and impossible bypaths, in resignation and
passivity.

Only, if this resignation, frankly based on the observation of a
deplorable condition of things and the impossibility of effecting any
alteration in them, was accessible to the rich in spirit, it was only the
more hardly to be received by the poor, whose grievances and
indignation the kindly hand of Religion was better adapted to appease.

These reflexions relieved Des Esseintes of a heavy burden; the
aphorisms of the great German thinker calmed the tumult of his
thoughts, while at the same time the points of similarity between the
two doctrines mutually helped each other to find a firm place in his
memory, and he could never forget Catholicism, so poetical, so

touching, in which he had been bathed as a boy and whose essence he had absorbed through every pore.

These returns towards religious convictions, these fears and doubts of uncertain faith had tormented him, especially since new complications had begun to show themselves in his health; they coincided with certain nervous disturbances that had lately arisen.

Since his earliest childhood he had been tormented by inexplicable repulsions, shuddering spasms that froze his backbone and clenched his teeth, whenever, for instance, he saw a servant-maid in the act of wringing out wet linen. These instinctive dislikes had never changed, and to that day it caused him genuine suffering to hear a piece of stuff torn in two, to rub his finger over a lump of chalk, to stroke the surface of watered silk.

The excesses of his bachelorhood, the abnormal strains put upon his brain had extraordinarily aggravated his original nervous weakness, still further impoverished the exhausted blood of his race; in Paris he had been obliged to resort to hydropathic treatment for trembling of the hands, for atrocious pains, for neuralgic agonies that seemed to cut his face in two, that beat with a never-ceasing hammering at his temples, sent stabbing throbs through his eyelids, provoked fits of nausea he could only subdue by stretching himself flat on his back in the dark.

These inconveniences had gradually disappeared, thanks to a better regulated and quieter life; now they were making themselves felt again, though in a different shape, diffused through the body generally; the pain left the head and attacked the stomach, which was swollen and hard; scorched the inwards as with a red-hot iron, brought on a condition of the bowels at once uneasy and constipated. Presently a nervous cough, dry and hacking, beginning always exactly at a set hour and lasting for precisely the same number of minutes, woke him half choking in his bed. Finally he lost all appetite; hot, gassy eructations rose like fire in his throat; the stomach was distended; he felt stifled, after each attempt to eat; he could not endure the least constriction about the body, a buttoned trouser-belt or a buckled waistcoat.

He gave up spirituous liquors, coffee and tea, confined himself to a milk diet, resorted to bathing the body with cold water, stuffed himself with assafœtida, valerian and quinine; he even consented to leave the house and take strolls in the country when the days of rain came that make the roads silent and deserted; he forced himself to walk, to take exercise; as a last resource, he renounced reading altogether for the time being and, consumed with ennui, determined by way of filling up this time of enforced leisure to carry out a project the execution of which he had again and again postponed out of laziness and dislike of change since the first day of his settling at Fontenay.

No longer able to intoxicate himself afresh with the magical enchantments of style, to fall into an ecstasy over the delicious

witchery of the rare and well-chosen epithet that, while still definite
and precise, yet opens infinite perspectives, to the imagination of the
initiate he resolved to complete the decoration of his dwelling, to fill it
with costly hothouse flowers and so procure himself a material
occupation that should distract his thoughts, calm his nerves and rest
his brain. Moreover, he had hopes that the sight of their strange and
magnificent colours might console him somewhat for the loss of the
fancied or real shades of literary style which his abstention from all
reading was to make him forget for the moment or lose altogether.

Chapter Eight

He had always been madly fond of flowers, but this passion which,
during his residence at Jutigny, had at the first embraced all flowers
without distinction of species or genus, had in the end grown more
discriminating and precise, limiting itself to a single type.

For a long time now he had scorned the everyday plants that
blossom on the counters of Parisian florists, in dripping flowerpots,
under green awnings or red umbrellas.

At the same time that his literary tastes, his preferences in art, had
become more refined, no longer caring for any works but such as had
been tried and sifted, the distillation of overwrought and subtle brains;
at the same time that his disgust with generally accepted notions had
reached its height, simultaneously his love of flowers had rid itself of
all base residuum, all dregs of commonness, had been clarified, as it
were, and purified.

He pleased his fancy by likening a horticulturist's shop to a
microcosm wherein were represented all the different categories of
society—poor, vulgar flowers, *hovel* flowers, so to speak, that are
really in their proper place only on the window-sill of a garret, roots
that are crammed in milk-tins and old earthen pots, the gilliflower for
instance; pretentious, conventional, silly flowers, whose only place is in
porcelain vases painted by young ladies, such as the rose; lastly,
flowers of high lineage, such as the orchids, dainty and charming,
trembling and delicate, such as the exotic flowers, exiles in Paris, kept
in hothouses, in palaces of glass, Princesses of the vegetable world,
living apart, having nothing whatever in common with the flowers of
the street, the blossoms that are the delight of grocers' wives.

In a word, he could do no more than feel a trivial interest, a slight
pity, for the people's flowers, fading under the poisonous breath of
sewers and sinks in squalid districts; to make up, he loathed those that
go with the cream and gold reception-rooms in new houses; he
reserved, in fact, for the full and perfect delectation of his eyes, rare
plants of high-bred type, coming from distant lands, kept alive by skill
and pains in an artificial equatorial temperature maintained by carefully

regulated furnaces.

But this choice of his, that had deliberately fallen on greenhouse flowers, had itself been further modified under the influence of his general ideas, his opinions that had now come to definite conclusions on all matters. In former days, in Paris, his innate preference for the artificial had led him to neglect the real flower for its copy, faithfully executed thanks to india-rubber and twine, glazed cotton and lustring, paper and velvet.

He possessed in accordance with this taste a marvellous collection of tropical plants, produced by the cunning fingers of supreme masters of the craft, following Nature step by step, recreating her, taking the flower from its birth, carrying it to maturity, imitating it to its final decease, observing every shade of its infinite variety, the most fleeting changes of its awakening and its sleep, noting the pose of its petals blown back by the wind or beaten down by the rain, sprinkling on its morning leaves little drops of gum to represent dew, fashioning it according to every season,—in full bloom, when the twigs bend under the weight of sap; or when it lifts its parched stem and ragged corolla as the petals drop away and the leaves fall.

This admirable art had long fascinated him; but now he was dreaming of the construction of another sort of flora.

He had done with artificial flowers aping the true; he wanted natural flowers imitating the false.

He set himself to work out this problem, nor had he to search long or go far, for was not his house situated in the very middle of the district specially favoured by the great flower-growers? He went straight off to pay a visit to the hot-houses of the Avenue de Châtillon and the valley of Aunay, to return tired out and his purse empty, thinking of nothing but the strange species he had bought, ceaselessly haunted by his memories of superb and extraordinary blooms.

Two days later the carts arrived.

List in hand, Des Esseintes called the roster, verified his purchases one by one.

The gardeners unloaded from their vans a collection of Caladiums whose swollen, hairy stalks carried enormous leaves, shaped like a heart; while keeping a general look of kinship, they were every one different.

They included some extraordinary specimens,—some rosy-red, like the Virginale which seemed cut out in glazed cloth, in shiny court-plaster; some all white, like the Albane, that looked as if made of the semi-transparent membrane that lines an ox's ribs, or the diaphanous film of a pig's bladder. Others again, especially the one called Madame Maine, mimicked zinc, parodied pieces of stencilled metal coloured emperor-green, blotched with drops of oil paint, streaks of red-lead and ceruse: these,—the Bosphorus was an example,—gave the illusion of

starched calico, spotted with crimson and myrtle-green; those, the
Aurora Borealis for instance, had broad leaves the colour of raw meat,
intersected by striations of a darker red and purplish threads, leaves that
seemed swollen and sweating with dark liquor and blood.

This plant, the Aurora Borealis, and the Albane between them
displayed the two opposite poles of constitution, the former bursting
with apoplexy, the latter pallid with bloodlessness.

The men brought other and fresh varieties, in this case presenting
the appearance of a fictitious skin marked by an imitation network of
veins. Most of them, as if disfigured by syphilis or leprosy, displayed
livid patches of flesh, reddened by measles, roughened by eruptions;
others showed the bright pink of a half-closed wound or the red brown
of the crusts that form over a scar; others were as if scorched with
cauteries blistered with burns; others again offered hairy surfaces eaten
into holes by ulcers and excavated by chancres. To finish the list, there
were some that had just come from the doctor's hands, it seemed,
plastered with black mercury dressing, smeared with green belladonna
ointment, dusted over with the yellow grains of iodoform powder.

Thus assembled all together, these strange blossoms struck Des
Esseintes as more monstrous yet than when he had first seen them
ranged side by side with others, like patients in a hospital ward, down
the long conservatories.

"*Sapristi!*" he exclaimed, stirred to the depths.

A new plant, of a type similar to the Caladiums, the "Alocasia
Metallica," moved his enthusiasm to a still higher pitch. Its leaves were
overlaid with a layer of green bronze, shot with gleams of silver; it was
the masterpiece, the fine flower of counterfeit; you might have thought
it a bit of stove-pipe, cut out of sheet iron in the shape of a spear-head,
by a jobbing blacksmith.

Next the men unloaded a tangled mass of leaves, lozenge-shaped,
bottle-green in hue; from their midst rose a switch on top of which
trembled a great ace of hearts, as smooth and shiny as a capsicum; then,
as if to defy all the familiar aspects of plants, from the middle of this
ace of hearts, of an intense vermillion, sprang a fleshy tail, downy,
white and yellow, upright in some cases, corkscrewed above the heart,
like a pig's tail, in others.

It was the Anthurium, one of the arum family, recently imported
from Colombia; it formed part of a section of the same family to which
also belonged an Amorphophallus, a plant from Cochin China, with
long black stalks seamed with scars, like a negro's limbs after a
thrashing.

Des Esseintes' cup of joy was brimming over.

Then they got out of the carts a fresh batch of monstrosities, the
Echinopsis, showing a pink blossom like the stump of an amputated
limb rising out of a compress of cotton-wool; the Nidularium,

displaying in its sword-like leaves gaping, ragged hollows; the "Tillandsia Lindeni," like a broken-toothed cury-comb, of the colour of wine-must: the Cypripedium, with its involved, incoherent, incongruous contours that seem the invention of a madman. It was shaped like a wooden shoe, or a little rag-bag, above which was a human tongue retracted, with the tendon drawn tight, as you may see it represented in the plates of medical works treating of diseases of the throat and mouth; two miniature wings, of a jujube red, that seemed borrowed from a child's toy windmill, completed this grotesque conjunction of the underside of a tongue, colour of wine-lees and slate, and a little glossy pocket, the lining of which distilled a viscous glue.

He could not take his eyes off this impossible-looking orchid, indigenous to India, till the gardeners, exasperated by these delays, began to read out aloud for themselves the labels fixed in the pots as they carried them in.

Des Esseintes looked on in wonder, listened open-mouthed to the barbarous names of the herbaceous plants,—the "Encephalartos horridus," a gigantic artichoke, an iron spike painted rust colour, like the ones they stick on the top of park gates to prevent intruders climbing over; the "Cocos Micania," a sort of palm, with a notched and slender stem, everywhere surrounded with tall leaves like paddles and oars; the "Zamia Lehmanni," a huge pineapple, like an immense Cheshire cheese, growing in peaty soil and bristling at the apex with barbed spears and cruel looking arrows; the "Cibotium Spectabile," going one better ever than its congeners in the wild caprice of its structure, defying the maddest nightmare, throwing out from amid a clustered foliage of palm leaves a prodigious orang-outang's tail, a brown, hairy tail curling over at the tip like a bishop's crozier.

These, however, he barely glanced at, waiting impatiently for the series of plants that particularly fascinated him, those vegetable ghouls, the carnivorous plants,—the Flycatcher of the Antilles, with its shaggy edge, secreting a digestive liquid, provided with curved thorns folding into each other to form a barred grating over the insect it imprisons; the Drosera of the peat mosses, furnished with rows of stiff, glandulous hairs; the Sarracena; the Cephalothus, with deep, voracious cups capable of absorbing and digesting actual lumps of meat; last, but not least amazing, the Nepenthes whose eccentricity of shape overpasses all known limits.

It seemed as though he could never weary of turning about in his hands the pot in which trembled this extravagant vagary of the flower tribe. It resembled the gum-tree in its long leaves of a sombre, metallic green, but from the end of these leaves depended a green string, a sort of umbilical cord, carrying a greenish coloured urn, veined with purple, a sort of German pipe in porcelain, a strange kind of bird's nest, that swung quietly to and fro, exhibiting an interior carpeted with a hairy growth.

"That one is a veritable miracle," Des Esseintes murmured to himself.

But he was forced to cut short his manifestations of delight, for now the gardeners, in a hurry to be gone, were unloading the last of their wares and setting down side by side tuberous Begonias and black Crotons, flecked with red-lead spots, like rusty iron.

Then he noticed that one name was still left on the list, the Cattleya of New Granada. They pointed out to him a little winged bell-flower of a pale lilac, an almost invisible mauve; he drew near, put his nose to it and started back; it exhaled an odour of varnished deal, just the smell of a new box of toys, recalling irresistibly all the horrors of the New Year and New Year's presents.

It struck him it would be well for him to beware of it, almost regretted having admitted among the scentless plants he had become possessor of the orchid that brought up the most unpleasant associations.

He cast only one glance over this flood-tide of vegetation that swelled in his vestibule; there they were, all confounded together, intercrossing their sword-blades, their kreeses, their lance-heads, forming a tangled mass of green weapons of war, over which floated like barbarian pennons of battle, blossoms dazzling and cruel in their brilliance.

The atmosphere of the room was clearer by now, and soon, in a dark corner, just above the floor, a light crept out, soft and white.

He went up to it, to discover it was a cluster of Rhizomorphs, each of which, as it breathed, was shedding this gleam like that cast by nightlights.

"All the same, these plants are amazing things," he muttered to himself; then he stepped back and embraced in one view the whole collection. Yes, his object was attained; not one of them looked real; cloth, paper, porcelain, metal seemed to have been lent by man to Nature to enable her to create these monstrosities. When she had found herself incapable of copying human workmanship, she had been reduced to mimick the membranes of animals' insides, to borrow the vivid tints of their rotting flesh, the superb horrors of their gangrened skin.

"It is all a matter of syphilis," reflected Des Esseintes, his eyes attracted, riveted on the hideous marking of the Caladiums, lit up at that moment by a shaft of daylight. And he had a sudden vision of the human race tortured by the virus of long past centuries. Ever since the beginning of the world, from sire to son, all living creatures were handing on the inexhaustible heritage, the everlasting malady that has devastated the ancestors of the men of to-day, has eaten to the very bone old fossil forms which we dig up at the present moment.

Never wearying, it had travelled down the ages, to this day it was raging everywhere, disguised under ordinary symptoms of headache or bronchitis, hysteria or gout; from time to time, it would climb to the surface, attacking for choice badly cared-for, badly-fed people breaking out in gold pieces, setting, in horrid irony, a Nautch-girl's parure of sequins on its wretched victim's brows, inscribing their skin, for a crown to their misery, with the very symbol of wealth and well-being.

And lo! here it was reappearing, in its pristine splendour, on the bright-coloured petals of flowers!

"It is true," pursued Des Esseintes, going back to the starting point of his argument, "it is true that, for most of the time, Nature is by herself incapable of producing species so morbid and perverse; she supplies the raw material, the germ and the soil, the procreative womb and the elements of the plant, which mankind rears, models, paints, carves afterwards to suit his caprice."

Obstinate, confused, limited though she be, she has at last submitted, and her master has succeeded in changing by chemical reactions the substances of the earth, to utilize combinations long ripened for use, crossings slowly prepared for, to employ artful buddings, systematic graftings, so that nowadays he can make her produce blooms of different colours on the same bough; invents new hues for her; modifies, at his good pleasure, the age-old shapes of her plants. He clears off the rough from her half-hewn blocks, puts the finishing touches to her rude sketches, marks them with his signet, impresses on them his sign-manual of art.

"There is no more to be said," he cried, resuming his train of thought; "mankind is able in the course of a few years to bring about a selection which sluggish Nature can never effect but after centuries of time; no doubt of it, in these present times, the gardeners are the only and the true artists."

He was a little weary and felt stifled in this atmosphere of hothouse plants; the walks he had taken during the last few days had exhausted him; the change from the open air to the warmth of the house, from the sedentary life of a recluse to the free activity of an outdoor existence, had been too sudden. He left the hall and went to lie down on his bed; but, bent on one single absorbing subject, as if wound up with a spring, the mind, though asleep all the while, went on paying out its chain, and he was soon wallowing in the gloomy fancies of a nightmare.

He was standing in the middle of a ride in a great forest at dusk; he was walking side by side with a woman he did not know, had never seen before; she was tall and thin, had pale flaxen hair, a bulldog face, freckled cheeks, irregular teeth projecting below a flat nose. She wore a servant's white apron, a long kerchief crossed like a soldier's buff-belt over her chest, a Prussian grenadier's half-boots, a black bonnet trimmed with ruchings and a big bow.

She had the look of a show-woman at a fair, a travelling mountebank or the like.

He asked himself who the woman was whom he somehow knew to have been a long while in the room, to have long been an intimate part of his life; in vain he strove to remember her origin, her name, her business, the explanation of her presence; no recollection would come to him of this inexplicable liaison, of which however there could be no doubt.

He was still searching his memory when suddenly a strange figure appeared in front of them; it was on horseback and trotted on for a minute, then turned round in the saddle.

His blood gave one bound within him and he remained nailed to the spot in utter horror. The ambiguous, sexless creature was green, and from under purple lids shone a pair of pale blue eyes, cold and terrible; two arms of an inordinate leanness, like a skeleton's bare to the elbows, shaking with fever, projected from ragged sleeves, and the fleshless thighs shuddered in churn-boots, a world too wide.

The awful eyes were fixed on Des Esseintes, piercing him, freezing him to the marrow of his bones; more terrified still, the bulldog woman pressed against him and yelled death and destruction, her head thrown back, her neck stiffened with a spasm of wild terror.

And lo! in an instant he knew the meaning of the appalling vision. He had before his eyes the image of the Pox.

Mad with fear, beside himself with consternation, he dashed into a side path, ran at headlong speed to a summer-house standing among laburnums to the left of the road, where he dropped into a chair in a passage.

In a few minutes when he was beginning to get his breath, the sound of sobs made him look up. The bulldog woman was before him; a piteous, grotesque spectacle. She stood weeping hot tears, declaring she had lost her teeth in her panic, and, drawing from the pocket of her servant's apron a number of clay pipes, she proceeded to break them and stuff bits of the stems into the holes in her gums.

"Come now, she's quite ridiculous," Des Esseintes kept telling himself; "the pipes will never stick in,"—and as a matter of fact, they all came tumbling out of her jaws one after the other.

At that moment, a galloping horse was heard approaching. A paralysing fear seized Des Esseintes; his limbs failed him. But the sound of hoofs grew momentarily louder; despair stung him to action like the lash of a whip; he threw himself upon the woman, who was now trampling the pipe bowls underfoot, beseeching her to be quiet and not betray him by the noise of her boots. She struggled; but he dragged her to the end of the passage, throttling her to stop her crying out. Suddenly, he saw an ale-house door, with green painted shutters, pushed it open, darted in and stopped dead.

In front of him, in the middle of a vast clearing in the woods, enormous white pierrots were jumping like rabbits in the moonlight.

Tears of disappointment rose to his eyes; he could never, no, never cross the threshold of the door.—"I should be dashed to pieces," he thought,—and as if to justify his fears, the troop of giant pierrots was reinforced; their bounds now filled the whole horizon, the whole sky, which they knocked alternately with their heels and their heads.

The horse came to a standstill, it was there, close by, behind a round window in the passage; more dead than alive, Des Esseintes turned round and saw through the circular opening two pricked ears, two rows of yellow teeth, nostrils breathing clouds of vapour that stank of phenol.

He sank to the earth, abandoning all idea of resistance or even of flight; he shut his eyes so as not to see the dreadful eyes of the Syphilis glaring at him through the wall, which nevertheless forced their way under his lids, glided down his spine, enveloped his body, the hairs of which stood up on end in pools of cold sweat. He expected any and every torment, only hoped to have done with it with one final annihilating blow; an age, that beyond a doubt lasted a whole minute, went by; then he opened his eyes again with a shudder.

All had vanished; without transition, as if by a change of scene, by a stage delusion, a hideous metallic landscape was disappearing in the distance, a landscape wan, desert, cloven with ravines, dead and dreary; a light illumined this desolate place, a calm, white light, recalling the glint of phosphorus dissolved in oil.

On the surface, something moved which took a woman's shape, a pallid, naked woman, green silk stockings moulding the legs.

He gazed at her curiously. Like horsehair curled by over-hot irons, her locks were frizzled, with broken ends; urns of the Nepenthes hung at her ears; tints of boiled veal showed in her half-opened nostrils. With entranced eyes, she called him in a low voice.

He had no time to answer, for already the woman was changing; gleams of iridescent colours flashed in her eyes; her lips assumed the fierce red of the Anthuriums; the nipples of her bosom blazed out like two bright red pods of capsicum.

A sudden intuition came to him; it is the Flower, he told himself; and the spirit of reasoning still persisted in the nightmare, drew the same conclusions as he had already in the daytime from the plants as the malevolence of the Virus.

Then he noticed the terrifying irritation of the bosoms and of the mouth, discovered on the skin of the body stains of bistre and copper, and recoiled in horror; but the woman's eye fascinated him, and he crept slowly, reluctantly towards her, trying to drive his heels into the ground to stay his advance, dropping to the earth, only to rise again to go to her. He was all but touching her when black Amorphophalli sprang up on every side, and made darts at her belly that was rising and falling like a sea. He put them away from him, pushed them back, feeling an infinite loathing to see these hot, moist, firm stems coiling between his fingers. Then, in a moment, the odious plants disappeared, and two arms were seeking to wind themselves about him. An agony of terror set his heart beating wildly, for the eyes, the dreadful eyes of the woman, had become pale, cold blue, terrible to look at. He made a superhuman effort to free himself from her embraces, but with an irresistible gesture she seized and held him, and haggard with horror, he saw the savage Nidularium blossom under her meagre thighs, with its sword blades gaping in blood-red hollows.

His body was almost in contact with the hideous open wound of the plant; he felt himself a dying man, and awoke with a start, choking, frozen, frantic with fear, sobbing out: "Thank God, thank God! it is only a dream."

Chapter Nine

These nightmares recurred again and again, till he was afraid to go to sleep. He would lie stretched on his bed, sometimes the victim of obstinate fits of insomnia and feverish restlessness, at others of abominable dreams only interrupted by the spasmodic awakening of a man losing foothold, pitching from top to bottom of a staircase, plunging into the depths of an abyss, without power to stop himself.

For several days, the exhausting nervous disturbance gained the upper hand again, showing itself more violent and more obstinate than ever, though under new forms.

Now the bedclothes were a weight not to be borne; he felt stifled under the sheets, while his whole body was tormented with tinglings; his thighs burned, his legs itched. To these symptoms were soon added a dull aching of the jaws and a sensation as if his temples were confined within a vice.

His distress of mind grew more and more acute, but unfortunately the proper means of mastering the merciless complaint were lacking. He had tried without success to fit up an installation of hydropathic appliances in his dressing room; but the impossibility of bringing water to the top of the hill on which his house was perched, the preliminary difficulty indeed of getting water at all in sufficient quantity in a village supplied by public fountains which only trickled sparingly at fixed hours, made his attempt abortive. Finding it impracticable to get himself douched with jets of water, which, shot freely and forcible against the bony rings of the vertebral columns, formed the only method powerful enough to subdue the insomnia and bring back peace of mind, he was reduced to the employment of short aspersions in his bath-room or his tub; mere cold aspersions followed by an energetic rubbing down with a horsehair glove at the hands of his valet.

But these half measures were very far from scotching the disease; the most he felt was a temporary relief of a few hours, dearly bought, moreover, by a fresh access of the paroxysms returning to the charge with increased violence.

He was consumed with infinite ennui. The pleasure he had felt in the possession of his amazing flowers was exhausted; he was tired already of looking at the texture of their leaves and the shades of their blossoms. Besides, for all the care he lavished upon them, most of his plants had died; these he had removed from the rooms, and then, to such a pitch of nervous irritability had he come, that the sight of the places left vacant for want of them wounded his eye and reduced him to a condition of further exasperation.

To distract his attention and kill the interminable hours, he had recourse to his portfolios of prints and sorted his Goyas. The early states of certain plates of the *Caprices*, proofs distinguishable by their reddish tone, which he had bought in former days at sales, at extravagant prices, struck his fancy, and he lost himself in their contemplation, as he followed the weird fancies of the artist with an unfailing delight in his bewildering imaginations,—witches riding black cats, women extracting a dead man's teeth at the foot of the gallows, bandits, succubi, devils and dwarfs.

After this, he went through all the other series of the artist's etchings and aquatints, his *Proverbs*, so grotesque in their gloomy horror, his battle subjects, so ferocious in their bloodthirstiness, his plate of the *Garotte*, of which he possessed a superb proof before letters, printed on heavy paper, unsized, with visible watermark-lines showing in its substance.

The savage vigour, the uncompromising, reckless talent of this artist captivated him. Yet, at the same time, the universal admiration his works had won put him off somewhat, and for years he had always refused to frame them, fearing, if he exhibited them, that the first noodle who might happen to see them would feel himself bound to talk inanities and fall into an ecstasy in stereotyped phrases as he stood in front of them.

It was the same with his Rembrandts, which he would examine now and again on the sly; and indeed it is very true that, just as the finest air in the world is vulgarized beyond all bearing once the public has taken to hum it and the street organs to play it, so the work of art that has appealed to the sham connoisseurs, that is admired by the uncritical, that is not content to rouse the enthusiasm of only a chosen few, becomes for this very reason, in the eyes of the elect, a thing polluted, commonplace, almost repulsive.

This diffusion of appreciation among the common herd was in fact one of the sorest trials of his life; unaccountable triumphs had for ever spoilt his enjoyment in pictures and books he had once held dear; the approbation of the general voice always ended by making him discover some hitherto imperceptible blemish, and he would repudiate them, asking himself if his taste was not getting blunted and untrustworthy.

He shut his portfolios and once more fell into a state of indifference and ill humour. To change the current of his ideas, he tried a course of emollient reading; essayed, with a view to cooling his brain, some of the *solanaceæ* of art; read those books so charming for convalescents and invalids whom sensational stories or works richer in phosphates would only fatigue: Charles Dickens' novels.

But the volumes produced an effect just the opposite of what he looked for; his chaste lovers, his Protestant heroines, modestly draped to the chin, whose passions were so seraphic, who never went beyond a coy dropping of the eyes, a blush, a tear of happiness, a squeezing of hands, exasperated him. This exaggerated virtue drove him into the opposite extreme; in virtue of the law of contrasts, he rushed into the contrary excess; thought of passionate, full-bodied loves; pictured the doings of frail, human couples; of ardent embraces mouth to mouth; of pigeon kisses, as ecclesiastical prudery calls them when tongue meets tongue in naughty wantonness.

He threw away his book, and banishing the mock-modesty of Albion far from his thoughts, dreamed of the licentious practices, the salacious little sins the Church condemns. A commotion shook him; the insensibility of brain and body that he had supposed final and irrevocable was no more. Solitude has its influence, too, on broken nerves; he was filled with a craving, not now for religious conviction, but for the pleasant sins religion condemns. The habitual object of its threats and curses was the one thing that tempted him; the carnal side of his nature, that had lain dormant for months, roused, first of all, by the feebleness of the pious stuff he had been reading, then stirred to full wakefulness in a spasm of the nerves by the hateful English cant, now asserted itself, and the stimulated senses harking back to the past, he found himself wallowing in the memories of his old dissipations.

He got up and gloomily opened a little box of silver-gilt, its lid set here and there with aventurines.

It was full of bonbons of a violet colour; one of these he took and turned it about in his fingers, thinking over the strange properties of these sweetmeats, sprinkled over with a powdering of sugar, like hoarfrost; formerly, in the days when his impotency was an established fact and he could dream of women without bitterness, regret or longing, he would place one of these sweetmeats on his tongue and let it melt in his mouth; then, in a moment, would recur with an infinite tenderness recollections, almost effaced, altogether soft and languishing, of the lascivious doings of other days.

These bonbons, an invention of Siraudin's known under the

ridiculous name of "Pearls of the Pyrenees," consisted of a drop of sarcanthus scent, a drop of essence of woman, crystallized in a piece of sugar; they entered by the papillae of the mouth, evoking reminiscences of water opalescent with rare vinegars; and deep, searching kisses, all fragrant with odours.

As usual, his face broke into a smile, as he drank in this amorous aroma; this shadowy semblance of caresses that revived in a corner of his brain a sense of female nudity and re-awakened for a second the savour, once so adorable, of certain women. But today, it was no longer a muffled peal that was ringing; the drug's effect was no longer limited to reviving the memory of far away, half forgotten escapades; rather was it to tear the veils from before his eyes and show him the bodily reality, in all its brutal force and urgency.

Heading the procession of mistresses that the taste of the sweetmeat helped to define in clear outlines, one riveted his attention, a woman with long, white teeth, a satiny skin, rosy with health, a short nose, mouse-grey eyes, short-clipped, yellow hair.

It was Miss Urania, an American girl with a supple figure, sinewy legs, muscles of steel, arms of iron.

She had been one of the most famous of the acrobats at the *Cirque*.

Whole evenings, Des Esseintes had watched her performing. The first few times she had struck him as being just what she was, a powerfully made, handsome woman, but he had felt no desire to come into any closer contact with her; she had nothing about her to appeal to the tastes of a worn man of the world, yet for all this he returned again and again to the Circus, drawn by some mysterious attraction, urged by some sentiment difficult to define.

Little by little, as he watched her, his mind filled with strange notions. The more he admired her strength and suppleness, the more he seemed to see an artificial change of sex operating in her; her pretty allurements, her feminine affectations fell more and more into the background, while in their stead were developed the charms attaching to the agility and vigour of a male. In a word, after being a woman to begin with, then something very like an androgyne, she now seemed to become definitely and decisively and entirely a man.

"This being so, just as a robust athlete falls in love with a thin slip of a girl, this woman of the trapeze should by natural tendency love a feeble, backboneless weakling like myself," Des Esseintes told himself; by dint of considering his own qualities and giving the rein to his faculties of comparison, he presently arrived at the conclusion that, on his side, he was himself getting nearer and nearer the female type. This point reached, he was seized with a definite desire to possess this woman, craving for her as an anæmic young girl will for some great, rough Hercules whose arms can crush her to a jelly in their embrace.

This change of sex between Urania and himself had stirred him deeply; we are made for each other, he would declare, while, added to this sudden admiration of brute force, a thing he had hitherto detested, was the spice of the self-degradation involved in such a union,—the same base delight a common prostitute enjoys in paying dear for the clumsy caresses of a bully.

Meantime, as his determination to seduce the acrobat, to make his dreams a reality, if the thing could be done, was maturing, he confined his cherished illusion by attributing the same series of inverted thoughts as his own to the unconscious brain of the woman, reading his own desires repeated in the fixed smile that hovered on the lips of the performer turning on her trapeze.

One fine evening, he made up his mind to open the campaign. Miss Urania deemed it necessary not to yield without some preliminary courting. Still she showed herself not very exacting, knowing from common report that Des Esseintes was wealthy and that his name was a help towards starting woman on a successful career.

But no sooner were his wishes granted than his disappointment passed all bounds. He had pictured the pretty American athlete to be as stolid and brutal as the strong man at a fair, but her stupidity, alas! was purely feminine in its nature. No doubt she lacked education and refinement, possessed neither good sense nor good wit, while at table she gave tokens of a brutish greediness but all the childish weaknesses of a woman were there in full force; she had all the love of chatter and finery that marks the sex specially given up to trivialities; any such thing as a transmutation of masculine ideas into her feminine person was a pure figment of the imagination.

Besides, she was quite a little Puritan and was altogether innocent of those rude, athletic caresses Des Esseintes at once desired and dreaded; she was not subject, as he had for a moment hoped she might be, to any morbid perversities of sex. Possibly, on searching the depths of her temperament, he might yet have discovered a penchant for a dainty, delicate, slimly-built paramour, for a nature precisely the opposite of her own; but in that case, it would have been a preference not for a young girl at all, but for some merry-hearted little shrimp of a man; for some skinny, queer-faced clown.

Inevitably Des Esseintes resumed his part, momentarily forgotten, as a man; his impressions of femininity, of feebleness, of a sort of protection bought and paid for, of fear even, disappeared entirely. He could deceive himself no longer; Miss Urania was just a mistress like any other, not justifying in any way the cerebral curiosity she had excited.

Though, just at first, the freshness and splendour of her beauty had surprised Des Esseintes and kept him captivated, it was not long before he sought to sever the connexion and bring about a speedy rupture, for his premature impotency grew yet more marked when confronted with the icy woman's caresses and prudish passivity.

Nevertheless, she was the first to halt before him in the unbroken procession of these wanton memories; but, at bottom, if she had made a deeper impression on his mind than a host of other women whose allurements had been less fallacious and the pleasures they gave less limited, this came of the smell she exhaled as of a sound and wholesome animal. Her redundant health was the very antipodes of the anæmic, perfumed savour, whose delicate fragrance breathed from Siraudin's dainty sweetmeats.

By sheer contrast of fragrance, Miss Urania was bound to hold a foremost place in his memory, but almost immediately, Des Esseintes, startled for a moment by the unexpectedness of a natural, unsophisticated aroma, came back to more civilized scents and began inevitably to think of his other mistresses. They trooped across the field of memory in crowds; but, above them all, stood out the woman whose monstrous gift had for months given him such contentment.

She was a brunette, a little lean woman, with black eyes and black hair worn in tight bandeaux, that looked as if they had been plastered on her head with a brush, and parted on one side near the temple like a boy's. He had made her acquaintance at a café-concert, where she was giving performances as a ventriloquist.

To the amazement of a crowded audience who were half frightened at what they heard, she would give voices, turn and turn about, to half a dozen dolls of graduated sizes seated on chairs like a row of Pandean pipes; she would hold conversations with the little figures that seemed all but alive, while, in the auditorium itself, flies could be heard buzzing about the chandeliers and the spectators whispering on the benches though they had never opened their mouths. Then a string of imaginary carriages would roll up the room from the door to the stage, seeming almost to graze the elbows of the seated audience, who started back, instinctively surprised to find themselves there at all.

Des Esseintes had been fascinated; a crowd of new thoughts coursed through his brain. To open the campaign, he made all haste to reduce the fortress by the battery of bank notes, the ventriloquist catching his fancy by the very fact of the utter contrast she presented to the fair American. This brown beauty reeked of artfully prepared perfumes, heady and unhealthy scents, and she burned like the crater of a volcano. In spite of all his subterfuges, Des Esseintes' vigour was exhausted in a few hours; none the less he persisted in allowing himself to be drained dry by her, for more than the woman as a woman, her phenomenal endowments attracted him.

In fact, the plans he had proposed to himself to carry out were ripe for execution. He resolved to accomplish a project hitherto impossible of realization.

One night, he had a miniature sphinx brought in, carved in black marble, couched in the classic pose with outstretched paws and the head held rigid and upright together with a chimæra, in coloured earthenware, flourishing a bristling mane, darting savage glances from ferocious eyes, lashing into furrows with its tail its flanks swollen like the bellows of a forge. He placed these monsters, one at each end of the room, put out the lamps, leaving only the red embers glowing on the hearth, to throw a vague and uncertain illumination about the chamber that exaggerated the apparent size of objects half lost in the semi-darkness.

This done, he stretched himself on the bed beside his mistress, whose unsmiling face was visible by the faint glow from the fireplace, and awaited developments. With weird intonations which he had made her long and patiently rehearse beforehand, she gave life and voice to the two monsters, without so much as moving her lips, without even a glance in their direction.

Then, in the silence of the night, began the wondrous dialogue of the Chimæra and the Sphinx, spoken in deep, guttural tones, now hoarse, now shrill, like voices of another world.

"Here, Chimæra, stop, I say."

"No, never."

Under the spell of Flaubert's marvellous prose, he listened trembling to the dreadful pair and a shudder shook his body from head to foot, when the Chimæra uttered the solemn and magic sentence:

"I seek new perfumes, ampler blossoms, untried pleasures."

Ah! it was to himself this voice, mysterious as an incantation, spoke; it was to him she told of her feverish desire for the unknown, her unsatisfied longing for the ideal, her craving to escape the horrible reality of existence, to overpass the confines of thought, to grope, without ever reaching it, after a certainty, in the mists of the regions beyond the bounds of art! All the pitifulness of his own efforts filled his heart with sick disgust. Softly he. pressed to his breast the silent woman by his side, clung to her for comfort like a frightened child, never even seeing the sulky looks of the actress forced to play a part, to exercise her craft, at home, in her hours of rest, far away from the footlights.

Their liaison went on, but before long Des Esseintes' feebleness grew more pronounced; the effervescence of his mental activities could no longer melt the icy fetters that held his bodily powers; the nerves refused to obey the mandates of the will; the lecherous caprices that appeal to old men dominated him. Feeling himself growing more and more inefficient as a lover, he had recourse to the most powerful stimulus of aged voluptuaries uncertain of their powers—fear.

While he held the woman clasped in his arms, a hoarse, furious voice would burst out from behind the door: "Let me in, I say! I know you have a lover with you. Just wait a minute, and I'll let you know, you trollop."—Instantly, like the libertines whose passions are stimulated by terror of being caught in *flagrante delicto* in the open air, on the river banks, in the Tuileries Gardens, in a summer-house or on a bench, he would temporarily recover his powers, throw himself at the ventriloquist, whose voice went storming on outside the room, and he found an abnormal satisfaction in this rush and scurry, this alarm of a man running a risk, interrupted, hurried in his fornication.

Unhappily these sittings soon came to an end. In spite of the extravagant prices he paid, the ventriloquist sent him about his business, and the same night gave herself to a good fellow whose requirements were less complicated and his back stronger.

Des Esseintes had regretted the woman, and when he recollected her artifices, other women seemed devoid of flavour; the affected graces of depraved children even appeared insipid, and so profound became his contempt for their monotonous grimaces that he could not bring himself to put up with them any more.

Still chewing the bitter cud of his disillusionment, he was walking one day all alone in the Avenue de Latour-Maubourg when he was accosted near the Invalides by a young man, almost a boy, who begged him to tell him the shortest way to go to the Rue de Babylone. Des Esseintes indicated his road and, as he was crossing the Esplanade too, they set off together.

The lad's voice, insisting, it seemed to his companion quite needlessly, on fuller instructions as to the way;—"Then you think, do you? that by turning left, I should be taking the longer road; but I was told that if I cut obliquely across the Avenue, I should get there all the quicker,"—was timid and appealing at the same time, very low and very gentle.

Des Esseintes looked him up and down. He seemed to have just left school, was poorly dressed in a little cheviot jacket tight round the hips and barely coming below the break of the loins, a pair of close-fitting black breeches, a turn-down collar cut low to display a puffed cravat, deep blue with white lines, La Vallière shape. In his hand he carried a class book bound in boards, and on his head was a brown, flat-brimmed bowler hat.

The face was at once pathetic and strangely attractive; pale and drawn, with regular features shaded by long black locks, it was lit up by great liquid eyes, the lids circled with blue, set near the nose, which was splashed with a few golden freckles and under which lurked a little mouth, but with fleshy lips divided by a line in the middle like a ripe cherry.

They examined each other for a moment, eye to eye; then the young man dropped his and stepped nearer; soon his arm was rubbing against Des Esseintes', who slackened his pace, gazing with a thoughtful look at the lad's swaying walk.

And lo! from this chance meeting sprang a mistrustful friendship that nevertheless was prolonged for months. To this day, Des Esseintes could not think of it without a shudder; never had he experienced a more alluring liaison or one that laid a more imperious spell on his senses; never had he run such risks, nor had he ever been so well content with such a grievous sort of satisfaction.

Among all the memories that pressed upon him in his solitude, the recollection of this attachment dominated all the rest. All the leaven of insanity that can torment a brain over-stimulated by nervous excitation was fermenting within him; moreover, to complete the satisfaction he found in these reminiscences, in this morose pleasure, as Theology names this recurrence of old doings of shame, he combined with the physical visions, spiritual ardours roused by his former readings of the casuists, writers like Busenbaum and Diana, Liguori and Sanchez, treating of sins against the Sixth and Ninth Commandments of the Decalogue.

While giving birth to an extra-human ideal in this soul which it had impregnated and which a hereditary tendency dating from the reign of Henry III. perhaps predisposed in the same direction, Religion had at the same time roused an illegitimate ideal of licentious pleasures; libertine and mystic obsessions haunted, in an inextricable union, his brain that thirsted with an obstinate craving to escape the vulgarities of life; to plunge, utterly regardless of revered usages, into new and original ecstasies; into excesses celestial or accursed, but equally ruinous in the waste of phosphorus they involve.

As a matter of fact, he issued from these reveries utterly exhausted, half dying; then he would at once kindle the candles and lamps, flooding the room with light, thinking in this way to hear less distinctly than in the darkness the dull, persistent, intolerable beating of the arteries that throbbed and throbbed unceasingly under the skin of the neck.

Chapter Ten

In the course of that singular malady which plays such havoc with races of exhausted vitality, sudden intervals of calm succeed the crises. Without being able to explain the reason, Des Esseintes awoke quite strong and well one fine morning; no more hacking cough, no more wedges driven with a hammer into the back of the neck, but an ineffable sensation of well-being and a delightful clearness of brain, while his thoughts became cheerful; and instead of being opaque and dull, grew bright and iridescent, like brilliantly coloured soap bubbles.

This lasted some days; then in a moment, one afternoon, hallucinations of the sense of smell appeared.

His room was strong of frangipane. He looked to see if perhaps there was a bottle of the perfume lying about anywhere uncorked; but there was no such thing in the place. He visited his working-room and then the dining-room; the smell was there too.

He rang for his servant. "Don't you smell something?" he asked, but the man, after sniffing the air, declared he noticed nothing. Doubt was impossible; the nervous derangement was come again, taking the form of a fresh delusion of the senses.

Wearied by the persistency of this imaginary aroma, he resolved to plunge himself in a bath of real perfumes, hoping that his nasal homeopathy might cure him or, at any rate, moderate the force of the overpowering frangipane.

He betook himself to his study. There, beside an ancient font that served him as a wash-hand basin, under a long looking-glass in a frame of wrought iron that held imprisoned like a well-head silvered by the moonlight the pale surface of the mirror, bottles of all sizes and shapes were ranged in rows on ivory shelves.

He placed them on a table and divided them into two series,—first, the simple perfumes, extracts and distilled waters; secondly, composite scents, such as are described under the generic name of *bouquets*.

He buried himself in an armchair and began to think.

Years ago he had trained himself as an expert in the science of perfumes; he held that the sense of smell was qualified to experience pleasures equal to those pertaining to the ear and the eye, each of the five senses being capable, by dint of a natural aptitude supplemented by an erudite education, of receiving novel impressions, magnifying these tenfold, coordinating them, combining them into the whole that constitutes a work of art. It was not, in fact, he argued, more abnormal than an art should exist of disengaging odoriferous fluids than that other arts should whose function is to set up sonorous waves to strike the ear or variously coloured rays to impinge on the retina of the eyes; only, just as no one, without a special faculty of intuition developed by study, can distinguish a picture by a great master from a worthless daub, a *motif* of Beethoven from a tune by Clapisson, so no one, without a preliminary initiation, can avoid confounding at the first sniff a *bouquet* created by a great artist with a pot-pourri compounded by a manufacturer for sale in grocers' shops and fancy bazaars.

In this art of perfumes, one peculiarity had more than all others fascinated him, viz, the precision with which it can artificially imitate the real article.

Hardly ever, indeed, are scents actually produced from the flowers whose name they bear; the artist who should be bold enough to borrow his element from Nature alone would obtain only a half-and-half-result, unconvincing, lacking in style and elegance, the fact being that the essence obtained by distillation from the flowers themselves could at the best present but a far-off, vulgarized analogy with the real aroma of the living and growing flower, shedding its fragrant effluvia in the open air.

So, with the one exception of the jasmine, which admits of no imitation, no counterfeit, no copy, which refuses even any approximation, all flowers are perfectly represented by combinations of alcoholates and essences, extracting from the model its inmost individuality while adding that something, that heightened tone, that heady savour, that rare touch which makes a work of art.

In one word, in perfumery the artist completes and consummates the original natural odour, which he cuts, so to speak, and mounts as a jeweller improves and brings out the water of a precious stone.

Little by little, the arcana of this art, the most neglected of all, had been revealed to Des Esseintes, who could now decipher its language,—a diction as varied, as subtle as that of literature itself, a style of unprecedented conciseness under its apparent vagueness and uncertainty.

To reach this end, he had, first of all, been obliged to master the grammar, to understand the syntax of odours, to grasp the rules that govern them; then, once familiarized with this dialect, to study and compare the works of the divers masters of the craft, the Atkinsons and Lubins, the Chardins and Violets, the Legrands and Piesses, to analyze the construction of their sentences, to weigh the proportion of their words and the disposition of their periods.

Next, in this idiom of essences, it was for experience to come to the assistance of theories too often incomplete and commonplace.

The classic art of perfumery was, in truth, little diversified, almost colourless, uniformly run in a mould first shaped by old-world chemists; it was in its dotage, hide-bound in its ancient alembics, when the Romantic epoch dawned and took its part in modifying, in rejuvenating it, in making it more malleable and more supple.

Its history followed step by step that of the French language. The Louis XIII. style, perfumed and full-flavoured, compounded of elements costly at that date, of iris powder, musk, civet, myrtle water, already known by the name of Angels' Water, barely sufficed to express the rude graces, the rather crude tints of the time which certain sonnets of Saint-Amand's have preserved for us. Later on, with the introduction of myrrh, frankincense, the mystic scents, powerful and austere, the pomp and stateliness of the *Grand Siècle*, the redundancy and artificiality of the orator's art, the full, sustained, wordy style of Bossuet and the great preachers became almost possible; later on again, the well-worn, sophisticated graces of French society under Louis XV. found a readier interpretation of their charm in the frangipane and *maréchale*, which offered in their way the very synthesis of the period. Then finally, after the indifference and incuriousness of the First Empire, which used Eau de Cologne and preparations of rosemary to excess, perfumery ran for inspiration, in the train of Victor Hugo and Gautier, to the lands of the sun; it created Oriental essences, *selams* overpowering with their spicy odours; invented new savours; tried and approved old tones and shades now rediscovered, which it made more complex, more subtle, more choice; definitely repudiating once for all the voluntary decrepitude to which the art had been reduced by the Malesherbes, the Andrieux, the Baour-Lormians, the vulgar distillers of its poetry.

Nor had the language of perfumes remained stationary since the epoch of 1830. Again it had progressed and following the march of the century had advanced side by side with the other arts. It, too, had complied with the whims of amateurs and artists, flying for motives to China and Japan, inventing scented albums, imitating the flowery nosegays of Takeoka; by a mingling of lavender and clove obtaining the perfume Rondeletia; by a union of patchouli and camphor, the singular aroma of India-ink; by compounding citron, clove and neroli (essence of orange blossoms), the odour, the Hovenia of Japan.

Des Esseintes studied, analyzed the soul of these fluids, expounded these texts; he took a delight, for his own personal satisfaction, in playing the part of psychologist, in unmounting and remounting the machinery of a work, in unscrewing the separate pieces forming the structure of a complex odour, and by long practice of this sort, his sense of smell had arrived at the certainty of an almost infallible touch.

Just as a wine-merchant knows the vintage by imbibing a single drop; as a hop-dealer, the instant he sniffs at a bag, can there and then name its precise quality and price; as a Chinese trader can declare at once the place of origin of the teas he examines, say on what farms of the Bohea mountains, in what Buddhist Monasteries, each specimen was grown, and the date at which its leaves were gathered, can state precisely the degree of heat used and the effect produced by its contact with plum blossom, with the Aglaia, with the Olea fragrans, with all or any of the perfumes employed to modify its flavour, to give it an added piquancy, to brighten up its rather dry savour with a whiff of fresh and alien flowers; even so could Des Esseintes, by the merest sniff at a scent, detail instantly the doses of its composition, explain the psychology of its blending; all but quote the name of the particular artist who wrote it and impressed on it, the personal mark of his style.

Needless to say, he possessed a collection of all the products used by perfume-makers; he had even some of the true Balm of Mecca, a very great rarity, to be procured only in certain regions of Arabia Petræa and guarded as a monopoly of the Grand Turk.

Seated now in his study at his working table, he was pondering the creation of a new *bouquet*, and had reached that moment of hesitation so familiar to authors who, after months of idleness, are preparing to start upon a fresh piece of work.

Like Balzac, who was haunted by an imperious craving to blacken reams of paper by way of getting his hand in, Des Esseintes felt the necessity of recovering his old cunning by dint of executing some task of minor importance. He determined to make heliotrope, and measured out the proper quantities from phials of almond and vanilla; then he changed his mind and resolved to try sweet-pea.

The phrases, the processes had escaped his memory. So he made experiments. No doubt in the fragrance of that flower, orange blossom was the dominant factor, he tried a number of combinations and ended by getting the right tone by blending the orange with the tuberose and rose, binding the three together with a drop of vanilla.

All his uncertainties vanished; a fever of eagerness stirred him, he was ready to set to work in earnest. He compounded a fresh brew of tea, adding a mixture of cassia and iris; then, sure of himself, he resolved to march boldly forward, to strike a thundering note, the overmastering crash of which should bury the whisper of that insinuating frangipane which still stealthily impregnated the room.

He handled amber; Tonquin musk, with its overpowering scent; patchouli, the most pronounced of all vegetable perfumes, whose blossom, in the natural state, gives off an odour compounded of wet wood and rusty iron. Do what he would, the associations of the eighteenth century haunted him, gowns with paniers and furbelows hovered before his eyes; memories of Boucher's "Venus," all flesh, without bones, stuffed with pink cotton-wool, beseiged him; recollections of the novel *Thémidore* and the exquisite Rosette with skirts high lifted in a fire-red despair, pursued him. In a rage, he sprang up and, to shake himself free from the obsession, sniffed in with all his might that unadulterated essence of spikenard that is so dear to Easterns and so disagreeable to Europeans, by reason of its over-strong savour of valerian. He staggered under the violence of the shock; as if crushed under the blow of a mallet, the delicate fibrils of the dainty scent disappeared. He took advantage of the moment's respite to escape from the dead centuries, the old-time emanations, to enter, as he had been used to do in other days, on creations less limited in scope and more modern in fashion.

Of old, he had loved to soothe his spirit with harmonies in perfumery; he would use effects analogous to those of the poets, would adopt, in a measure, the admirable metrical scheme characterizing certain pieces of Baudelaire's, for instance *"l'Irréparable"* and *"le Balcon,"* where the last of the five lines composing the strophe is the echo of the first, returning like a refrain to drown the soul in infinite depths of melancholy and languor.

He wandered, lost in the dreams these aromatic stanzas called up in his brain, till suddenly recalled to his starting point, to the original *motif* of his meditations, by the recurrence of the initial theme, re-appearing at studied intervals in the fragrant orchestration of the poem.

For the actual moment, he was fain to roam in freedom amid a landscape full of surprises and changes, and he began by a simple phrase,—ample, sonorous, at once opening a view over an immense stretch of country.

With the help of his vaporizers, he injected into the room an essence composed of ambrosia, Mitcham lavender, sweet-pea, compound *bouquet*,—an essence which, if distilled by a true artist, well deserves the name bestowed on it of "extract of meadow flowers"; then, into this meadow, he introduced a carefully modulated infusion of tuberose, orange and almond blossom, and instantly artificial lilacs came into being, while lindens swayed in the breeze, shedding on the ground about them their pale emanations, mimicked by the London extract of tilia.

This scene, once arranged in a few imposing lines, melting to the horizon under his closed eyes, he insinuated a light rain of human, not to say half feline, essences, smacking of the petticoat, announcing woman powdered and painted,—the stephanotis, the ayapana, the opoponax, the chypre, the champaka, the sarcanthus, over which he superimposed a dash of seringa, to suggest, amid the factitious life of make-up and make-belief which they evoked, a natural flower of hearty, uncontrolled laughter, of the joys of existence in the eye of the sun.

Then he let these fragrant waves escape by a ventilator, keeping only the country scent, which he renewed and reinforced, strengthening the dose so as to force it to recur like the burden of a song at the end of each strophe. Little by little, the feminine aroma disappeared, the country was left without inhabitants. Then, on the enchanted horizon, rose a row of factories whose tall chimneys flamed at their tops like so many bowls of punch.

A breath as of manufactories, of chemical works now floated on the breeze which he raised by waving fans, though Nature still continued to sweeten with her fragrant emanations this foulness of the atmosphere.

Des Esseintes proceeded to turn about and warm between his hands a ball of styrax, and a very curious odour filled the room, a smell at once repugnant and exquisite, blending the delicious scent of the jonquil with the filthy stench of gutta-percha and coal tar. He disinfected his hands, shut away his resin in a box hermetically sealed, and the stinking factories vanished in their turn. Then, he tossed amid the revivified vapours of lindens and meadow-grass some drops of "new mown hay," and on the magic spot, instantly bared of its lilacs, rose mounds of hay, bringing with them a new season, scattering their delicate odours reminiscent of high summer.

Last of all, when he had sufficiently savoured the sight, he hurriedly scattered about exotic perfumes, exhausted his vaporizers, concentrated his strongest essences, gave the rein to all his balms, and lo! the stifling closeness of the room was filled with an atmosphere, maddening and sublime, breathing powerful influences, impregnating with raging alcoholates an artificial breeze,—an atmosphere unnatural, yet delightful, paradoxical in its union of the allspice of the Tropics, the pungent savours of the sandalwood of China and the hediosmia of Japan with native odours of jasmine, hawthorn and vervain, forcing, to grow together, in despite of seasons and climates, trees of diverse essences, flowers of colours and fragrances the most opposite, creating by the blending and shock of all these tones one common perfume, unknown, unforeseen, extraordinary, wherein re-appeared at intervals as a persistent refrain, the decorative phrase of the opening, the odour of the broad meadows breathed over by the lilacs and the lindens.

Suddenly a sharp agony assailed him; it felt as though a centre-bit were boring into his temples. He opened his eyes, to find himself once more in the middle of his study, seated before his working table; he got up and walked painfully, half-stunned, to the window, which he threw part open. A current of fresh air sweetened the stifling atmosphere that enveloped him; he marched up and down the room to recover the proper use of his limbs, going to and fro, his eyes fixed on the ceiling on which crabs and seaweed powdered with sea salt stood out in relief from a grained background, yellow as the sand of a beach. A similar design decorated the plinths bordering the panels, which in their turn were covered with Japanese crape, a watery green in colour and slightly waved to imitate the ripple of a wind-blown river, while down the gentle current floated a rose leaf round which frolicked a swarm of little fishes dashed in with two strokes of the pen.

But his eyes were still heavy; he left off pacing the short length of floor between the font and the bath and leant his elbows on the window sill. Presently his dizziness ceased, and after carefully recorking the bottles of scents and essences, he seized the opportunity to tidy his apparatus for making up the face,—his paints and powders and the like. He had not touched these things since his arrival at Fontenay, and he was almost astonished now at the sight of this collection once visited by so many women. One on top of the other, phials and porcelain pots littered the table confusion. Here was a china box, of the green sort, containing *schnouda*, that marvellous white cream which, once spread on the cheeks, changes under the influence of the air to a tender pink, then to a scarlet so natural that it gives an absolutely convincing illusion of a complexion mantling with red blood; there, jars incrusted with mother-o'-pearl held Japanese gold and Athens green, coloured like the wing of the cantharides beetle, golds and greens that blend into a deep purple directly they are moistened; beside pots full of filbert paste, of *serkis* of the harem, of emulsions of Cashmere lilies, of lotions of strawberry and elderflower for the skin, beside little phials of solutions of India-ink and rose-water for the eyes, lay a host of different instruments, of mother-o'-pearl, of ivory and of silver, mixed up with dainty brushes for the teeth and gums,—pincers, scissors, strigils, stumps, crimpers, powder-puffs, back-scratchers, patches and files.

He handled all this elaborate apparatus, bought in former days to please a mistress who found an ineffable pleasure in certain aromatics and certain balms, an ill-balanced, nerve-ridden woman, who loved to have her nipples macerated in scents, but who only really experienced a genuine and over-mastering ecstasy when her head was tickled with a comb and she could, in the act of being caressed by a lover, breathe the smell of chimney soot, of wet plaster from a house building in rainy weather, or of dust churned up by the heavy thunder drops of a summer storm.

He pondered these recollections, recalling particularly an afternoon spent, partly for want of anything better to do, partly out of curiosity, in this woman's company at her sister's house at Pantin, the memory of which stirred in his breast a whole forgotten world of long-ago thoughts and old-time scents. While the two women were chattering and showing each other their frocks, he had gone to the window and, through the dusty panes, had looked out on the long, muddy street and heard its pavements echo under the incessant beat of heavy boots trampling through the puddles.

The scene, now far away in the past, suddenly stood out before him with extraordinary vividness. Pantin lay there in front of his eyes, bustling and alive, imaged in the green, dead water of the mirror into which his eyes involuntarily gazed. A hallucination carried him far away from Fontenay; the looking-glass reproduced for him the same reflections the street had once presented to his bodily eye, and buried in a dream, he said over the ingenious, melancholy yet consoling, anthem he had noted down on that former occasion on getting back to Paris:—

"Yes, the time of the great rains is come; behold, the gutter-pipes vomit their drippings on to the pavements, with a song of many waters, and the horse-dung lies fermenting in the puddles that fill the holes in the macadam with a coffee-coloured fluid; everywhere, for the humble wayfarer, are foot-baths full to overflowing.

"Under the lowering sky, in the dull air, the walls of the houses drip black sweat and the cellar-openings stink; loathing of life is strong within the soul and the spleen is a torment to the flesh; the seeds of filthiness that every man has in his heart begin to bud; cravings for foul pleasures trouble the austerest and in the brain of respectable folks criminal desires spring up.

"And yet, there I am, warming myself before a blazing fire, while a basket of blowing flowers on a table fills the room with a sweet savour of benzoin, geranium and bent-grass. In mid November, it is still spring-time at Pantin, in the Rue de Paris, and I find myself laughing in my sleeve to think of the timorous family parties that, in order to avoid the approach of winter, fly to Antibes or Cannes as fast as steam will take them.

"Inclement Nature goes for nothing in this strange phenomenon; it is to industry, to commerce, and that alone, be it said, that Pantin owes this artificial spring.

"The truth is, these flowers are of lustring, mounted on brass-wire, and the spring-like fragrance floating in through the cracks of the window-frame, is exhaled by the neighbouring factories where Pinaud and Saint-James make their perfumes.

"For the artisan exhausted by the hard labour of the workshops, for the small clerk, alas! only too often a father, the illusion of a breath or two of good air is a possibility—thanks to these manufacturers.

"Indeed, out of this scarce believable illusion of the country may be developed a quite rational medical treatment. Fast livers affected by chest complaints who are now carted off to the South mostly die, broken down by the rupture of all their habits of life, by the homesick craving to return to the Parisian pleasures that have brought them to this pass by their excess. Here, in an artificial climate, heated and regulated by stoves, libertine recollections will return, gently and harmlessly, along with the languishing feminine emanations given off by scent factories. In lieu of the deadly dreariness of provincial existence, the physician can by this device supply his patient platonically with the longed-for atmosphere of Parisian boudoirs, of Parisian haunts of pleasure.

"In the majority of cases, all that will be required to complete the cure is for the sick man to possess a little touch of imagination.

"Now, seeing that, in these times of ours, there is no single thing really genuine to be found; seeing that the wine we drink and the liberty we acclaim are equally adulterate and derisory; considering how remarkable a dose of credulity it takes to suppose the governing classes to deserve respect and the lower to be worthy either of relief or commiseration, it appears to me," concluded Des Esseintes, "neither more absurd nor more insane to demand of my neighbour a sum total of illusion barely equal to that he expends every day in his life for quite idiotic objects, that he may successfully persuade himself that the town of Pantin is an artificial Nice, a factitious Menton."

* * *

"All which," he exclaimed, rudely interrupted in his reflexions by a sudden failure of all his bodily powers, "does not alter the fact that I must beware of these delicious and abominable experiments that are killing me." He heaved a sigh: "Well, well, more pleasures to moderate, more precautions to take,"—and he retired for refuge to his study, thinking in this way to escape more easily from the haunting influence of the perfumes.

He threw the window wide open, delighted to enjoy an air bath; but next moment, the wind seemed to bring with it a vague breath of essence of bergamot, mingled with a smell of jasmine, cassia and rose-water. He shuddered, asking himself if he was not surely under the tyranny of one of those possessions by the devil that the Priests used to exorcise in the Middle Ages. Soon the odour changed and altered, however. An uncertain savour of tincture of tolu, balm of Peru, saffron, blended together by a few drops of amber and musk, now floated in from the sleeping village at the bottom of the hill; then, suddenly, in an instant, the metamorphosis was wrought, the scent of frangipane, of which his nostrils had caught the elements and were so familiar with the analysis, filled all the air from the valley of Fontenay away to the Fort, assailing his exhausted sense of smell, shaking afresh his shattered nerves, prostrating him to such a degree that he fell swooning and half dying across the window sill.

Chapter Eleven

The terrified domestics hurried off in search of the Fontenay doctor, who did not understand one word of Des Esseintes' condition. He muttered sundry medical terms, felt the invalid's pulse and examined his tongue, tried in vain to make him speak, ordered sedatives and rest, promised to come back next day, and on Des Esseintes shaking his head,—he had regained strength enough to disapprove his servant's zeal and send the intruder about his business,—took his departure and went off to describe to every inhabitant of the village the eccentricities of the house, the furniture and appointments of which had struck him with amazement and frozen him where he stood.

To the astonishment of the servants, who dared not stir from their quarters, their master recovered in a day or two, and they came upon him drumming on the window-panes and gazing up anxiously at the sky.

One afternoon, the bells rang a peremptory summons, and Des Esseintes issued orders that his trunks were to be got ready for a long journey.

While the old man and his wife were selecting, under his superintendence, such articles as were necessary, he was pacing feverishly up and down the cabin of his dining-room, consulting the time tables of steamers, going from window to window of his study, still scrutinizing the clouds with looks at once of impatience and satisfaction.

For a week past the weather had been atrocious. Sooty rivers pouring unceasingly across the grey plains of the heavens rolled along masses of clouds that looked like huge boulders torn up from the earth.

Every few minutes storms of rain would sweep down and swallow up the valley under torrents of wet.

But that day the firmament had changed its aspect. The floods of ink had dried up, the rugged clouds had melted; the sky was now one great flat plain, one vast watery film. Little by little this film seemed to fall lower, a moist haze wrapped the face of the land; no longer did the rain descend in cataracts, as it had the day before, but fell in a continuous drizzle, fine, penetrating, chilling, soaking the garden walks, churning up the roads, confounding together earth and sky. The daylight was darkened, and a livid gloom hung over the village now transformed into a lake of mud speckled by the rain-drops that pitted with spots of silver the muddy surface of the puddles. In the general desolation, all colour had faded to a drab uniformity, leaving only the roofs glittering with wet above the lifeless hues of the walls.

"What weather!" sighed the old servant, depositing on a chair the clothes his master had called for, a suit ordered some time before from London.

The only answer Des Esseintes vouchsafed was to rub his hands and take his stand before a glass-fronted bookcase in which a collection of silk socks was arranged in the form of a fan. He hesitated a while over the best shade to choose, then rapidly, taking into consideration the gloom of the day and the depressing tints of his coat and trousers, and remembering the object he had in view, he selected a pair of drab silk and quickly drew them on. Next he donned lace-up, brogued, shooting boots; put on the suit, mouse-grey with a check of a lighter grey and whitey spots, clapped a little round hat on his head, threw an inverness-cape round his shoulders, and followed by his servant staggering under the weight of a trunk, a collapsible valise, a carpet bag, a hat-box and a travelling rug wrapped round umbrellas and sticks, he made for the railway station. Arrived there, he informed the domestic that he could fix no definite date for his return, that he might be back in a year's time, next month, next week, sooner perhaps, gave orders that nothing should be changed or moved in the house during his absence, handed over the approximate sum required to keep up the establishment, during his absence, and got into the railway carriage, leaving the old fellow dumbfounded, arms dangling and mouth wide open, behind the barrier beyond which the train got into motion.

He was alone in his compartment; a blurred, murky landscape, looking as if seen through the dirty water of an aquarium, whirled past the flying, rain-splashed train. Buried in his thoughts, Des Esseintes closed his eyes.

Once more, this solitude he had so ardently desired and won at last had resulted in poignant distress; this silence that had once appealed to him as a consolation for all the fools' chatter he had listened to for years, now weighed upon him with an intolerable burden. One morning, he had awoke as frenzied in mind as a man who finds himself locked up in a prison cell; his trembling lips moved to cry out, but no sound came, tears rose to his eyes, he felt choked like one who has been sobbing bitterly for hours.

Devoured by a longing to move, to see a human face, to talk with a fellow human being, to mingle with the common life of mankind, he actually asked his servants to stay with him, after summoning them to his room on some pretext or other. But conversation was impossible; besides the fact that the two old people, bowed and bent under the weight of years of silence and broken in to the habits of sick-nurses, were next door to dumb, the distance which Des Esseintes had always maintained between himself and his dependents was not calculated to make them anxious to unclose their lips. Their brains, too, had grown sluggish and inert, and refused to supply more than monosyllabic answers to any questions they might be asked.

There was nothing therefore to be hoped for from them in the way of relief or solace. But now a fresh phenomenon came to pass. The reading of Dickens which he had in the first instance carried out with the object of composing his nerves, but which had produced just the opposite effect to what he had looked for in the matter of benefitting his health, now began to act little by little in an unexpected direction, inducing visions of English life over which he sat pondering for hours; gradually into these fictitious reveries came creeping notions of turning them into a positive reality, of making an actual voyage to England, of verifying his dreams, engrafted on all which was further a growing wish to experience novel impressions and so escape the divagations of a mind dizzied with grinding, grinding at nothing, which had so disastrously sapped his strength.

Then the abominable weather with its everlasting fog and rain helped on his purpose, confirming as it did what he remembered from his reading, keeping constantly before his eyes a picture of what a land of mist and mud is like, and in this way focussing his ideas and holding them to their original starting point.

He could resist no more, and one day had quite suddenly made up his mind. So great was his hurry to be off that he fled precipitately, impatient to be done with his present life, to feel himself hustled in the turmoil of a crowded street, in the crush and bustle of a railway station.

"I can breathe now," he said to himself as the train slowed down in its dance and came to a halt in the rotunda of the Paris terminus of the Sceaux Railway, its last pirouettes accompanied by the crashes and jerks of the turn-tables.

Once out in the street, on the Boulevard d'Enfer, glad to be encumbered as he was with his trunks and rugs, he hailed a cabman. By the promise of a generous pourboire he soon came to an understanding with the man of the drab breeches and red waistcoat. "By the hour"; he ordered, "drive to the Rue de Rivoli and stop at the office of *Galignani's Messenger*"; his idea was to purchase before starting a Baedeker's or Murray's Guide to London.

The conveyance blundered off, throwing up showers of mud from the wheels. The streets were like a swamp; under the grey sky that seemed to rest on the roofs of the houses, the walls were dripping from top to bottom, the rain-gutters overflowing, the pavements coated with mud of the colour of gingerbread in which the passers-by slipped and slid. On the side-walks, as the omnibuses swept by, people would stop in crowded masses, and women, kilted to the knees and bending under sodden umbrellas, would press against the shop windows to escape the flying mire.

The wet was coming in at the windows; so Des Esseintes had to put up the glass, which the rain streaked with little rivulets of water, while clots of mud flew like a firework in all directions from the moving vehicle. To the monotonous accompaniment of the storm beating down with a noise like a sack of pears being shaken out on his luggage and the carriage roof, Des Esseintes dreamed of his coming journey; it was already an instalment on account of rainy London he was now receiving at Paris in this dreadful weather; the picture of a London, fog-bound, colossal, enormous, smelling of hot iron and soot, wrapt in a perpetual mantle of smoke and mist, unrolled itself before his mind's eye. Vistas of endless docks stretched farther than eye could see, crowded with cranes and capstans and bales of merchandise, swarming with men perched on masts, a-straddle across ship's yards, while on the quays myriads of others were bending, head down and rump in air, over casks which they were storing away in cellars.

All this activity he could see in full swing on the riverbanks and in gigantic warehouses bathed by the foul, black water of an imaginary Thames, in a forest of masts, in vast entanglements of beams piercing the wan clouds of the lowering firmament, while trains raced by, some tearing full steam across the sky, others rolling along in the sewers, shrieking out horrid screams, vomiting floods of smoke through the gaping mouths of wells, while along every avenue and every street, buried in an eternal twilight and disfigured by the monstrous, gaudy infamies of advertising, streams of vehicles rolled by between marching columns of men, all silent, all intent on business, eyes bent straight ahead, elbows pressed to the sides.

Des Esseintes shuddered deliciously to feel himself lost in this terrible world of men of business, in this isolating fog, in this incessant activity, in this ruthless machine grinding to powder millions of the poor and powerless, whom philanthropists urged, by way of consolation, to repeat verses of the Bible and sing the Psalms of David.

Then, in a moment, the vision vanished as the vehicle gave a jolt that made him jump on the seat. He looked out of the window. Night had fallen; the gas lamps were winking through the fog, each surrounded by a dirty yellow halo; ribands of fire swam in the puddles and seemed to circle round the wheels of the carriages that jogged on through a sea of liquid, discoloured flame. He tried to see where he was, caught sight of the Arc du Carrousel, and in an instant, without rhyme or reason, perhaps simply from the reaction of his sudden fall from the high regions where his imagination had been roaming, his thoughts fell back on a quite trivial incident he now remembered for the first time,—how, when he stood looking on at his servant packing his trunks, the man had forgotten to put in a tooth-brush among his other toilet necessaries. Then he mentally reviewed the list of objects included; yes, they had all been duly arranged in his portmanteau, but the annoyance of this one omission pursued him obstinately till the coachman pulled up his horse and so broke the current of his reminiscences and regrets.

He was now in the Rue de Rivoli, in front of *Galignani's Messenger*. On either side of a door of frosted glass, the panels covered with lettering and hung with Oxford frames containing cuttings from newspapers and telegrams in blue wrappers, were two broad windows crammed with books and albums of views. He came nearer, attracted by the look of these volumes, some of them in paper covers, butcher's-blue and cabbage-green, lavishly decorated with gold and silver patterning, others bound in cloth of various colours, carmelite blue, leek green, goose yellow, current red, cold tooled on back and sides with black lines. All this had an anti-Parisian touch, a mercantile flavour, more vulgar but yet less cheap and tawdry than the way the book-hawkers' wares are got up in France; here and there, among open albums showing comic scenes by Du Maurier and John Leech or chromos of mad gallops across country by Caldecott, appeared a few French novels, tempering this riot of discordant colours with the plain and soothing commonplace of their yellow backs.

At last, tearing himself away from this display, he pushed open the door and entered a vast library, crowded with people. Foreign females sat examining maps and jabbering remarks to one another in strange tongues. A clerk brought Des Esseintes a selection of guide-books. He, too, sat down and fell to turning over the volumes, whose flexible covers bent between his fingers. He glanced through them, but was presently arrested by a page of Baedeker describing the London Museums. His interest was roused by the brief, precise details supplied by the Guide; but it was not long before his attention wandered from the works of the old English painters to those of the new school which appealed to him more strongly. He recalled certain examples he had seen at International Exhibitions, and he thought that very likely he would see them again in London,—pictures by Millais, the "Eve of St. Agnes," with its moonlight effect of silvery green; pictures by Watts, with their strange colouring, speckled with gamboge and indigo; works sketched by a Gustave Moreau fallen sick, painted in by a Michael Angelo gone anæmic, and retouched by a Raphael lost in a sea of blue. Among other canvases he remembered a "Cure of Cain," an "Ida," and more than one "Eve," wherein, under the weird and mysterious amalgamation of these three masters, lurked the personality, at once complex and essentially simple, of an erudite and dreamy Englishman, unfortunately haunted by a predilection for hideous tones.

All these pictures came crowding into his head at once. The shopman, surprised to see a customer sitting at a table lost in a brown study and quite oblivious of his surroundings, asked him which of the Guides he had chosen. Des Esseintes looked up in a dazed way, then, with a word of excuse for his absence of mind, purchased a Baedeker and left the shop. The cold wind froze him to the bone; it was blowing crosswise, lashing the arcades of the Rue de Rivoli with a pelting rain. "Drive there," he cried to the cabman, pointing to a shop at the end of a section of the arcade standing at the corner of the street he was in and the Rue de Castiglione. With its shining panes lighted from within, it looked like a gigantic lantern, a beacon fire amid the perils of the fog and the horrors of the vile weather.

It was the "Bodega." Des Esseintes stood wondering to find himself in a great hall that ran back, like a broad corridor, the roof carried by iron pillars and lined along the walls on either side with tall casks standing up-ended on stocks.

Hooped with iron, and having round their waist a miniature line of battlements resembling a pipe-rack in the notches of which hung tulip-shaped glasses upside down, with a hole drilled in the lower part in which was fixed an earthenware spigot, these barrels, blazoned with a Royal shield, displayed on coloured cards the name of the vintage each contained, the amount of liquor they held and the price of the same, whether by the hogshead, in bottle, or by the glass.

In the passage-way left free between these rows of casks, under the gas jets that flared noisily in a hideous chandelier painted iron-grey, ran a long counter loaded with baskets of Palmer's biscuits, stale, salty cakes, plates piled with mince-pies and sandwiches, hiding under their greasy wrappers great blotches of miniature mustard-plasters. Beside this stood a double row of chairs extending to the far extremity of this cellar-like room, lined all along with more hogsheads having smaller barrels laid across their tops, these last lying on their sides and having their names and descriptions branded with a hot iron in the oak.

A reek of alcohol assailed his nostrils as he took a seat in this room where so many strong waters were stored. He looked about him. Here, the great casks stood in a row, their labels announcing a whole series of ports, strong, fruity wines, mahogany or amaranth coloured, distinguished by laudatory titles, such as "Old Port," "Light Delicate," "Cockburn's Very Fine," "Magnificent Old Regina"; there, rounding their formidable bellies, crowded side by side enormous hogsheads containing the martial wine of Spain, the sherries and their congeners, topaz coloured whether light or dark,—San Lucar, Pasto, Pale Dry, Oloroso, Amontillado, sweet or dry.

The cellar was crammed. Leaning his elbow on the corner of a table, Des Esseintes sat waiting for the glass of port he had ordered of a "gentleman" busy opening explosive sodas in egg-shaped bottles that reminded one, on an exaggerated scale, of those capsules of gelatine and gluten which chemists use to mask the taste of certain nauseous drugs.

All round him were swarms of English,—ungainly figures of pale-faced clergymen, dressed in black from head to foot, with soft hats and monstrously long coats decorated down the front with little buttons, shaven chins, round spectacles, greasy hair plastered to the head; laymen with broad pork-butcher faces and bulldog muzzles, apoplectic necks, ears like tomatoes, wine-sodden cheeks, bloodshot, foolish eyes, beards and whiskers joining in a collar like some of the great apes. Further off, at the far end of the wine-shop, a tall, thin man like a string of sausages, with towy locks and a chin adorned with straggling grey hairs like the root of an artichoke, was deciphering with a microscope the small print of an English newspaper; more to the front, a sort of American commodore, short and stout and round-about, with a smoke-dried complexion and a bottle nose, sat half asleep, a cigar stuck in the hairy orifice of his mouth, staring at the placards on the walls advertising champagnes, the trademarks of Perrier and Roederer, Heidsieck and Mumm, and a hooded monk's head with the name in Gothic lettering of Dom Pérignon, Rheims.

A feeling of lassitude crept over Des Esseintes in this rude, garrison-town atmosphere; deafened by the chatter of these English folk talking to one another, he fell into a dream, calling up from the purple of the port wine that filled their glasses a succession of Dickens' characters, who were so partial to that beverage, peopling in imagination the cellar with a new set of customers, seeing in his mind's eye here Mr. Wickfield's white hair and red face, there, the phlegmatic and astute bearing and implacable eye of Mr. Tulkinghorn, the gloomy lawyer of Bleak House. Perfect in every detail, they all stood out clear in his memory, taking their places in the Bodega, with all their works and ways and gestures; his recollections, lately revived by a fresh perusal of the stories, were extraordinarily full and precise. The Novelist's town, the well lighted, well warmed house, cosy and comfortably appointed, the bottles slowly emptied by Little Dorrit, by

Dora Copperfield, by Tom Pinch's sister Ruth, appeared to him sailing like a snug ark in a deluge of mire and soot. He loitered idly in this London of the imagination, happy to be under shelter, seeming to hear on the Thames the hideous whistles of the tugs at work behind the Tuileries, near the bridge. His glass was empty; despite the mist that filled the room over-heated by the smoke of pipes and cigars, he experienced a little shudder of disgust as he came back to the realities of life in this moist and foul smelling weather.

He asked for a glass of Amontillado, but then, as he sat before this pale, dry wine, the nerve-soothing stories, the gentle lenitives of the English author were scattered and the harsh revulsives, the cruel irritants of Edgar Allan Poe rose in their place. The chill nightmare of the cask of Amontillado, the story of the man walled up in an underground chamber, seized upon his fancy; the kindly, commonplace faces of the American and English customers who filled the hall seemed to him to reflect uncontrollable and abominable cravings, odious and instinctive plans of wickedness. Presently he noticed he was nearly the last there, that the dinner hour was close at hand; he paid his score, tore himself from his chair and made dizzily for the door. He got a wet buffet in the face the instant he set foot outside; drowned by the rain and driving squalls, the street lamps flickered feebly and gave hardly a gleam of light; the clouds ruled lower than ever, having come down several pegs, right to the middle of the house fronts. Des Esseintes looked along the arcades of the Rue de Rivoli, bathed in shadow and dripping with moisture, and he thought he was standing in the dismal tunnel excavated beneath the Thames. But the cravings of hunger recalled him to reality; he went back to his cab, threw the driver the address of the tavern in the Rue d'Amsterdam, near the Saint-Lazare railway station, and looked at his watch,—it was seven o'clock. He had just time enough to dine; the train did not start till eight-fifty, and he fell to counting up the time on his fingers, calculating the hours required for the crossing from Dieppe to Newhaven, and telling himself,—"If the figures in the railway-guide are right, I shall be in London tomorrow on the stroke of half-past twelve noon.

The vehicle stopped in front of the tavern, once more Des Esseintes left it and made his way into a long hall, with drab wills innocent of any gilding, and divided by means of breast-high partitions into a series of compartments like the loose-boxes in a stable. In this room, which opened out into a wider space by the door, rows of beer engines rose along a counter, side by side with hams as brown as old violins, lobsters of a bright metallic red, salted mackerel, along with slices of onion, raw carrots, pieces of lemon peel, bunches of bay leaves and thyme, juniper berries and coarse pepper swimming in a thick sauce.

One of the boxes was unoccupied. He took possession of it and hailed a young man in a black coat, who nodded, muttering some incomprehensible words. While the table was being laid, Des Esseintes examined his neighbours. It was the same as at the Bodega; a crowd of islanders with china blue eyes, crimson faces and pompous, supercilious looks, were skimming through foreign newspapers. There were some women amongst the rest, unaccompanied by male escort, dining by themselves,—sturdy English dames with boys' faces, teeth as big as tombstones, fresh, apple-red cheeks, long hands and feet. They were attacking with unfeigned enthusiasm a rumpsteak pie,—meat served hot in mushroom sauce and covered with a crust like a fruit tart.

After his long loss of appetite, he looked on in amazement at these sturdy trencherwomen, whose voracity whetted his own hunger. He ordered a plate of oxtail, a soup that is at once unctuous and tasty, fat and satisfying; then he scrutinized the list of fish, asked for a smoked haddock, which struck him as worthy of all praise, and seized with a rabid fit of appetite at the sight of other people stuffing themselves, he ate a great helping of roast beef and boiled potatoes and absorbed a couple of pints of ale, his palate tickled by the little musky, cow-like smack of this fine, light-coloured beer.

His hunger was nearly satisfied. He nibbled a bit of blue Stilton, a sweet cheese with an underlying touch of bitter, pecked at a rhubarb tart, and then, to vary the monotony, quenched his thirst with porter, that British black beer which tastes of liquorice juice from which the sugar had been extracted.

He drew a deep breath; for years he had not guzzled and swilled so much. The change of habits, the choice of unexpected and satisfying viands had roused the stomach from its lethargy. He sat back in his chair, lit a cigarette and prepared to enjoy his cup of coffee, which he laced with gin.

The rain was still falling steadily; he could hear it rattling on the glass skylight that roofed the far end of the room and running in torrents along the gutters. Nobody stirred a finger; all were dozing; comfortable like himself with liqueur glasses before them.

Presently tongues were lossened; as nearly everyone looked up in the air in talking, Des Esseintes concluded that these Englishmen were all discussing the weather. No one ever laughed, and all were dressed in suits of grey cheviot with nankin-yellow and blotting-paper red stripes. He cast a look of delight at his own clothes, the colour and cut of which did not sensibly differ from those of the people round him, highly pleased to find himself not out of tone with his surroundings, glad to be, in a kind of superficial way, a naturalized citizen of London. Then he gave a start,—"but what of the train time?" he asked himself. He consulted his watch,—ten minutes to eight; he had still nearly half-an-hour to stay there, he told himself, and once more he fell to thinking over the plan he had framed.

In the course of his sedentary life two countries only had tempted him to visit them, Holland and England.

He had fulfilled the first of these two wishes; attracted beyond his power to resist, he had left Paris one fine day and inspected the cities of the Low Countries one by one.

The general result of the journey was a series of bitter disappointments. He had pictured to himself a Holland after the pattern of Teniers' pictures and Jan Steen's, Rembrandt's and Ostade's, fashioning beforehand for his own particular use and pleasure Jewries as richly sun-browned as pieces of Cordova leather, imagining prodigal *kermesses*, everlasting junketings in the country, expecting to see all that patriarchal goodfellowship, that riotous joviality limned by the old masters.

No doubt Haarlem and Amsterdam had fascinated him; the common folk, seen in their unpolished state and in true rustic surroundings were very much as Van Ostade had painted them with their unlicked cubs of children and their old gossips as fat as butter, big-bosomed and huge-bellied. But of reckless merrymakings and general carousings not a sign. As a matter of fact, he found himself forced to admit that the Dutch School as represented in the Louvre had led him astray; it had merely supplied him with a spring-board, as it were, to start him off on his fancies; from it he had leapt off on a false trail and wandered away into an impossible dreamland, never to discover anywhere in this world the land of faery he had hoped to find real; nowhere to see peasants and peasant-maidens dancing on the greensward littered with wine-casks, crying with sheer happiness, shouting with joy, relieving themselves under stress of uncontrollable laughter in their petticoats and their trunks!

No, decidedly, nothing of the sort was to be seen; Holland was a country like any other, and to boot, a country by no means simple and primitive, by no means specially genial, for the Protestant faith was rampant there with its stern hypocrisies and solemn scruples.

This past disillusionment recurred to his memory; again he consulted his watch,—there was then some minutes more before his train left. "It is high time to ask for my bill and be going," he muttered to himself. He felt an extreme heaviness of stomach and an overpowering general lethargy. "Come now, he exclaimed, by way of screwing up his courage, "let's drink the stirrup cup,"—and he poured himself out a glass of brandy, while waiting for his account. An individual in a black coat, a napkin under one arm, a sort of major-domo, with a pointed head very bald, a harsh beard turning grey and a shaved upper lip, came forward, a pencil behind his ear, took up a position, one leg thrown forward like a singer on the platform, drew a paper-book from his pocket, and fixing his eyes on the ceiling without once looking at his writing, scribbled out the items and added up the total. "Here you are, sir," he said, tearing out the leaf from his book and handing it to Des Esseintes, who examined it curiously, as if it had been some strange animal. "What an extraordinary specimen, this John Bull," he thought, as he gazed at this phlegmatic personage whose clean-shaven lips gave him a vague resemblance to a helmsman of the American mercantile marine.

At that moment, the door into the street opened, and a number of people came in, bringing with them a stench of drowned dog mingled with a smell of cooking which the wind beat back into the kitchen as the unlatched door banged to and fro. Des Esseintes could not stir a limb; a soothing, enervating lassitude, was creeping through every member, rendering him incapable of so much as lifting his hand to light a cigar. He kept telling himself: "Come, come now, get up, we must be off"; but instantly objections occurred to him in contravention of these orders. What was the good of moving, when a man can travel so gloriously sitting in a chair? Was he not in London, whose odours and atmosphere, whose denizens and viands and table furniture were all about him? What could he expect, if he really went there, save fresh disappointments, the same as in Holland?

He had only just time enough left now to hurry to the station, and a mighty aversion for the journey, an imperious desire to stay quiet, came over him with a force that grew momentarily more and more powerful and peremptory. He sat dreaming and let the minutes slip by, thus cutting off his retreat, telling himself: "Now I should have to dash up to the barriers,, hustle with the luggage; how tiresome, what a nuisance that would be!"—Then, harking back, he told himself over again: "After all, I have felt and seen what I wanted to feel and see. I have been steeped in English life ever since I left home; it would be a fool's trick to go and lose these imperishable impressions by a clumsy change of locality. Why, surely I must be out of my senses to have tried thus to repudiate my old settled convictions, to have condemned the obedient figment of my imagination, to have believed like the veriest ninny in the necessity, the interest, the advantage of a trip abroad?—There," he concluded, glancing at his watch, "the time is ripe to go back home again." And this time he did get to his feet, left the tavern and ordered the cabman to take him back to the Gare de Sceaux; thence he returned with his trunks, his packages, his portmanteaux, his rugs, his umbrellas and walking-sticks to Fontenay, feeling all the physical exhaustion and moral fatigue of a man restored to the domestic hearth after long and perilous journeyings.

Chapter Twelve

During the days that followed his return home Des Esseintes occupied himself in reviewing the books of his library, drawing from the thought that he might have been parted from them for a long period as genuine a satisfaction as he would have enjoyed if he had really been coming back to them after a serious absence. Under the stimulus of this feeling, the volumes appeared to him in a new light altogether, for he found beauties in them he had quite forgotten ever since the day he first purchased them.

Everything: books, bric-à-brac, furniture, acquired a peculiar charm in his eyes. His bed struck him as more downy, in comparison with the pallet he would have occupied in London; the discreet, silent bearing of his domestics enchanted him, harassed as he was to think of the noisy loquacity of hotel waiters; the methodical organization of his daily life seemed more than ever desirable, since the haphazard of travelling had become a possibility.

He plunged himself again in the bath of fixed habits to which artificial regrets added a more bracing and tonic quality.

But it was his books that chiefly attracted his interest. He examined them, arranged them afresh on the shelves, looking to see whether, since his coming to Fontenay, the heat and wet had not injured their bindings or foxed their costly papers.

He began by turning over all his Latin library, after which he re-marshalled the special works of Archelaüs, Albertus Magnus, Raymond Lully and Arnaud de Villanova treating of the kabbala and the occult sciences; lastly he verified, one by one, his modern books and was delighted to find they were all intact, dry and in good condition.

This collection had cost him considerable sums of money; the fact is that he could not endure to see the authors he specially cherished printed, like those in other people's libraries, on rag paper, wearing hob-nailed shoes like a clumsy peasant's.

In former days at Paris, he had certain volumes specially set up for him and printed off by specially hired workmen on hand-presses. Sometimes he would go to Perrin of Lyons, whose slim, clear types were suitable for archaic re-impressions of old tracts; sometimes he would send to England or the States, for new characters to print works of the present century; sometimes he would apply to a house at Lille which had for hundreds of years possessed a complete font of Gothic letters; sometimes again he would call in the help of the long-established Enschedé press, of Haarlem, whose type-foundry preserves the stamps and matrices of the so-called "letters of civility."

He had followed the same course for his papers. Wearying one fine day of the ordinary papers de luxe,—the silvery Chinese, the pearly golden Japanese, the white Whatmans, the brown Dutch, the Turkey-grains and Seychal-mills tinted to resemble chamois leather, and long ago disgusted with the machine-made articles, lie had commissioned a laid paper run in special moulds from the ancient paper-mills at Vire, where they still use the old-fashioned stamps formerly employed to break the hemp. Then, to introduce a little variety in his collection, he had at various times imported from London dressed fabrics—flock-papers, repp-papers—while to further accentuate his scorn of the bibliophiles, a Lübeck tradesman was making him a glorified candle-paper, bluish in tint, crackling and rather brittle, in the substance of which the straw-lines were replaced by gold spangles like those that glitter in Dantzig liqueur-brandy.

By such means, he had secured a unique library, always choosing unusual sizes and shapes of page. These treasures he had had clothed by Lortic, by Trautz Bauzonnet, by Chambolle, by the firm of Capé's Successors, in irreproachable bindings of antique silk, of stamped ox-leather, of Cape goat-skin, full bindings, panelled and mosaïced, with wavy or watered silk linings instead of end-papers, adorned like Church service-books with clasps and metal corners, sometimes even ornamented by Gruel-Engelmann in oxydized silver and transparent enamel.

On these lines, he had had printed in the admirable episcopal character of the ancient firm of Le Clere, a copy of Baudelaire in a large *format*, recalling that of a Missal, on a very light Japanese felt, spongy in texture, as soft as elder-pith and just faintly tinged with pink over its milky white. This edition, limited to a single copy and printed in a velvety India-ink black, had been clothed outside and covered within with a marvellous and authentic sow-skin, one picked out of a thousand, flesh colour all dotted with the bristle marks and decorated with a lacework in black executed with the cold iron, the designs miraculously assorted by a great artist.

To-day, Des Esseintes took down this incomparable volume from his shelves, and after fondling it reverently in his hands, re-read certain pieces, which in this simple but inimitable frame seemed to him more striking and significant than ever.

His admiration for the writer in question was limitless. To his mind, Literature had hitherto confined itself to exploring the mere surface of the soul or, at most, penetrating into such of its underground chambers as were readily accessible and well lighted, verifying here and there the stratification of the deadly sins, studying their seams and their origin, noting for instance with Balzac the geological formation of the soul possessed by the monomania of an overmastering passion,—by ambition, or avarice, or paternal infatuation, or senile love.

After all, it was entirely concerned with virtues and vices of a quite healthy and robust order, with the peaceable activity of brains of a perfectly ordinary conformation, with the practical reality of current ideas, with never a thought of morbid depravations, with no outlook beyond the pale of everyday; in a word, the speculations of these analysts of human nature stopped short at the ordinary classification of human acts by the Church into good and evil; it was all the simple investigation, the mere examination into normal conditions of a botanist who watches minutely the foreseen development of the everyday flora growing in common earth.

But Baudelaire had gone further; he had descended to the bottom of the inexhaustible mine, had pushed his way along abandoned or unexplored galleries, had penetrated those districts of the soul where the monstrous vegetations of the sick mind flourish.

There, near the confines where aberrations of the intellect and diseases of the will sojourn,—the mystic tetanus, the burning fever of wantonness, the typhoids and yellow fevers of crime, he had found, hatching in the gloomy forcing-house of Ennui, the appalling reaction of age on the feelings and ideas.

He had revealed the morbid psychology of the mind that has reached the October of its sensations, detailed the symptoms of souls challenged by grief, set apart by spleen; had demonstrated the ever incroaching caries of the impressions at a time when the enthusiasms and beliefs of youth are faded; when there remains only the barren memory of miseries endured, of tyrannies suffered, of vexations undergone, in intelligences crushed by an incongruous fortune.

He had traced all the phases of this lamentable Autumn, as he watched the human creature, quick to grow embittered, ingenious at self-deception, forcing his thoughts to cheat each other, all to render his suffering more acute, spoiling in advance, thanks to his powers of analysis and observation, all possibility of happiness.

Next, following on this sensitivenes, this irritability of soul, on this ferocity of bitter reflexion that repulses the importunate ardour of acts of devotion, the benevolent insults of charity, he saw arise little by little the horror of those passions of age, those loves of maturity, where one is still ready to comply while the other remains aloof and on guard, where lassitude claims of the pair filial caresses whose false juvenility seems a something new, or maternal fondlings whose gentleness is so restful and affords, as it were, the stimulating remorse of a vague sort of incest.

In magnificent pages he had exposed these hybrid loves, pages exasperated by their powerlessness to express the whole truth, these dangerous subterfuges of stupefying and poisonous drugs called upon to help soothe pain and conquer the weariness of the flesh. At a period when Literature was wont to attribute the grief of living exclusively to the mischances of disappointed love or the jealousy of adulterous deceptions, he had said not a word of these childish maladies, but had sounded those more incurable, more poignant and more profound: wounds that are inflicted by satiety, disillusion and contempt in ruined souls tortured by the present, disgusted with the past, terrified and desperate of the future.

And the more Des Esseintes re-read his Baudelaire, the more fully he recognized an indescribable charm in this writer, who, in days when verse had ceased to serve any purpose save to depict the external aspect of men and things, had succeeded in expressing the inexpressible, thanks to a sinewy and firm-bodied diction which, more than any other, possessed the wondrous power of defining with a strange sanity of phrase the most fleeting, the most evanescent of the morbid conditions of broken spirits and disheartened souls.

After Baudelaire, the number of French books that found a place on his shelves was very limited. He was assuredly insensible to the merits of those works which it is a mark of taste and cleverness to wax enthusiastic over. The side-shaking mirth of Rabelais, "the full-bodied *vis comica* of Molière" failed to rouse his sense of humor; indeed his antipathy towards these comicalities even went so far that he did not hesitate to liken them, from the point of view of art, to those rows of flaring sconces that contribute to the jollity of country fairs.

So far as older poets were concerned, his reading hardly went beyond Villon, whose mournful "ballades" touched him, and some stray morsels of D'Aubigné that stirred his blood by the incredible virulence of their apostrophes and anathemas.

In prose, he made small account of Voltaire and Rousseau, or even of Diderot, whose extravagantly lauded "Salons" struck him as being stuffed to a singular excess with moral twaddlings and nonsensical aspirations. Detesting all this balderdash, he confined his reading almost entirely to the masterpieces of Christian eloquence, to Bourdaloue and Bossuet, whose sonorous and elaborate periods impressed him; but, for choicer preference, he savoured those pithy aphorisms condensed in stern, strong phrases of the sort Nicole wrought, in his meditations, and still more Pascal, whose austere pessimism and agonizing sense of sin stirred him to the bottom of his heart.

Apart from these few books, French literature, so far as his library was concerned, began with the present century.

It was classified into two groups, one comprising the ordinary, profane writers, the other the Catholic authors,—a special literature, almost unknown to the generality, albeit disseminated by long established and enormous bookselling firms to the four corners of the world.

He had had the courage to wander in these hidden places, and, the same as in secular literature, he had discovered, underneath a gigantic mass of insipidities, some works written by true masters.

The distinctive characteristic of this literature was the persistency, the unchangeableness of its ideas and diction; just as the Church has perpetuated the primordial shape and form of sacred objects, in the same way has she kept intact the relics of her dogmas and piously preserved the reliquary that enshrined them,—the oratorical phraseology of the *Grand Siècle*. As one of its own exponents even, Ozanam to wit, declared, the Christian style had nothing to learn from the language of Rousseau; its duty was to employ exclusively the dialect made use of by Bourdaloue and by Bossuet.

Despite this dictum, the Church, more tolerant than her disciple, winked at sundry expressions, sundry turns of phrase, borrowed from the lay speech of the same century, and the Catholic idiom had to some extent shaken itself free of its ponderous periods, weighed down, especially in Bossuet, by the length of its parentheses and the painful redundancy of its pronouns. But there the concessions had stopped; indeed. others would no doubt have been unavailing, for so lightened, this prose was adequate for the limited number of subjects which the Church condemned herself to treat.

Incapable of dealing with contemporary life, of making visible and palpable the simplest aspect of men and things, ill adapted to explain the complex ruses of a brain indifferent to the state of grace, this diction nevertheless excelled in the treatment of abstract subjects. Useful in the discussion of a controversy, in the demonstration of a theory, in the uncertainties of a commentary, it possessed more than any other the authority needful to lay down, without discussion, the value of a doctrine.

Unfortunately, there as everywhere, an innumerable army of pedants had invaded the sanctuary and degraded by their ignorance and want of talent its stern and uncompromising dignity. Then, to crown the calamity, pious ladies had taken up the pen, and ill-advised sacristies and rash drawing-rooms had extolled as veritable works of genius the wretched prattlings of these females.

Among other works of this sort that stirred his curiosity, Des Esseintes had read those of Madame Swetchine, the Russian General Officer's wife whose house at Paris was the rendezvous of the most fervent Catholics. They had filled him with an inexhaustible and overpowering sense of weariness; they were worse than bad, they were trivial; the whole thing suggested an echo hanging about a little chapel wherein a crowded congregation of bigoted, narrow-minded people knelt muttering prayers, asking after each others' news in whispers, repeating with looks of profound mystery a string of commonplaces on politics, the state of the barometer, the condition of the weather at the moment.

But there was a lower depth; there was Madame Augustus Craven, an accredited laureate of the *Institut*, the author of the "Récit d'une

Sœur," of "Eliane," of "Fleurange," applauded with blaring trumpets and rolling organ by the whole Catholic press. Never, no never, had Des Esseintes imagined that anyone could write such poor stuff. The books were, from the point of view of general conception, so utterly silly and were written in so nauseous a style, that they actually attained a sort of individuality of their own, became curiosities in their way.

In any case, it was not among female writers that Des Esseintes, whose mind was naturally sophisticated and unsentimental, could find a literary refuge adapted to his peculiar idiosyncrasies.

Still he persevered and with a conscientiousness no impatience could modify, did his best to appreciate the work of that child of genius, the blue-stocking Virgin of this group, Eugénie de Guérin. His efforts were in vain, he could not stomach the famous "Journal" and "Letters" in which she extols, without tact or discretion, the prodigious talents of a brother who rhymed with such consummate ingenuity and grace that we must surely go back to the works of M. de Jouy and M. Ecouchard Lebrun to find any verses so boldly conceived and so fresh and new.

To no purpose had he tried to understand the charm of these productions in which we find such thrilling remarks as these:—"This morning I hung up beside papa's bed a cross a little girl gave him yesterday,"—"We are invited tomorrow, Mimi and I, to M. Roquiers', to attend the service of blessing a bell; I am very pleased to go,"—in which are recorded such momentous events as this: "I have just hung about my neck a medal of the Blessed Virgin, sent me by Louise as a safeguard against cholera,"—in which we come upon poetry of this calibre: "Oh, the lovely moonbeam that has just fallen on the Gospel I was reading!" or, to make an end, observations of the brilliant perspicacity of the following: "Whenever I see a man, on passing a crucifix, cross himself and take off his hat, I tell myself—That is a Christian going by."

This was the sort of thing that runs on page after page, without truce or respite, till the death of Maurice de Guérin, whom his sister bewails in still more rhapsodies, written in a wishy-washy prose interspersed here and there with tags of verse the poverty of which ended by moving Des Esseintes' pity.

Well, there was no denying it, the Catholic party was not hard to please in its choice of protégées, and far from critical! These pious muses it had made so much of and for whom it had exhausted the complaisance of its press, wrote one and all like Convent schoolgirls, in a colourless diction, in a flux of words no astringent can arrest!

The end was Des Esseintes turned away in horror from the stuff. But neither were the modern masters of sacred literature of a nature to offer him any sufficient compensations for his disappointment. These preachers and polemists were impeccable and correct in style, but the

Christian dialect, in their sermons and books, had ended by becoming impersonal, stereotyped in a rhetoric whose movements and pauses were all fixed beforehand, arranged in a series of periods each constructed on one and the same model. In fact, the ecclesiastical authors all wrote alike, with a trifle more or a trifle less unconstraint and emphasis; the differences were all but imperceptible among these grey, colourless canvases, whether the work of Messeigneurs Dupanloup or Landriot, La Bouillerie or Gaume, of Dom Guéranger or the Père Ratisbonne, of Monseigneur Freppel or Monseigneur Perraud, of the Réverends Pères Ravignan or Gratry, the Jesuit Olivain, the Carmelite Dosithée, the Dominican Didon or of the erstwhile Prior of Saint-Maximin, the Réverend Chocarne.

Again and again, the conclusion had been forced upon Des Esseintes that it would need a very authentic talent, a very genuine originality, a firmly anchored conviction to thaw this frozen diction, to give life to this conventional style incapable of expressing a single unexpected idea, of upholding any thesis of the smallest audacity.

Nevertheless, one or two authors were to be found whose burning eloquence could melt and mould this inert phraseology,—Lacordaire first and foremost, one of the only real authors the Church has produced for many years.

Imprisoned, like all his colleagues, within the narrow circle of orthodox speculation, obliged, like them, to mark time and refrain from touching any ideas but such as had been originated and consecrated by the Fathers of the Church and developed by the masters of the pulpit, he yet managed to turn the obstacle, to rejuvenate, almost to modify, these time-honoured commonplaces by throwing them into a more personal and more living form.

Scattered up and down his *Conférences de Notre-Dame*, happy phrases, bold expressions, accents of loving-kindness, outbursts of enthusiasm, cries of gladness, ecstatic outpourings of spirit occurred that made the age-old style smoke under his pen. Then, over and above his talent as an orator,—and he was a true orator, this capable gentle-hearted monk whose intellect and industry were exhausted in the hopeless effort to conciliate the liberal doctrines of an advanced society with the authoritative dogmas of the Church, he was further endowed with a temperament of fervent charity, of diplomatic tenderness.

Then, again, the letters he used to write to young men often contained the loving words of a father exorting his sons,—smiling reprimands, indulgent expressions of forgiveness. Some were charming where he would avow all his greed for affection, others almost impressively serious when he was sustaining his correspondents' courage or dissipating their doubts by the statement of the irrefragable certainties of his own Faith. In a word, this feeling of fatherhood, which under his pen assumed a dainty, feminine touch, impressed on his prose an accent unique amid all the mass of clerical literature.

After him, very few were the ecclesiastics and monks who showed any individuality. At most, some pages of his pupil the Abbé Peyreyve were readable. He had left touching biographical notices of his master, written some amiable letters, composed articles conceived in the sonorous language of the pulpit, pronounced panegyrics in which the declamatory note is too dominant. Undoubtedly, the Abbé Peyreyve had neither the tenderness nor the fire of Lacordaire. He was too much a priest and too little a man; here and there nevertheless his rhetoric as a preacher was illuminated by telling analogies, broad and weighty phrases, purple patches rising almost to sublimity.

But it was only among writers who had not submitted to Ordination, among secular authors attached to the interests of Catholicism and devoted to its propaganda, that a prose style was to be found worthy to arrest the attention.

The episcopal diction, so feebly handled by our Prelates, had acquired new strength, regained something of masculine force and vigour in the hands of the Comte de Falloux. Under an appearance of moderation, this Academician distilled gall; his discourses pronounced in 1848 in Parliament were diffuse and dull, but his articles contributed to the *Correspondant*, and afterwards collected in book form, were biting and bitter under the exaggerated courtesy of their outward expression. Conceived as set speeches, they displayed a certain caustic wit, while they startled by the intolerance of their convictions.

Dangerous as a controversialist by reason of the pitfalls he dug for his adversaries and the crookedness of his logic, forever turning the enemy's flank and striking an unexpected blow, the Comte de Falloux had also written some striking pages on the death of Madame Swetchine, whose remains he had edited and whom he revered as a Saint.

But where this author's temperament really showed itself was in two pamphlets which appeared one in 1846 and the other in 1880, the latter entitled *l'Unite nationale* ("National Unity").

Filled with a cold fury, this implacable Legitimist delivered for once, contrary to his custom, a frontal attack, and by way of peroration hurled at the sceptics' heads this thunder of savage invective:—

"And you, Utopians of a system, who make an abstraction of human nature, panegyrists of atheism, nourished on hallucinations and detestations, emancipators of woman, destroyers of the family, genealogists of the simian race, you, whose name was once insult enough, be well content; you will have been the prophets and your disciples will be the high-priests of an abominable future!"

The other pamphlet bore for title: *le Parti catholique* ("The Catholic Party") and was directed against the despotism of the *Univers* and its editor Veuillot, whose name it refused to utter. Here the flank attacks were resumed, poison lurked under every line of the little book in which the gentleman, bruised and battered, answered with scornful sarcasms the brutal blows of the professional bully.

Between them they represented the two parties in the Church whose differences degenerate into ungovernable hatred. De Falloux, at once more arrogant and more crafty than his opponents, belonged to that liberal coterie which already embraced both Montalembert and Cochin, both Lacordaire and de Broglie; he adhered heart and soul to the principles advocated by the *Correspondant*, a review which strove to overlay with a varnish of tolerance the peremptory theories of the Church. Veuillot, more outspoken and frank, threw off the mask, avowed unhesitatingly the tyranny of ultramontane aspirations, openly admitted and loudly acclaimed the pitiless yoke of her dogmas.

The latter champion had forged himself for the struggle a special language, borrowed part from La Bruyère and part from the bully of the Gros-Caillou. This style, half pompous, half familiar, wielded by this brutal personality, had the crushing weight of a bludgeon. Extraordinarily stubborn and extraordinarily courageous, he had felled with this terrible weapon free-thinkers and bishops alike, hitting out might and main, rushing like a wild bull at his foes to whichever party they belonged. Distrusted by the Church, which approved neither his contraband diction nor his blackguard attitude, this religious mountebank had nevertheless made his mark by his undoubted talents, bringing about his heels the whole pack of the press, which he lashed till the blood came in his *Odeurs de Paris*, keeping at bay every assault, kicking off the whole base horde of low quill-drivers that tried to bite his calves.

Unfortunately, his incontestable talents only showed in a fight; in cold blood Veuillot was but an indifferent writer. His poetry and novels only inspired pity; his peppery invective lost its pungency when blows were no longer flying; the Catholic warrior was metamorphosed, in peaceful days, into a dyspeptic wheezing out trite litanies and stammering puerile canticles.

More narrow, more limited, more serious was the cherished apologist of the Church, the inquisitor of Christian diction, Ozanam. Difficult though he was to apprehend, Des Esseintes could not fail to be astonished by the aplomb of this author who would prate of the inscrutable purposes of God when he should have been adducing the proofs of the impossible assertions he was making; with the most perfect coolness he would travesty events, deny, more impudently still than the panegyrists of the other parties, the acknowledged facts of history, declare that the Church had never hidden the high esteem in which it held Science, describe heresies as foul miasmas, treat Buddhism and all other religions with such fine scorn that he excused himself from sullying Catholic prose by so much as an attack upon their doctrines.

There were occasions when religious passion breathed a certain ardour into his oratorical periods, beneath the ice of which boiled an undercurrent of suppressed violence; in his numerous writings on Dante, on St. Francis, on the author of the "Stabat," on the Franciscan poets, on Socialism, on Commercial Law, on everything, the man never failed to plead the defence of the Vatican which he deemed impeccable, judging all cases alike according as they approached more or less close or differed more or less widely from his own.

The same manner of looking at all questions from one point of view and one only equally belonged to that paltry scribbler whom some people held up as his rival, Nettement. The latter was less straitlaced and made less exalted and more worldly pretensions. He had repeatedly trespassed beyond the literary cloister in which Ozanam was a voluntary prisoner, and had dipped into profane writings with a view to appraising them. This region, indeed, he had penetrated groping, like a child in a cave, seeing nothing but darkness round him, perceiving in the general blackness only the flicker of the taper that lighted him onwards, throwing its glimmer a few feet ahead.

In this ignorance of the localities, in this obscurity, he had blundered at every step. Speaking of Mürger, he described him as "heedful of a polished and carefully finished style"; Victor Hugo was one who searched out the impure and filthy and he dared to compare N. de Laprade with him; Delacroix disdained all rules, while Paul Delaroche and the poet Reboul he extolled because they seemed to him to possess faith.

Des Esseintes could not help a shrug of the shoulders at these unfortunate criticisms, which were expressed in a laboured prose, the material of which, already worn threadbare, caught and tore on every corner of his sentences.

In another class, the productions of Poujoulat and Genoude, Montalembert, Nicolas and Carné failed to inspire him with any much more vivid interest; nor were his inclinations for History treated with painstaking erudition and in dignified language by the Duc de Broglie, nor his predilections for social and religious questions discussed by Henry Cochin, who had, however, revealed his true sentiments in a letter wherein he recounted a heart-stirring assumption of the veil at the Sacré-Cœur, very much more pronounced. For years, he had not looked into these books, and it was now a far-off day when he had thrown away as waste paper the puerile lucubrations of the dismal Pontmartin and pitiable Féval, and handed over to the servants for household purposes the little histories of Aubineau and Lesserre, those feeble hagiographers of the miracles wrought by M. Dupont de Tours and the Virgin.

In a word, Des Esseintes failed to extract from this literature even a

passing distraction to his boredom; so he pushed away into the remote
corners of his library this mass of volumes which he had studied in
former days after leaving the Jesuits' seminary,—"I should have done
better to leave them behind in Paris," he muttered, as he drew out from
their lurking-place behind the rest two sets of books he found
particularly unendurable, the works of the Abbé Lamennais and those
of that unmitigated fanatic, so supremely, so pompously tiresome and
futile, Count Joseph de Maistre.

A single volume only was left still in place on a shelf within reach
of the hand, that entitled *l'Homme*, by Ernest Hello.

This writer was the absolute antithesis of his brethren in religion.
Almost isolated in the pious group which was shocked by his ways of
thought, Ernest Hello had ended by abandoning the great main road
that leads from earth to heaven.

Sickened no doubt by the triteness of this highway and the throng
of pilgrims of letters that had for centuries filed obediently along the
same track, walking each in the foot-marks of his predecessor, stopping
at the same halting-places, to exchange the same commonplaces on
Religion, on the Fathers of the Church, on their identical beliefs, on
their identical masters, he had diverged along by-paths, had come out
into the gloomy forest clearing of Pascal, where he had tarried a long
while to recover his wind; then he had pursued his journey and
penetrated further into Jansenism, which all the time he abused, in the
regions of human thought.

Full of subtlety and preciosity, erudite and elaborate, Hello with
his hair-splitting minutiae of analysis reminded Des Esseintes of the
laboured and meticulous studies of some of the psychological sceptics
of the last and present centuries. There was in him a kind of Catholic
Duranty, but more dogmatic and more astute, a practised master of the
microscope, a trained engineer of the soul, a skilful watchmaker of the
brain, delighting to examine the mechanism of a passion and explain
minutely every wheel of the machinery.

In this oddly constituted mind were to be found associations of
thought, analogies and contrasts scarcely to have been expected; added
to which, a curious trick whereby he made the etymology of the words
he used a spring-board for leaping off to fresh ideas, the combination of
which was often trivial enough, but almost invariably ingenious and
stimulating.

In this way, and in spite of the faulty equilibrium of his
constructions, he had taken to pieces, so to speak, with remarkable
perspicacity *The Miser, The Mediocre Man*, analysed "Popular Taste,"
"The Passion of Calamity," besides revealing the interesting
comparisons that can be established between the processes of
photography and those of memory.

But this adroitness in wielding this perfected weapon of analysis which he had stolen from the Church's enemies represented only one of the sides of the man's temperament.

Yet another being existed in him; his mind had a double aspect, and after the good side appeared the bad,—that of a religious fanatic and a Biblical prophet.

Like Hugo himself, whose contortions both of thought and phrase he recalled, Ernest Hello had loved to pose as a little St. John on Patmos to play the pontiff and enact the oracle from the top of a rock manufactured in the sacred image shops of the Rue Saint-Sulpice, haranguing the reader in an apocalyptic tongue salted here and there with the gall of an Isaiah.

He affected at that time exaggerated pretensions to profundity; some flatterers even hailed him as a genius, pretended to regard him as the great man of his day, the well of knowledge of his epoch,—a well perhaps, but one where you could very often not see one drop of water.

In his volume *Paroles de Dieu* ("Words of God"), in which he paraphrased the Scriptures and did his best to complicate their meaning when fairly obvious; in another book of his entitled *l'Homme*; in his pamphlet *le Jour du Seigneur* ("The Day of the Lord"), composed in a Biblical style, broken and obscure, he showed the qualities of a vindictive, haughty apostle, full of gall and bitterness; he revealed himself in the character of a crack-brained deacon, half mystic, half epileptic, of a De Maistre for once endowed with talent, of a harsh and ferocious sectary.

At the same time, reflected Des Esseintes, this morbid excess of zeal barred the way to inventive sallies of casuistry; with more intolerance than Ozanam, he repudiated absolutely whatever did not pertain to his own narrow world, announced the most amazing axioms, maintained with a disconcerting air of authority that "Geology had gone back to Moses," that Natural History, Chemistry, all contemporary Science was by way of verifying the scientific accuracy of the Bible; every page was full of the "sole and only Verity," "the superhuman wisdom of the Church," the whole interspersed with aphorisms more than dangerous, and savage imprecations poured out in foul torrents on the art and literature of the last century.

To this strange alloy was superadded a love of pious studies—translations of the *Visions* of Angèle de Foligno, a book of an unparalleled fluidity and folly; and of selected portions from Ruysbroek l'Admirable, a mystic of the thirteenth century, whose prose presents an incomprehensible but fascinating combination of gloomy ecstasies, outpourings of unction, transports of bitterness.

All this attitude of the overbearing high-priest, which was characteristic of Hello, had come out in full force in an astounding Preface he wrote for this book. It is his own remark that "extraordinary things can only be told in stammers," and he stammered accordingly, declaring that "the holy obscurity wherein Ruysbroek spreads his eagle's wings is his ocean, his prey, his glory, and the four horizons would be for him a garment all too narrow."

Let him be what he would, Des Esseintes felt himself attracted by this ill-balanced, but subtle mind; to complete the fusion between the adroit psychologist on the one hand and the pious pedant on the other, had proved impossible, and these jolts, these incoherences even constituted the personality of the man.

Recruits to his standard were certain other writers forming little bands that operated as skirmishers on the outskirts of the Clerical camp. They did not belong to the main body, but were, properly speaking, rather the scouts of a Religion that distrusted men of talent like Veuillot and Hello, whom it deemed too independent and not colourless enough. What it really wanted was soldiers who never reasoned, regiments of the purblind, mediocre sort of men whom Hello stigmatized with the indignation of one who had endured their yoke. Accordingly, Catholicism had made all haste to expel from the columns of its organs one of its own partisans, Leon Bloy, a savage pamphleteer, who wrote a style at once furious and artificial, coquettish and uncultivated, and had turned out of doors at its official bookshops, as one plague-stricken and unclean, another author who had yet bawled himself hoarse in celebrating its praises: Barbey d'Aurévilly.

Truth to tell, he was too compromising an ally, and too indocile a disciple. The rest would always in the long run bow the head under rebuke and fall back into line; he was the incorrigible urchin" the party could not recognize; he was a literary runagate after the girls, whom he brought bare-bosomed into the very sanctuary.

It was only due to that huge scorn with which Catholicism looks down on talent that an excommunication in due and proper form had not outlawed this strange servant who, under pretext of doing honour to his masters, was for breaking the church windows, mountebanking with the sacred vessels, executing fancy dances round the tabernacle.

Two works in particular of Barbey d'Aurévilly's fired Des Esseintes' imagination: the *Prêtre marié* ("Married Priest") and the *Diabolique*. Others, such as *l'Ensorcelé* ("The Bewitched"), the *Chevalier des Touches, Une vieille Maîtresse* ("An Old Mistress"), were no doubt better balanced and more complete works, but they appealed less warmly to Des Esseintes, who was genuinely interested only in sickly books with health undermined and exasperated by fever.

In these comparatively sane volumes Barbey d'Aurévilly was perpetually tacking to and fro between those two channels of Catholicism which eventually run into one,—mysticism and Sadism.

But in these two books which Des Esseintes was now turning over, Barbey had abandoned all prudence, had given the rein to his steed, had dashed off whip and spur along the roads he had then traversed to their extremest limits.

All the mysterious horror of the Middle Ages hovered over that improbable book the *Prêtre marié*; magic was mixed up with religion, gibberish with prayer, and more pitiless, more cruel than the Devil, the God of original sin tortured without respite or remorse the innocent Calixte, the victim of His abhorrence, branding her with a red cross on the brow, as of old He had had one of his angels mark the houses of unbelievers whom he was fain to slay.

Conceived by a fasting monk run delirious, these scenes succeeded one another in the broken language of a fever patient. But, unfortunately, among these creations as fantastic as the Coppélias galvanized into life by Hoffmann, there were some, the Néel de Néhou for example, that seemed to have been imagined in one of those periods of exhaustion that follow a crisis and were quite out of keeping amid these tales of gloom and madness, into which they imported the comic element that moves our involuntary mirth at sight of the little tin mannikin that plays the horn, in hunting boots, on the top of a mantelpiece clock.

Succeeding to these mystical divagations, the author had a period of comparative calm; then a terrible relapse followed.

The belief that man is a Buridan's ass, a being dragged this way and that by two forces of equal strength, which fight, turn and turn about victorious and vanquished, for his soul, the conviction that human life is no better than a doubtful struggle between hell and heaven, the faith in two opposed entities, Satan and the Christ, were bound fatally and inevitably to engender those inward discords where the soul, stimulated by an incessant combat, excited in a sort by promises and threats, ends by giving up the effort to resist and prostitutes itself to whichever of the two factions had been most obstinate in its pursuit.

In the *Prêtre marié*, the praises of the Christ, whose temptations had been successful, were sung by Barbey d'Aurévilly; in the *Diaboliques*, the author had surrendered to the Devil whom he then extolled. And then came the apparition of Sadism, that bastard birth of Catholicism, which Faith has for centuries, under all its shapes, pursued with its exorcisms and its fires.

This condition of mind, so strange and so ill-defined, cannot in fact arise in the soul of an unbeliever. It does not consist solely in a mad riot amid the excesses of the flesh, further stimulated by bloody outrages of cruelty, for in that case it would be merely an aberration of the sexual feelings, an instance of satyriasis arrived at its point of supreme maturity; it consists primarily and particularly in a course of sacrilegious acts, in a moral revolt, in a spiritual debauch, in an aberration purely ideal, purely Christian. Another essential characteristic is a joy tempered by fear, analogous to the naughty pleasure of disobedient children who insist on playing with forbidden articles for no other reason than because their parents have expressly forbidden them to go near them.

In truth, if it did not involve a sacrilege, Sadism would have no *raison d'être* on the other hand, sacrilege, which flows from the very existence of a religion, cannot be intentionally and effectively committed save by a believer, for a man would experience no satisfaction from profaning a faith that he did not believe in, or knew nothing of.

The force of Sadism then, the attraction it offers, lies wholly in the forbidden pleasure of transferring to Satan the homages and prayers we owe to God; it lies then in the non-observance of the Catholic precepts which we are actually respecting, though in an inverse sense, when we commit, in order the more scornfully to mock the Christ, the sins he had most expressly banned,—pollution of holy things and carnal orgies.

In reality, the vice to which the Marquis de Sade has given his name was as old as the Church herself; it had been rampant in the eighteenth century, reintroducing, to go back no farther, by a mere phenomenon of atavism, the impious practices of the mediæval Witches' Sabbath.

By simply consulting the *Malleus Maleficorum*, Jacob Sprenger's terrible code of justice, which permitted the Church to exterminate by the fires of the stake thousands of necromancers and sorcerers, Des Esseintes was enabled to recognize in the ancient Sabbath all the obscene practices and all the blasphemies of Sadism. Over and above the unclean orgies dear to the Evil One, nights consecrated successively to lawful and unnatural coition, nights befouled by the bloody bestialities of ruttish animals, he found repeated the same parodies of Church processions, the same standing insults and defiances against God, the same ceremonies of devotion to his Rival, when was celebrated, with curses in lieu of blessings on the bread and wine, the Black Mass on the back of a woman crouching on all fours, whose rump, naked and polluted again and again; served for altar table, and the congregation communicated, in derision, with a black host on the face of which a figure of a he-goat was impressed.

The very same debauch of foul-mouthed raillery and degrading insults was to be seen in the Marquis de Sade, who added to his cruel and abominable sensualities the spice of sacrilegious profanities.

He defied Heaven, made invocation to Lucifer, called God a contemptible scoundrel, an idiot, an imbecile, spat on the communion, did all he could to degrade with vile obscenities a Deity he hoped would damn him, while declaring, the better to defy Him, that he had no existence.

This condition of soul Barbey d'Aurévilly came very near sharing.

If he did not go as far as De Sade in uttering atrocious maledictions against the Saviour; if, more prudent or more timid, he always made a profession of honouring the Church, he none the less, as they did in the Middle Ages, addressed his pleadings to the Devil and fell, like the rest, by way of defying God, into demoniac erotomania, contriving sensual monstrosities of vice; borrowing even from the *Philosophie dans le Boudoir* a certain episode, which he seasoned with new condiments, when he wrote the tale: le *Dîner d'un athée* ("An Atheist's Dinner-Party").

This extraordinary book was Des Esseintes' delight; he had printed for him in violet ink, Bishop's violet, within a border of Cardinal purple, on an authentic parchment which the Church officials had blessed, a copy of the *Diaboliques* set up in "letters of civility," whose outlandish serifs and flourishes, twisted into horns and hoofs, affect a Satanic contour.

After certain pieces of Baudelaire's which, in imitations of the psalms chanted on the nights of the Witches' Sabbath, took the form of infernal Litanies, this volume was among all the works of contemporary apostolic literature the only one that bore witness to that condition of soul at once pious and impious, towards which the remembered claims of Catholicism, stimulated by the attacks of nervous disorder, had often urged Des Esseintes.

With Barbey d'Aurévilly, the series of religious writers came to an end. To tell the truth, this pariah belonged more, from every point of view, to secular literature than to the other in which he was for claiming a place that was denied him. His language, characterized by a romanticism run wild, crammed with contorted expressions, unusual turns of phrase, extravagant similes, whipped up his sentences which tore along with roar and rattle and clang of noise of bells from top to bottom of the page. In a word, d'Aurévilly appeared like a full-blooded stallion among the geldings that people the Ultramontane stables.

Such were Des Esseintes' reflexions as he re-read passages chosen at random from the book and compared its nervous and varied style with the lymphatic, stereotyped diction of his fellows, thinking at the same time of the evolution of language so rightly insisted on by Darwin.

Associating with the profane, educated in the romantic school, familiar with the new literature, accustomed to the business of modern publications, Barbey found himself inevitably in possession of a dialect which had undergone many and profound modifications, which had been changed and renovated, since the days of the *Grand Siècle*.

Very different had been the case with the ecclesiastical writers; confined to their own domain, imprisoned within an ancient and identical range of reading, knowing nothing of the literary movements of the centuries and firmly determined, if need be, to tear out their eyes rather than see, they necessarily employed a language incapable of change, like that speech of the eighteenth century which the descendants of the French settlers in Canada still speak and write as their mother tongue, without any selection of phraseology or words having ever been possible in their idiom, isolated as it is from the ancient metropolis and surrounded on all sides by the English language.

Matters were at this point when the silvery sound of a bell tinkling a tiny *angelus* informed Des Esseintes that breakfast was ready. He left his books, wiped his forehead and made for the dining-room, telling himself that among all the volumes he had been arranging on his shelves, the works of Barbey d'Aurévilly were still the only ones whose matter and style offered those gamey flavours, those stains of disease and decay, that cankered surface, that taste of rotten-ripeness which he so loved to savour among the decadent writers, Latin and Monastic, of the early ages.

Chapter Thirteen

The weather went from bad to worse. That year the seasons seemed to have changed places; after a long succession of rain-storms and fogs, blazing skies, like sheets of white-hot metal, now hung over the earth from horizon to horizon. In two days, without any transition whatever, cold, wet mists and lashing showers were followed by a torrid heat, an atmosphere as heavy as lead. As if stirred to a fiery fury with giants, the sun glared,—a glowing furnace-mouth shooting forth an almost white light that scorched the eyes; a dust of flame rose from the burnt-up roads, grilling the parched trees, frying the dry grass. The reverberation from the white-washed house-walls, the flames thrown back from the zinc of roofs and panes of windows, blinded the sight; the temperature of a smelting-house in full blast weighed on Des Esseintes' house.

Half stripped, he threw open a casement, to receive full in the face a puff of wind as hot as if coming from an oven; the dining-room, whither he fled for refuge, was burning, the rarefied air seemed to boil. In utter exhaustion, he sat down, for the excitement that had kept his mind active with dreams and fancies during the time when he was arranging his books had come to an end.

As is the case with all sufferers from nervous disorders, the heat undermined his strength terribly; his anæmia, checked for the time being by the cold, recurred, exhausting a body debilitated by copious perspirations.

With shirt clinging to his moist back, perspiring perineum, dripping arms and legs, brow streaming with salt drops that poured down his cheeks, Des Esseintes lay back half fainting in his chair. The sight of the food on the table sickened him; he ordered it to be taken away and boiled eggs brought instead. He tried to swallow sippets of toast dipped in the yolk, but they stuck in his throat. He turned sick and drank a few drops of wine, but it seemed to burn his stomach like fire. He mopped his face; the sweat, hot just now, was now cold as it trickled from his temples; he tried sucking bits of ice to relieve the feeling of nausea,—but all to no purpose. An infinite lassitude glued him to his chair by the table; at last he got up, longing for air, but the sippets of toast had swelled and risen in his throat till they came near choking him. Never before had he felt so oppressed, so feeble, so ill at ease; his eyes, too, were affected, he saw things double and turning round and round; soon the sense of distance grew confused, his glass seemed to be a mile away from his hand. He told himself he was the victim of an optical delusion, but he could not throw off the sensation. Finally, he went and lay down on the sofa in the drawing-room; but then the rolling of a ship at sea began, increasing his nausea still further. He sprang up again, resolved to take a digestive to settle the eggs in his stomach.

He returned to the dining-room and sadly compared himself, in his cabin, to passengers on a vessel attacked by seasickness. With staggering steps he made his way to the cupboard that contained his "mouth-organ," and examined the latter, but without opening it he reached instead up to a higher shelf for a bottle of Bénédictine, which he selected to keep by him because of its shape which struck him as suggestive of ideas at once pleasantly festive and vaguely mystical.

But for the moment, he remained indifferent, looking with a dull eye at the thick-set flagon of dark green glass which was wont at other times to call up before his mind's eye the Priors of the mediæval Monastery as he looked at its antique monkish paunch, its head and neck wrapped in a parchment cowl, its stamp of red wax quartered with three silver mitres on a field azure, the cork tied over and sealed with lead like a Papal bull, and the label written in sonorous Latin, on paper yellowed and faded as if by age,—*liquor Monachorum Benedictinorum Abbatiæ Fiscanensis* (Liqueur of the Benedictine Monks of the Abbey of Fécamp).

Under this full monastic habit, certified by a cross and certain ecclesiastical initial letters,—P. O. M., within these parchments and bands that guarded it like an authentic charter, slumbered a saffron-coloured liquor of an exquisite delicacy. It distilled an aroma of the quintessence of angelica and hyssop mingled with sea-shore herbs rich in iodines and bromines disguised by sugary matters; it stimulated the palate with a spirituous heat dissimulated under a toothsomeness altogether virginal and innocent; flattered the nose with a smack of rankness enwrapped in a soothing savour at once childlike and pious.

This hypocrisy resulting from the startling discrepancy between the containing vessel and its contents, between the liturgical form of the bottle and the soul inside it, so feminine, so modern, had before now set him dreaming; he had indeed fallen many a time into a brown study as he sat before this liqueur, thinking of the monks who sold it, the Benedictines of the Abbey of Fécamp who, while belonging to the Congregation of Saint-Maur, famous for its researches in History, served under the rule of St. Benedict, yet did not follow the observances of the white monks of Citeaux and the black monks of Cluny. Irresistibly they came crowding before his mind's eye, in their daily life as they lived in the Middle Ages, cultivating simples, heating retorts, distilling in alembics sovereign panaceas, infallible cure-alls.

He drank off a drop of the liqueur and felt a relief that lasted a minute or two; but very soon the same fire that a mouthful of wine had before kindled in his inwards burned there again. He tossed away his napkin and went back into his study, where he began pacing up and down; he felt as if he were under the bell of an air-pump in which a vacuum was being gradually produced, and a sensation of faintness, at once soothing and excruciating, ran from his brain down every limb. He pulled himself together and, unable to bear more, for the first time perhaps since his arrival at Fontenay, fled for refuge to his garden, where he found shelter in the ring of shadow cast by a tree. Seated on the turf, he gazed with a dazed look at the beds of vegetables the servants had planted. But it was only after an hour had elapsed that his eyes saw what he was looking at, for a greenish mist floated before his eyes and prevented his making out more than the blurred images, as if viewed through deep water, of objects, whose appearance and colour kept continually changing.

In the end, however, he recovered his balance and found himself able to distinguish clearly onions and cabbages, further off a broad patch of lettuce and in the background, all along the hedge, a row of white lilies standing motionless in the heavy air.

A smile flitted over his lips, for suddenly he remembered a quaint comparison old Nicander makes, likening, from the point of view of shape, the pistil of a lily to an ass's genitals, while a passage from Albertus Magnus also occurred to him where that miracle-worker gives a singular formula for discovering by the use of a lettuce whether a girl is still virgin.

These recollections gave him a moment's merriment. Then he fell to examining the garden, marking how the plants lay withered by the heat and the ground smoked in the glare of the dusty sunbeams. Presently, above the hedge separating the garden which lay at a lower level from the raised roadway leading up to the Fort, he caught sight of a band of young rascals tumbling over each other in the blazing sunshine.

His attention was still concentrated on them when another village lad appeared, a smaller mite than the rest. He was a squalid object; his hair looked like sea-weed sodden with sand, his nose was filthy, his mouth was disgusting, the lips smeared with a white paste from what he had been nibbling at,—skim-milk cheese spread on a piece of bread and sprinkled over with slices of raw green onion.

Des Esseintes sniffed the air; a sudden longing, a perverse craving seized him; the nauseous dainty brought the water to his mouth. He thought somehow that his stomach, that rebelled against all food, would digest this horrid repast and his palate enjoy it like a royal feast.

He sprang up, ran to the kitchen and gave instant orders to send to the village for a round loaf, some white cheese and a raw onion, directing that they should make him a meal exactly like what he had seen the child gnawing at. This done, he went back and resumed his seat under the tree.

The lads were fighting now, snatching scraps of bread out of each other's hands, shoving them into their mouths and then licking their fingers. Kicks and fisticuffs were freely exchanged, and the weaker vessels got tumbled over in the road, where they lay squalling as the jagged stones scraped their backsides.

The sight gave new life to Des Esseintes; the interest he took in the combat diverted his thoughts from his own miseries. Looking on at the fury of these naughty youngsters, he reflected on the cruel and abominable law of the struggle for existence, and ignoble as the children were, he could not help sympathizing with their lot and concluding it would have been better for them had their mother never borne them.

In fact, what was it all but scald-head, colics, fevers, measles, kicking and cuffings in infancy, hard knocks and degrading jobs of work at thirteen or so, women's trickeries, vile diseases and wives' unfaithfulness in manhood; then, in declining years, infirmities and a painful death in a workhouse or a hospital.

When all was said and done, the future was the same for all, and neither one nor the other class, if they had had a particle of common sense, could possibly have desired it. For the rich, it was, in different surroundings, the same passions, the same vexations, the same sorrows, the same diseases, and likewise the same poor satisfactions, whether these were alcoholic, literary or carnal. There was even a vague compensation for all the sufferings, a kind of rude justice that restored the balance of misery as between the classes, enabling the poor to endure more easily the physical sufferings that broke down more mercilessly the feebler and more emaciated bodies of the rich.

What madness to beget children! reflected Des Esseintes. And to think that ecclesiastics, who have taken a vow of sterility, have actually pushed unreason so far as to canonize St. Vincent de Paul because he saved innocent little ones for useless torments!

Thanks to his odious precautions, he had postponed for years the death of beings, devoid of intelligence and feeling, in such wise that, having in time grown almost understanding and at any rate capable of pain, they could foresee the future, could expect and dread the death they had hitherto not known so much as the name of; that they could, some of them, even call upon it to come, in very hatred of the condemnation to live he inflicted on them in virtue of an illogical code of Theology.

Yes, and since the old Saint's death, his ideas had come to govern the world; children abandoned to die were rescued, instead of being left to perish quietly without their being conscious of aught amiss; while, at the same time, the life they preserved them for was growing day by day harsher and more barren! Under pretext of liberty and progress, Society had discovered yet another means of aggravating the miseries of man's existence, by dragging him from his home, tricking him out in an absurd costume, putting specially contrived weapons in his hands, brutalizing him in a slavery identical with that from which they had, out of compassion, enfranchised the negro, and all this merely to put him in a condition to slaughter his fellows without risking the scaffold, as common murderers do who work in units, without uniform, with arms less noisy and less swift to kill.

What a strange epoch, Des Esseintes told himself, is this, which, while invoking the sacred name of humanity, and striving to perfect anæsthetics to abolish physical pain, at the very same time provides such irritants to aggravate moral agonies!

Ah! if ever, in the name of pity, useless procreation should be abolished, that time was now! But here, again, the laws promulgated by men like Portalis and Homais appeared, ferocious and self-contradictory.

Justice deemed quite natural the ways men use to trick Nature in the marriage bed; it was a recognized, admitted fact; there was never a household, no matter how well-to-do, that did not employ means to hinder procreation, use contrivances to be bought openly in the shops,—all artifices it would never occur to anybody to disapprove. Yet, if these means, these subterfuges proved ineffectual, if the trickery failed, and to make good the failure, recourse was had to more certain methods, there were not prisons and gaols and penal settlements enough to hold in durance vile people condemned to this punishment by judge and jury, who the same night in the conjugal bed used every trickery they could devise not to beget youngsters of their own.

The trickery itself therefore was no crime, but to make good its failure was one!

In a word, Society regarded as a crime the act that consisted in killing a creature endowed with life; and yet, in expelling a fœtus, the operator was surely destroying an animal, less fully formed, less alive and certainly less intelligent and more ugly than a dog or a cat, which may be strangled at birth without penalty.

It is right to add, thought Des Esseintes, for further proof how monstrous the injustice is, that it is not the unskilful operator, who generally makes off with all haste, but the woman, victim of his awkwardness, who pays the penalty for saving an innocent being from the burden of life.

Verily the world must be extraordinarily prejudiced to want to suppress manoeuvres so natural that primitive man, that the very savages of the South Seas have been led to practise them by the mere action of their own instinct.

At this moment, his servant interrupted these charitable reflexions of his master by bringing Des Esseintes a silver-gilt salver on which lay the nauseous dainty he had asked for. A spasm of disgust shook him; he had not the courage to touch the thing, for the morbid craving had now ceased. A sensation of extreme malaise returned; he was forced to rise from where he sat; the sun, in moving westwards was little by little encroaching on the place, the air becoming more oppressive and the heat more scorching.

"Go and pitch the thing," he ordered the man, "to those children yonder fighting in the road; I hope the weakest ones will be maimed and never get a scrap and, what's more, be soundly whipped by their parents when they get back home with trousers torn and eyes blackened; that will give them a foretaste of the merry life that awaits them!" Then he returned to the house, where he sank half fainting in an armchair.

"Still I *must* try and eat something," he sighed,—and he proceeded to soak a biscuit in a glass of old Constantia (J. P. Cloete brand), a few bottles of which were still left in his cellar.

This wine, the colour of onion skins slightly burnt, smacking of old Malaga and Port, but with a sugary bouquet of its own and an after-taste of grapes whose juices have been condensed and sublimated by burning suns, had often comforted his stomach and given a fillip to his digestion enfeebled by the forced fasts he was compelled to undergo; but the cordial, generally so efficacious, failed of its effect. Then, hoping an emollient might cool the hot irons that were burning his intestines, he had recourse to Nalifka, a Russian liqueur, contained in a flask patterned over with dead-gold filigree; but this unctuous, fruity syrup was equally ineffective. Alas! the days were long past when Des Esseintes, still in the enjoyment of robust health, would, in the middle of the dog-days, mount a sledge he had at home, and then, closely wrapped in furs which he would pull up to his chin, force himself to shiver as he told himself through teeth that chattered of set purpose: "Ah! but the cold is Arctic; it's freezing, freezing hard!" till he actually persuaded himself it was cold weather!

Alas! suchlike remedies were of no avail now that his sufferings were real.

With all this, it was useless for him to have recourse to laudanum; instead of acting as a sedative, that drug only irritated his nerves and robbed him of sleep. In former times he had resorted to opium and haschisch in order to see visions, but the only result had been to bring on vomiting and intense nervous disturbances; he had been obliged forthwith to give up their use and without the help of these coarse excitants to ask his brain of itself alone to bear him far away from everyday life into the region of dreams.

"What a day!" he moaned to himself on this occasion, as he sponged his neck, feeling as if every ounce of strength he had left was melting away in a fresh access of perspiration. A feverish restlessness still made it impossible for him to stay in one place; again he set off roaming through his rooms, trying all the seats one after the other. Wearied out at last, he presently sank down before his writing-desk, and resting his elbow on the table, fell mechanically and without any ulterior motive to turning about in his hands an astrolabe, lying as a paper-weight on a heap of books and memoranda.

He had purchased the instrument, which was of copper engraved and gilt, of German workmanship and dating from the seventeenth century, at a bric-à-brac shop in Paris, after a visit he had paid one day to the Musée de Cluny, where he had stood for hours enraptured before a wonderful astrolabe of carved ivory, the cabalistic look of which had fascinated him.

The paper-weight in question stirred up in him a whole crowd of reminiscences. Influenced by the associations evoked by the sight of the little ornament, his thoughts flew from Fontenay to Paris, to the old curiosity shop where he had bought it, then returned to the Musée des Thermes, where he called up the mental picture of the ivory astrolabe, while his eyes still continued to dwell, but without seeing it, on the copper astrolabe on his writing table.

Then, still led by memory, he quitted the Museum and, without leaving town, strolled up and down the streets. After roaming along the Rue Sommerard and the Boulevard Saint-Michel, he struck off into the adjoining streets and came to a halt in front of certain establishments whose frequency and peculiar character had often struck him.

Beginning with the astrolabe, this mental excursion ended by leading him to the beer-halls of the Quartier Latin.

He recalled the great number of these places all along the Rue Monsieur-le-Prince and at the end of the Rue Vaugirard adjoining the Odéon; sometimes they stood cheek by jowl like the old *riddecks* in the Rue du Canal-aux-Harengs at Antwerp, stretching one after the other down the side-walk, which they overlook with a row of signboards all very much alike.

Through the half open doors and the windows only partially

obscured by coloured panes or curtains he could remember having caught glimpses of women walking up and down with dragging step and out-thrust neck, the way geese waddle; others lounging on benches were rubbing elbows on marble-topped tables, dreaming away the hours or singing to themselves, their heads drooped between their fists; yet others would be preening themselves before the looking-glass, patting with the tips of their fingers their false hair just dressed by a barber; others again would be drawing out of reticules with broken fastenings piles of silver and copper which they amused themselves by ranging methodically in little heaps.

The majority had massive features, hoarse voices, flaccid bosoms and painted eyes, and all, like so many automata wound up at the same time with the same key, uttered in the same tone the same invitations, lavished the same smiles, talked in the same silly phrases, indulged in the same absurd reflexions.

Thoughts began to crystallize in Des Esseintes' mind and he found himself coming to a definite inference, now that he could look back in memory and take a bird's-eye view, as it were, of these crowded taverns and streets.

He realized the meaning of these cafes, saw that they corresponded to the state of mind and imagination of a whole generation; he gathered from them material for the synthesis of the period.

Indeed, the symptoms were plain and unmistakable; the legalized brothel was disappearing, and each time one of these closed its doors, a beer-tavern opened.

This diminution of official prostitution, organized for the satisfaction of clandestine amours, was evidently to be accounted for by the incomprehensible illusions men indulge in from the carnal standpoint.

Monstrous as this might seem, the fact was, the beer-tavern satisfied an ideal.

True, the utilitarian tendencies transmitted hereditarily and further developed by the precocious discourtesies and constant brutalities of school and college had made the youth of the present day singularly coarse and also singularly opinionated and cold-hearted, but for all this, it had preserved, deep down in its heart, an old-fashioned flower of sentiment, a vague, half decayed ideal of love.

So nowadays, when the blood was hot within, it could no more consent just to march in, work its will, pay and go home again. This, in its eyes, was a bestial thing, like a dog covering a bitch without preliminary or preamble. Besides, vanity was in no sort of way gratified in these official houses of vice where there was no pretence of resistance on the woman's part, no semblance of victory on that of the man, where no special preference was to be expected, nor even any special liberality of favours from the prostitute who, as a tradeswoman should, measured her caresses in proportion to the price paid. On the other hand, to pay court to a girl at a beer-saloon *was* allowing for all these sentimentalities, all the delicacies of love. There were rivals in this case striving for her affection, and those to whom she agreed, for a sufficient consideration, to grant a rendezvous, imagined themselves, in all good faith, to have won a victory, to be the object of a flattering preference, the recipient of a precious favour.

Yet, all the time, the creatures were every whit as stolid, as mercenary, as base and degraded as those who ply their trade in the houses with numbers. Like these, the tavern waitresses drank without being thirsty, laughed without being amused, were mad after the caresses of a fancy man from the streets, blackguarded each other and quarrelled and fought on the slightest provocation. Yet, in spite of everything, the young Parisian rake had never learned that the servant wenches at these beer-halls were, from every point of view, whether of personal good looks or attractive poses or pretty dresses, altogether inferior to the women confined in the luxurious rooms of the other sort of establishment! Great God! Des Esseintes could not help exclaiming, what simpletons these fools must be who flutter round beer-halls, for, to say nothing of their ridiculous self-deception, they have positively brought themselves to ignore the danger they run from the low-class, highly suspicious quality of the goods supplied, to think nothing of the money spent in drinks, all priced beforehand by the landlady, to forget the time wasted in waiting for delivery of the commodity,—a delivery put off and put off continually in order to raise the price, frittered away in delays and postponements endlessly repeated, all to quicken and stimulate the liberality of the client.

This imbecile sentimentalism combined with ferocity in practice seemed to represent the dominant feeling of the age; these same fellows who would have gouged out their best friend's eye to make a sixpence, lost all clearness of vision, all perspicacity, in dealing with the disreputable tavern-wenches who bullied them without compunction and exploited them without mercy. Workmen toiled, families cheated one another in the name of trade, all to let themselves be swindled out of money by their sons, who in their turn allowed themselves to be plundered by these women, who in the last resort were drained dry by their fancy lovers.

From end to end of Paris, East to West and North to South, it was one unbroken chain of petty trickeries, a series of organized thefts repeated continually from one to another,—all this simply because, instead of satisfying lechers straight away, the suppliers of these goods were artful enough to keep their clients dangling about and waiting with what patience they might.

At bottom, human wisdom might be summed up in the precept,— drag things out indefinitely, say no, then after a long time, yes; for indeed there was no way of managing mankind half so good as procrastination.

"Ah! if only the same held good of the stomach," sighed Des Esseintes, seized with a sudden spasm of pain which instantly brought his thoughts back to Fontenay, recalling them from the far-away regions they had been roaming.

Chapter Fourteen

Two or three days had jogged by more or less satisfactorily, thanks to various devices for cheating the stomach's reluctance, when one morning the highly spiced sauces which masked the smell of fat and savour of blood that go along with flesh-meat stirred Des Esseintes' gorge, and he asked himself anxiously whether his weakness, already alarming, was not getting worse and likely soon to force him to take to his bed. Suddenly, a gleam of light shone through his distress of mind; he remembered how one of his friends, who had been very ill at one time, had succeeded by using a "patent digester" in checking the anæmia, stopping the wasting, keeping what was left him of vigour from further dissipation.

He despatched his servant to Paris to procure the precious apparatus, and in accordance with the directions the maker sent with it, himself instructed the cook how to cut up the beef into little bits, put it dry into the tin digester, to add a slice of leek and carrot, then screw on the lid and set the whole thing to boil in a hot-water pan for four hours.

At the end of that time, the threads of meat were squeezed dry, and you drank a spoonful of the muddy, salty juice left at the bottom of the pot. Then you felt something slip down that was like absorbing warm marrow, something that soothed the stomach with a gentle, velvety caress.

This quintessence of nourishment stopped the spasms and nauseas of the empty stomach, stimulating its action till it no longer refused to keep down a few spoonsful of soup.

Thanks to his "digester," Des Esseintes' nervous malady made no further progress, and he told himself: "Well, that is something gained, at any rate; perhaps the temperature will fall soon; the clouds will modify the glare of that odious sun that wears me out, and I shall then get along, without overmuch suffering, to the first fogs and frosts of Autumn."

In his present state of apathy and the weariness of having nothing to occupy his thoughts, his library, the re-arrangement of which still remained uncompleted, got on his nerves; no longer stirring from his chair, he had continually before his eyes the shelves appropriated to profane literature with the books on them lying about in disorder, propped up one against the other, piled up in heaps or tumbled like a pack of cards flat on their sides. This confusion shocked him the more when he contrasted it with the perfect order of his religious works, carefully drawn up, as if on parade, along the walls.

He tried to remedy this confusion, but after ten minutes' labour he found himself bathed in perspiration; the effort was too much for his strength; he lay down exhausted on a couch and rang for his servant.

Following his directions, the old domestic set to work, bringing him the books one by one, which he then examined and pointed out the chosen place for each.

The task was quite a short one, for Des Esseintes' library contained only a singularly limited number of non-religious books of the present day.

By dint of passing them through the test of a severe mental review, in the same way as the wire-drawer passes strips of metal through a steel draw-plate from which they issue attenuated and light, reduced to almost invisible threads, he had finally come to possess only books which had proved capable of withstanding such a treatment and were solid enough of frame to bear the second rolling-mill of perusal. By this process of elimination, he had checked and pretty well sterilized all pleasure in reading, accentuating yet further the irreconcilable conflict between his ideas and those of the society in which chance had ordained he should be born. It had come to this at last that he found it impossible any longer to discover a book to satisfy his secret aspirations; nay, he had even ceased to admire the very volumes that had without a doubt done much to embitter his mind and fill it so full of subtle suspicions.

Yet in literature and art, his opinions had started in the first instance from a simple enough point of view. For him, there were no such things as schools, only the writer's individual temperament mattered, only the working of the creator's brain interested him, whatever the subject treated of. Unfortunately, this true criterion of appreciation, worthy of La Palisse, was as good as useless, for the simple reason that, while desiring to be rid of prejudice, to refrain from all passion, every man goes for choice to those works which correspond most intimately with his own temperament and he ends by relegating all the rest to the background.

This work of selection had gone on slowly. He had at one time adored the great Balzac, but in proportion as his organism had lost balance, as his nerves had gained the upper hand, his inclinations had been modified and his preferences changed.

Soon even, and this although he was well aware of his injustice towards the marvellous author of the *Comédie Humaine*, he had given up so much as ever opening his books, the sturdy art of which irritated him; other aspirations stirred him now, that were in a sense incapable of precise definition.

By careful self-examination, however, he realized in the first place that a book to attract him must bear the character of singularity that Edgar Allan Poe craved; but Des Esseintes was ready and willing to adventure further along this road, demanding strange flowers of Byzantine fancy and complicated sophistries of diction; he preferred a vague, vexing indefiniteness, that left him to brood meditatively over it till he had made it, at will, yet more vague, or more firmly outlined, according to the condition of his spirit at the moment. He wanted, in one word, a work of art both for what it was in itself and for what it allowed him to lend it of himself; he wanted to go along with it, thanks to its support, helped on his way by it as if supported by a friend's arm, as if borne forward by a vehicle, into a sphere where the sublimated stress of sensation roused in him an unexpected commotion, the exact causes of which he would strive long and even vainly to unravel.

Lastly, ever since his leaving Paris, he shrunk more and more from the realities of life and above all from the society of his day which he regarded with an ever growing horror,-a detestation which had reacted strongly on his literary and artistic tastes; he refused, as far as possible, to have anything to do with pictures and books whose subjects were in any way connected with modern existence.

Thus, losing the faculty of admiring beauty independently of the shape, whatever that may be, under which it presents itself, he now preferred, in Flaubert, the *Tentation de Saint-Antoine* to the *Education sentimentale*; in De Goncourt, *Faustin* to *Germinie Lacerteux*; in Zola, *La Faute de l'Abbé Mouret* to *L'Assommoir*.

This point of view seemed to him logical; these works, less direct indeed, but equally thrilling, equally human, let him penetrate further into the inmost secrets of temperament of these masters who displayed with a more unfeigned frankness the most mysterious impulses of their being, while at the same time they raised him also, higher than the rest, out of that trivial life he was weary of.

Moreover, he could enter in reading them into complete community ideas with the writers who had conceived them; because at the moment of writing, the authors had been in a state of mind closely analogous to his own.

The truth is, when the period at which a man of talent is condemned to live is dull and stupid, the artist is, unconsciously to himself, haunted by a sensation of morbid yearning for another century.

Unable to bring himself into harmony, save at rare intervals, with the surroundings amid which he develops, ceasing to find in the study of these surroundings and in the beings who are subjected to them sufficient pleasures of observation and analysis to divert him, he feels the birth and growth in himself of phenomena of a singular sort. Confused cravings for a change of time and place spring up, which find their satisfaction in reflexion and reading. Instincts, sensations, preferences transmitted from his ancestors awake, grow more and more precise and govern his thoughts as masters. He recalls memories of persons and things he had never personally known, and there comes a time when he escapes impetuously from the prison-house of his century, and wanders forth, in freedom, in another epoch, with which, by a crowning piece of self-deception, he believes he would have been in better accord.

In some cases, it is a return to past ages, to vanished civilizations, to dead centuries; in others, it is an impulse towards the fantastic, the land of dreams, it is a vision more or less vivid of a time to come whose images reproduce, without his being aware, as a result of atavism, that of by-gone epochs.

In Flaubert's case, it was, a series of vast and solemn pictures, of grandiose and pompous spectacles, in the magnificent and barbaric frame of which moved beings sensitive and delicate, mysterious and proud, women endowed, in the perfection of their beauty, with sick and suffering souls, wherein he discerned secret horrors of infatuation and insane caprice, driven to desperation as they were even in their day by the miserable inadequacy of the pleasures they could hope to enjoy.

The temperament of the great author was revealed in all its brilliance in those incomparable pages of the *Tentation de Saint-Antoine* and *Salammbô* in which, far from all associations of our petty modern life, he called up the Asiatic splendours of far-off ages, their mystic aspirations and discouragements, the morbid fancies of their idleness, the ferocities springing from the oppressive ennui that flows, even before its pleasures have been drained to the dregs, from a life of opulence and prayer.

In De Goncourt, on the other hand, it was a longing for the preceding century, a craving to return to the elegant trivialities of the eighteenth century, never to be renewed.

The gigantic panorama of seas breaking upon piers of granite, of deserts beneath blazing skies stretching farther than eye can see, found no place in *his* work of imaginary reconstruction, which confined itself, within the boundaries of a great noble's park, to a boudoir warm with the alluring emanations of its fair occupant, a woman with a tired smile, a discontented mouth, restless yet pensive eyes. The soul wherewith he animated his characters was not now the soul Flaubert breathed into his creations, a soul in revolt beforehand at thought of the inexorable certainty that no new happiness was possible; rather was it a soul driven to revolt after trial, after experience, after all the fruitless efforts it had made to invent novel, less hackneyed liaisons, to give a new spice to the one, world-old pleasure that is repeated from age to age in the gratification, more or less ingeniously carried out, of a pair of lovers' lust.

Albeit Faustin lived among us moderns and was body and soul of our age; yet, by ancestral influences, she was a being of the by-gone century, the captious heart and mental lassitude and sensual satiety of which she shared in full.

This book of Edmond de Goncourt's was one of the volumes Des Esseintes most delighted in. Indeed, that suggestiveness, that invitation to dreamy reverie which he loved, abounded in this, work, where underneath the written line peeped another visible to the soul only, indicated rather than expressed, which revealed depths of passion piercing through a reticence that allowed spiritual infinities to be defined such as no idiom of human language could have encompassed. It was very different from the diction of Flaubert, no doubt one of inimitable magnificence; here the style was at once clear and morbid, vigorous and deformed, careful to note the impalpable impression that strikes the senses and determines sensation; a style expert to modulate complicated shades of distinction of a period which was itself extraordinarily complex. In a word, it was the phraseology inevitably called for by decrepit civilizations which for the due expression of their needs demand, to whatever age they belong, special acceptations, special turns of phrase, novel moulds of sentences and words.

At Rome, expiring Paganism had modified its prosody, transmuted its language, with Ausonious, Claudian, Rutilius, whose style, careful and scrupulous, full-bodied and sonorous, presented, particularly in passages descriptive of reflections, shadows, shades of meaning, an inevitable analogy with that of the De Goncourts.

At Paris, a unique phenomenon in literary history had come about; this perishing society of the eighteenth century, which had produced painters, sculptors, musicians, architects, all influenced by its predilections, imbued with its be. liefs, had never succeeded in fashioning a veritable writer capable of rendering its dying elegancies, or expressing the essential juice of its feverish pleasures, that were to be so cruelly expiated. It had had to wait for De Goncourt, whose temperament was made up of memories, of regrets stirred to life by the grevious spectacle of the intellectual poverty and the base aspirations of his own day, to resuscitate, not alone in his books of history, but likewise in a retrospective work like *Faustin*, the very soul of the epoch, to incarnate its nervous daintinesses in his actress heroine, so painfully eager to torment heart and head alike that she might savour to the verge of exhaustion the cruel revulsives of love and art.

In Zola, the same feeling of neurotic longing, the craving to overpass the bounds of the present day, took a different form. In him there was no wish to travel to regions and systems of the past, to worlds vanished in the darkness of by-gone ages. *His* temperament, strong and powerful, enamoured of the luxuriances of life, of full-blooded vigour, of moral sturdiness, deterred him from the artificial graces, the painted and powdered pallors of the last century, as likewise from the hieratic solemnity, the brutal ferocity and the effeminate, dubious imaginations of the ancient East. The day when he, too, in his turn, had been attacked by this same yearning, this desire that is in essence poetry itself, to fly far from this contemporary society he was studying, he had hastened to an ideal country where the sap boiled in full sunshine; he had dreamed of fantastic concupiscences of heaven, of long passionate swoonings of earth, of fertilizing showers of pollen falling on the panting genitals of flowers; he had arrived at a gigantic pantheism, had, all unconsciously perhaps, created, in these surroundings where, as in a Garden of Eden, he placed his Adam and Eve, a wondrous Hindu epic, celebrating in a style whose broad colours, laid on unmixed, had a sort of quaint brilliancy as of an Indian painting, the hymn of the flesh, matter, animated, living, revealing to human beings by its very frenzy of generation the forbidden fruit of love, its suffocating spasms, its instinctive caresses, its natural attitudes.

With Baudelaire, these were the three masters who in all the range of French literature, modern and profane, had most caught and moulded Des Esseintes' tastes; but by dint of re-reading them, of saturating his mind in their works, of knowing them by heart from end to end, he had been constrained in order to gain the power of absorbing them again, to force himself to forget them and leave them for a while undisturbed on his bookshelves.

Accordingly, he barely opened them as the old servant handed them to him one by one. He confined himself to pointing out the place they were to occupy, taking care to see them arranged in good order and with plenty of elbow room.

The domestic next brought him another series of books, which caused him more trouble. These were works to which he had grown more and more partial, works which by the very fact of their imperfection, relieved the strain after the high perfections of writers of vaster powers. Here again, in his refining way, Des Esseintes had come to look for and find in pages otherwise ill put together occasional sentences which gave him a sort of galvanic shock and set him quivering as they discharged their electricity in a medium that had seemed at first entirely a non-conductor.

The very imperfections themselves pleased him, provided they did not come from base parasitism and servility, and it may well be there was a modicum of truth in his theory that the subordinate writer of the decadence, the writer still individual though incomplete, distils a balm more active, more aperitive, more acid than the author of the same period who is really truly great, really and truly perfect. In his view, it was in their ill-constructed attempts that the most acute exaltations of sensibility were to be seen, the most morbid aberrations of psychology, the most extravagant eccentricities of language pushed to its last refusal to contain, to enclose the effervescent salts of sensations and ideas.

So, in spite of himself, neglecting the masters, he now addressed himself to sundry minor writers, who were only the more agreeable and dear to him by reason of the contempt in which they were held by a public incapable of understanding them.

One of these, Paul Verlaine, had already made his debut with a volume of verse, the *Poèmes Saturniens*, a volume almost to be described as feeble, in which imitations of Leconte de Lisle jostled against experiments in romantic rhetoric, but which nevertheless revealed in certain pieces, such as the sonnet entitled *Un Rêve familier*, the real personality of the poet.

Going back to his antecedents, Des Esseintes discovered underlying these attempts with their uncertain touch a talent already profoundly affected by Baudelaire, whose influence subsequently became much better marked, though without the contributions offered by the impeccable master being too flagrantly plagiarisms.

Then later, some of his books, the *Bonne Chanson*, the *Fêtes Galantes*, the *Romances sans paroles* and finally his last volume, *Sagesse*, contained poems in which the original writer was revealed, making his mark among the mass of his contemporaries.

Provided with rhymes contrived by using the tenses of verbs, sometimes even by lengthy adverbs preceded by a monosyllable. from which they fell as from a stone sill in a massive cascade of water, his verse, divided by impossible caesuras, was often singularly obscure with its daring ellipses and strange breaches of rule, that were yet not without a certain grace.

Handling metre better than most, he had endeavoured to rejuvenate the stereotyped forms of poetry, the sonnet, for instance, which he turned about, tail in air, like those Japanese fish of variegated earthenware we see which rest on their pedestal gills downwards. In other cases, he had degraded its form, employing only masculine rhymes, for which he seemed to show a predilection. Similarly and not unfrequently he had adopted a quaint form, a strophe of three lines, the middle one being left unrhymed, and a tercet, with one rhyme only, followed by a single line by way of refrain and recurring as an echo of itself, as in the popular pieces like "Dansons la Gigue." Yet other rhymes were to be found whose half-heard ring was only faintly to be caught in far-off strophes, like the distant sound of a bell.

But his individuality was mainly conspicuous in the fact that he had known how to suggest vague and delicious secrets, in whispered voices, in the dusk of twilight. He alone had had the art to half reveal certain mysterious and troublous instincts of the soul, certain whisperings of thought so soft and low, certain avowals so gently murmured, so brokenly expressed, that the ear catching them was left hesitating, passing on to the mind languors stirred by the mystery of this breath of sound divined rather than heard. Verlaine's very spirit is in those admirable lines of the *Fêtes Galantes*:—

> Le soir tombait, un soir équivoque d'automne,
> Les belles se pendant rêveuses à nos bras,
> Dirent alors des mots si spécieux tout bas,
> Que notre âme depuis ce temps tremble et s'étonne.[1]

It was not now the limitless horizon revealed through unforgettable portals by Baudelaire, but rather, on a moonlit night, a chink half opened upon a field of view more restricted and more intimate; in a word, a field peculiar to the author. Indeed the latter, in verses that Des Esseintes greatly savoured, had formulated his own poetic system:—

> Car nous voulons la nuance encore,
> Pas la couleur, rien que la nuance
> . . . .
> Et tout le reste est littérature.[2]

Gladly Des Esseintes had followed him through the series of his works, even the most diverse. After the publication of his *Romances sans paroles*, issued from the printing-office of a local newspaper at Sens, Verlaine had written nothing for a considerable interval; then, in charming lines touched with the gentle, moving charm of Villon, he had reappeared, celebrating the Virgin, "far from our days of carnal spirit and dreary flesh." Often would Des Esseintes read and re-read this book, *Sagesse*, and enjoy under its inspiration secret reveries, imaginations of an occult passion for a Byzantine Madonna, transmuting at a given moment into a Cyprian goddess who had strayed into our century. She was so mysterious and so troublous to the senses that none could say whether she was craving for depravities of vice so monstrous that, once accomplished they would become irresistible by mankind; or whether she herself was immersed in a dream, an immaculate reverie, where the adoration of the soul should float about her in a love for ever unconfessed, for ever pure.

There were other poets, too, who enticed him to trust their guidance. One was Tristan Corbière, who, in 1873, amid general indifference, had launched a volume of verses of the wildest eccentricity under the title of *Les Amours Jaunes*. Des Esseintes, who, in his hatred of the trivial and commonplace, would have welcomed the most unmitigated follies, the most grotesque extravagancies, spent

---

[1] Night was falling, a dubious night of Autumn; it was the hour when fair ones hanging pensive on our arms said words so specious in whispered tones that since that time our soul is lost in trembling and amaze.

[2] For what we still desire is the shade of colour, not the colour, nothing but the shade . . . and all the rest is literature.

some agreeable hours with this book where the burlesque was strangely combined with an inordinate vigour, where lines of a disconcerting brilliance occurred in poems that were as a whole utterly incomprehensible, such as the litanies in his *Sommeil*, which he himself in one passage stigmatized as:—

Obscène confesseur des dévotes mort-nées.[3]

It was barely French; the author was talking negro, using a sort of telegram language, passing all bounds in the suppression of verbs, affecting a ribald humour, condescending to quips and quibbles only worthy of a commercial traveller of the baser sort; then, in a moment, in this tangle of ludicrous conceits, of smirking affectations, would rise a cry of acute pain, like a violoncello string breaking. But with all this, in this style, rugged, arid, fleshless, bristling with unusual vocables and unexpected neologisms, flashed many a happy expression, many a stray verse, rhymeless yet superb; finally, to say nothing of his *Poèmes Parisiens*, from which Des Esseintes used to quote this profound definition of woman-kind:—

Eternal féminin de l'éternel jocrisse.[4]

Tristan Corbière had, in a style almost imposing in its conciseness, sung the seas of Brittany, the mariners' seraglios, the *Pardon* of St. Anne, and had even risen to the eloquence of hate in the invective he hurled, in connexion with the Camp of Conlie, at the individuals whom he reviled under the title of "mountebanks of the Fourth of September."

This over-ripe flavour which Des Esseintes loved and which was offered him by this poet of the contorted epithets and beauties that are always of the rather suspect sort, he found likewise in another poet, Théodore Hannon, a disciple of Baudelaire and Gautier, a writer animated by a very special sense of far-sought elegancies and factitious pleasures.

Unlike Verlaine, who came direct, without cross, from the Baudelaire breed, particularly on the psychological side, the whimsical turn of his thought and the artful concentration of his sentiment, Théodore Hannon derived from the master, mainly on the plastic side, by his external envisagement of men and things.

His fascinating corruption bore a fatal correspondence with Des Esseintes' predilections, and, in days of fog and rain, the latter would shut himself up in the retreat imagined by this poet, intoxicating his eyes with the glitter of his rich stuffs, with the flash of his jewels, with

---

[3] Obscene confessor of fair bigots still-born.
[4] Eternal feminine of the eternal clown.

his sumptuosities, exclusively material, which all helped to excite the brain to frenzy and rose like a cantharides powder in a cloud of hot incense towards a Brussels Idol with painted face and belly tanned with perfumes.

With the exception of these and of Stéphane Mallarmé, whom he directed his servant to set on one side, in order to give him a class apart, Des Esseintes was only very moderately drawn to the poets.

For all his magnificence of technique, for all the impressive roll of his verse which moved with so fine a stateliness that even Victor Hugo's hexameters seemed in comparison flat and dull, Leconte de Lisle could now no longer satisfy him. The ancient world, re-animated with so marvellous a vigour by Flaubert, remained dead and cold in his hands. There was no movement in his verse; it was all outside façade, with, most part of the time, never an idea to prop it up; there was no life in the dusty poems whose dull mythologies ended by chilling him.

On the other hand, after having long cherished him as a prime favourite, Des Esseintes was coming to lose interest in Gautier's work; his admiration for that incomparable painter of pictures had been melting from day to day, and now he was more amazed than delighted before his descriptions, in a way *impersonal* as they are. The impression of objects had fixed itself on his eminently perceptive eye, but there it had, so to say, localized itself, had penetrated no further into brain and into body; like a marvellously contrived reflector, it had confined itself to repeating all things about it with an indifferent precision.

No doubt Des Esseintes still loved the works of these two poets in the same way as he loved rare jewels, precious articles of dead matter, but none of the variations of these accomplished instrumentalists could any longer move him to ecstasy, for not one of them was conducive to reverie, not one of them opened, at any rate for him, one of those living outbursts that enabled him to speed the slow flight of the hours.

He left their books hungry and the same was true of Victor Hugo's. The Oriental and patriarchal side was too conventional, too empty to retain his interest, while the other side, at once good-natured and grandfatherly, got on his nerves. It was not till he came to the *Chansons des rues et des bois* that he felt himself bound to applaud the faultless jugglery of his metrical technique yet, when all was said and done, how gladly would he have given all these *tours de force* for one new poem of Baudelaire to match the old, for beyond a doubt the latter was almost the only author whose verses contained beneath their shining rind a really balsamic and nutritious kernel!

To leap from one extreme to the other, from form devoid of ideas to ideas devoid of form, left Des Esseintes no less cold and circumspect in his admiration. The psychological labyrinths of Stendhal, the analytical divagations of Duranty attracted him; but their diction, official, colourless, dry; their mercenary prose, at most good for the ignoble consumption of the stage, repelled him. Besides, the interesting intricacies of their analyses appealed, after all, only to brains still stirred by passions that no longer moved him. Little he cared for the common emotions of humanity, for the ordinary associations of ideas, now that his mental reserve was growing more and more pronounced; and he was sensitive to none but superfine sensations and the doubts raised by Catholicism and sensual phenomena.

To enjoy a literature uniting, as he desired, with an incisive style, a penetrating, feline power of analysis, he must resort to that master of Induction, that strange, profound thinker, Edgar Allan Poe, for whom, since the moment when he had begun to re-read him, his predilection had suffered no possible diminution.

Better than any other writer perhaps, Poe possessed those close affinities of spirit that fulfilled the demands Des Esseintes had formulated in the course of his meditations.

While Baudelaire had deciphered in the hieroglyphics of the soul the period of recurrence of feelings and thoughts, *he* had, in the realm of morbid psychology, more particularly scrutinized the region of will.

In literature, he had been the first, under the emblematic title of "The Demon of Perversity," to explore those irresistible impulses which the will submits to without understanding their nature and which cerebral pathology now accounts for with a fair degree of certainty; again, he was the first, if not to note, at any rate to make generally known, the depressing influence of fear acting on the will, like those anæsthetics that paralyze sensibility and that *curare* that annihilates the nervous elements of motion; it was on this point, this lethargy of the will, that he had focussed his studies, analysing the effects of this moral poison, pointing out the symptoms of its progress, the troubles incidental to it, beginning with anxiety, proceeding to anguish, culminating finally in terror which stupefies the powers of volition, yet without the intelligence, however severely shaken, actually giving way.

To death, which the dramatists had so lavishly abused, he had, in a manner, given a new and keener edge, made it other than it was, introducing into it an algebraic and superhuman element; yet, to say truly, it was not so much the actual death agony of the dying he depicted as the moral agony of the survivor, haunted before the bed of suffering by the monstrous hallucinations engendered by pain and fatigue. With a hideous fascination, he concentrated his gaze on the effects of terror, on the collapse of the will; applied to these horrors the cold light of reason; little by little choking the breath out of the throat of the reader who pants and struggles, suffocated before these mechanically reproduced nightmares of raging fever.

Convulsed by hereditary nervous disorders, maddened by moral choreas, his characters lived only by the nerves; his women, the

Morellas, the Ligeias, possessed a vast erudition, deeply imbrued with the foggy mists of German metaphysics and the cabalistic mysteries of the ancient East; all had the inert bosoms of boys or angels, all were, so to say, unsexual.

Baudelaire and Poe, whose minds have often been compared because of their common poetical inspiration and the predilection they shared for the examination of mental maladies, yet differed radically in their conceptions of love,-and these conceptions filled a large place in their works. Baudelaire's passion was a thirsty, ruthless thing, a thing of cruel disillusion that suggested only reprisals and tortures; Poe's a matter of chaste and ethereal amours, where the senses had no existence, and the brain alone was stirred to erethism with nothing to correspond in the bodily organs, which, if they existed at all, remained for ever frozen and virgin.

This cerebral clinic where, vivisecting in a stifling atmosphere, this spiritual surgeon became, directly his attention flagged, the prey of his imagination, which sprayed about him, like delicious miasmas, apparitions whether of nightmare horrors or of angelic hosts, was for Des Esseintes a source of indefatigable conjectures. Now, however, when his nerves were all sick and on edge, there were days when such reading exhausted him, days when it left him with trembling hands and ears strained and watchful, feeling himself, like the lamentable Usher, seized by unreasoning pangs of dread, by a secret terror.

So he felt bound to moderate his zeal, to indulge sparingly in these formidable elixirs, just as he could now no longer visit with impunity his red vestibule and intoxicate himself with the sight of Odilon Redon's gloomy paintings or Jan Luyken's representations of tortures.

And yet, when he was in these dispositions of mind, all literature struck him as vapid after these terrible philtres imported from America. Thereupon he turned his attention to Villiers de l'Isle-Adam, in whose works he noted, here and there, observations equally unorthodox, vibrations equally spasmodic, but which, at any rate, with the exception of his *Claire Lenoir*, did not distil so overwhelming a sense of horror.

First published in 1867 in the *Revue des lettres et des arts*, this *Claire Lenoir* opened a series of romances included under the generic title of *Histoires moroses*. On a background of obscure speculations borrowed from old Hegel, moved a phantasmagoria of impossible beings, a Doctor Tribulat Bonhomet, pompous and puerile, a Claire Lenoir, comic and uncanny, wearing blue spectacles, as round and big as five franc pieces, concealing her almost lifeless eyes.

The romance turned on an ordinary adultery, but ended on an unspeakable note of horror, when Bonhomet, uncovering Claire's eyeballs on her death-bed and searching them with hideous probes, beheld distinctly reflected on the retina the picture of the offended husband brandishing in his extended hand the severed head of the lover; and, like a Kanaka savage, howling a war-song of triumph.

Based on the physiological fact, more or less surely verified, that the eyes of some animals, oxen for instance, preserve till decomposition sets in, in the same way as photographic plates, the image of the persons and things lying at the instant of their death within the range of their last look, the tale evidently derived from those of Edgar Allan Poe, from whom he copied the meticulous and appalling discussion of the details.

The same might be said of the *Intersigne*, subsequently incorporated in the *Contes cruels*, a collection of stories displaying indisputable talent, and in which occurred *Vera*, a romance Des Esseintes regarded as a little masterpiece.

Here the hallucination was impressed with an exquisite tenderness; there was nothing here of the gloomy imaginings of the American author, it was a vision of warmth and gentleness, almost celestial in its beauty. It formed, in an identical mode, the antithesis of Poe's Beatrices and Ligeias, those sad, wan phantoms engendered by the inexorable nightmare of black opium!

This romance likewise brought into play the operations of the will, but it no longer treated of its enfeeblements and failures under the action of fear. On the contrary, it made a study of its exaltations under the impulse of a conviction become a fixed idea; it demonstrated its power, which even came to saturate the atmosphere and impose its faith on surrounding things.

Another book of Villiers', *Isis*, struck him as curious on other grounds. The philosophical lumber of Claire Lenoir cumbered this book no less than its predecessor, and it presented an incredible confusion of verbose, chaotic observations and reminiscences of old-fashioned melodramas, oubliettes, poniards, rope ladders, all those transpontine situations Villiers was to prove himself unable to revivify in his *Elen* and his *Morgane*, pieces long since forgotten, published by an obscure local printer, Monsieur Francisque Guyon, of Saint-Brieuc.

The heroine of this book, a Marquise Tullia Fabriana, who was supposed to have assimilated the Chaldean learning of Poe's women together with the diplomatic wisdom of the Sanseverina-Taxis of Stendhal, had into the bargain put on the enigmatic air of a Bradamante added to an antique Circe These incompatible mixtures developed a smoky vapour through which philosophical and literary influences elbowed each other, without having been able to take order in the author's brain at the time he was writing the prolegomena to this work, which was planned to embrace not less than seven volumes.

But in Villiers' temperament there existed another side, altogether more telling, more clearly defined, an element of grim pleasantry and savage raillery; it was no longer, when this came into play, a case of Poe's paradoxical mystifications, but rather. a cruel jeering, a gloomy jesting, of the same sort as Swift's black rage against humanity. A whole series of pieces, *les Memoiselles de Bienfilâtre, l'Affichage céleste, la Machine à gloire, le Plus beau dîner au monde*, revealed a gift of satirical banter singularly inventive and effective. All the filth of utilitarian ideals, all the mercenary baseness of the century were glorified in pages the bitter irony of which moved Des Esseintes to ecstasy.

In this special class of serious and biting pleasantry no other book existed in France; at most, a romance of Charles Cros, *La Science de l'amour*, published originally in the *Revue du Monde-Nouveau*, might well amaze readers by its wild eccentricities, its satiric humour, its coldly comic observations, but the pleasure was no more than relative, for the execution was fatally defective. Villiers' style, strong, varied, often original, had disappeared to give place to a sort of force-meat scraped from the shop-board of the first literary pork-butcher to hand.

"Great God! how few books then there are that one can re-read," sighed Des Esseintes, watching the servant as he stepped off the stool he had been perched on and drew aside to let his master cast a general look along the shelves.

Des Esseintes nodded his approval. There now remained on his table only two thin volumes. He beckoned the old man to leave the room, and fell to skimming the pages of one of these, bound in wild ass's skin, first glazed under a hydraulic press, dappled in water-colour with silver clouds and provided with "end-papers" of old China silk, the pattern of which, now rather dim with age, had that grace of faded splendour that Mallarmé celebrated in a singularly delightful poem.

These pages, nine in all, contained extracts from unique copies of the two earliest *Parnasses*, printed on parchment, and preceded by a title-page bearing the words: *Quelques vers de Mallarmé*, designed by a wonderful calligrapher in uncial letters, coloured and picked out, like the characters in an ancient manuscript, with points of gold.

Among the eleven pieces included in the collection some, *Les fenêtres, l'Epilogue, Azur*, attracted him; but one of all the rest, a fragment of the *Hérodiade*, mastered him like a veritable spell at certain times.

How many evenings, under the light of the lowered lamp flooding the silent room, had he not felt his senses stirred by this same Herodias who, in Gustave Moreau's masterpiece that, now half invisible in the dimness, gleamed merely as a vaguely seen white statue in the midst of a dull glowing brazier of jewels.

The darkness hid the blood, dimmed the flash of colours and gold, buried in gloom the far corners of the temple, obscured the minor actors in the murderous drama where they stood wrapped in sad-coloured garments, sparing only the high lights of the painting, showing the white figure of the woman emerging from her sheath of jewels and accentuating her nakedness.

Involuntarily he lifted his eyes and looked. There gleamed the never-to-be-forgotten outlines of her shape; she lived again, recalling to his lips those weird, sweet words that Mallarmé puts in her mouth:

"..................... O miroir!
"Eau froide par l'ennui dans ton cadre gelée,
Que de fois, et pendant les heures désolée
Des songes et cherchant mes souvenirs qui sont
Comme des feuilles sous ta glace au trou profond,
Je m'apparus en toi comme une ombre lointaine!
Mais, horreur! des soirs, dans ta sévère fontaine,
J'ai de mon rêve épars connu ta nudité."[5]

He loved these verses as he loved all the works of this poet who, in an age of universal suffrage and an epoch of filthy lucre, lived aloof from literary society; sheltered against the folly of the world about him by his fine scorn; finding joy, far from the crowd, in the surprises of the intellect, the visions of his brain; refining on thoughts already fine and specious, engrafting on them Byzantine conceits, perpetuating them in deductions just lightly hinted, deductions barely bound together by an imperceptible thread.

These thoughts, interwoven and precious, he knotted into one with an adhesive diction, aloof and secret, full of contorted phrases, elliptical turns of speech, audacious tropes.

Catching analogies the most remote, he would often designate by a word that suggests by an effect of likeness at once form, scent, colour, quality, brilliancy, the object or being to which he must have appended a host of different epithets to indicate all its aspects, all its lights and shades, if it had been merely referred to by its technical name. He thus contrived to do away with the formal statement of a comparison, which arose of itself in the reader's mind by analogy, once he had comprehended the symbol, and avoided dissipating the attention over each of the several qualities which might otherwise have been presented one by one by a series of adjectives strung in a row, concentrating it instead on one single word, on one whole, producing, as an artist does in a picture, one unique and complete effect, one general aspect.

The result was a sort of condensed literature, an essence of nutriment, a sublimate of art. It was a device which Mallarmé after first

---

[5] ...O mirror! chill water-pool frozen by ennui within thy frame, how many times, and for hours long, tortured by dreams and searching my memories that are like dead leaves under the glassy surface that covers thy depths profound, have I seen myself in these like a far-off shadow! But, horror! of evenings, in thy cruel fountain, have I known the bare nudity of my broken vision!

employing it only sparingly in his earlier works, had openly and boldly adopted in a piece he wrote on Théophile Gautier and in the *l'Après-midi du faune*, an eclogue in which the subtleties of sensual joys were unfolded in mysterious, softly suggestive verses, broken suddenly by this frantic, wild-beast cry of the Faun:

> "Alors m'éveillerai-je à la ferveur première,
> Droit et seul sous un flot antique de lumière,
> Lys! et l'un de vous tous pour l'ingénuité."[6]

The last verse, which with its monosyllable "Lys" thrown back to the beginning called up the idea of something rigid, tall, white, an indication further strengthened by the noun "ingénuité" brought in as a rhyme, expressed allegorically, in a single word, the passion, the effervescence, the passing moment of excitement of the virgin Faun, maddened to lust at sight of the Nymphs.

In this extraordinary poem, surprises, novel images, unexpected conceptions awaited the reader in every line, as the poet went on to describe the emotions and regrets of the goat-foot standing by the marsh-side and gazing at the clumps of rushes still keeping a fleeting impress of the rounded forms of the Naïds that had lain there.

Then Des Esseintes also found a fanciful delight in handling the miniature volume, the covers of which, in Japanese felt, as white as curdled milk, were fastened with two silk cords, one China pink, the other black.

Concealed behind the binding, the black riband met the pink one, which gave a note of velvety softness, a suspicion as of modern Japanese rouge, a suggestion of love and licence, to the antique severity of the pure white, the frankly natural tint of the book, which it entwined, knotting together in a small rosette its combre hue with the brighter tint of the other, suggesting a discreet intimation of the Faun's regrets, a vague foreshadowing of the melancholy that succeeds the transports of passion and the appeasing of the senses excited to frenzy by desire.

Des Esseintes replaced on the table the *Après-midi du faune*, and glanced through another thin volume which he had had printed for his private use,—an anthology of prose poetry, a little shrine dedicated to Baudelaire as patron saint and opening with one of his pieces.

The collection included selected passages from the *Gaspard de la nuit* of that fantastic author Aloysius Bertrand who has transferred Da Vinci's methods to prose and painted with his metallic oxides a series of little pictures whose brilliant tints glitter like transparent enamels. To

---

[6] Then shall I awake to the pristine fervour, standing upright and alone under an old-world flood of light, Flower of the lily! and the one of you all for innocence!

these Des Esseintes had added the *Vox populi* of Villiers, a piece
superbly struck off in a style of gold recalling the type of Leconte de
Lisle and Flaubert, and some extracts from that delicious trifle, the
Livre de Jade, whose exotic perfume of ginseng and tea is mingled with
the fresh fragrance of water babbling in the moonlight from cover to
cover of the book.

But, in this selection, had likewise been gathered sundry pieces
rescued from dead and gone reviews:—*le Demon de l'analogie, la
Pipe, le Pauvre enfant pâle, le Spectacle interrompu, le Phénomène
futur*, and in particular the *Plaintes d'automne et Frisson d'hiver*. This
last was one of Mallarmé's masterpieces, one of the masterpieces of
prose poetry to boot, for they united a diction so magnificently ordered
that it lulled the senses, like some mournful incantation, some
intoxicating melody, with thoughts of an irresistible seductiveness,
stirrings of soul of the sensitive reader whose quivering nerves vibrate
with an acuteness that rises to ravishment, to pain itself.

Of all forms of literature that of the prose poem was Des Esseintes'
chosen favourite. Handled by an alchemist of genius, it should,
according to him, store up in its small compass, like an extract of meat,
so to say, the essence of the novel, while suppressing its long, tedious
analytical passages and superfluous descriptions. Again and again Des
Esseintes had pondered the distracting problem, how to write a novel
concentrated in a few sentences, but which should yet contain the
cohobated juice of the hundreds of pages always taken up in describing
the setting, sketching the characters, gathering together the necessary
incidental observations and minor details. In that case, so inevitable and
unalterable would be the words selected that they must take the place of
all others; in so ingenious and masterly a fashion would each adjective
be chosen that it could not with any justice be robbed of its right to be
there, and would open up such wide perspectives as would set the
reader dreaming for weeks together of its meaning, at once precise and
manifold, and enable him to know the present, reconstruct the past,
divine the future of the spiritual history of the characters, all revealed
by the flash-light of this single epithet.

The novel, thus conceived, thus condensed in a page or two, would
become a communion, an interchange of thought between a magic-
working author and an ideal reader, a mental collaboration by consent
between half a score persons of superior intellect scattered up and down
the world, a delectable feast for epicures and appreciable by them only.

In a word, the prose poem represented in Des Esseintes' eyes the
concrete juice, the osmazone of literature, the essential oil of art.

This succulence, developed and concentrated in a drop, already
existed in Baudelaire, as also in those poems of Mallarmé's which he
savoured with so deep a delight.

When he had closed his anthology, Des Esseintes told himself, here was the last book of his library, which would probably never receive another addition.

In fact, the decadence of a literature, attacked by incurable organic disease, enfeebled by the decay of ideas, exhausted by the excess of grammatical subtlety, sensitive only to the whims of curiosity that torment a fever patient, and yet eager in its expiring hours to express every thought and fancy, frantic to make good all the omissions of the past, tortured on its deathbed by the craving to leave a record of the most subtle pangs of suffering, was incarnate in Mallarmé in the most consummate and exquisite perfection.

Here was to be found, pushed to its completest expression, the quintessence of Baudelaire and Poe; here was the same powerful and refined basis yet further distilled and giving off new savours, new intoxications.

It was the dying spasm of the old tongue which, after a progressive decay from century to century, was ending in a total dissolution, in the same deliquium the Latin language had suffered, as it expired finally in the mystic conceptions and enigmatic phrases of St. Boniface and St. Adhelm.

For the rest, the decomposition of the French language had come about at a blow. In Latin, a lengthy period of transition, a pause of four hundred years, had intervened between the variegated and magnificent phraseology of Claudian and Rutilius and the dialect of the eighth century with its taint of decomposition. Not so in French; here no interval of time, no long-drawn series of ages, occurred; the variegated and magnificent style of the De Goncourts and the tainted style of Verlaine and Mallarmé rubbed elbows at Paris, dwelling together at the same time, in the same period, in the same century.

And Des Esseintes smiled to himself as he looked at one of the folios lying open on his church reading-desk, thinking how the moment might come when a learned scholar would compile for the decadence of the French language a glossary like that in which the erudite Du Cange has noted down the last stammering accents, the last spasmodic efforts, the last flashes of brilliancy, of the Latin tongue as it perished of old age, the death rattle sounding through the recesses of monkish cloisters.

Chapter Fifteen

After blazing up like a fire of straw, his enthusiasm for the "digester" was extinguished with a like rapidity. Soothed for the time being, his dyspepsia began again; presently, this over-stimulating essence of nourishment brought on such an irritation of the bowels that Des Esseintes was obliged to drop its use with all possible speed.

The complaint resumed its course, hitherto unknown symptoms going with it. First nightmares, hallucinations of smell, disturbances of vision, a hacking cough, coming on at a fixed hour with the regularity of clockwork, a beating of the arteries and heart accompanied by cold sweats; then, delusions of hearing, all the mischiefs, in fact, that mark the last stage of the malady.

Eaten up by a burning fever, Des Esseintes would suddenly hear the sound of running water, the buzz of wasps; then these noises would melt into a single one resembling the whirring of a lathe; then this would grow shriller and thinner, changing finally into the silvery tinkle of a bell.

Then he would feel his maddened brain wafted away on waves of music, rolling among the billows of harmony familiar to his boyhood. The chants he had learned from the Jesuit Fathers recurred to him, recalling the college, the college chapel, where they had echoed; then the hallucination would pass on to the olfactory and visual organs, wrapping them in the vapour of incense and the gloom of a sanctuary dimly lit through painted windows under lofty vaults.

Among the Fathers, the rites of religion were performed with great pomp and ceremony; an excellent organist and a noteworthy choir made these spiritual exercises an artistic delight, to the great end of edification. The organist was a lover of the old masters, and on days of festival he would select one of Palestrina's or Orlando Lasso's masses, Marcello's psalms, Handel's oratorios, Sebastian Bach's motets, would play in preference to the sensuous, facile compilations of Father Lambillotte so much favoured by the average priest, certain "Laudi spirituali" of the sixteenth century whose stately beauty had many a time fascinated Des Esseintes.

But above all, he had experienced ineffable pleasures in listening to the "plain-song," which the organist had kept up in spite of modern prejudices.

This form, now looked down upon as an effete and Gothic type of the Christian liturgy, as an antiquarian curiosity, as a relic of barbarous centuries, was the life-word of the ancient Church, the very spirit of the Middle Ages; it was the prayer of all time set to music in tones modulated in accord with the aspirations of the soul, the never-ceasing hymn of praise that had risen for hundreds of years to the throne of the Most High.

This traditional melody was the only one that, with its mighty unison, its solemn, massive harmonies, like blocks of ashlar, could fitly go with the old basilicas and fill their romanesque vaults, of which it seemed the emanation and the living voice.

How many times had not Des Esseintes been entranced and mastered by an irresistible awe when the "Christus factus est" of the Gregorian chant had swelled up in the nave whose pillars trembled amid the floating clouds of incense, or when the rolling bass of the "De profundis" groaned forth, mournful as a stifled sob, poignant as a despairing cry of mankind bewailing its mortal destiny, imploring the tender mercy of its Saviour.

In comparison with this magnificent plain-song, created by the genius of the Church, impersonal, anonymous as the organ itself, whose inventor is unknown, all other religious music seemed to him secular, profane. At bottom, in all the works of Jomelli and Porpora, of Carissimi and Durante, in the most admirable conceptions of Handel and Bach, there was no real renunciation of popular triumph, no sacrifice of artistic success, no abdication of human pride listening to itself at prayer; at best, in those imposing masses of Lesueur's performed at Saint-Roch was the true religious style renewed, grave and august, making some approach to the unadorned nudity, the austre majesty of the old plain-song.

Since those days, utterly revolted by pretentious works like the *Stabat mater* of Rossini or the similar compositions of Pergolese, disgusted with all this intrusion of worldly art into the liturgical sanctum, Des Esseintes had held aloof altogether from these equivocal productions tolerated by an indulgent Mother Church.

In fact, this fatal complacence, due partly to the greed for offertories, partly to a supposed attraction the music exercised on the faithful, had led directly to abuses,—airs borrowed from Italian operas, trivial cavatinas, unseemly quadrilles, performed with full orchestral accompaniment in the churches transformed into fine ladies' boudoirs, entrusted to theatre actors who bellowed aloft under the roof while down below the women fought a pitched battle of fine clothes with one another and quivered with soft emotion to hear the heroes of the opera whose wanton tones defiled the sacred notes of the organ!

For years now he had positively refused to take part in these pious entertainments, resting satisfied with his memories of childhood, regretting even having heard sundry *Te Deums* by great masters, for did he not remember that admirable *Te Deum* of the plain-song, that hymn so simple and grandiose, composed by some Saint, a St. Ambrose or a St. Hilary, who, lacking the complicated resources of an orchestra, failing the mechanical music of modern music, displayed an ardent faith, a delirious joy, the essence of the soul of all humanity expressed in burning, trustful, almost heavenly accents?

In any case, Des Esseintes' ideas on music were in flagrant contradiction with the theories he professed as to the other arts. In religious music, he really cared only for the monastic music of the Middle Ages, that ascetic music that acted instinctively on the nerves, like certain pages of the old Christian Latinity; besides, he admitted it himself, he was incapable of understanding the artful devices contemporary masters might have been able to introduce into Catholic art. The truth is, he had not studied music with the same passionate ardour he had applied to painting and to literature. He could play the piano like any other amateur, had come, after many fumblings, to be competent to read a score; but he knew nothing of harmony or the technique needful for really appreciating lights and shades of expression, for understanding nice points, for entering, with proper comprehension, into refinements and elaborations.

Then, on another side, secular music is a promiscuous art which one cannot enjoy at home and alone, as one reads a book; to taste it, he must needs have mixed with that inevitable public that crowds to theatres and besieges the *Cirque d'hiver* where, under a broiling sun, in an atmosphere as muggy as a wash-house, you see a man with the look of a carpenter bawling a remoulade and massacring disconnected bits of Wagner to the huge delight of an ignorant crowd!

He had never had the courage to plunge into this bath of promiscuity in order to hear Berlioz; some fragments of whom had nevertheless won his admiration by their high-wrought passion and abounding fire, while he realized with no less perspicacity that there was not a scene, not a phrase in any opera of the mighty Wagner that could be detached from its context without ruining it.

The scraps thus cut from the whole and served up at a concert lost all meaning, all sense, for, like the chapters in a book that mutually complete each other and all concur to bring about the same conclusion, the same final effect, his melodies were used by Wagner to define the character of his personages, to incarnate their thoughts, to express their motives, visible or secret, and their ingenious and persistent repetitions were only intelligible for an audience which followed the subject from its first opening and watched the characters grow little by little more clearly defined, observed them develop in surroundings from which they could not be separated without seeing them perish like branches severed from a tree.

So Des Esseintes thought, convinced that of all the horde of melomaniacs who every Sunday fell into ecstasies on the benches, twenty at most knew the score the musicians were massacring, when the box-openers were kind enough to hold their tongues and let the orchestra be heard.

The circumstance also being remembered that the intelligent patriotism of the French nation forbade the production of an opera of Wagner's at a Paris theatre, there was nothing left for the curious amateur who is unskilled in the arcana of music and cannot or will not travel to Bayreuth, save to stay at home, and that was the reasonable course Des Esseintes had adopted.

On another side, more popular, easier music and detached morceaux taken from the old-fashioned operas scarcely appealed to him; the trivial tunes of Auber and Boieldieu, of Adam and Flotow, and the commonplaces of musical rhetoric favoured by Ambroise Thomas, Bazin and their like repelled him just as much as the antiquated sentimentalities and cheap graces of the Italian composers. He had therefore resolutely refused to have anything to do with music, and for all the years this renunciation lasted, he found nothing to look back upon with any pleasure save a few chamber concerts at which he had heard Beethoven and above all Schumann and Schubert, who had stimulated his nerves as keenly as the most telling and tragical poems of Edgar Allan Poe.

Certain settings for the violoncello by Schumann had left him positively panting with emotion, gasping for breath under the stress of hysteria; but it was chiefly Schubert's *lieder* that had stirred him to the depths, lifted him out of himself, then prostrated him as after a wasteful outpouring of nervous fluid, after a mystic debauch of soul.

This music thrilled him to the very marrow, driving back an infinity of forgotten griefs, of old vexations, on a heart amazed to contain so many confused miseries and obscure sorrows. This music of desolation, crying from the deepest depths of being, terrified, while fascinating him. Never, without nervous tears rising to his eyes, had he been able to repeat the "Young Girl's Plaints," for in this *lamento* there was something more than heart-broken, something despairing that tore his entrails, something recalling the end of love's dream in a dismal landscape.

Every time they came back to his lips, these exquisite and funereal laments called up before his fancy a lonely place beyond the city boundaries, a beggarly, forsaken locality, where noiselessly, in the distance, lines of poor folks, harassed by life's wretchedness, filed away, bent double, into the gloom of twilight, while, meantime, he himself, full of bitterness, overflowing with disgust, felt himself standing alone, all alone in the midst of weeping Nature, overborne by an unspeakable melancholy, by an obstinate distress, the mysterious intensity of which brooked no consolation, no comparison, no respite. Like a passing bell, the despairing air haunted his brain now that he lay in bed, enfeebled by fever and tormented by an anxiety the more implacable because he could no longer discover its cause. Eventually he surrendered himself to the current, let himself be swept away by the torrent of the music, suddenly barred for a brief minute by the plain-song of the psalms that rose with its long-drawn bass notes in his head, whose temples seemed bruised and battered by the clappers of a hundred bells.

One morning, however, these noises fell quiet; he was in better possession of his faculties and asked the servant to hand him a mirror. He hardly knew himself; his face was earthen in hue, the lips dry and swollen, the tongue furrowed, the skin wrinkled; his straggling hair and beard, which his man had not trimmed since the beginning of his illness, added to the horror of the sunken cheeks and staring, watery eyes that burned with a feverish brightness in this death's-head bristling with unkempt hair.

Worse than his weakness, worse than his irrepressible fits of vomiting which rejected every attempt at taking food, worse than the wasting from which he suffered, this disfigurement of face alarmed him. He thought he was done for; then, in spite of the exhaustion that crushed him down, the fierce energy of a man at bay brought him to a sitting posture in his bed, lent him strength to write a letter to his Paris doctor and order his servant to go instantly to find him and bring him back with him, cost what it might, the same day.

In an instant, he passed from the most absolute despair to the most comforting hope. The physician in question was a noted specialist, renowned for the cure of nervous disorders; "he must before now have cured more obstinate and more dangerous cases than mine," Des Esseintes told himself; "not a doubt of it, I shall be set up again in a few days' time." But presently again this over-confidence was followed by a feeling of utter disenchantment; no matter how learned and how perspicacious they may be, doctors really know nothing about nervous disease, the very cause of which they cannot tell. Like all the rest, he would prescribe the everlasting oxide of zinc and quinine, bromide of potassium and valerian; "and who can say," he went on to himself, clinging to the last twig of hope, "if the reason why these remedies have hitherto failed me is not simply because I have not known how to employ them in proper doses."

Despite everything, this waiting for expected relief gave him new life; but presently a fresh dread assailed him,—suppose the doctor should not be in town or should decline to disturb his arrangements; then came yet another panic lest his servant should have failed to find him at all. This threw him into the depths of despair. His mind began to fail again, jumping, moment by moment, from the most inordinate hopefulness to the most baseless apprehension, exaggerating both his chances of sudden recovery and his fears of immediate danger. Hour after hour slipped by, and a time arrived when, despairing and exhausted, convinced the doctor would never come, he told himself over and over again in impotent anger that, if only he had seen to it in time, he would undoubtedly have been saved; then after a while, his rage with his servant, his indignation at the doctor's delay, abated, and he began to cherish a bitter vexation against himself instead, blaming his own procrastination in having waited so long before sending for help, persuading himself that he would have been perfectly well by now, if, even the night before only, he had provided himself with good, strong medicines and proper nursing.

Gradually these alternate paroxysms of hope and fear that tormented his half-delirious brain grew milder, as these repeated panics wore down his strength. He dropped into a sleep of exhaustion broken by incoherent dreams, a kind of coma interrupted by periods of wakefulness too brief for consciousness to be regained. He had finally lost all notion of what he wished and what he feared so completely that he was merely bewildered, and felt neither surprise nor satisfaction, when suddenly the doctor made his appearance in the room.

The servant no doubt had informed him of the manner of life Des Esseintes led and of various symptoms he had himself been in a position to notice since the day when he had picked up his master by the window where he lay, felled by the violence of his perfumes, for he asked the patient very few questions, knowing indeed his antecedents for many years past. But he examined and sounded him and carefully scrutinized the urine, in which certain white streaks told him the secret of one of the chief determining causes of his nervous collapse. He wrote a prescription and took his leave without a word, saying he would come again.

His visit comforted Des Esseintes, albeit he was alarmed at the doctor's silence and besought his servant not to hide the truth from him any longer.

The man assured him the doctor had showed no signs of anxiety and, suspicious as he was, Des Esseintes could detect no tokens whatever of prevarication or falsehood in the old man's calm face.

Then his thoughts grew more cheerful; indeed the pain had stopped and the feebleness he had experienced in every limb had merged into a sort of agreeable languor, a feeling of placid content at once vague and slowly progressive. Then he was at once astonished and pleased to find his bedside table unlittered with drugs and medicine bottles, and a pale smile hovered over his lips when finally his servant brought him a nourishing enema compounded with peptone, and informed his master that he was to repeat the little operation three times every twenty-four hours.

The thing was successfully carried out, and Des Esseintes could not help secretly congratulating himself on the event which was the coping stone, the crowning triumph, in a sort, of the life he had contrived for himself; his predilection for the artificial had now, and that without any initiative on his part, attained its supreme fulfilment! A man could hardly go farther; nourishment thus absorbed was surely the last aberration from the natural that could be committed.

"What a delicious thing," he said to himself, "it would be if one could, once restored to full health, go on with the same simple régime. What a saving of time, what a radical deliverance from the repugnance meat inspires in people who have lost their appetite! what a definite and final release from the lassitude that invariably results from the necessarily limited choice of viands! what a vigorous protest against the degrading sin of gluttony! last but not least, what a direct insult cast in the face of old Mother Nature, whose never varying exigencies would be for ever nullified!"

In this vein, he went on talking to himself under his breath. Why, it would be easy enough to sharpen one's appetite by swallowing a strong aperient, then when one could truly tell oneself: "Come, what hour is it now? seems to me it must be high time to sit down to dinner, I have a wolf in my stomach," the table would be laid by depositing the noble instrument on the cloth,—and lo! before you had time so much as to say grace, the troublesome and vulgar task of eating would be suppressed.

Some days later, the man handed his master an enema altogether different in colour and smell from the peptone suppositories.

"Why, it's not the same!" exclaimed Des Esseintes, looking with consternation at the liquid poured into the apparatus. He demanded the menu as he might have done in a restaurant and unfolding the physician's prescription, he read out—

Cod-liver oil	20 grammes
Beef-tea	200 "
Burgundy	200 "
Yolk of one egg	

He sat pensive. He had never succeeded, on account of the ruined state of his stomach, in taking a serious interest in the art of cookery; now he was surprised to find himself all of a sudden pondering over combinations of *a posteriori* gourmandise! Then a grotesque notion shot across his brain. Perhaps the doctor had imagined his patient's abnormal palate was wearied by this time of the flavour of peptone; perhaps, like a skilful chef, he had wished to vary the savour of the foods administered, to prevent the monotony of the dishes leading to a complete loss of appetite. Once started on this train of thought, Des Esseintes busied himself in composing novel recipes, contriving dinners for fast days and Fridays, strengthening the dose of cod-liver oil and wine, while striking out the beef-tea as being meat and therefore expressly forbidden by the Church. But, before very long, the necessity disappeared of deliberating about these nourishing liquids, for the doctor managed little by little to overcome the nausea and gave him, to be swallowed by the ordinary channel, a syrup of punch mixed with powdered meat and having a vague aroma of cocoa about it that was grateful to his genuine mouth.

Weeks passed and the stomach at last consented to act; occasionally fits of nausea still recurred, which, however, ginger beer and Rivière's anti-emetic draught were effectual in subduing. Eventually, little by little, the organs recovered with the help of the pepsines, and ordinary foods were digested. Strength returned and Des Esseintes was able to stand on his feet and try to walk about his bedroom, leaning on a stick and holding on to the furniture. Instead of being pleased with this success, he forgot all his past sufferings, was irritated by the length of his convalescence, and upbraided the doctor for protracting it in this slow fashion. True, sundry ineffectual experiments had delayed matters; no better than quinine did the stomach, tolerate iron, even when mitigated by the addition of laudanum, and these drugs had to be replaced by preparations of arsenic; this after a fortnight had been lost in useless efforts, as Des Esseintes noted with no small impatience.

At last, the moment was reached when he could remain up for whole afternoons at a time and walk about his rooms without assistance. Then his working-room began to get on his nerves; defects to which custom had blinded his eyes now struck him forcibly on his coming back to the room after his long absence. The colours chosen to be seen by lamplight seemed to him discordant under the glare of daylight; he thought how best to alter them and spent hours in contriving artificial harmonies of hues, hybrid combinations of cloths and leathers.

"Without a doubt I am on the highroad to health," he told himself, as he noted the return of his former preoccupations and old predilections.

One morning, as he was gazing at his orange and blue walls, dreaming of ideal hangings made out of stoles of the Greek Church, of gold-fringed Russian dalmatics, of brocaded copes patterned with Slavonic lettering, adorned with precious stones from the Urals and rows of pearls, the doctor came in and, noting what his patient's eyes were looking at, questioned him.

Then Des Esseintes told him of his unrealizable ideals and began to plan out new experiments in colour, to speak of novel combinations and contrasts of hues that he meant to contrive, when the physician soused a sudden douche of cold water over his head, declaring in the most peremptory fashion that, come what might, it would not be in that house he could put his projects into execution.

Then, without giving him time to recover breath, he announced that so far he had only attacked the most urgent necessity, the re-establishment of the digestive functions, but that now he must deal with the nervous derangements which were by no means mitigated and would require for their cure years of regimen and careful living. He concluded with the ultimatum that, before trying any course of cure, before beginning any sort of hydropathic treatment,—impracticable in any case at Fontenay,—he was bound to abandon this solitary existence, to return to Paris and take part again in the common life of men; in a word, endeavour to find diversions the same as other people.

"But they don't divert *me*, the pleasures other people enjoy," protested Des Esseintes, indignantly.

Without discussing the question, the doctor simply assured his hearer that this radical change of life which he ordered was in his opinion a matter of life and death, of restored health or insanity followed at short notice by tuberculosis.

"Then it is a case either of death or deportation!" cried Des Esseintes, in exasperation.

The physician, who was imbued with all the prejudices of a man of the world, only smiled and made for the door without vouchsafing an answer.

Chapter Sixteen

Des Esseintes shut himself up in his bedroom and turned a deaf ear to the knocking of the men's hammers who were nailing up the packing-cases the servants had got ready; each stroke seemed to beat on his heart and send a pang of pain through his flesh. The sentence pronounced by the doctor was being executed; the dread of enduring all over again the same sufferings he had borne before, the fear of an agonizing death, had exercised a more powerful influence over Des Esseintes than his hatred of the detestable existence to which the physician's orders condemned him could counteract.

"And yet," he kept telling himself, "there are people who live alone, without a soul to speak to, self-absorbed and utterly aloof from society, like the Reclusionists and Trappists for instance, and there is nothing to show that these unfortunates, these wise men, run mad or develop consumption."

These examples he had quoted to the doctor,—without effect; the latter had merely repeated in a dry tone admitting of no reply, that his verdict, confirmed moreover by all the writers on nervous diseases, was that distraction, amusement, cheerfulness, were the only means of benefitting this complaint which, on the mental side, remained unaffected by any remedies in the nature of drugs. Finally, annoyed by his patient's reproaches, he had once for all declared his refusal to go on with his case unless he consented to take change of air and live under altered conditions of hygiene.

Des Esseintes had immediately repaired to Paris, where he had consulted other specialists and frankly submitted his case to them; all had with one accord and unhesitatingly approved their colleague's prescriptions. Thereupon, he had taken a flat still vacant in a newly-built house; had returned to Fontenay and, white with rage, had given his servant orders to pack his boxes.

Buried in his armchair, he was now pondering these express directions of the faculty which upset all his plans, broke all the ties binding him to his present life, made his future projects futile. So, his time of bliss was over! This haven, that sheltered him from the storms, he must abandon and put out again into the storm-tost ocean of human folly that had battered and bruised him so sorely.

The doctors prated of amusement, of distraction; with whom, pray with what, did they expect him to be blithe and gay?

Had he not deliberately put himself under a social ban? did he know one single friend who would be willing to essay a life, like his, of contemplation, of dreamy abstraction? did he know a single individual capable of appreciating the delicate shades of a style, the subtle joints of a picture, the quintessence of a thought, one whose soul was so finely framed as to understand Mallarme and love Verlaine?

Where, when, in what depths must he sound to discover a twin soul, a mind free of commonplace prejudices, blessing silence as a boon, ingratitude as a solace, suspicion as a port of security, a harbour of refuge?

In the society he had frequented before he took his departure for Fontenay?—Why, the majority of the clowns he associated with in those times must, since that date, have yet further stultified themselves in drawing-rooms, grown more degraded sitting at gaming tables, reached lower depths in the arms of prostitutes. Nay, the most part must by now be married; after having enjoyed all their life hitherto the leavings of the street-loafers, it was their wives who at present owned the leavings of the street-walkers, for, master of the first-fruits, the vulgar herd was the one and only class that did not feed on refuse!

"What a pretty change of partners, what a gallant interchange, this custom adopted by a society that still calls itself prudish!" Des Esseintes growled to himself.

Yes, nobility was utterly decayed, dead; aristocracy had fallen into idiocy or filthy pleasures! It was perishing in the degeneracy of its members, whose faculties grew more debased with each succeeding generation till they ended with the instincts of gorillas quickened in the pates of grooms and jockeys, or else, like the once famous houses of Choiseul-Praslin, Polignac, Chevreuse, wallowed in the mud of legal actions that brought them down to the same level of baseness as the other classes.

The very mansions, the time-honoured scutcheons, the heraldic blazons, the stately pomp and ceremony of this ancient caste had disappeared. Its estates no longer yielded revenue, they and the great houses on them had come to the hammer, for money ran short to buy the smiles of women that bewitched and poisoned the besotted descendants of the old families.

The least scrupulous, the least dull-witted, threw all shame to the winds; they mixed in low plots, stirred up the filth of base finance, appeared like common pickpockets at the bar of justice, serving at any rate to set off the tact of human justice which, finding it impossible to be always impartial, ended the matter by making them librarians in the prisons.

This eagerness after gain, this itch for filthy lucre, had found a counterpart also in another class, the class that had always leant for support on the nobility,—the clergy to wit. Now were to be seen on the outside sheets of the papers advertisements of corns cured by a priest. The monasteries were transformed into apothecaries' laboratories and distilleries. They sold recipes or manufactured the stuff themselves; the Cistercians, chocolate, Trappistine, semolina, tincture of arnica; the Marist Brotherhood, bisulphate of chalk for medical purposes and vulnerary water; the Jacobines, anti-apoplectic elixir; the disciples of St. Benedict, Bénédictine; the monks of St. Bruno, Chartreuse.

Business had invaded the cloisters, where, in lieu of antiphonaries, fat ledgers lay on the lecterns. Like a leprosy, the greed of the century devastated the Church, kept the monks bending over inventories and invoices, turned the Fathers Superior into confectioners and quacksalvers, the lay brothers and novices into common packers and vulgar bottle-washers.

And yet, spite of everything, it was still only among ecclesiastics that Des Esseintes could hope for relations congruent, up to a certain point, with his tastes. In the society of the clergy, generally learned and well educated men, he might have spent some affable and agreeable evenings; but then he must have shared their beliefs and not be a mere waverer between sceptical notions and spasms of conviction that came surging from time to time to the surface, buoyed up by the memories of childhood.

He must needs have held identical views, refused to accept, as he was ready enough to do in his moments of ardour, a Catholicism spiced with a touch of magic, as under Henri III., and a trifle of Sadism, as at the end of the eighteenth century. This special brand of clericalism, this vitiated and artistically perverse type of mysticism, towards which he was tending at certain seasons, could not even be discussed with a priest, who would either have failed to understand what he meant or would have excommunicated him there and then in sheer horror.

For the twentieth time, the same insoluble problem tormented him. He would fain this state of suspicion and suspense against which he had struggled in vain at Fontenay should have an end; now that he was to turn over an entirely new leaf, he would fain have forced himself to possess faith, to seize it and clothe himself in it, to fasten it with clamps in his soul, to put it beyond the reach of all the reasonings that shake it and uproot it. But the more he desired it and the less the emptiness of his mind was filled, the more the visitation of the Saviour delayed its coming. Just in proportion, indeed, as his religious faith increased, as he craved with all his strength, as a ransom for the future and a help in the new life he was to lead, this faith that showed itself in glimpses, though the distance still dividing him from it appalled him, did doubts rise crowding his ever excited brain, upsetting his ill-poised will, repudiating on grounds of common sense, of mathematical demonstrations, the mysteries and dogmas of the Church.

He should have been able to stop these discussions with himself, he told himself with a groan; he should have been able to shut his eyes, let himself be carried along with the stream, forget all the accursed discoveries that have shattered the religious edifice from top to bottom during the last two centuries.

"Yet, really and truly," he sighed, "it is neither the physiologists nor the sceptics who destroy Catholicism, it is the priests themselves, whose clumsy writings might well root up the most firmly grounded convictions."

In the Dominican collection, was there not to be found a certain Doctor of Theology, Révérend Père Rouard de Card, a Preaching Brother, who in a brochure entitled:—"Of the Falsification of the Sacramental Substances," has demonstrated beyond a doubt that the major part of Masses were null and void, by reason of the fact that the materials used in the rite were sophisticated by dealers?

For years, the holy oils had been adulterated with goose-grease; the taper-wax with burnt bones; the incense with common resin and old benzoin. But worse than all, the substances indispensable for the holy sacrifice, the two things without which no oblation was possible, had likewise been falsified,—the wine by repeated dilutings and the illicit addition of Pernambuco bark, elder-berries, alcohol, alum, salicylate, litharge; the bread, that bread of the Eucharist that must be kneaded of the fine flour of wheat, by ground haricotbeans, potash and pipeclay!

Nay, now they had gone further yet; they had dared to suppress the wheat altogether and shameless dealers manufactured out of potato meal nearly all the hosts!

Now God declined to come down and be made flesh in potato flour. This was a surety, an indisputable fact; in the second volume of his Moral Theology, His Eminence Cardinal Gousset had also dealt at length with this question of adulteration from the divine standpoint, and, according to the authority of this master which there was no gainsaying, the celebrant *could* not consecrate bread made of oats, buckwheat or barley, and though the case of rye-bread at least admitted of doubt, no question could be raised, no argument sustained, when it came to using potato meal, which, to employ the ecclesiastical expression, was in no sense a substance competent for the Blessed Sacrament.

By reason of the easy manipulation of this meal and the good appearance presented by the unleavened cakes made of this substance, the unworthy and fraudulent substitution had become so widely prevalent that the mystery of the transubstantiation could hardly be said to exist any longer, and priests and faithful laymen communicated, all unwittingly, with neutral elements!

Ah! the days were far away when Rhadegond, Queen of France, used with her own hands to prepare the bread destined for the altars; the days when, by the custom of Cluny, three priests or three deacons, fasting, clad in alb and amice, after washing face and fingers, sorted out the wheat grain by grain, crushed it in the hand-mill, kneaded the dough with cold spring-water and baked it themselves over a clear fire, singing psalms the while!

"All this," Des Esseintes told himself, "cannot hinder the natural result, that this prospect of being constantly duped, even at the holy table itself, is not of a sort to establish beliefs already tottering; besides, how accept an omnipotence that is hindered by a pinch of potato meal or a drop of alcohol?"

These thoughts still further darkened the aspect of his future existence and rendered his horizon yet more dark and threatening.

Of a surety, no haven of refuge was open to him, no shore of safety left. What was to become of him in Paris yonder, where he had neither relatives nor friends? No tie bound him any more to the Faubourg Saint-Germain that was now quavering in its dotage, scaling away in a dust of desuetude, lying derelict—a worn-out, empty hull!—amid a new society! And what point of contact could there be between him and that bourgeois class that had little by little climbed to the top, taking advantage of every disaster to fill its coffers, stirring up every kind of catastrophe to make its crimes and thefts pass muster?

After the aristocracy of birth, it was now the turn of the aristocracy of money; it was the Caliphate of the counting-house, the despotism of the Rue du Sentier, the tyranny of commerce with its narrow-minded, venal ideas, its ostentatious and rascally instincts.

More nefarious, more vile than the nobility it had plundered and the clergy it had overthrown, the bourgeoisie borrowed their frivolous love of show, their decrepit boastfulness, which it vulgarized by its lack of good manners, stole their defects which it aggravated into hypocritical vices. Obstinate and sly, base and cowardly, it shot down ruthlessly its eternal and inevitable dupe, the populace, which it had itself unmuzzled and set on to spring at the throat of the old castes!

Now the victory was won. Its task once completed, the plebs had been for its health's sake bled to the last drop, while the bourgeois, secure in his triumph, throned it jovially by dint of his money and the contagion of his folly. The result of his rise to power had been the destruction of all intelligence, the negation of all honesty, the death of all art; in fact, the artists and men of letters, in their degradation, had fallen to their knees and were devouring with ardent kisses the unwashed feet of the high-placed horse-jockeys and low-bred satraps on whose alms they lived!

In painting, it was a deluge of effeminate futilities; in literature, a welter of insipid style and spiritless ideas. What was a-lacking was common honesty in the business gambler, common honour in the freebooter who hunted for a dowry for his son while refusing to pay his daughter's, common chastity in the Voltairean who accused the clergy of incontinence while he was off himself to sniff, like a dull fool and a hypocrite, pretending to be the rake he was not, in disorderly dens of pleasure, at the greasy water in toilet vessels and the hot, acrid effluvium of dirty petticoats.

It was the vast, foul bagnio of America transported to our Continent; it was, in a word, the limitless, unfathomable, incommensurable firmament of blackguardism of the financier and the self-made man, beaming down, like a despicable sun, on the idolatrous city that grovelled on its belly, hymning vile songs of praise before the impious tabernacle of Commerce.

"Well, crumble then, society! perish, old world!" cried Des Esseintes, indignant at the ignominy of the spectacle he had conjured up,—and the exclamation broke the nightmare that oppressed him.

"Ah!" he groaned, "to think that all this is not a dream! to think that I am about to go back into the degraded and slavish mob of the century!" He tried to call up, for the healing of his wounded spirit, the consoling maxims of Schopenhauer; he said over to himself Pascal's grievous axiom: "The soul sees nothing that does not afflict it when it thinks of it"; but the words rang in his brain like sounds without sense; his weariness of spirit disintegrated them, robbed them of all meaning, all consolatory virtue, all effective and soothing force.

He realized, at last, that the arguments of pessimism were powerless to comfort him; that the impossible belief in a future life could be the only calmant.

A fit of rage swept away like a hurricane his efforts after resignation, his attempts at indifference. He could deceive himself no more, there was nothing, nothing left for it, everything was over; the bourgeoisie were guzzling, as it might be at Clamart, on their knees, from paper parcels, under the grand old ruins of the Church, which had become a place of assignation, a mass of débris, defiled by unspeakable quibbles and indecent jests. Could it be that, to prove once for all that He existed, the terrible God of Genesis and the pale Crucified of Golgotha were not going to renew the cataclysms of an earlier day, to rekindle the rain of fire that consumed the ancient homes of sin, the cities of the Plain? Could it be that this foul flood was to go on spreading and drowning in its pestilential morass this old world where now only seeds of iniquity sprang up and harvests of shame flourished?

Suddenly the door was unclosed; in the distance, framed in the opening, appeared men carrying lights in their caps, with clean-shaven cheeks and a tuft on the chin, handling packing-cases and shifting furniture; then the door closed again after the servant, who marched off with a bundle of books under his arm.

Des Esseintes dropped into a chair, in despair. "In two days more I shall be in Paris," he exclaimed; "well, all is over; like a flowing tide, the waves of human mediocrity rise to the heavens and they will engulf my last refuge; I am opening the sluice-gates myself, in spite of myself. Ah; but my courage fails me, and my heart is sick within me!—Lord, take pity on the Christian who doubts, on the sceptic who would fain believe, on the galley-slave of life who puts out to sea alone, in the darkness of night, beneath a firmament illumined no longer by the consoling beacon-fires of the ancient hope."

THE END

Printed in the USA
CPSIA information can be obtained
at www.ICGtesting.com
LVHW020313190824
788609LV00007B/144

9 781420 965674

who believe in the existence of Creator might do my kingdom harm. So I prefer to keep humans ignorant, even if it means they are ignorant of me.

Who is responsible for keeping humankind out of my clutches? Creator. I want to kill every human on planet Earth, but Creator keeps finding ways to keep them alive. If Creator had not made me, then I would not be in the dilemma I find myself. If Creator had not made humankind, then I would not be jealous and filled with envy of the relationship between Creator and His prized Creation.

Yes! Creator and humans, in my opinion, are responsible for my problems. Hence, I seek revenge on humankind to get back at Creator. With great vengeance, I carry on a mission to destroy His Creation. When I can, I steal all that humans have, kill whatever is dear to them, and as much as possible, destroy their dreams.

Humans are easy. Give them something valuable, and I can have their souls in exchange. An invention, a device, an answer to a scientific or medical question, and they become putty in my hands. They will argue the merits of the invention, the innovativeness of a device, or applaud answers to scientific or medical questions, but they will never question the source. They do not care about the source. Once they benefit or gain notoriety, why bother with learning anything else? They take credit and off they go. They are impressed with themselves. I understand their attitudes, for I impress myself too.

Daily, I hear many humans shouting praises

to Creator. I desperately want to steal His thunder, but I keep running into obstacles. Humans? Humans.

On Earth, I move up and down to see what humankind is up to. In my opinion, humans are always up to something. They are creative like the Creator, but they are too stupid to know this. Periodically, I come across humans who are stricken with chronic stubbornness, which I have labeled the "Job Factor," severe to chronic desire to serve Creator in a righteous manner. These become my primary targets!

What are my immediate plans for man's damnation? Attack all that humankind hold dear, corrupt everyone he loves, hinder his progress, alter his system of rules, and blind him to my devices, my modus operendi.

I copy; I cannot create. I kill; I cannot restore life. That's my whole purpose, to steal, kill, or destroy. I have chosen my current role! Just like you musty creatures called humans have free choice, so did I. And eons ago, I chose to be a liar, thief, and destroyer. I do my own thing. Unlike humans, however, fallen angels do not have the option to repent and start afresh. We are damned to hell, and we know it. We merely compensate by taking down as many humans as we can trick.

Many people do not understand how I can influence them. I put "hooks in the noses" of humans and pull them toward damnation. What are these hooks? Addictions! An addiction of any kind is a hook in the nose of the addicted, and he or she can

be driven or pulled into evil by his or her addiction. When humans become addicted to any substance—food, drugs, alcohol, or sex, disembodied spirits might just have a chance to infiltrate that person's subconscious. What does being drunk do to the spirit? It opens up the doorway to the spirit world.

The first thing I do to undermine the human race is to steal everything I can from mankind. I steal their wisdom, knowledge, and understanding. Why should I have regard for mankind? In the end, humankind will choose me and my ways, debauchery, violence, sexual immorality.

Making humans afraid has been my focus since I was thrown out of Heaven. I want people to think that I am omnipresent, that I am everywhere at once.

I want humans to be wild—wilder than films portray so called prehistoric humans, wilder than any animal! Right now, I am doing a superb job on the current generation. So many are disrespectful to their parents and other adult figures; multitudes are unthankful, and most are unholy. I want these youngsters to grow up wild, without discipline and no natural affection—a generation to foster mayhem.

I am against young people abstaining from sexual intercourse until marriage; I am against monogamous relationships. If I have my way, the age of consent will be lowered to 12.

Actually, I've hated mankind since his creation. I have envied man's role in Creator's scheme of things. Creator made everything that you see for

the baffled idiotic specimen called mankind. The sun, moon, stars—the seas, oceans and all that are in them—the animal and plant kingdoms—all created for the enjoyment and use of human beings. To think that Creator actually formed a stumbling, mumbling, error-prone, petty creature like a human being, dumber than the animals, just increases my hatred of humankind and my rage against all humans. Creator has done me an injustice by giving so much power and authority to humans who have no idea what to do with power. I am doing everything in my power (limited as it may be) to cause Creator's very own Creation to turn against Him. I have been practicing for years! Ha!

Humankind is hopeless. I lead them on a path to self-destruct. I am ready to see Creator's kingdom crumble!

So I have, since my eviction from Heaven, come down to Earth with a voluminous rage against and malicious hatred for humankind. My purpose is to turn them all from Creator so they, too, will be barred from Heaven. A Lake of Fire has been reserved for me where I'm damned to spend eternity. An eternity in a pit that burns with fire and brimstone is not an exciting future that I look forward to, so I plan to take with me to the pit of hell as many humans as I can.

What are my overall aims? I want to see humankind at his lowest—spiritually, financially, socially, physically, and emotionally. I want humans to conform to every decadent act, fad, or trend, and create their own forms of self-indulgent behaviors,

each one worse than the first. I want each person to believe he or she is okay and needs no such thing as accountability to or forgiveness from anyone.

Dead relationships. If relationships can die, then I want to see the death of every relationship among humans. I want every man, woman, boy, and girl to passionately hate each other. I want every person on Earth to pass judgment continuously on everyone. I want every person the enemy of the other. I want families at odds continually, neighbors to harbor sweltering hatred for neighbors, and countries continually at war. I especially want to decimate or annihilate relationships among groups that declare that there is such a being as Creator.

I want to institute cycles of agony and defeat. I want to kill family members to multiply the number of bereaved, multiply pain and suffering of the sick, and devastate the poor and needy by making even bare necessities impossible to acquire. I want all humans to be impatient about everything, to be driven by evil spirits. I want humans to accept my words as truth and Creator's as fantasy. I want every human being that has ever lived to join my hordes of demons and me in the Lake of Fire that burns with brimstone. When the Book of Truth is opened and lifestyles are judged, I want to hear: Guilty! Guilty! Guilty!

What is my prognostication for the future? Changes, multiple changes.

Pornographic halls of worships. A pornographic theater placed in every neighborhood in

place of Christian church. I will relish the day when majority of parents, without flinching, and their young children sit and watch pornographic videos on their television sets in their homes. Pornographic paraphernalia—posters, magazines, books, tapes— on sale in convenient stores, discount department stores, and all major grocery chains. Pornographic art classes will be electives in colleges and universities and part of the day-to-day curriculum in high schools with corresponding porn textbooks.

Cannibalism will be the order of the day. The flesh of human beings sold as delicacies on the black market. The brain and heart being the most expensive, since there is so much ado about the "heart" of a human.

A new industry, the best yet—human organs on sale, not only to the very rich, but also to those of moderate income. Humans kept alive and penned as animals so organs or body parts can be removed to sell as these are ordered. With human organs for sale, imagine just how many humans will be abducted and killed just for body parts. No family member will be safe then. Can you imagine how many families will get rich at the expense of their children, husbands, or wives? Even grandparents will be at risk! The powerless and the weak will disappear totally!

Humans reduced to animalistic behavior. Rape, incest, bestiality, sodomy, lesbian coupling— openly on television, on the big screen, in backyards, on picnic grounds, on public beaches, or even on

neighborhood sidewalks. No human even turns his or her head or looks the other way.

My best yet is the return of prayer to public schools. This time, however, prayers will be offered to any and all gods, those of the past and any new gods the populace can create. This will be the appropriate time for an exit from the closet of witches, warlocks, and satan worshipers.

What are my plans for humans? A new and improved desensitized human on the face of the Earth, until he brings about his own annihilation or the wrath of Creator.

I plan for morality to be removed from any semblance of godliness; that is, I want "right and wrong" to be totally orchestrated by the will of the people. The consensus of the majority will determine what is right or inappropriate. There will be no wrongness in any situation.

Take for instance, the issue of sex. Debauchery is in order. Human acceptance of incest and bestiality are primary on my list of priorities. I do not include homosexuality because tolerance and soon majority acceptance of men lying with men and women sleeping with women will soon be legislated. I have my agents at work trying to bring about the legislation that will make homosexuality a commonplace occurrence. With the acceptance and tolerance of homosexual lifestyles, legislation to accept incest and bestiality is forthcoming.

After homosexuality is firmly established as an acceptable lifestyle, then my imps will work on

the intellect of those who propagate incestuous relationships. Brothers and sisters, fathers and daugh-
ters, sons and mothers, sisters, brothers, cousins—all
coming together to create a sexual cesspool that only
demons can appreciate. Initially, the believers in Creator will denounce the move as diabolical. (How right
they are!) But a strong minority who wish to sanction
this deviant lifestyle will move to make sexual intercourse between family members an appropriate act,
not punishable by law. They will use the adage of
sexual preference and herald the relationship as an
"alternative family style." The sexual union of family
members will more than likely produce children who
might be deficient mentally, physically, and socially.

When humankind has plummeted to its lowest point because of acceptance of incest, then bestiality will be introduced; that is, laws will be introduced that will make it okay for humans to cohabit
with larger animals. First, it will be simply a matter
of privacy; that is, sex between humankind and larger
animals within a person's home will not be subject to
judgment by the law. However, those who become
consumed with this form of sexual perversion will
seek the world's approval by chanting "an alternative human-animal lifestyle." Justification? The act
would improve relations between the "human and
animal kingdoms." The consenting minority, though
small, will try to exert pressure on the disapproving
majority by screaming, *Intolerance*! Many who disapprove will re-think their stance, suffer from a guilt
complex, and will refuse to either speak against bes-

tiality or sanction the act. After the practice becomes open and accepted by a recognizable majority, then laws will be passed to sanction sexual intercourse between humankind and animals.

To further desensitize the public, scene of men and women engaged in sexual acts with the animals of their preference will be included in prime time television shows and in movies. Parents and their children (if children are still being produced at this point) will sit in front of television sets or movie screens and view sitcoms or movies that hint at or show scenes of human-animal sexual encounters. From man's union with animals, there will be no procreation. Thus, I will have driven another stake in God's command to be "fruitful, multiply and fill the Earth." Human reproduction will be at an all time low. My hordes and I will have taken the race of humans down to the status of beasts. How can I predict these things? I have had eons to study the actions and attitudes of humankind. This is how they do it!

EPILOGUE

There are no special rehabilitative programs for fallen angels. I cannot repent. I can never again live in the presence of Creator, so I hate all who has that possibility to do so.

What are my immediate goals? Corrupt each present generation; hinder their ability to pro-create. Influence humans to legislate morality. Convince humankind that there is no such being as Creator. Turn the affections of humankind "inward" and promote sexual promiscuity and sexual experimentation.

I would like to count on twenty-first-century humans to assist me in carrying out my plans. Yet, I cannot count on these to do my bidding, because deep in the heart of supposedly "liberated societies," many humans have deep rooted senses for doing the "right" thing. Their propensity to do this "right" thing during my prime time causes havoc in the kingdom of darkness. Just when I think the Earth is mine, humans band together to perpetrate kind acts to other humans or cities or nations. Humans are so inconsistent!

For example, for most of the twentieth century, the stronghold on nations was discrimination. The populace had no clue that they were instruments in a satanic war waged from hell to foster prejudice,

segregation, and racial cleansing. I had every demon of strife and dissemination actively moving about nations to keep the war ongoing. What do some busybody humans do? Wage a worldwide struggle against apartheid. The struggle made me look bad in the world of the spirits. I am still striving to salvage what is left of strongholds of racial discrimination.

I have been working to steal, kill, and destroy humankind for the past six thousand years. I walked through the Garden of Eden, presided at the Tower of Babel, and experimented in Sodom and Gomorrah. I inspired the use of slave labor at slavery's inception through the building of pyramids around the globe, the enslavement of the Hebrews in Egypt, slavery throughout the Roman and Grecian periods, the Africa to America saga, slavery in countries of Africa today, and many other so-called "secret" slavery rings. I levitated in the arenas while Christians were being eaten by lions, and I roared with laughter while Nero's fires burned within inches of destroying Rome. The Bubonic plague in Europe was a satanic filler. I prided myself during the backward thrust in learning during the Middle Ages when someone suggested that humans should learn to read. Barbarianism, cannibalism—I have had my hands in every bloody war or act that killed humans since the inception of time, including human sacrifices by ancient people, religious persecutions as well. The witch hunts in Europe and the Americas were strategic, if I do say so myself. Famine, conflicts, and wars—massacres, homicide, infanticide, suicide, genocide—any

act of human destruction, I participated in. I did not cause them all, but when the opportunity presented itself, I joined in to make matters as worst as the situations could get!

How do I do all of this? Through branding suggestions into human minds. A being as powerful as I, who has been around for as long as I have, can surely outdo the local psychic or hypnotist! I reach most humans through their minds, their intellect. When the mind is pliable and willing to allow demonic infiltration, then demons move in! Then I have control of that human. Unless . . . but let's not talk about that now.

Overall, for nearly six thousand years, I have wreaked havoc among and against mankind, yet my overall success ratio has been fair to moderate. Always there was a "savior" of some kind—a prophet here, a saint there—someone to enlighten humankind that evil truly exist, and that they should look to and serve Creator to avoid being engulfed in my specialty: unadulterated corruption.

It was about two thousand years ago, give or take a few years, when I sensed that Earth was "ripe" for something new and different. I have orchestrated the deaths of judges, prophets, kings, missionaries, and pastors. I indirectly organized cults, orders, sects, and religions. I have manipulated rulers, kings, fallen angels, and demons to do my biddings. I have devised plots, takeovers, and wars. I have manufactured famines and disasters, natural and man-made. Then He came on the scene. He was like no human

I had ever tempted. I had come so close to conquest only to experience total defeat!

How do humans view the world where I reside? Most humans do not consider it at all! I sit in galleries and country clubs of the supposedly "sophisticated" where I hear them discuss the world of the spirit as tribal nonsense of the ignorant, the downtrodden, and the poor. In pool halls, pubs, barbershops, beauty salons, and other human haunts, I hear humans speak of misfortunes and bad luck.

I vie for ownership of the souls of humans, and whether humans believe it or not, my hordes and I constantly battle with the angelic host of Heaven over the souls of humans. Humans' freedom to choose between Creator's kingdom and mine is the cause of angelic confrontations. I want to command the world, both the invisible and the visible; for I have seized control of the minds of so many humans that society seems to favor me over Creator.

I was forewarned in the Garden of retribution. I have known since then that my undoing would come by way of a human, one like the very ones I have spent most of my existence trying to conquer or wipe out. I was forewarned that a male of the human race would bring about my defeat and an end to my evil kingdom. How did I know all of this? Unlike most of you, I read. Whenever I want to know what is happening in the realm of humans, I check the Scriptures. I read the words and I read between the lines.

If I am destined to go down, I plan to go down

with a bang! I plan to take the downward plunge with as many humans as I can carry. So humans, "Beware!"

In the meantime . . .

Contact A. E. Hepburn
or order more copies of this book at

TATE PUBLISHING, LLC

127 East Trade Center Terrace
Mustang, Oklahoma 73064

(888) 361 - 9473

Tate Publishing, LLC

www.tatepublishing.com